freefall

JESSICA BARRY

Harvill *Secker*
LONDON

1 3 5 7 9 10 8 6 4 2

Harvill Secker, an imprint of Vintage,
20 Vauxhall Bridge Road,
London SW1V 2SA

Harvill Secker is part of the Penguin Random House group of companies
whose addresses can be found at global.penguinrandomhouse.com

Copyright © Hudson & Guide Post Limited 2019

Jessica Barry has asserted her right to be identified as the
author of this Work in accordance with the Copyright,
Designs and Patents Act 1988

First published by Harvill Secker in 2019

A CIP catalogue record for this book is available from the British Library

penguin.co.uk/vintage

ISBN 9781787301092 (hardback)
ISBN 9781787301108 (trade paperback)

Printed and bound in Great Britain by Clays Ltd, Elcograf S.p.A.

freefall

'A gripping page-turner. *Freefall* is exactly what a great thriller should be' Renee Knight

'Charged with genuine depth and raw power' A. J. Finn

'Most debut thriller writers would be happy to have one amazing story to tell. Jessica Barry's come up with two, and the way she weaves them together will have you on the edge of your seat. *Freefall* is an electric mix of action and emotional drama that never stops, never slows down' Liv Constantine

'Once you start reading, you won't want to stop' Karin Slaughter

'Wow. I barely drew breath as I galloped through this gripping debut thriller' Laura Marshall

'An enthralling, impossible-to-put-down mystery that keeps the pages flying' Aimee Molloy

'*Freefall* is the explosive debut thriller from Jessica Barry . . . It's a page-turner of a book, nail-biting and compelling, and I loved the relationship between mother and daughter, both powerful female characters' Fiona Cummins

'Easily devourable and pacy – but what really got me was the mother–daughter relationship. Prepare for your heart to be wrenched . . .' Emily Koch

'Jessica Barry has written a page-turner; a taut and compelling story which is difficult to put down. At the same time, through her convincing and sympathetic characters, she captures the complex relationship between mother and daughter brilliantly' Jenny Quintana

For my parents, with love and gratitude

Allison

Breathe. Breathe.

My eyes open. A canopy of trees above. A flock of birds stare down before taking flight.

I survived.

He might have, too.

I have to see. I pick my way through the wreckage on bare feet. Where are my shoes? It doesn't matter. Bits of twisted metal everywhere. One of the wings lodged in the V of a nearby tree. A roll of toilet paper draped across the branches. The cabin is a tin can sliced open, exposing two rows of cream leather seats. I take a step closer and peer inside.

He is there, chest slumped over the controls.

"Hello?" My voice is startling in my ears. "Can you hear me?"

Silence. The engine hisses. The gasoline ticks into the grass.

Into the cabin. Avoid the jagged rim. He is still holding the radio transmitter in his hand, the cable severed. I nudge him, gently. His body falls against the side of the cabin.

His face is missing.

Out. Out.

I retch, then sit. *Focus.*

Here are the facts: I am alone. I am on a mountain. The plane I was on has crashed. My body is covered in bruises and cuts and my left leg has a wound that will soon become infected if I don't clean it. My finger is strained or broken and quickly swelling. I have very little food and water. The sun is still high but it will be dark in a few hours and my only shelter is a twisted hulk of metal that could, at any minute, explode.

I feel sick with fear. I want, very badly, to lie back on the bank of grass and let my heavy eyelids close. I wonder what it will be like to die. Will it be like the tilt and drop of sleep? Will there be a light to follow, or just the dark?

Stop.

I don't want to die. What I need is a plan.

You have to go.

The voice in my head is urgent, insistent.

Youhavetogoyouhavetogoyouhavetogo.

Stay alive.

My overnight bag. In a tree. Tug it down. Ignore the searing pain in my shoulder. I plunge through the clothes I'd packed for a weekend in Chicago. Out go the cocktail dresses, the spindly heels, the flimsy bra, and two pairs of lacy underwear. Gym gear. Thank God. Something useful. Off goes the cotton dress, the ridiculous bra and underwear. *Do not think about the bruises blooming on your thighs. Do not think about the lacerations on your hips. Do not think about that crooked pinkie finger and the worrying blue cast it is taking on. Do not think about the blood all over your white dress, your stomach, your thighs. Do not think. Move.* Tug on the running leggings, the sports bra, the socks, the freebie T-shirt from some 10K.

My phone. I have to find my phone. Where is it? I scan the debris field. Nothing.

Move. Move. The expensive bottle of perfume, the shampoo and conditioner, the precleanse oil, the cream cleanser and exfoliator, the separate lotions for body, face, hands, under eyes: gone. The hair dryer and the curling iron: gone. Wait. The cords. Jerk free and save. The empty toner bottle, the mirrored compact, and the travel-size bottle of hair spray. All useful. Maybe. Put them to one side. Out go the deodorant and the makeup and the hairbrush. The lip balm goes into one of the bag's zippered pockets.

The bag's weight is manageable. On to his suitcase. A Turnbull & Asser sleeve peeking through a tear in the lining. A spare T-shirt.

His Harvard sweatshirt goes on. *Do not think about how much it smells like him.* God, it smells like him.

You have to go.

Out comes the high-tech windbreaker. A pair of socks. That's it. *What else. Think. These things will keep you alive.*

The plane's canopy cover flaps in a low tree branch. Roll it up. Tie it to the bag. The first aid kit is lodged behind a rotten tree stump. The plastic case has cracked, but the contents are still intact: iodine, rubbing alcohol, bandages, scissors, painkillers, antihistamines, tweezers, sewing kit, tape.

My eye snags on the cabin. My phone. *You have to go back in.* There is food there. Water. I won't last two days without those things. There is smoke coming from the engine, black and thick. *In. In. In.*

The plastic bag. Right where I left it, tucked behind the front passenger seat. Four Luna bars, a bag of mixed nuts, an unopened bottle of water. The can of Diet Coke. I feel momentarily giddy. My hand searches the floor and finds the sharp cut of glass. I pull it out and look at the smashed face of my phone. I try to switch it on but the spidered screen stays black. Broken. *Fuckfuckfuck.* I take it with me anyway. My eyes water from the smoke. *Focus. Focus.* I reach behind the back seat. A fleece blanket, a roll of duct tape, a coil of rope. I reach again. The thin metal body of a lighter. Everything in the bag. The light is dimming. I have to go.

Out. Out. Out. My animal brain is screaming at me, but wait. What is the plan? *Stay alive.* I climb on top of the wreckage, avoiding the razor edges, the pain in my shoulder, and the blown-off face of the man I had so recently touched. *Look.* Snow-capped mountains thrusting their way into an epic stretch of blue sky. Below, green hills roll out in gentle waves, each fringed with trees and specked with wildflowers. On and on the vast lands stretch, out to the farthest point on the horizon. There is no sign of another human, except for a path. A steep slope but relatively even, and free of the sudden sheer cliff edges peppering the other routes. There, nestled into the crook of the valley below, I see a thin strip of mirrored glass. There is water below. The plan. The path is the plan.

Out. Out. Out. I jump free of the wreckage.

I heft the bag back onto my shoulders, screaming at the pain, and slip my arms through the handles and use the long strap to buckle it securely around my waist. The engine's hiss has finally fallen silent but the smoke still comes. I cast one last look around the clearing and see the shattered glass and bits of broken plastic and the pile of belongings that I have cast aside.

There is nothing left here now, nothing to salvage.

The sun is setting. *You have to go.*

Maggie

It was still early in the morning, the sky outside a dark pink not yet paled to blue. I had NPR on low in the background, a mug of coffee was slowly going cold on the counter, and Barney was threading himself around my ankles, hoping for a second breakfast. The floorboards creaked underfoot as they always did. I glanced at the recipe card, not that I needed to check it. I'd been making the same loaf for years and knew it by heart, but the recipe was written in Charles's strong, sure hand, and I liked to keep it near me when I was making it. It was part of the ritual.

The dough was warm and soft as I pulled it away from me and folded it back, feeling it stretch and tighten beneath my hands. I shouldn't be kneading dough—it exacerbates the arthritis that had settled in my knuckles after years of typing—but I made a loaf of bread at the start of every week, even though most weeks now it ended up stale and moldy by Friday.

The doorbell rang. I ignored it. If I stopped, it wouldn't turn out, and besides, my hair was a bird's nest and I was still wearing my dressing gown and the L. L. Bean slippers Charles had given me six years earlier. It was probably the mailman. He'd stick a note under the door about a package and be on his way.

The doorbell rang again. I sighed and wiped my floury hands on a square of kitchen towel. *Whoever this is*, I thought, *it better be good*.

When I opened the door and saw Jim standing there in his full chief of police uniform, I thought maybe he'd come for Linda's casserole dish. She'd left it at the house after bringing over a lasagna, and she was always eagle-eyed about her bakeware. But I took one look at his face, and at the nervous little slip of a thing standing behind him all buttoned up in her starched blues, and I knew he wasn't here about the dish.

"Do you mind if I come in?" he asked, taking off his hat and holding it over his heart. Jim Quinn and I had known each other since high school, when he used to flick me in the back of the head with the nub of his pencil and ask me for answers in American history. He had never once asked for permission to enter my house. Suddenly, all I could see was his uniform and his bright, shiny badge.

"Jim, what's going on?" My voice was too loud.

"Why don't we sit down." It wasn't a question, and he ushered me back into my own house. The lady cop followed behind. "This is Officer Draper," he said, gesturing toward her.

"Call me Shannon," she said, so quietly I almost missed it.

"Nice to meet you." I turned back to Jim. "Now tell me what's going on."

Jim took me by the elbow and led me to the kitchen table. "Sit down," he said, gently, though he pressed me down into the chair before taking a seat across from me. "Maggie, there's been an accident."

My heart sank. "Is it Linda? Is she all right?" Even as I asked, I knew it wasn't about his wife.

He shook his head. "Linda is fine."

I knew then. I just knew. It's what all parents know deep down is coming for them. That one day, they'll get a phone call or a knock on their door and in that very instant, their world will cease to exist.

"Ally." I said.

He nodded.

He looked at me with his watery blue eyes. "There was a plane crash."

The world went white.

6

Allison

The weight of the bag propels me down the mountain at speed, the dim moonlight guiding my way through the trees. Branches thwack against my arms and legs. I fall once, hard. I let out a wail but get back to my feet and carry on. The blood thunders in my ears. All night I run. I don't let myself look back. I don't let myself stop.

I make it to the basin before dawn. I crouch by the edge of the water and touch it with my fingertips. Its coolness is like a shock. I splash some on my face. The water that drips down my forearms is a light pink color. The blood. Thirst grips me like a fever. It would be so easy to lift cupped hands to mouth and drink.

No. The water could poison me. I haven't survived a plane crash to be killed by dysentery. I fill up the two empty bottles and add a drop of iodine to each. I wait. *There are so many ways to die.*

I look down at my body. The pain is like an echo, reverberating through me but distant somehow, remote.

I could get an infection, I could bleed out. I could die. So many ways to die.

Stay alive.

I pull off my leggings. The gash on my left leg is deep, nasty, and uneven. I pull the button-down out of my bag, rip a strip from it, and dip it into the bottle of rubbing alcohol. I work the cloth into the cut, the pain cleaving me in half. When I can see again, my breath comes out ragged. I can see a sliver of white—the cut went down to the bone.

Breathe.

His skull, the whiteness of his skull. Which I could see because his face was gone.

The world tilts on an angle and I struggle to remain conscious.

Stop. Breathe. Focus.

I squeeze the edges of the skin together and tape a butterfly bandage over it. It will leave an ugly scar.

Poor pretty little Allison.

I pull my leggings back on.

I feel a chill and a prickling heat runs up my spine. The adrenaline coursing its way through me, then leaving. I pull the hair away from my neck, and that's when I notice it's gone. The necklace. My hand stays at the base of my throat. I can feel my heart hammering beneath the skin.

My stomach clenches. How could I have been so careless? It was all that I had, the only thing worth protecting, and now it's gone.

I shove the thought away. There's no point dwelling—there's nothing I can do about it. It's already done.

I check my watch—a thin gold band with a diamond-studded face, absurd—and see I have another five minutes to wait before I can drink the water. My father always told me it took a full thirty minutes for iodine to purify water. He liked to teach me those sorts of things, practical things, even when I'd roll my eyes and groan that it was pointless, that I'd never have the need for it. Joke's on me, I guess.

I think about the Luna bars, the bag of nuts. My stomach wrenches. I should eat, but all I see is the empty space where his face should have been. I close my eyes and breathe.

When I open my eyes, six minutes have passed. The water is safe. I drink both bottles quickly. Too quickly. I fight to keep it down, and it stays. The water is perfect, cold and metal edged. Refill the bottles. Drop in the iodine. Into the bag.

Move move move.

Onto my feet, hoist the pack. Something in my shoulder shifted and cracked. A hairline fracture, maybe, or just a strain. I fight the urge to cry.

No time to think about it now.

I jump from rock to rock. Every step hurts. Is it better to push off or land on my injured leg? Land, I decide. I reach the bank. There is the expanse of rocky flatland and the mountain crowning above it, and over there is the sun, casting a pinkish glow across the mountain as it climbs to the sky.

I don't know how much time I have before they come looking for me, but I know they'll come eventually, and that means I have to keep moving.

I have to go east, into the rising sun. The mountain will have to be climbed.

Maggie

"Maggie. Maggie."

I heard it through the roaring in my ears. My vision was a field of white, but the edges grew fuzzier, darker, more familiar.

"Maggie."

It was Jim.

"Maggie, she was on a four-seater coming out of Chicago. They think it went down somewhere in the Colorado Rockies."

"Are you telling me my daughter is dead?" My voice wasn't my own. It was someone else speaking, in a reality that wasn't mine, either.

"We don't know yet," he said, shaking his head. "They haven't been able to get to the crash site to confirm, but from the radio signals before it cut out . . ."

This changed everything. She could still be alive. Hope bloomed in my chest like a sunflower. "How do you know she was even on that plane?" Maybe she wasn't in danger at all. Maybe she was at home, safe.

"She was on the flight register—her and the man who was flying the plane. I've seen the airport records, there was a photo of her on file . . . it's her."

"All right. All right." My mind kicked into gear. My baby was missing in the mountains. Scared and alone and maybe hurt. But not dead. "What can I do to help? We get a search party together, right? Should I make calls? Fly out?"

Jim spoke slowly. "There are already people looking for her, Maggie."

"Who, though?" I didn't like the idea of strangers searching for her. They wouldn't know how to find her, they'd make mistakes, they wouldn't understand her like I would. "I want to know who is out there right now looking for my daughter. She's all alone out there, Jim. I want to know their names."

"They're doing everything they can, Maggie. They've got rangers all over the mountains looking for the crash site. The local police are involved, too. But, Maggie. I need you to listen. It was a plane crash. The likelihood that she's survived . . . the odds aren't good."

I looked at him, hard, and saw the sadness in his eyes. "She's alive," I said, with more conviction than I felt. "Ally is a tough kid. I'm sure she's alive."

He nodded slowly. "We'll do everything we can to make sure we find her. I can promise you that. Shannon, see if you can find any liquor, will you?"

He thought I was in shock. He thought I wasn't in my right mind. "I'm fine, Jim," I snapped.

"It'll do you good." He turned around in his chair and pointed. "Up there, in the cabinet above the refrigerator. Should be to the right—yep, that's it."

Shannon held up a bottle of Baileys.

"Is that all you could find?" Jim asked. She nodded. "Shit, where's the brandy? They always have brandy." He poured glugs of Baileys into my dirty coffee mug and placed it in my hands. "Drink."

"Thank you." I felt like a child being given her milk. I took a reluctant sip. It was too sweet, like drinking a milkshake. I set the mug down on the table, placed my hands on the worn top. "How the hell hard is it to find a plane? Aren't there satellites they could use? Helicopters?" I tried to drive the idea of Ally out there, scared and alone and hurt, from my head. That picture wouldn't help. Facts would help. I needed to establish the facts.

"Everything that can be done is being done," he said. "I promise."

My mind raced. Jim had said it had been just her and another person on the plane. "Who was the man she was with? The pilot. What's his name?"

He shifted in his seat. "They're still trying to notify his next of kin."

Out of the corner of my eye, I saw the little officer wiping down the counter with a dish towel. A wave of rage coursed through me. "But you know? You know and you're not telling me."

"Honestly, Maggie, right now you know just as much as I do."

I got up, took the cloth out of the little officer's hand, and started wiping at a bit of countertop. The dough was slowly deflating on its wooden board. "I should keep kneading," I muttered to myself. The thought of throwing out the dough struck me suddenly as the most horrible waste. I refloured my hands and the board and began pushing the dough away from me with the heels of my hands and then folding it back. Away and back. Away and back. Away and back.

Jim stood up and placed his hands on my shoulders. "Why don't you go lie down? Shannon here will get you a cup of coffee, maybe—Shannon, can you put the coffee maker on?"

"I don't want to lie down and I don't want a cup of coffee, thank you anyway, Shannon. I want to finish kneading this dough and get it proving or else it won't rise in the oven."

Jim's hands tightened and I heard him let out a sigh. "Maggie, leave the damn dough. Just— Just calm down for a minute. Just take a breath."

I wheeled on him. "My little girl is out there in the middle of God knows where and you're telling me to calm down?"

Jim looked at me for a long moment. "I'm sorry," he said quietly, "but getting yourself worked up like this isn't going to help anything."

I was silent.

He picked up his hat and held it in both hands. "I'm going to call the doctor and see if he can prescribe something to help you sleep. I'll ask Linda to pick it up from the drugstore on her way over."

"I'm not crazy, Jim. My daughter was in a plane crash. I'm sorry my reaction is making you uncomfortable." A look of hurt crossed his face that I immediately regretted. I tried again. "You've told Linda?"

"I came here as soon as I heard, but I thought you'd want——" He sighed. "She'll want to help, and if you don't mind me saying so, you need a good friend around you right now."

In that moment, I didn't want to see a single person on this earth who wasn't my daughter, but I knew there was no point in trying to fight off Linda Quinn's goodwill. I nodded. "Tell her to come by when she's got a minute."

"I'll go by the house now," he said, gathering his keys from the table. He couldn't wait to leave, the relief was painted across his face. "She'll be over real soon. In the meantime, Shannon here will stay with you."

I looked at the little officer, who was now fingering the hem of the tablecloth. She shot me a nervous smile. Everything about her—her round, lash-fringed eyes, her hair pulled into a perky little ponytail, her smooth, lineless skin—felt like an affront. She was so young. Younger than Ally. What right did she have to be there? "I'll be fine on my own," I said coolly.

Jim gripped the brim of his hat a little more tightly. "I'm sure you would, but I'd be more comfortable knowing someone was here with you until Linda gets here. You've had an awful shock, and I would just——" He looked at me pleadingly. "Please, for my peace of mind."

I nodded. "Fine." I dropped the dough into an oiled glass bowl, covered it with a tea towel, and walked into the pantry, where I set it on a shelf to rise. I stood there for a minute, staring up at the neat rows of canned corn and olive oil and dried pasta, and placed my head against the cool wall. I could hear the two of them whispering about me on the other side of the door. I had never felt more helpless in my life.

I took a deep breath and walked back into the kitchen. Jim pulled me in for an awkward hug. "I'll be in touch as soon as I hear anything. Anything you need, don't hesitate."

"You just find my girl."

He nodded. "I'll see you soon. Shannon, you take good care of her."

Shannon nodded and we both listened to the door shut behind him. Her cheeks were pink. She wore a claddagh on the ring finger of her right hand with the tip of the heart pointed out. I wanted to hit her. "Are you sure you don't want a cup of tea?" she asked, eyes wide with concern. "Or maybe some more coffee?"

I shook my head. "I'm fine, really. You can go whenever you want. I'm sure you have better things to be doing with your time." I didn't know how much longer I could look at her innocent little face without screaming.

"Chief Quinn ordered me to stay, so that's what I'm going to do." The firmness of her voice took me by surprise, and my face must have showed it. "It's only my first month," she added apologetically. "I don't want to get in trouble with the boss."

"I see." I turned and braced myself against the sink. I practiced breathing. It felt important that I didn't let her see me cry. *Pull it together, Margaret. For the love of God, pull it together.* I don't know how long I stood there. A minute? Ten?

Then she spoke. "You know what?"

I turned to her. I could tell by her face that she had seen it, the fissures.

"I'll wait just outside the door, but if you need anything, shout. When Mrs. Quinn comes I'll be on my way, I promise."

It was a kindness, and I took it. "That's fine," I said.

She stepped outside, leaving the door ajar with an apologetic "Regulations, ma'am."

I had read enough books to know that this first moment when I was alone with my thoughts was the moment I was supposed to sink to my knees and wail a primal scream. I sat there and stared into nothing and waited for the phone to ring. It dawned on me then that I might be waiting forever.

Allison

The flat plain stretches out in front of me, an endless carpet of scrub grass and wildflowers. Fat bees drone lazily as they make their way from stem to stem.

In the distance, the mountain looms large. No matter how far I walk, it doesn't seem to get any closer. A cloud of gnats whine around my head.

I think of the view from the plane, a patchwork of green intercepted by the occasional expanse of rock and snow. I try to imagine how I look from above, up there in the blue, cloudless sky.

These mountains are the land of gods and giants. Their sole purpose is to remind you that you're nothing but a speck, that your time on earth is short and fleeting, and that these rocks were here eons before you were born and will continue to stand long after you've turned to dust.

For a single second, I feel something other than terror.

I feel relief.

It doesn't last long. I know what's coming for me.

"Cover your tracks. If he finds out, he'll come after you." His eyes had bored into mine as he said it. "They all will. You have no idea how powerful they are. Do you understand?" I'd nodded. "Listen to me very carefully. You need to be prepared to run. If you think for a second that he's on to you, you need to disappear."

The phone. Shit: I still have the phone. I pull it out of my bag and throw it onto the ground. My heel comes down on it once, twice, until the plastic casing comes away. My fingers scramble to find the chip. I throw the remains of the phone in one direction and the chip in the other. I watch it wink in the sunlight as it spins into the brush.

Maggie

"A Maine native is missing following a plane crash. Allison Carpenter, thirty-one, was last seen boarding a single-engine aircraft at Midway airport in Chicago. The plane sent out a distress signal several hours later, and is believed to have crashed somewhere in the Colorado Rockies. Rescuers are searching for signs of the wreckage. The pilot, believed to be operating the plane under a private license, has not been identified. Coming up next, Doctor Alan Phillips will be here to answer our questions on the virus currently sweeping through Bolivia, and will answer the question we've all been asking: Will it make its way here?"

I reached over and switched off the radio. After all these years of watching other people's lives dragged out across the news, their tragedies turned into spectacle and sport, I remembered the pity I'd felt and also the relief in knowing it wasn't me or any of mine . . . and now it was.

Linda would be here any minute, I thought. I could hear the rumble of her car, rounding the corner a quarter of a mile away. She'd bought it off a former Mary Kay rep a decade earlier. Jim hated it, couldn't wait for it to give up the ghost so he could get her into a nice, sensible Lincoln, something that befitted the wife of the chief of police. But the pink Cadillac, like Linda, proved indomitable. It was still kicking, with an engine so loud and a transmission so shot you could hear her from halfway across Maine. The front door swung open and she appeared in the doorway, blond hair still damp from the shower.

"Maggie."

It was enough. I felt myself crack open. The howl I'd kept pressed down inside my rib cage came out. She was on me in a second, holding me in her arms. I don't know how long I sobbed for, but as my tears tapered off, I heard an engine start and a car pull out of the driveway. The little officer was true to her word.

I opened my eyes and Linda crouched in front of me. "What do you need me to do?" She wiped my tears away with the backs of her hands.

"I don't know," I said. "I don't know." I looked up at her. "Where is she, Linda? Where is she?" All I could see was Ally lying among twisted shards of metal. I wondered if I was going to be sick.

"Shhh. They'll find her, they'll find her." We sat like that for a while, Linda stroking my hair. Eventually I could breathe again.

"Now," said Linda, "I brought drugs to help you sleep and drugs to take the edge off things when you're awake." She rummaged around in her enormous handbag and pulled out two orange pill bottles. "These are the nighttime ones," she said, shaking one of the bottles. "Ambien, they'll knock you right out—and these are for the daytime." She leaned in. "Valium," she whispered, as though someone might overhear, "left over from when Jim had his slipped disk."

I took them without looking and placed them on the counter behind me, where I knew they'd remain untouched. I had never been one for taking medicine, not even Advil for a headache. Charles used to tease me about it, ask if I'd converted to Seventh-Day Adventism without him knowing. I just didn't like the feeling that I wasn't in control of my own body.

"What else can I get for you? Have you eaten? I wrapped up half a banana loaf I made earlier if you want, or I could make you a sandwich?"

The thought of food made my stomach turn. "No," I said, shaking my head. "Thank you."

She patted the back of my hand. "I'll make us both some tea." She got up and put the kettle on the burner.

"You don't have to stay," I said, my back still turned to her. "I'm honestly fine on my own, not that anyone seems to think so." I was suddenly embarrassed by letting her see me cry like that. She was my best friend, sure, but it didn't matter. I didn't like anyone to see me cry. Not even Charles, when he was still here.

"What are you talking about?" she tutted. "Why would I be any-place other than here?"

I listened to the sounds of her making tea and stared at a crack in the wall. When had that appeared? I felt the urge to get up and fix it right there and then, to trudge down to the basement for a tub of Spackle and a putty knife and fill it in. It would be good to do something productive. Anything.

She set a mug of tea in front of me and sat down at the table with her own. We sipped in silence for a few minutes. Barney leaped onto the table and nudged my cheek with his nose, and I stroked his long orange fur. He stayed for a moment, purring happily, before jump-ing down and snuffling at his empty food dish. I got to my feet and bent to refill his bowl.

"Did you know she was traveling this weekend?" Linda asked.

I shook my head.

"What do you think she was doing in Chicago? Do you think she had business there?"

I felt my shoulders stiffen. "I don't know."

"And on a private plane, too. I don't know many people who travel on private planes. Maybe it was owned by a client?"

"Linda, please. I told you I don't know." The anger in my voice cut through the room.

"I'm sorry," she said quietly. She stared down at her tea. "I don't know what got into me, asking you all those questions. Of course you don't want to talk about it right now."

It was true, I didn't want to talk about it, but it was more than that. I didn't know the answers to any of Linda's questions because I didn't know anything about Ally's life.

What I knew, but Linda didn't, was that I hadn't seen or spoken to my daughter in more than two years.

The Man stood on the bluff and gazed out at the mountains. The afternoon sun was strong, and he raised a hand to shield his eyes.

The mountainside was smeared with twisted metal, and the air was heavy with the smell of gasoline. He saw the body resting inside the cabin, at peace if it weren't for its lack of a face. The seat next to it was empty, the seat belt coiled on the leather like a snake.

He walked the perimeter, pulled a scrap of fabric from a branch, scuffed the clawed earth with his heel. There wasn't much left, but there was enough for him to know.

He took out his phone, dialed.

—It's me. I'm here. He's dead.

He looked behind him. One body in the plane. One bag on the ground, open, contents scattered. A pair of silver high heels, spikes pointing up like steeples. No sign of her.

—I'm sure.

—No, no sign.

—Yes sir. I will.

He lit a cigarette, tossed the match into the cracked fuel tank. Acrid smoke filled his lungs, and he began to cough.

One last look at the wreckage, now starting to smoke.

Time to go.

Allison

I hike through the day without a break. The grass merges into a field of flat rock that reminds me of a photograph of the moon's surface, pockmarked and barren. I'm pursued by the thrumming buzz of greenbottles, which swarm and bite every time I stop to wipe the sweat off my face with the edge of my T-shirt. The sun beats down relentlessly. I ration the water in tiny sips, letting each one dissolve on my tongue. I scratch at the bites on my arms until I draw blood. The wound on my leg catches on the fabric of my leggings. The air is so still that all I can hear is the steady creak of the leather straps on my bag as it shifts on my shoulders and the crunch of gravel underfoot. Adrenaline courses through me in waves, electrifying me one moment and depleting me the next. I walk. I walk. I walk.

By the time I make it across the moonscape, the sun is setting. I want desperately to make a run for the woods in front of me, to use the last of my energy in a frenetic burst toward the trees and shade and the illusion of safety, but I force myself to maintain the same steady, plodding pace I've walked all day. I don't have enough food or water for sudden bursts of energy. I barely have enough for plodding.

The grass sprouts up again in brownish-green patches at first and then grows lusher. Soon there are the trees, huge towering beasts that arc over me and block out what remains of the sun's heat. The air feels fresh now, alive, and I breathe it in.

My vision narrows and blurs. There is a faint humming coming from the center of my skull, and I wonder if it's audible to the outside world or localized in my own head. I stare at birds and insects and the occasional scurrying hare for clues. *Can you hear it?* I want to ask, but there's no one here to listen to the question, let alone the hum. If a tree falls . . .

A swoon comes over me.

His eyelashes. Each thick black strand curved, the thin membrane of his eyelid pulsing in sleep. I would lie next to him at night and marvel at those eyelashes, as long as a newborn's and swooped up to the sky. *What are you dreaming about?* I would whisper. *Are you dreaming about me?* The waves below beat time with the rise and fall of his breath, and the question would roll in and out of me, rhythmic and steady and always unanswered.

Are you dreaming about me?

My foot catches on a branch and I stumble.

I can't afford to remember. Not yet.

On and on into the forest, until the trees circle around me. I find a clear stretch of ground and lay out the canopy cover, spread the blanket over me, and am asleep before the last of the light dies out. I don't dream. The blankness is a gift.

Maggie

Linda finally left at dinnertime. Once the light began to fade, she started looking out the window in a nervous way—she didn't like driving at night, her cataracts played up—and I told her to go on home.

The silence that settled in when she left was a blessing at first, but after a few hours of the ticking of the clock and the pad of Barney's paws on the stone floor, I started feeling claustrophobic. Everything, absolutely everything in the house, reminded me of Ally. This was where she had placed her muddy soccer cleats. That was the corner of the hutch that had held her bronzed baby shoes. That was the mug she had given Charles for Father's Day, unused these past two years now. There was the coat closet and in that closet was a scarf she'd knitted me, inexpertly, her first year out of college, when she was low on money but too proud to take a little extra from us. There, through the glass of the back door, was the flagstone patio where she'd split her chin when she was four and I had held her, sobbing, against me, the blood trickling through my fingers as I'd whispered into her chestnut hair, *Breathe. Breathe.* She was a brave little thing and stopped crying almost immediately, but I kept whispering it. I had needed the reminder, too.

Eventually, the sun came up.

As soon as I heard Jim's footsteps on the walk, I knew what he'd come to tell me. Something about the slow, heavy plod of his shoes on the brick as he came up the path told me everything I needed to know.

I pulled open the door. "She's dead, isn't she?"

He looked stunned for a moment, and then his face softened and he nodded, just once.

I expected myself to be hysterical, to collapse at his feet and weep and wail, but there was a stillness inside me, as though I were floating several inches above my own head. I shifted to one side to let him pass and watched his back retreat into the kitchen.

I stood in the doorway. "Where is she?"

"They found the plane halfway up Electric Peak. The pilot must have misjudged the altitude, I guess, though they'll know more when they find the flight recorder."

I felt myself nod, as though hearing it was the most natural thing in the world, as though I'd been expecting it all along, which I guess I had. All those times I'd waved her off on the school bus, or at the airport, or in cars driven by strange boys, I would find myself thinking that I might never see her again, that she might be taken from us, and now she had been. "When can I see her?"

He rubbed the back of his neck. "It might take a while for them to get everything sorted. There'll have to be an investigation, and who knows how long those things can take . . ." He shifted on his feet, and I could tell there was something he hadn't said.

"When can I see my daughter, Jim." It was no longer a question.

He raised his eyes to mine. They were small in his face and rimmed with pink. "There was a fire at the crash site . . . some kind of explosion on impact, they think. There wasn't much . . ." He shook his head. "There was a lot of damage at the site."

I pictured scorched earth and melted metal, singed hair and burning flesh. "Excuse me." I ran to the bathroom and threw up the morning's coffee. Brackish liquid splashed up the white porcelain of the bowl, and the acid burned the back of my throat. My little girl, my gorgeous little girl. I thought of her face as a child, her smile as wide as the moon, and imagined it disintegrating in front of me. How could I still be living when my only daughter was dead, obliterated on some mountain halfway across the country? What did it mean that I hadn't died, too, that my heart hadn't immediately stopped beating the moment hers had? I spat into the toilet. What sort of a mother could continue to live when her child was dead? I placed my forehead against the cool rim of the bowl and forced myself to breathe.

I found Jim staring blankly at the backs of his hands. "I'm sorry. I shouldn't have told you that," he said, shaking his head. "There was no need."

"No. I don't want you to hide anything from me. I want to know everything about what happened. Every single damn thing." Facts. The thing I could cling to, like a buoy in the middle of the ocean. "Do they know the name of the pilot yet?"

"Still looking for next of kin. Do you know if she was seeing anyone? Maybe it could have been a boyfriend?"

"Not that she'd mentioned," I said. It was the truth, in a way.

He nodded. "Did you know of any . . . I don't know how to put this. Did you know of any trouble Allison was in?"

"What sort of trouble?"

"Aw, hell. Drugs, drinking—that sort of thing?"

"Ally wasn't a big drinker, and I never knew her to do drugs, but—" I left the rest unsaid. I didn't know my daughter. I hadn't known her for a while. "Why do you ask?"

"No reason, just a couple things turned up in the system— Anyway, it looks like it was in the past. Forget I said anything."

I folded my arms across my chest. "You're not holding out on me, are you?"

He shook his head. "Of course not." Jim Quinn had always been a terrible liar.

"Will there— Is there something of hers that was left? That I could have?"

He looked up at me, and the sadness in his eyes was enough to flatten anyone. For a second, I hated him for it. I didn't want his sadness or his pity. I wanted only the sharp edges of facts. "They're still sorting through everything up there. Trying to identify . . ." He stopped himself. "Like I said, there'll be an investigation, so it might take a bit of time before they release anything, but I'll make sure you get anything you can as soon as possible."

Anything. My daughter had been reduced to a thing. What would Jim do, I wondered, if I screamed right then? Just one long, loud wail. Probably send for the doctor to sedate me. Or more likely, send Linda over with her bagful of drugs.

He stared down at the flat of his hands and sighed. "They want a photo of Allison."

"Why? I thought you said they had one of her at the airport."

"Not them . . . the media. We keep getting calls from television stations asking for one, and if we don't give them one ourselves they'll end up finding one on the internet or something." He paused. "I thought you'd want to be the one to choose it."

Allison's photo. My daughter. Out there for everyone to see. I thought of people sitting on their couches, saying how pretty she was, how young, what a shame. Pitying her. Me. It made me feel angry. But I knew Jim was right. "Okay," I said quietly. "I'll take a look and see what I can find."

Good, I thought. *Yes.* It was a task. A task that was small and could be accomplished.

I climbed down the uneven wooden steps into the basement and switched on the light. The bare bulb flickered across the concrete walls. I'd always wanted to finish it, maybe put a library down there, or a game room, but Charles insisted on using it as a shop. Now the disused workbench languished in the corner, along with a tangle of old power tools and, inexplicably, a full beekeeper's outfit hanging from a peg on the wall. Charles was a man who'd loved a hobby. The stone floor was cool on my bare feet. Snowshoes and cross-country skis mixed with tent poles and camp stoves. Every other spare inch was covered in cardboard boxes, some opened, most not. I picked my way through them until I found the one I was looking for, a small box with the words PHOTOS 2004–2016 scrawled on it in black Sharpie. There wasn't much reason to take photos after 2016.

Back in the kitchen, I sliced open the top with a pair of scissors and peered inside. Jim watched wordlessly. At the top of the pile was a photo of Charles and Allison smiling together in the snow. I flipped it over: 12/24/2011. CHRISTMAS EVE. We'd been on our way to the car to get to the carol service at Christ the King when Ally had stopped and flopped back in a bank of snow on the front lawn. I thought at first she'd fallen—she was no longer used to dealing with the snow—but then I saw that she was making a snow angel. Before I knew it, Charles was on his back, too, arms and legs moving like windshield wipers. When they stood up, there were two perfect angels left in the snow, and I took a photo of them with her new iPhone, laughing with their arms around each other. She'd had it printed that day and tucked it in the tree so it was waiting for us in the morning. It had been a perfect Christmas that year.

I put the photo to one side and took out another handful. I had to be ruthless about it—I couldn't afford to relive every memory. I flicked through the cruise to Bermuda that Charles and I had taken when he'd retired, a camping trip to the White Mountains he'd taken with a few of his friends, a weekend on the Cape. Photos of us with Ally when we'd gone to visit her in California, her tanned and glowing and happy, me and Charles pale and jet-lagged but relieved to find her doing so well. I can still picture that apartment, just ten minutes from the beach and filled to bursting with equally tanned and glowing friends of hers, all doing internships or graduate degrees and falling in and out of love. On our last night in San Diego, Charles and I had taken them out to dinner to their favorite Mexican restaurant. We'd sat back from the table and smiled as the girls fell on the fajitas like they hadn't eaten in weeks. Charles managed to flinch only a bit when the bill came, and I remember getting on the plane the next morning feeling so proud of my little family. I put aside a photo from that trip, one of

26

Ally wearing a pale blue cotton dress, her dark hair shining as she smiled into the sun. My eyes slid to the remaining photographs. This one was from the Fourth of July 2015, Charles standing by the seafront as fireworks explode behind him. In it he isn't facing the camera, but I could see the thinness of his legs inside his trousers, like matchsticks, and the defeated slump of his shoulders. I pushed it away.

I stared at my hands outstretched on the worn wooden table. My knuckles were swollen and sore. I turned my wedding ring around slowly, feeling it tug on the skin underneath. I hadn't taken it off in so long, I couldn't imagine what my finger looked like without it. The skin beneath the band would be pale and shiny, and there would be an indentation where the ring pinched. It was too small for me, it had been for years, but the ring's design—delicate latticework cut into gold—meant it would have been ruined if I'd tried to have it enlarged, and anyway at that point it would have to have been cut off my finger, because there was no way to get it past my knuckle. They were welcome to do that just before they shoved my body into the furnace, but not a minute sooner.

Jim reached over and took my hand. The warm pressure of it stunned me. How long had it been since someone had taken my hand and held it?

They hadn't had to cut Charles's ring to get it off. I had slipped it off his finger before they took him away. I'd thought I'd have wanted him to be buried with it, but he'd chosen to be cremated, and I couldn't bear the thought of it melting—it was cheap gold, we'd been poor when we got married—so I slid it off his finger and onto my thumb and it stayed there until I got home and tucked it into my jewelry box, next to the opal earrings he'd given me for our thirtieth anniversary, which I was always too afraid to wear in case I lost one of them. I had to keep his ring safe for him, just in case. Just in case he came back.

I couldn't have told Ally why I kept it. I knew what she would have said if I'd told her that, deep in my heart, I believed that somehow her father would come back to me. She would have told me that denial was a natural part of the grieving process, but that ultimately it was important to let go. She's very rational, Ally. She takes after me in that regard (magical thinking about my dead husband aside) though I'm sure she'd hate to admit it. She always wanted to be like her father, dreaming big dreams about the stars, rather than down on earth filing facts away in little boxes like me. And who could blame her?

I suppose I did, a little. I can admit that much.

I picked up the photograph of her smiling in her blue dress and ached at the sight. It was a deep, primal ache, the same one I'd had since the day she was born—the day she'd started on her trajectory out of my orbit and out into the world, away from me.

I handed the photograph to Jim. "Here," I said. "They can use this one. It's from a few years ago, but she can't have changed that much."

He studied it for a minute. "She always did have a beautiful smile."

I looked down at the photograph. "She gets it from her father."

He slid the photo into his shirt pocket and stood up from the table. "I know you said you wanted to be alone, and I don't want to push it, but—"

I held up a hand to stop him. "Tell Linda to come whenever she can."

He nodded. "I'm sure she'll be right over. I'll be in touch as soon as I know anything more," he said, walking to the door. "And Maggie? Maybe start screening your calls. These media people will start calling the house once the news breaks, if they haven't started already. They're a bunch of ghouls."

The thought of speaking to a reporter about Ally made my stomach churn. I didn't want them having a piece of her. I wanted her all to myself. "Thanks, Jim. For everything."

"I wish I could do more to help," he said, and then he shut the door behind him and the house was silent again.

I sat at the kitchen table and let myself feel the heaviness in my chest. It was like my rib cage was being pulled apart bone by bone. Barney snaked his way around my ankles but I couldn't bring myself to reach down and pet him. I couldn't do anything.

The clock ticked. I wondered if it was possible for me to rip off my own skin, just claw my way out of it and leave my old bones and my ravaged heart behind.

I glanced up at the counter and saw the two little pill bottles standing to attention on the butcher's block. I picked one of them up—the Valium—and tilted a pill into my palm, then two. I swallowed them without water, feeling them scratch at my throat, and then sat back down at the table and waited for the feeling to stop.

Linda arrived just as the pills were kicking in. She came through the door without knocking and as soon as she saw my glazed eyes, she nodded. "Good for you." She sat down across from me and held my hands. The drugs did their job. It was almost—almost—like not feeling, except for the moments that the pain would pierce through.

"Do they know anything?" Linda asked finally. She'd been silent for three-quarters of an hour, surely the longest she'd gone without speaking in her entire life.

I shook my head. "There's going to be an investigation." My tongue felt thick in my mouth.

"Well, that's good," she said. "At least you'll know. Any more news on the pilot?"

I shook my head. "Nothing yet." I was failing her again. We all were. There were answers out there and I couldn't get them. Ally needed facts and I'd intentionally blurred my edges. I was weak.

"Jim said they were still waiting to hear about next of kin, but surely they can't keep holding back his name. The press'll dig it up soon enough, anyway."

The phone rang as if on cue. We both sat still and listened to the answering machine pick up. It was still Charles's voice— "You've reached the Carpenters, leave a message after the beep.

Beeeeep!" I knew I should change it; Linda even offered to do it herself, knowing how much I hate the sound of my own voice, but I couldn't erase him. We'd never owned a video camera, so this was it. A joke on an answering machine.

The machine clicked on and a smooth, low voice filled the house. "Hello, Mrs. Carpenter, this is Leon Terzi from the *Boston Herald*. I'm so sorry to hear of your loss. I'd love to speak with you about your daughter if you have a moment—she seemed like a very special girl. I'm putting together an article on the accident and I'm sure our readers would love to hear your memories of Allison. You can reach me at 617-555-4923."

Linda and I listened to the sound of the phone going dead. "Asshole," Linda muttered, gathering herself up and switching on the coffee machine. "What the hell am I doing?" she asked, flicking it off again. "Let's have a drink."

"No thanks," I said, waving her away. I watched her flick the coffee machine back on and pull two mugs down from the cabinet. I was still foggy from the Valium but I could feel it starting to clear out of my system. The weight had returned to my hands and feet and the room moved at the pace of my vision. I wanted a drink very badly, actually, and another of those little blue pills, but the phone call had shaken me back into myself. I shouldn't be trying to hide from the pain. I should be letting it wash over me like so many crashing waves.

My daughter is dead.

My daughter is dead.

My daughter is dead.

"The nerve of that man calling the house," Linda said, settling herself back down at the table and taking a sip of her coffee. I could smell the Baileys she'd slipped into it instead of creamer. "I'll talk to Jim, see if there isn't something to be done about it."

"I just won't answer the phone," I said. I wouldn't have answered the phone anyway, but this made the choice clearer.

"Make sure you don't watch the news, either. You don't need to see the reports. I'll bring over some movies if you want. Or that Jane Austen program on PBS I was telling you about."

I shook my head. "There's no need."

"I'll stay with you tonight, anyway. Keep you company."

I shook my head again. Poor Linda. She wanted to help so badly, but I had nothing to offer. I was on an island that she couldn't reach. No one could.

"You really shouldn't be alone—"

I sighed. She wasn't going to let it go. "I know you're trying to help and I love you for it, I do, but I'd rather be alone."

I saw her face drop and I knew I'd hurt her feelings, but I couldn't help it. I couldn't stand the idea of anyone—not even her—sitting in my house watching me go through this. I didn't need anyone to bear witness. I was witness enough.

She pushed back from the table and started rummaging through the refrigerator. "Let me at least make you something for dinner before I go," she said. "I can't let you starve to death." She froze. "I'm sorry," she said quietly.

"You're allowed to say the word 'death,'" I said, even though hearing it had sent a chill through me. "It's fine."

"No, it's not fine," she said, spinning around. "It's anything but fine, and I just wish I could— I just wish—"

"I know," I said, getting up and moving toward her. I put my hand on her back. I could feel the heat coming off her.

"I'm sorry," she said, wiping tears from the corners of her eyes. "I'm not meant to be the one crying, I know I'm meant to be the strong one, it's just, I feel so—so—"

"You're not meant to be anything other than what you are," I said, rubbing my hand across her back. I felt very tired then, and my arm was heavy as I dragged my palm back and forth. "You don't need to apologize."

"I do," Linda said, eyes suddenly flashing. "Someone should apologize for this, so why shouldn't it be me? You don't deserve this, Maggie. Charles didn't deserve what happened to him and Ally didn't deserve what happened to her and you sure as hell don't deserve what's happening to you now."

My eyelids felt heavy and I wondered how my body was managing to remain upright. It felt like the sole of a boot was pressing down on the top of my head, slowly but firmly working me into the ground. "No one deserves anything," I said finally. And the truth of that was enough to make my knees give way.

Allison

In the half-light of the morning, just before I'm fully awake, I smell the damp sweetness of mulch and the faint gray tang of smoke. For a second, I think I'm in my childhood bedroom. I can hear my mother's voice calling to me from the bottom of the stairs, promising pancakes and orange juice. I can feel the weight of the comforter, the soft fur of the plush toy dog I slept with, the cool smoothness of the pillowcase against my cheek.

I open my eyes. A shroud of fog has descended overnight. I sit up, every muscle in my body complaining, pull the blanket around my shoulders, and shiver. I feel old, like my body has aged a hundred years in a matter of hours. I try to remember what it was like not to feel pain, but it's impossible. The night was colder than I expected, and my fingers and toes prick as the blood comes back into them. My head feels heavy, like it's filled with sand, and my mouth tastes faintly of metal.

I'm alive.

I need to find water before I go any farther. I'm running low and there's no way I can climb a mountain without a decent supply. That's my first priority.

A papery laugh floats from my lungs. *Climb a mountain.* Jesus Christ.

I pull down my leggings and inspect the gash on my thigh. The bandage is dark with old blood and the edges are filthy. It has to be changed. I peel it off slowly but that doesn't stop it from hurting like hell. The cut looks angry underneath, the skin around it pale and slightly swollen. I take out the rubbing alcohol and brace myself. I swear I see the blood fizz slightly when the alcohol hits it, or maybe it's just my brain's way of dealing with the pain. I patch it up with a fresh bandage and try not to think about when I had my last tetanus shot.

My finger has turned a nasty purple underneath the splint but seems less swollen and sore. It could be healing or it could be nerve damage. Add that to the list of things I'm not thinking about.

I rummage around in my bag and pull out the bag of nuts. I am suddenly, ravenously hungry, but I can't afford to eat too much. I don't know how long I'll be out here, and I have to make the few things I have last. I nibble at the edge of a brazil nut and pretend it's a bagel. Not that I allowed myself to eat a bagel in my previous life.

My previous life—that's what it has already become, sepia tinged and pressed flat between pages, a place where I counted carbs among my enemies. I try to remember standing on the tarmac, the heat so intense that it made my ears ring, or in the house overlooking the beach, all whitewashed floors and chrome finishes, but I feel nothing, just the sickly fear starting to creep back in. They could be out there somewhere already, searching for me.

Move.

It's early still, and the sun is weak beyond the tree cover. The wildflowers are still tightly tucked into themselves, just the smallest tip of petal peeking through the leaves. Yesterday felt like one sort of dream—a visceral, terrifying nightmare—and today feels like another. Drowsy. Unreal.

A chipmunk stops short in front of me, cheeks pumping rapidly, then disappears into a pile of leaves. I climb over a fallen tree trunk, the underside of it covered in thick green-blue moss and speckled with tiny mushrooms. The air smells fresher now. And then I hear a gentle shushing. Water.

It's barely a stream, more of a trickle, but it's enough. I finish off the rest of yesterday's water, dunk the empty bottles into the stream, and sit back to wait for the iodine to work. I tug off my sneakers, peel off my socks, and dip my feet in. Fresh blisters sting.

I rub at the sores through the water. They'll toughen up, I figure. They'll have to.

I splash water onto my face and neck, careful not to reopen the lacework of cuts, and pat myself dry with a fresh scrap of shirt. I briefly consider my toenails, still painted a delicate shell pink from a recent pedicure. Absurd, really. Hilarious, even. I pull on a fresh pair of socks and rinse yesterday's in the stream before hanging them to dry on the back of my bag.

By midday, I reach the first ridge. The forest is still thick and it's difficult to tell if I've been heading in the right direction, so when I reach the clearing and can finally see, it takes me a minute to get my bearings. The tops of trees dip into the valley below, and beyond them, through the deep V, rises the peak of the mountain where we crashed.

It's all undulating waves of treetops rising to harsh, jagged peaks. The mountain looks like a picture on a postcard or an ad for hot chocolate, benign and surreally beautiful. How could catastrophe be hidden so quickly? I had expected a scar on the landscape, a blight, but there is just the smooth surface of nature staring blankly back, like a painting bought in a suburban mall.

And then I see it. It's quick and at first I think I've imagined it, but then I notice something else and I know that it's real. The glint of sunlight off metal and then, faint but steady, a wispy line of smoke snaking its way through the trees. It exists. It happened. And now the plane is on fire. Fire means smoke. Smoke gets attention.

They're coming.

The panic rises in me like the tide. My animal brain returns.

Fuck fuck fuck. Move.

Go, climb, faster. Up up up you can't stop. Keep going. Do not stop.

You have to move.

I can feel the grief behind the fear, just pushing through. I've lost the man I loved. I will have to come to terms with that at some point.

Not yet.

Maggie

I spent a night plagued by visions. Ally's face contorted in terror. Ally crying out in pain. Ally bloodied and bruised. Ally on fire. Ally's flesh melting from her bones. It was the world's most brutal newsreel.

I tried over and over to change the tape but it was stuck on a loop, and I was stuck there with it. This was my life now. This tape would always be playing in my mind. Years later, even if some shadow of normal life had resumed, I would be grocery shopping or in the doctor's waiting room or on hold with the gas company, and there would only ever be this: Terror. Pain. Blood. Fire. Bone. Ally.

I got up, went downstairs, clicked the lid off Linda's sleeping tablets, and took four of them. I climbed back up the stairs, got into bed, waited for Barney to settle himself back on my feet, turned out the lights, and lay there watching the tape until the heavy hood of oblivion settled over my head and pulled me into a deep, blank sleep.

I woke up feeling like I'd gone ten rounds in the ring and lost, badly. Every muscle in my body was sore. Grief had been my well-worn companion for the past few years. I thought I was used to it—over time it had slowly ground down my edges and dulled my senses—but this was something else. This was a gut punch. Charles's illness and slow death had been a long, arduous plod up an unforgiving hill. This, though, was a violence.

The reel started up again: Terror. Pain. Blood. Fire. Bone. Ally. My body ached with the weight of the grief, like there was lead lining my skin.

Barney, now up on my pillow, shot me a dirty look as I shifted out of bed. Seven a.m. I'd been asleep for ten hours. I would have to thank Linda for the pills. I would have to ask her if she could get some more.

The stone tiles in the kitchen were cold underfoot. It was early July, but the mornings were still cool and there would be dew on the grass. The answering machine blinked at me, demanding to be heard. I hit Play. It was message after message from Jennifer and Chip and Mark and Sandra from various news organizations across the country, all telling me about the sensitive portraits of Allison they were working on and how they needed only a few minutes of my time. How it was sensitive to keep calling a woman whose only child had just died in a plane crash, I couldn't tell you.

I deleted them all and thought about pulling the phone cord out of the wall, but there was a part of me—the same part that had pried the wedding ring off Charles's finger in the end—that knew I had to keep it plugged in. They hadn't found her body. This could still all be a horrible mistake. I could still get a call putting it right.

The kitchen was filled with a sour, fermented smell, and I followed it into the pantry. I knew the source immediately. I lifted the tea towel off the glass bowl on the shelf and saw the lump of dough lying there, collapsed. A thin skin had formed on top, which bloomed with blue-green mold. The sight of it lying there, ruined and forgotten, was too much. So much waste. Tears streamed down my face as I tipped the bowl into the garbage. The dough landed with a resigned thud.

I saw the orange pill bottle on the table and shoved it into the junk drawer. Ally needed me clearheaded and sharp eyed.

There was a knock at the front door and the particular set of noises of someone letting herself in. Linda. She bustled into the kitchen moments later, arms laden with plastic carrier bags from the Shop-n-Save and a stack of casserole dishes.

"News travels fast," she said, dumping the dishes unceremoniously on the counter.

The women of Owl's Creek were great believers in the healing power of casseroles. Birth, illness, tragedy, death: there was a casse-role that would help. When Charles died, they were stacked high on my doorstep with a Post-it attached to each one identifying its con-tents and its creator. Joan Doherty's tuna noodle, Sue Provencher's green bean surprise, Diane Beaulieu's meatloaf, Elaine McNulty's sweet potato, Kathleen Sullivan's macaroni mayo, Holly Parker's ham and potato, Mary Bianchi's baked ziti, Joy Chamberlain's chili cheese. They sat in my fridge for weeks until I finally had the strength to scrape them out into the trash, scour the glass dishes with a Brillo pad, and return them to their rightful owners.

I understood that these casseroles came from a place of genu-ine concern, and that they were an expression of sympathy and thoughtfulness that would be difficult to put into words. But I'd lived in that town all my life, and I knew there was something else, too—something a little less generous. I'd never gotten involved in the Owl's Creek casserole-making frenzy, which is probably why I got so many of the damned things: so that all of those women could prove that they were better than me. And God forbid you forgot to return their Pyrex.

"I picked up a few things from the store," Linda said, gesturing toward the bags on the floor. Her hair was piled on top of her head and secured with a tortoiseshell clip, and her fingers wandered up to the stray hairs that floated around her face. "Feel free to chuck them out with the casseroles, but I couldn't face coming over here empty handed, and you're going to have to eat at some point."

"Thanks," I said, and I meant it. Linda was not one of the cas-serole women. She did kind things all the time, not because she wanted something in return but because it would never occur to her to be anything other than kind. I watched as she dipped a hand into one of the bags and pulled out a hunk of bread, which she started absently chewing. She looked tired.

"Did you get any sleep?"

I watched her shove the casserole dishes into the fridge. "I took your pills."

"Good girl. Do you want any more? I can call the doctor for you. I'm sure he'd just call it in."

I shook my head. "That's all right."

She nodded. "If you change your mind, just let me know. Any more phone calls from the jackals?"

"I switched off the ringer."

She pulled a couple of cans of soup out of a bag and stacked them in the pantry. "Good for you."

"Have you seen anything?" I asked. "On the news?"

"I caught a little something on the seven o'clock," she said. She reached up and tucked a wisp of hair back into the clip. "I didn't stick around to watch it all. They were mostly talking about that damn president of ours, as usual."

I looked at her carefully. Linda had always had a terrible poker face. "What is it?"

She took another bite of bread and chewed it too thoroughly. She was stalling.

"Linda. Please."

She swallowed, hard. "Jim showed me that picture of Allison in the blue dress you gave him. For the news people."

Ally in sunlight in the blue dress. I nodded.

"Well, he gave it to them, but it's not the photo they're using."

Was this my life? Not even the pictures of her were mine anymore. "What picture are they using?"

"It's not one I've seen before," she said. "Jim says they must have got it from the internet or something." She paused, then leaned across the table. "The thing is, and I know I haven't seen her in a couple of years, but I barely recognized her. She looks . . . different."

A jolt ran through me. "Different how?"

"Just not like Allison. She was blond in the photo, and thin. I know she's always been small but she looked *tiny*. Was she on a diet?"

"I don't know," I said quietly.

"Well, she must have been. I'm not saying she doesn't look great

39

in the photo, because she does. Like a movie star or something. When it first came on I said to Jim, that can't be our Allison, can it? She looks so fancy! I know she works for a magazine and everything, and she always dressed nice, but—" Linda looked over at me and fell silent. "I'm sorry. I shouldn't be running my mouth like this."

I lifted my eyes to hers. It was time to come clean. "There's something I need to tell you."

"What is it?"

I took a deep breath. "I haven't seen Allison since Charles died."

Her brow furrowed. "What do you mean? You went out to visit her last Thanksgiving!"

"I went to my sister's in Florida instead. Ally didn't invite me."

"I don't understand. Why would she do that? Why didn't you say something? You could have had Thanksgiving with us!"

"I didn't want to make a big fuss." I'd been embarrassed, of course. What kind of a mother must I have been for my daughter not to want to see me? Even after everything we'd been through together. Especially after everything.

"Grief does strange things to people," Linda said, shaking her head. "Whatever her reason, I'm sure she didn't mean to shut you out like that."

"Linda . . ." I felt sick at the thought of telling her the truth, but it had to be done. I'd come this far, and there was no room for any more lies. "When Charles was real sick, toward the end, he asked me to—to help him, if you see what I mean." Linda's face was blank. "He didn't want to suffer anymore. He wanted it to end. Do you understand what I'm saying?"

I watched it register. She flinched, just for a second, and then she nodded, eyes filling with tears. "Oh, Maggie," she said quietly.

I looked away. I didn't want to see the look on her face in case it held judgment. "I didn't tell Ally about it, because I didn't want to upset her." I wanted to get all of it out, like sucking the poison from a snakebite. "I knew she wanted her dad to live as long as he possibly could, and I didn't think . . ." I shrugged. "I don't know what I thought. I didn't tell her, but she found out anyway." Linda shook her head, like she was trying to ward off what was coming.

I took a deep breath. "The doctor left the morphine unlocked. We hadn't talked about it with him—we didn't want him to get into trouble or, God forbid, lose his license—but he seemed to know what we were planning, and he made it easy. I thought Ally was still out for her run. Charles hadn't wanted her to see it, and neither did I. We both wanted her to think it was natural. I don't know why—it seems so stupid now, so cruel of us not to let her say goodbye—but it was like we were in this fog together, and neither of us could see clearly. I kissed him and then I turned on the tap and held his hand until he was gone. It was quick. Quicker than I'd thought." I reached up and dashed away a tear. "When I turned around, I saw her standing there in the doorway." I glanced over and could still see it, as clear as if it were happening right then. "I could tell by the look on her face that she'd seen me kill him."

She reached over and gripped my hand, tight. "Look at me, Maggie."

I raised my eyes reluctantly to hers. There was nothing in her face except love and worry and kindness. I sagged with relief. It was Linda—I should have known. I should have told her years ago.

"You did not kill him," she said gently. "You were helping him."

I suddenly felt like I was being disloyal to Ally, looking for reassurance that I didn't deserve. I pulled my hand away like I'd been burned. "That's not how she felt. In her eyes, I killed her father." I pictured the look on her face, a mix of grief and loathing and betrayal. A look a mother never wants to see on her child's face. "She didn't say a word, she just got her stuff and ran out of the house. That's why she wasn't at the funeral—it wasn't because she was too upset, or because she had the flu, or whatever damn thing I told people at the time. It was because she knew I was responsible, and she couldn't stand being near me."

"The only thing responsible for Charles's death is the goddamn cancer that ate him alive," Linda said. "You were only doing what he asked you to do. I saw how much pain that man was in. Ally saw it, too. What you did was merciful, and I'm sure deep down she knew that."

I shrugged. "All I know is the last time I looked my daughter in the eyes, I saw hatred in them. And now I'll never look into them again." The realization ripped through me once more. How was I still alive? How was my heart still beating in my chest when it felt so irreparably broken?

"Oh, Maggie." Linda came over and crouched down by my chair. "I am so sorry. God, I can't imagine . . ." Jim and Linda had three boys, each of whom had moved back to Maine after college. Craig, the oldest, had bought a house on the same street as them with his wife. Ben, their middle boy, lived an hour away in Portland. Every weekend, they had a houseful. It was why I hadn't told her before: I knew that she would feel the pain of my loss too keenly, and I hadn't wanted her to feel that sort of hurt. "She knew you loved her," she whispered. "And she loved you."

I was grateful she said it, but the tense. *She loved me. I loved her.* It was in the past. My whole life was now in the past.

"Maggie," Linda said, studying my face. "Time for a rest?"

I welled up. We'd known each other a long time. I nodded.

She squeezed my arm. "I'll let myself out, but call me when you get up. The second you get up."

She stood, gathered the empty mugs that littered the table, and put them in the sink. "Leave those dishes," she said as she walked out the door. "I love you."

I heard her gunshot engine starting and her car pulling away.

She was gone, and I was alone.

Allison

Stop.

Breathe.

I've been climbing for hours now. Palms scraped, knees bloodied, lungs screaming, back aching. But now I'm at the summit. The top of the world, if the world didn't seem so far away.

The land stretches out like a ragged carpet. The descent is steep and treacherous, but I can see the faint outline of a trail snaking down the side of the mountain. If I take it, I'll have to be careful not to get turned around. If I don't take it, I'll increase my chances of falling down a crevice and splitting open my skull.

The whiteness of bone.

So many ways to die.

The plan is Take the Path.

I take a sip of water, the first in hours, and eat half a Luna bar. The greenbottles swarm but I don't bother to swipe them away anymore. I'm already covered in angry welts and bloodied scabs—I figure there isn't much skin left for them to bite. I'm wrong about that, of course. They just bite the welts and scabs, the fuckers.

The humming sound has returned, louder now, insistent. I'm dehydrated, but I can't tell how badly. All I know is that I can't afford to faint. I take another sip and shove the bottle back in my bag. That's enough. It'll have to be. On my feet. It's time to go.

I set out for the path, navigating the sharp rocks with inching side steps, shifting my way down the steep ridges, the bag bumping on the small of my back with each step. The movement becomes almost meditative, the slow shift from left foot to right, the steady rasp of my breath, the persistent drone of encircling flies.

Then, suddenly and with a clarity that takes my breath away, it comes. A memory. Me zipped into a snowsuit, small arms and legs too hot beneath the pillowy fabric, wool hat itching my forehead, and my father dressed in corduroys and boots and his old ski jacket pulling me up a hill on a red plastic sled. Climbing in behind me, pushing us off with a shove, trees whizzing past as we careered down the hill on the icy track, him holding on to me tightly as I screamed the sort of scream that comes when you are completely safe inside a brief terror.

And then, too soon, it's replaced with another image. Him, thin skinned, yellowed and brittle, lying on the sofa, lips cracked and bleeding, whispering something urgent that I couldn't understand. My mother crouched down beside him, holding both of his hands in one of hers, the skin underneath her eyes pouched and bruise dark.

I can still conjure up the anger I felt toward her. For months after I saw her open the valve on his morphine drip, I carried the hatred around with me, like a flame protected by cupped palms. She killed him. She took him away from me. She didn't warn me. She didn't even give me the chance to say goodbye.

And then, like waking up after a long fever, the anger broke, replaced by waves of grief and regret. But by then it was too late.

I push this away, down to where memories like that are kept. Deep down and out of sight. I can't think about that right now. I can't afford to think about anything other than keeping myself alive.

I shuffle my way down the smooth face of a boulder. Think of a song to sing. Or a poem to recite. But I don't know any poems by heart and the only songs I can think of are Christmas ones, and Christmas songs remind me of my father and winter and us sledding down the hill, and the image of my father in the sled brings me back to his legs so thin beneath the afghan, and his skin like wax, and the way I recoiled when I knew he was reaching for me. I had watched my mother hold both of my father's hands, and the thing I had felt the most had been revulsion. I hate myself for that. Among other things.

I trip and fall, hard, wrenching my bad shoulder. "Fuck!" I holler into the nothing. I look back at what tripped me. A tree stump.

Stupid, silly girl.

My palms sting and my shoulder throbs but the pain clears my mind.

The plan is Stay Alive.

I get back to my feet and start toward the path. Slowly. Carefully. There are a few hours until dusk, four at most. I need to set up camp before dark. One foot in front of the other, careful where I place each step.

I take a sip of water as a reward when I reach the path, but I don't have much left, only half a bottle, and the sun's heat is unrelenting even as it starts to dip in the sky. The hum in my skull is now a steady roar.

Hurry.

The dark is encroaching by the time the path levels out. I step off the trail and into the forest, letting the trees swallow me.

In a small clearing, I shrug off my bag, wincing. I run my fingers across the ridges left by the straps; the skin is tender and bloodied underneath. My body is a symphony of pain, each part of me registering a specific octave.

The sky is a deep velvet navy. The temperature has dropped. All the day's heat has been replaced with a dry chill. I shiver and dig the sweatshirt out of my bag, but it isn't enough: the cold works its way into my bones. I need to build a fire.

Gather wood. Tote it to the clearing. Check the direction of the wind and the location of the trees. I build the fire just like my father taught me. A bundle of tinder. A tepee of bark and kindling. Large dry sticks at the ready, to feed any hopeful sparks.

I take out the silver lighter and flick it open. The pale blue flame flickers as I touch it to the pine needles. They glow orange as they catch. I wait until it has spread evenly through the kindling and then gently place a few larger branches onto the fire. It begins to crackle and spit.

The heat of the fire warms the metal of my watch, so I slip it into the zippered pocket on my bag. It doesn't matter what time it is, anyway. I try to ignore the growl of my stomach and the dryness in my mouth and the hulking terror squatting at the base of my throat.

I watch the flames lick at the branches, turning them to ash. I was nine the day my dad taught me to build a fire. He had a desk job at the town hall, but every free minute he had he was outdoors. He spent the winters snowshoeing and the summers camping and climbing, and as soon I could walk, he took me along.

That night, we were building a bonfire in the backyard to burn the dried leaves we'd raked up the day before. He'd sent me off to fetch kindling from the trees near our house and then showed me how to place everything just right, and when it came time to light it, he held out a pair of stones: a piece of quartz and a flat rock.

"Watch close, Allycat," he'd said. "It's like a magic trick." And he struck the stones until—there! A spark.

"You try," he'd said, handing me the two rocks and showing me how to hold them. "You want to hit the handstone with the striker right there," he'd said, pointing to the center of the flat stone.

I hit the stone again and again, but nothing happened. "Keep at it," he'd said. "You'll get there."

I kept going. Nothing happened. My arms started to ache and my fingers seized. "This is stupid. Why am I doing this?" I'd asked. "We have matches in the house!"

"It's important." That's all he said. Because he said it, I started to think it was important, too.

I broke the flat rock. He found me another. "Don't give up," he'd said. "You're tough. You're patient. You can do this."

And then it happened. A single bright orange spark and then, with the next strike, a tiny shower of them. He'd whooped with glee. "Do it again!" he'd said. "Over the tinder this time!" I did it again, and one of the tiny orange sparks fell on the pile of fluff and pine needles and my dad cupped his hands around it and blew gently until it caught, and then we both sat back and watched the tiny flame grow in strength until it reached up into the pile of sticks and twigs and then, suddenly, it was a fire. I had made fire. I remember him putting his arm around me and pulling me in close. "I knew you could do it."

In that moment, I thought I could do anything.

But then he died and I betrayed him. I'd allowed myself to become useless, decorative. Good for only one thing.

I look back at the fire. The chill has been chased from the air now, and the feeling is starting to return to my fingers and toes. I pull out the bag of nuts and eat two peanuts and a walnut, one by one, chewing and chewing until they're nothing but paste. Then, to celebrate the successful fire, I follow it with half a Luna bar. The food wakes up my stomach and it twists with hunger.

There are two and a half Luna bars left and a half bag of nuts. Enough for another couple of days, max. I'll have to figure something out, though Lord knows what. But first, sleep.

Down go the canopy cover and the blanket. Off come my shoes. Inspect the new blisters. One of my toenails is sore to the touch, and I can see the tinge of blackness underneath the pink polish. I'll lose that one.

I lie down and tuck the blanket around me. The fire crackles. I can smell my father in the smoke and I feel something beneath the sore muscles, the cuts and bruises, and the deep, unshakable anxiety rooted in my breastbone. It feels a little like comfort.

You're tough. You can do this.

That's the last thing I think as I go to sleep under a black sky and a half moon and a sea of tiny, sparkling stars.

Maggie

I hadn't meant to tell Linda what happened between me and Ally, but now that I had, it felt like a weight had been lifted.

Ally had been gone from me for two years. In the months after Charles had died, I had tried to make things right. I called her apartment, left messages on the answering machine and with her roommate, sent her letters begging her to talk to me, but all of it was met with silence. She didn't want me in her life—she'd made that very clear, and I was too rubbed raw with grief and guilt and regret to keep knocking on a door that was bolted shut. I told myself it was for the best, that I was obeying Ally's wishes, respecting her decision. The truth was, I was weak. I should have kept pushing. I should have turned up on her doorstep and refused to leave until she agreed to see me. She was my daughter, and she was hurting. I should have done everything in my power to make things right.

Now she was gone forever. It was too late to patch that rift, but I owed it to her to find out what had happened to her. I hadn't fought for her then, I thought, but I could fight for her now.

I had to see that picture.

I waited for the six o'clock news to come on, coiled in Charles's old armchair like a snake. I leaned forward as the opening credits rolled.

A redheaded woman in a startlingly bright red suit sat behind a desk and grimaced at the camera. "In our top story tonight, a Bangor woman is accused of attacking her own son in what witnesses are describing as a brutal moment of madness . . ."

I muted it and sat back in the chair. I had no interest in listening to other people's misery when I had so much of my own.

I clicked the sound back on as they were wrapping up a segment about the Red Sox's no-hitter against the Orioles.

"It looks like Sox fans finally have something to smile about," said the sportscaster with the rolled-up sleeves.

The redheaded anchor nodded at him. "Sure does, Jim," she said, before turning back to the camera and pulling her face into a frown. "Investigators are still searching for the cause of a plane crash that left a woman with ties to the Maine area dead."

A photograph appeared to the left of the redhead's face. Her hair *was* blond and she *was* thin. Too thin. She was smiling over her shoulder in a backless black dress, each of her vertebrae visible. Her hair falling in caramel waves. Her cheekbones were high and her skin glowed and her teeth were blindingly white in her broad smile. She was beautiful, breathtakingly so, but she looked nothing like the daughter I had known. Ally had always been beautiful, of course, but this woman looked like a film star. It had taken me a second to recognize my daughter.

"Allison Carpenter, thirty-one, was the only passenger on board the single-engine aircraft when it went down in the middle of the Colorado Rocky Mountains. The pilot has yet to be identified. Ms. Carpenter grew up in Maine but was most recently a resident of San Diego, California. Authorities are still trying to determine the cause of the crash but at the moment, it is not a criminal investigation. We'll have more as this story unfolds."

The anchorwoman's face shifted again. "Tonight's lottery rollover is set to be a record $1.6 million. Have you got your ticket, Brad?"

"I sure do, Melanie—"

I switched off the television. The silence settled around me along with the dust glittering in the remains of the day's light.

I thought about the photo of Ally, the glossiness of her. How could she have afforded that dress? That haircut? I didn't know much about fashion, but I knew that she didn't make enough for all that. She did something with advertising for a women's magazine that had just gotten off the ground called *Faces*. She'd shown us issues when we'd visited. It was full of beautiful women of every color under the sun, some heavy, some thin. One with a scar lashing across her face. None of them looked a thing like the woman whose photograph was on that news report. "We're interested in representation," Ally had said, her brows knitting together. "The magazine is all about women celebrating women, in all the ways it looks, in all the things it means. We want to do more than be a tool for big companies. We want to interrogate the industry." Neither Charles nor I knew what she was talking about, but we knew her fiery passion well. "That sounds great, dear," we'd said. I'd taken the issue and read it on the plane. I liked it, but I didn't know who would ever buy advertising in it. But maybe it had taken off. Though surely I would have heard if it had become a success, and I couldn't remember ever seeing it on the magazine racks at Target.

I walked into the kitchen and fired up the ancient iMac that we had sent Ally to college with and inherited when she had enough money to buy herself a sleek silver laptop. The fan whirred and the bootup screen cycled on. Most of my friends didn't understand how the internet worked and only the most savvy had Facebook accounts. Linda had finally convinced her daughter-in-law to stop sending links to pictures from their vacations entirely; instead, she would just upload them to a drugstore's website and give her a call to say there were some photos for her to pick up. Not me. Twenty years on the research desk at the Bowdoin College library had made me perfectly capable of navigating the Web. The computer we kept at home was slow, but it worked fine enough, and my retired staff badge got me access to everything I could ever need at the college library, whenever I wanted it. Despite all that, having the knowledge and the equipment, I hadn't looked up Ally's name online since I gave up trying to contact her. The least I could do, I had thought, was respect her wishes and stay out of her life. Stupid me.

I started by typing her name into the search bar, but all that came up were stories about the crash. No Facebook profile, either, though I knew she'd had one at one point because she'd showed it to me a few years earlier when she was home over Christmas break. We'd spent a couple of hours looking up old friends of hers from high school, seeing who was up to what. "Jenny has three kids," she'd said, mouth hanging open. "Can you believe it?" But there were no Allison Carpenters from San Diego on the list, and none of the thumbnail photographs grinning out at me looked anything like her, not even the movie-star version of her.

I tried googling "Faces magazine" next, but nothing much came up there, either. The first link was a Wikipedia entry. As any good student can tell you, Wikipedia isn't a reliable source, but it can be a good place to start. The entry was brief, detailing the mission statement Ally had told us about. There was a scandal involving a pop star whose name I vaguely recognized saying something awful about the models. Under a picture of the first issue on the right-hand side was a list of facts. Editor in chief: Agathe Silverman. Frequency: Monthly. First issue: September 2009. Final issue: January 2016.

That couldn't be right. January 2016 was four months before Charles had died. I had seen Ally in March of that year and she hadn't said a thing about it.

My daughter was a cipher. I needed to talk to someone who knew something about her. I yanked open the drawer that held the old clothbound address book, stuffed full of scraps of paper and business cards and the names of people I hadn't seen in years and probably never would again. I pulled it down from the shelf and flicked to the page. There it was, the number for Allison's apartment, written in Charles's blocky handwriting. I hadn't dialed it for over two years.

What was her roommate's name? Sara? Tara. Tara. I dialed the number. I wasn't relishing telling her about the crash, but I needed answers.

"Hello?" The voice that answered was familiar, but it wasn't Ally's. My treacherous heart sank. It was the same traitor who'd kept

Charles's wedding ring and kept the phone plugged in, that part that whispered, *What if it's all a mistake? What if she is there, has been home the whole time? What if she is padding around her apartment in her sweatpants, safe and sound?*

"Is that Tara?"

"Speaking."

"Tara, it's Maggie Carpenter. Ally's mom."

She gasped. "Mrs. Carpenter! Oh, my God. I'm so sorry. I just heard on the news, and I couldn't believe it . . ." I could picture Tara on the other end of the phone, blond hair tugged into a ponytail, thin shoulders shuddering. I'd met her only once, on that trip down to San Diego, but she was a sweet girl, the kind you wanted to wrap your arms around and take for a sandwich or an ice cream.

"I know, sweetheart. Me neither."

"It's just such a shock. I mean, I haven't seen Allison for a while, but the idea of her being gone . . ."

"Had she been away from home for long? Was she on a business trip?"

I listened to her sniffle down the line. "I— A business trip? I don't know. I guess it's possible."

"Do you think there's anything in her room that could tell us? Did she pack a lot of clothes, or just a few?"

There was a long pause. "Mrs. Carpenter, you know Allison doesn't live here anymore, right?"

My breath caught in my throat. "Oh. I see. When did she move out?"

"About a year and a half ago."

"A year and a half." I let it sink in. "Where did she go? Do you have the address?"

"No. I . . . I don't know," she said. "We weren't . . . we didn't talk all that much by the time she moved out." She began to cry.

"It's all right, dear," I murmured quietly. Ally had moved without telling me. For more than a year, I hadn't known where my daughter lived. If I'd needed to get in touch with her, I wouldn't have been able to. She had absented herself from me completely, totally.

"Most of her stuff is still here—she just took a suitcase, really—and I keep seeing the blanket we picked out together and the TV stand and the dishes and—" She was crying hard now, and her words came out in gasps.

"Take a deep breath, sweetheart. Do you know where she was working? I tried looking up that magazine she was at before, but . . ."

"She stopped working there a long time ago," Tara said gently.

"Did she get a job at another magazine? Something that might have involved her traveling? We're still not sure about why she was on that plane, you see, and I thought maybe it would have something to do with her line of work."

There was a pause on the other end of the line. "I heard she ended up working as a cocktail waitress at this place downtown."

"A cocktail waitress?" I tried to picture Ally—beautiful, brilliant Ally, with her college degree and her stacks of books—holding one of those trays stacked with umbrella-filled glasses. "She couldn't find anything else?"

"She tried, but there wasn't anything out there . . . she was always applying for jobs when she still lived here but nothing ever came from it, I guess."

My mind whirred as it tried to place this new information. I needed to know more. "Tara, do you remember the name of the bar she worked at?"

"I think it was a place called Sapphire's in the Gaslamp Quarter." She started crying again. I pictured her thin little shoulders being racked with sobs, and my heart broke. "I miss her," she gasped. "I really miss her."

"I know you do. We all do," I said. I couldn't bring myself to ask her any more questions. I'd already pushed her too far. I told her to take care of herself and put down the phone.

I tried to connect this new version of Allison with the one I remembered. She'd been full of dreams as a little girl, her head always stuck in a book or scribbling away in her notebook, photographs of London and Paris tacked to her walls. Charles and I used to catch each other's eye when she said something particularly smart and shake our heads in wonder at this incredible person we'd made. She was going to do anything and everything she wanted, and she'd ended up a cocktail waitress. I couldn't make the two ends meet. Being the mother of a grown child seemed to be a twinned experience, simultaneously loving the person she had become with all your soul while mourning everything she had not.

Now it was too late, and I would never get to know the woman she had become. She'd always be stuck in time, her edges blurring as each thing I learned made me unlearn something else.

Still. I had to try.

Allison

I wake up to a distant mechanical whir. An airplane, maybe, or a helicopter. I sit bolt upright and listen as the noise retreats into the sky, replaced by the quiet hum of the forest. The light leaks through the trees in fragments and I squint up at it before the pounding in my head starts again. Louder now, an insistent drum.

I struggle to my elbows and fight against the swoon. My shoulder throbs.

I check the bottle of water. Just a few swallows left. I gulp them down greedily before I can stop myself. I need to find water now, that's the first thing. I remember the path. I just need to find my way back to the path.

It wasn't that I didn't try. I applied to every opening for magazine work I could find, and then for every office admin job, and then for every job. I registered with temp agencies and had meetings with recruiters, who scanned my résumé with a frown and promised to be in touch, but they never were. When they did call, they told me I was overqualified, that employers wanted someone fresh out of college answering their phones, someone who wouldn't want too much from them. I told them I wasn't looking for anything more than a paycheck, but it didn't matter—jobs still didn't materialize.

Six months went by. Six months in the unrelenting glare of constant sunshine, marooned on the sofa in the dingy apartment I could no longer afford, watching daytime television and scrolling through job listings while waves of grief battered me, relentless. The little money I'd managed to save from my old job slowly drained away, until I was faced with a choice between rent and my car. It was California, so I chose the car.

Tara covered my share of the rent for a while, but I knew it was a strain on her, so when she finally told me that she'd have to look for a new roommate, I lied and told her I had another place lined up. She said I could stay on the couch, but she'd done too much for me already—I didn't want her to worry about me anymore. I called an old friend and asked if I could stay with her for a few days. A few days stretched into a week, and then two, until I couldn't look her in the eye anymore and I called another old friend, and then another. I stayed in spare rooms and couches across the city until I ran out of old friends and goodwill.

And then I moved into my car.

I knew my mother would have helped me if I'd asked. All through the nights on lumpy sofas and my cramped back seat and the days spent eating ramen and boiled eggs and killing time before sundown, I knew that I could have ended it all with a single phone call home. But I couldn't bring myself to do it. The anger I'd felt toward her had started to fade, though I could still locate it if I searched hard enough, like a bruise that had nearly healed. It had been replaced by something slippery and harder to define. Betrayal, yes, that she'd shut me out like that, but also shame at the way I'd reacted. I had missed my father's funeral. I had abandoned her at her lowest moment. And now I was just some washed-up spoiled brat who couldn't even find a job. A waste of space. A failure.

No. I couldn't call her, not yet. I had to do this on my own.

I heave myself onto my feet and start to pack up camp. The grass underneath the canopy is flattened now and there's a me-shaped depression in the soft earth. I kick at the ground with the toe of my sneaker, then toss down a few branches over the scorched remains of the fire. I don't want to leave any evidence.

The trees seem to have grown taller in the night. I look up at the canopy, and the expanse of green seems to stretch on into the sky. I scan the trunks for the scrap of fabric I'd left to mark the path. It was just a few steps to the left of camp. Or was it to the right? I turn in a slow semicircle, twigs snapping underfoot. Everything looks the same and nothing looks familiar. It had been dusk when I'd made camp—too dark to see the details, and anyway, I hadn't been looking.

Stupid, silly girl.

I squint up at the sky. The tree cover is too thick to pinpoint the sun's arc in the sky. I can't tell which way is east or west, or what time it is—above and below and all around me the trees stare blankly back. A drift of bluebells chime in the breeze. My nerves begin to twist.

Think. What would Dad do?

But he's not here to tell me. I'll have to guess.

Right. I'll go right.

No. Left.

I set off with purpose, the weight of the bag a familiar comfort as it rubs against the raw patches on my back. The birds fall silent when I'm near, but I can hear them calling to each other, calls borne out of love or loneliness or fear.

"Do you hear that?" my father whispered when we were deep in the woods by our house. I stood stock still and strained my ears—actually strained them; I can still feel the tug—until I heard a strange metallic rattling sound coming from the trees above, like someone was knocking softly but rapidly on a cellar door. "Yellow-billed cuckoo," he said, nodding sagely. "Come on, there's going to be a storm soon."

"How do you know?" I asked as we gathered our things and hurried back to the house.

"The cuckoos," he said, tapping a finger to the side of his nose. "They're telling us."

By the time we reached the back door, the first pellets of a hard rain had begun to fall.

I strain my ears now but can't make sense of the chatter. I'd never had the gift, not like my dad. He'd treated the Maine woods like an old lover. "She's a beaut, isn't she?" he'd ask, holding out a sliver of mica or pointing to a thatch of bergamot. I would stare as hard as I could at whatever he was showing me, willing it to reveal whatever mystery it had already given up to my father, but it would always just look like a piece of rock to me, or a bunch of scraggly weeds. Eventually I'd get too cold to stop my teeth from chattering and we'd head back home, a nagging sense that I'd let him down nipping at my heels.

And then I left the rocks and the weeds and the chattering teeth behind in favor of the constant steady beat of the California sun. "Isn't it a little weird, not having seasons?" my parents had asked when they'd first come to visit, the smell of stale plane air still clinging to their clothes.

"No," I'd said, more harshly than intended, and I'd watched them shrink back into themselves a little. They'd looked so small out there under the wide blue sky. It was the first time I realized they were getting old, and would get older.

My foot catches on a root and I stumble. There isn't enough sun to cast a shadow, and I hunch down to see where I'm placing my feet. Maybe I've gone the wrong way. Left instead of right. I turn around, take a few steps back. Stop. Turn again. The branches crowd around me, low slung and intertwined. There are no more bluebells here, just scuffed black earth and a carpet of fallen leaves and the chitter of invisible insects.

The path. What happened to the path?

I turn again, start to retrace my steps. The deep scar across the belly of this tree trunk. The snapped arm of this branch, hanging at an awkward angle. Are these familiar? Have I seen them before? The thick tree stump crawling with lines of busy carpenter ants— surely I would have noticed that.

Panic soars through me, its wings expanding in my throat.

I'm lost.

Maggie

The phone scared the daylights out of me. Two days with the ringer off and I had forgotten the racket it made. Linda had made me promise that I'd switch it on when she left the night before, just in case she needed to get ahold of me. She tried to get me to take her cell phone, but I pressed it back into her hands. I hated the things, had never had one, and I wasn't about to start then. I didn't like the idea of people being able to reach me whenever they wanted. It felt like an intrusion.

I lifted the receiver tentatively, like a grenade. "Hello?"

"Maggie, it's Jim. I've got some news."

My heart thudded to life. "What is it? Did they find her body?"

"Not yet." He cleared his throat. "They got the initial report back from the investigators. Looks like there isn't any evidence of engine failure, which is what they originally thought."

"So what was it then?"

There was a long pause. "Seems like the crash was caused by pilot error."

"Pilot error?"

"They're still looking into it, but that's what they think."

"It was the pilot's fault? He did something that made the plane crash?"

"What I'm telling you is that right now they can't find any mechanical fault with the plane. Maybe he didn't chart his altitude correctly. Maybe he didn't realize how high those mountains are. Maybe he had a medical emergency. We just don't know."

"Do you know his name now? The pilot?"

I heard the rustle of paper. Jim cleared his throat. "His name was Ben Gardner. Thirty-four, San Diego native. He was an owner-operator."

I wrote down his name on a scrap of paper and underlined it, twice. "What do you mean, 'owner-operator'?"

"He got his pilot's license a couple of years ago and bought his own plane soon after." There was a pause down the line. "I looked it up, and the model he was flying cost half a million bucks."

The breath went out of me. "Half a million dollars?"

He grunted. "Apparently the guy was some drug industry hotshot. Head of some drug company, worth a fortune."

I thought of the glossy photograph of her. "Were he and Ally . . . involved?"

"We were hoping you'd be able to tell us that."

I hesitated. God bless Linda for keeping her mouth shut, though in this instance, I wished I didn't have to tell Jim myself. I took a deep breath. "Ally and I weren't in touch."

Silence. "I didn't realize. I'm sorry to hear that, Maggie."

"It's fine." It wasn't, but there was nothing else to say. "Can you talk to someone who knew him? Maybe his parents, or a friend . . ." I trailed off. "Maybe they could tell us how he knew Ally."

"We're working on it," he said. "Someone's trying to reach his next of kin right now—we should know more after that."

"Is there anything else you can tell me about him?"

The rustle of paper again. "Not much. I had a quick look before I called you and there isn't anything about him in the system. No police record or anything like that."

I felt a glimmer of relief. At least she hadn't been mixed up with some criminal. A thought occurred to me. "Do you have a photograph of him I could see?"

He paused. "I don't know if that's within regulations, exactly. I . . . You sure you want to see him?"

"Jim."

"All right. I'll send Shannon over with it."

"Who's Shannon?"

"Officer Draper. You met her a couple of days ago, remember? Little scrap of a thing?"

The little woman rifling through my cabinets. "Oh. Her." She'd seen me at my weakest. I didn't want to see her again.

Jim picked up on the irritation in my voice. "She'll just drop off the photo and leave."

I sighed. "Fine. Send her over."

"She'll be over right after lunch."

"All right then. Thanks, Jim. I appreciate it."

Jim cleared his throat. "Maggie. There's something else."

I gripped the phone tight. "What is it?"

I heard him take a breath. "They've declared her presumed dead," he said quietly. "The coroner's office."

I felt sick to my stomach. "But they haven't found her," I said. "How can they declare her anything if they haven't found her?"

He sighed. "They judged it on the evidence at the site. They don't think anyone could have survived the crash."

"I don't understand." It felt negligent to me, and reckless. How could they declare my daughter dead without a single scrap of evidence? Maybe she hadn't even been on that damn plane after all. They couldn't know for sure until they'd found her.

"They found a necklace at the crash site," Jim said, like he could read my mind. "They've sent a photo of it . . . Would you mind taking a look, see if you recognize it?"

I knew what it was straightaway, and my heart seemed to swell and contract at the same moment. "It's a gold Saint Christopher's locket." Jim was silent down the line. "Isn't it?"

Charles had given it to her a week before he died. "The patron saint of travelers and children," he murmured as he fastened it around her neck. Ally and I had exchanged a look. Charles had never been a religious man. He seemed to read our thoughts. "Anything that promises to protect my little girl is worth a shot," he said, and he caught my eye and smiled sadly. I can still remember the inscription on the back. *God protect him as he travels, by air or land or sea, keep him safe and guide him, wherever he may be.*

Her hand reached for it as she bent down to kiss the top of his head, and I saw his eyes close as he inhaled the smell of her. I knew then that he was saying goodbye.

After all this time, after everything, she'd still been wearing it. That had to mean something. "Where was it?"

"They found it in some brush near the crash site." His voice was strange, like he'd swallowed something that had gotten stuck in his windpipe. "It probably came off on impact and flew off . . ."

I was quiet for a minute. Them finding her necklace meant she'd been on that plane. I was sure of that now, I had to accept it. But them finding the necklace but not her body . . . something didn't add up. "I'd like to have it if I can, once they've finished with it."

"I'll ask the coroner's office to send it over as soon as they're through with it."

Good. Then I'd have something of hers, something I could see and touch. I felt sure it would help me somehow, like a talisman. "Did they find anything else of hers at the crash site?" Clothing. A scarf. Something I might be able to hold in my arms. Something that might still carry her smell.

"Things got pretty burnt up. There wasn't much . . ." There was another pause on the line. I could hear Jim's steady breath. "I'm sorry, Maggie."

"I know, Jim. Thank you." The necklace, though. At least I'd have the necklace.

I hung up and stared out the window. It was a sunny day and the heat was starting to creep. I should let some air in. I'd been shut up in there for days. But the idea of fresh air, the sharp-sweet smell of newly cut grass on a hot summer's day, felt like an affront. Grief shouldn't mix with sunshine.

I thought about what Jim had told me about the pilot of the plane. What was Ally doing on some rich man's private plane? I tried to imagine the kind of money you'd have to have to be able to afford something like that, but failed. The richest person in Owl's Creek was a cardiologist who worked out of Penobscot Valley Hospital. She and her husband lived in a redbrick mansion on Hillcrest and owned a pair of Range Rovers with matching vanity plates. Showy, Linda would tut when one of them drove past. But owning your own airplane? I didn't know how to make sense of that world. It was another piece of proof that I didn't understand my daughter.

The truth was, things had started going wrong between me and Ally long before Charles got sick. She'd come back from college over break and I'd find her in the kitchen, peering into the refrigerator, or coming out of the bathroom with her hair wrapped up in a towel, and for the briefest second I'd wonder who this woman in my house was. She could feel it, too. I could tell. It was like we couldn't see each other, like our vision went out of focus when we were in each other's presence. We were reaching out blindly for each other but could never quite touch.

Shannon turned up a little after two, all nerves. She jangled into the hall in her too-big uniform.

"Do you want some coffee?" I asked, niceties on autopilot.

She took a step back, as if I might bite. "That would be great," she said shyly, "if it's not any trouble."

"No trouble at all." I tried not to let my irritation show.

She followed me into the kitchen. "I'm so sorry about your daughter," she said. "It's just awful."

Get out, I chanted to myself. *Get out get out get out.* "Thank you," I said. "Do you take your coffee regular?"

"Yes please." She sat down at the kitchen table and started fumbling through her bag. I heaped a teaspoon of sugar into the mug of coffee and added a splash of half-and-half.

"Here you go," I said, setting it in front of her.

"Thanks." Her hand was shaking as she picked up the mug and took a sip. She winced—she must have burned her tongue. She slid a brown paper envelope across the table toward me. "From the chief."

I opened it carefully. Two photographs slid out.

He was handsome, I'd give him that. Dark hair sweeping across his forehead, blue eyes, straight nose, wide, full mouth. Like a soap star, or a game show host. The type of man I might have chased after when I was young, before I knew better.

In the first photo, he was wearing a dark suit and shaking the hand of another man in a suit, both of them wearing self-congratulatory smiles. The second was more casual, him wearing chinos and a light blue button-down while sitting on the deck of what looked like a massive yacht. Maybe he owned that, too. He had a Master of the Universe grin on his face, all even white teeth and suntanned charm, and he was holding a glass of champagne up toward the camera.

"Nice-looking kid," I said.

Shannon peered at the photograph and frowned. She took a deep breath. "He looks like the quarterback at my old high school." She blushed deeply. Words seemed to come out of the poor girl only in gulps.

"He looks like the quarterback at every high school," I said, nodding in agreement. I stared at the photograph for a minute longer. I didn't like the look of him. There was something in the way he held his mouth that seemed cruel. I sighed. "Do you want some more coffee?"

She shook her head. "No thanks. I should probably get going."

"Okay," I said, but neither of us moved. It was strange—now that she was there, sitting across from me, I didn't want her to go. She brushed her hair back from her face. She looked so young, so—unblemished. Everything about her that had made me angry before was now a strange comfort. I wanted to look at her a little longer. "So, how are you finding Owl's Creek? Have you been here long?"

"I moved here about a month ago," she said, tucking a strand of hair behind her ear. "I transferred from Jacksonville."

"Florida?"

"Yeah." She fiddled with the mug's handle. "That's where my family is from."

"Maine must be a shock to the system, temperature-wise. Though I guess you haven't faced a winter here yet."

She lit up, her whole face breaking into a grin. "I can't wait for it to snow," she said. "I always wanted to live somewhere cold. Hot chocolate, fireplaces, white Christmas, all that stuff."

"Well, you talk to me in March when you're knee-deep in sludge and scraping an inch of ice off your windshield. Then we'll see if you're still keen."

"Oh, I will be. I hate the heat. I hated Florida, all the sun and the humidity and the thunderstorms every afternoon." She looked up at me. "Have you ever been to Florida?"

"I have, twice." Aside from that visit to my sister's last Thanksgiving, Charles and I had taken Ally to Disney World for her seventh birthday. Charles had eaten a bad order of fish and chips at the England pavilion in Epcot Center and had spent the rest of the vacation lying in a darkened hotel room drinking stale ginger ale and eating overpriced Saltines. Ally and I had forged ahead with Breakfast with Mickey and Big Thunder Mountain and the Country Bear Jamboree, but our hearts hadn't been in it. Shannon was right: every day at four o'clock sharp, the skies would open and we'd have to scurry for cover underneath whatever themed scrap of tarpaulin we could find. I could picture Ally now, clear as day, hair plastered to her small skull, mouse ears askew, her skinny little arms and legs shaking as we waited for it to clear up. The thought of her then, so tiny and sweet, made my heart ache.

"You know what I mean then." I liked that she didn't ask to hear what I'd been doing in Florida, or even if I liked it, but had just assumed that I had the same opinion of it as she did. Which, it turns out, I did.

I got up and poured her more coffee. "So what made you choose Owl's Creek? Apart from the prospect of a real winter."

She shrugged. "There weren't that many places up north that had positions open on the force. It looked like a nice place to live, and Chief Quinn has a great reputation—"

"He does?"

She nodded eagerly. I hadn't meant to sound surprised. Of course I knew that Jim was good at his job. People in town respected and admired him, but having once been the victim of his spitballs, I found it hard to imagine him in a professional capacity, even if he had been police chief for almost fifteen years. I sat back in my chair and stared at her across the table. I couldn't get over how young she looked, how . . . unformed. Like if I pressed a thumb into the flesh of her cheek, it would leave an indentation.

"I've got to admit," I said, "you don't strike me as the police type. How did you end up in it?"

"Oh, you know," she said, twisting her claddagh ring. "I used to read loads of crime novels, so once I went on to college, I thought criminal justice would be an interesting thing to study. I guess I just fell into it."

I nodded encouragingly. "Do you enjoy it?"

"Most of the time. I was kind of a jock in high school—I ran cross-country—so I like the fitness part of it. I'm too much of a rookie to get to see much of the interesting stuff, but I guess that will come over time. At least I hope so." She shook her head. "I don't want to be stuck at a desk filling out paperwork for the rest of my life."

"What about being a woman? Do you get much trouble from the men because of it?" She was so small, so delicate looking. I was suddenly gripped with a desire to keep her safe.

"Nah, they're all right. If any of them give me any trouble, I just challenge them to a pull-up competition." She grinned. "I win every time."

I laughed. "I can't imagine you doing any pull-ups with those skinny little arms of yours."

"I'm a lot stronger than I look." She sat back and flexed her bicep with a shy smile.

"I'll bet you are. Are you sure I can't get you something else? Maybe some lunch? I'm drowning in casseroles over here, so you'd be doing me a favor."

She shook her head. "I really have to get going or I'll be in deep shit." She shot me a mortified look. "Excuse my language. Too much time around the guys."

"I've heard worse coming out of my own mouth only this morning," I said, waving her away.

She laughed and nodded toward the photographs on the table. "Do you want to keep those?"

I looked down at his tanned, glossy face staring back at me and nodded. "I don't know what I'm going to do with them, but I'd like to hang on to them for now."

"Sure. We've got more copies at the station. I saw the picture of Allison, by the way."

"The one from the news?" The image of Ally as a blond movie star flashed through my head and I blanched.

She shook her head. "No, the one you gave to Chief Quinn. She was really pretty."

The light blue dress. The way her hair lit up gold in the sunshine. I smiled. "She was."

Shannon got up from the table and took her mug to the sink. She turned on the tap and started washing it out, but I shooed her away. "Leave that," I said. "It'll give me something to do."

I walked her to the hall, and she paused at the front door. "I know you have loads of people looking out for you and everything, but if there's anything I can do to help . . . I'd be happy to come by sometime?"

"I'd like that," I said, and I was surprised to find that it was the truth.

"Good," she said, giving me that same shy grin. "I'll see you soon, then."

I went back into the kitchen and stared at the man smiling up at me from the photograph. For the first time in a long time, I felt the dark clouds in my mind part.

Who are you? And what on earth were you doing with my Ally?

Allison

I can't tell what time it is. The woods seem to grow darker every time I take a step, the branches above closing in on me, forcing me to stoop. My back is in agony. I'm trying to fight the waves of panic with the breathing I'd learned at countless hot yoga sessions back in San Diego. The instructor had been a tall, rangy guy with a ponytail and a pungent odor. He would scold us like children throughout the class, lecturing us about our closed hearts and our poor alignment. Still, the classes were full each week, the room crowded with women lying on their mats, waiting for a man to tell them what they were doing wrong in the name of enlightenment. We were used to it, I guess. It felt natural. The smell of his sweat pushed its way into our pores and up our noses as we practiced our ujjayi breath and tried to bend ourselves into shapes that would please him.

I should have known how easily I'd be turned around. I should have known I'd lose my way.

It's high summer but there's a chill in the air, and I know it'll be cold by nightfall. What I'd give for one of those endless California days right now, my skin bronzed and warm to the touch. I close my eyes, just for a minute, and I can see him standing on the beach, his blue eyes shining like two polished marbles, his bare shoulders pinked and sandy, his hand outstretched, waiting for mine.

I'd loved him then.

I heave the bag off my back and sit down heavily on the ground. In front of me there's a tree with a perfect hollow cut in the center of its broad trunk, like something Winnie-the-Pooh would get stuck in looking for honey. I look up, eyes straining through the trees, but the sun can't reach me down here.

A dragonfly hovers above a tuft of crabgrass, its febrile wings stuttering before it darts and swoops away. Dragonflies are usually near water—I can't be too far. The drumbeat in my head starts up again. I get to my feet and lift the bag onto my back once more.

I saw the ad on Craigslist while using the free Wi-Fi in the library. "Wanted: waitresses/hostesses for upscale private bar. No experience necessary. Send résumé and photographs—head shot and full length—to the email address below. $75 a shift plus tips. Uniform provided."

I sent them photographs in the morning taken under the too-bright fluorescents of a McDonald's bathroom—and got a call from the manager that afternoon. When could I start?

It was a place in the Gaslamp Quarter. A heavyset bouncer opened the unmarked door and I stepped inside someone's idea of luxury, though it wasn't mine. It was darkly lit and velvet flocked and filled with men in suits being waited on by women in short black skirts and high heels. A jaundiced man with slicked-back hair and an earpiece handed me a little package of black cloth wrapped in cellophane. Uniform provided. "The first night is a trial," he said as he showed me where I could change. "You don't get paid until you're hired."

I can still feel the weight of the knife in my hand as I sliced lemons for garnish behind the bar. The wince of citrus on bitten-down cuticles. The dull ache in my back and my hips and the arches of my feet as I stood behind the bar, watching the other waitresses swoop and dive like seagulls across the room. Backs straight, chins tilted upward, asses only barely covered by the mandatory short black skirt, feet dancing in vertiginous high heels. Minimum four inches. Some of them managed six with a platform.

"You're not ready for the big time yet, chickadee," the head waitress said when I hesitated over the cash register. She shoved me out of the way, stabbed an order onto the screen with a fingernail, grabbed a bottle of champagne from the fridge with one hand and two glasses from the chiller with the other before sauntering over to her waiting table, lipsticked mouth stretched into a blinding smile.

I edged a heel out of one of my shoes and placed it down on the sticky concrete floor. The balls of my feet had gone numb. It would take days to get the feeling back.

One of the other waitresses, a brassy-haired girl with a yoga instructor's body and big green eyes fringed with false eyelashes, appeared at my elbow. "The boss will freak out if he sees you out of your shoes," she whispered, darting a glance at the closed door off the other end of the bar.

I shoved my foot back into the shoe. "Thanks," I said, bowing my head over the cutting board and slicing a lemon in half. The knife slipped and nicked the delicate skin between thumb and forefinger. Blood bloomed. "Shit." I raised my hand to my mouth and sucked.

The brassy-haired waitress rolled her eyes. "Come on," she said, casting another nervous look at the manager's door before pulling me into the stairwell.

The staff room was downstairs, a tiny box room that perpetually smelled of hairspray and damp and sweaty feet. One side of the room was lined with lockers—this was where the waitresses kept their stuff during their shifts. The rest of the room was empty save for a beat-up old chair and a small table on which sat an ashtray piled with cigarette butts. The strict smoking ban didn't apply in there.

The waitress reached into her locker and pulled out a glittery purple makeup bag. I was expecting her to produce a Band-Aid, or a skein of gauze, but instead she pulled out a small plastic vial filled with white powder. She untwisted the top and tapped a little bit out onto the flat of her hand. "Here," she said, offering it up.

I hadn't done coke since college, when giggling friends had pulled me into the bathroom of a dive bar off Commonwealth Avenue. I hadn't liked it then. It had made me feel out of control. But then I thought of my father lying still on the sofa, and the look on my mother's face when her eyes met mine, and the blankets tucked under the back seat of my car, and the pain that was already shooting its way up my calves from my heels. She was offering me something that I suddenly, desperately wanted: to lose myself completely. I bent my head over the girl's hand and inhaled sharply. I felt it hit the back of my skull, and my whole body seemed to lift off the floor.

"We call it Snow White around here," the brassy-haired girl said with a wink. "It makes you whistle while you work." She tapped out a bump for herself and inhaled it in one quick sniff. "I'm Dee, by the way." She slipped the purple bag back into her locker and slammed the door shut.

At some point, I must have started to sing. Who knows how long I've been doing it, but when my voice finally registers in my ears, I'm startled by the sound. It's a Beatles song, of course, because what other songs does anyone know by heart? God knows how much of the back catalog I've gone through already—Was it chronological? Did I start with the Hamburg days before moving into psychedelia?—but I catch myself on "Eleanor Rigby." Not exactly one to lift the spirits. I stop and switch to "Good Day Sunshine," though it feels perverse given the circumstances and the fact that the slivers of sky available to me through the trees have turned a pale purple. It'll be dark soon, and I still haven't found water. Maybe the dragonfly was lost. I sure as hell am.

I don't have a good voice—it's too low, gravelly. I was a soprano as a kid, voice high and clear as glass, but something shifted during puberty and I was relegated to the back of the school choir. Still, he loved it when I sang. "Janis Joplin, eat your heart out!" he'd call when he'd catch me singing in the shower. I was always embarrassed afterward, but he'd just shake his head and laugh. "You

73

sound perfect," he'd say, pulling me close and kissing the damp coils of hair. "You sound happy."

It's you, I would say. You've made me happy. It's you.

He loved when anyone sang, really. Not just me. He loved hearing the housekeeper sing to herself as she polished the floor. He loved spotting a teenager wearing those huge can headphones and singing quietly to himself on the street, lips barely moving, eyes focused on the cracks in the pavement. Whenever he saw someone playing on a street corner, an old acoustic strapped around his shoulder, maybe a beat-up amp squatting next to him, he'd always stop. It didn't matter how good the performer was. He would listen to him, a slow smile spreading across his face, head nodding approvingly. People would push past, a few of them shoving a couple of quarters into the open case, but he'd stay until the song was finished, and then he'd walk up to the musician, take him by the hand, look him in the eye, and say, Wow, that was great, that was wonderful, I loved it. And then he'd give the performer money. Real money, not a handful of change dug from a back pocket but a crisp bill in a high denomination. The first time I saw him do it, I watched with a quiet awe: his kindness, his patience, his generosity not just with his money but with his time, his appreciation, his approval. His approval was the most valued thing of all.

You see it now, don't you? Anyone would fall in love with him. You would have fallen in love with him, too. Especially if you needed to be rescued.

My shoulder throbs under the weight of the bag. It's killing me, I think, but no, it's not the bad shoulder that will kill me, or the ache in my lower back, or the still-bent finger, now a sickly greenish yellow. It's the gash on my leg, which, last time I checked, was neatly packed with pus, or the burning thirst at the back of my throat, or the fact that the temperature has dropped another ten degrees in the past hour and will keep dropping.

There are so many things that are killing me now, slowly, until I finally lie down on the forest floor and give my flesh up to the ground until only the picked and bleached bones remain.

The smell of gasoline and burning rubber. The shock of the skull stripped of its skin.

Has it only been a few days? I thought I'd be stronger than this. I thought I was strong.

All those days in the gym. All those miles running to nowhere. Little sachets of protein. Kickboxing on Tuesdays. *C'mon, ladies. Push! Don't forget to hydrate.* I've been so stupid.

Twigs snap underfoot. The woods are in half-light, the shadows cast are long. A face stares out at me from the dark, eyes screwed shut, mouth frozen in a silent scream. I stop short, heart seized in my chest, and try to blink it away. "Hello?" I take a step forward and the face dissolves. It's just a tree trunk, thickly set, with a wide hollow carved in its center. Like something Winnie-the-Pooh would get stuck inside, looking for honey.

Shit. I've been here before.

I've walked all day and ended up right back where I started. What an idiot I am. What a fucking fool.

A laugh bubbles up inside me and escapes my lips. Hysteria elbows its way past the fear nestled in the base of my throat and pushes out into the quiet evening air.

If you didn't laugh, you'd cry, my father would say when I was a kid, usually about the Red Sox. Even when he got sick, even when the cancer had stripped him of every last ounce of earthly pleasure, he'd goggle his eyes at me and shrug. If you didn't laugh, you'd cry. He stopped laughing, though, at the end. It took that away from him, too.

Maggie

I could have saved Shannon a trip: it turned out that photographs of Ben were ten a penny.

I had waited until I heard the police car rumble out of the driveway before I booted up the computer and typed his name into the search engine. The screen filled with entries. His name had been released to the media by then so the first few hits were about the crash. I clicked on the first one.

ASSOCIATED PRESS
Jennifer McNulty

Pioneering CEO of Prexilane Killed in Plane Crash

Ben Gardner, 34, was the owner of the single-engine Mooney Aviation that went down over the Colorado Rockies last Sunday and is believed to have been piloting the aircraft when it crashed, killing him and the plane's only other occupant, Allison Carpenter, 31. Investigators are still trying to determine the cause of the crash.

Gardner had been the CEO of Prexilane Industries since 2011. Under his control, Prexilane grew to be one of the most profitable pharmaceutical companies in the world.

Jim hadn't been kidding when he'd said the guy was a big shot. I went back to the Google search page and scrolled through a few more articles about him, jotting down notes as I went. There was something satisfying about writing the neat bullet points down on the page, like I was wresting back control. I was halfway through one of them when I heard someone come through the front door.

"Maggie? Are you in here?"

"In the kitchen!"

Linda staggered in carrying two cake carriers and a pile of envelopes. "These were on the doorstep," she said, spilling it all onto the kitchen counter. She opened up one of the cake carriers and stuck her nose inside. She pulled a face. "I think this one's a pound cake."

"Why don't you bring them home with you? Give them to the kids when they come around."

She shook her head. "You know Kelly won't let me give those kids sugar." Kelly was her daughter-in-law, a Waspish blonde with whom Linda had been waging a war of attrition ever since her son Craig had slid a diamond onto her finger. "She only lets them eat dried fruit and carrot sticks, poor little things," Linda tutted. She paused. "Though the last time I gave those kids cake, Benji tore down my nice curtains and used them to build a fort, so she might have a point." She sat down at the table and studied my face. "How are you doing?"

I shrugged. "Oh, you know."

"No, I don't, but I can guess. Jim told me about Allison." I nodded and kept my eyes down on the table. "I don't know what to say other than I'm sorry." I reached over and took her hand in mine and we sat there for a few minutes, silent.

Linda shifted in her chair and the spell was broken. "He said they'd found the name of the pilot. He said you've seen a picture."

"That's right." I pushed the pair of photographs toward her.

"Good-looking kid," she grumbled. She stood up and walked to the coffee machine. "Do you want one?"

"I'm fine, thanks."

I tried not to feel impatient as she bustled around the kitchen. I was grateful that she was there and I loved her dearly, but part of me wanted her to leave so I could get back to my research. She sat back down at the table with her mug and looked at me. "So. What have you found out?"

"What do you mean?" I tried to look innocent. I figured Linda would worry if she knew what I was up to.

She rolled her eyes. "Don't give me that. I've known you for longer than either of us care to remember and I know what you're like when you want to find out about something—like a dog with a bone. You didn't spend twenty years up at Bowdoin to sit around twiddling your thumbs when something like this happens. So spill it. What do you know about him?"

I pushed my chair back from the table and sighed. "So far, not much. He's rich, that's for sure, and it looks like he comes from money, too—there was a piece about a family house in San Diego in the *New York Times* a few years ago. His father commissioned an architect to build it—one of those minimalist cement boxes. The neighbors hated it, apparently."

"I can see why. It sounds like an eyesore. What else?"

I picked up the notepad on the table and read from my notes. "Ben Gardner graduated from Syracuse in 2009 with an MBA. Nothing about any honors or anything, so it looks like he was an average student. Parents gave him the reins to run the family business in 2011."

"I know the type. Born on third base, thinks he got a triple. What kind of business?"

"Pharmaceuticals. A company called Prexilane. Anyway, he headed that up until—" My voice gave out suddenly. Terror. Pain. Blood. Fire. Bone. Ally. "Until the crash," I finished.

Linda put her hand over mine. "You're pushing yourself too hard."

I shook my head. "No. It's good for me to be doing this." I lifted my eyes to hers, saw the uncertainty clouding them, the concern. "Really."

Linda took a sip of her coffee. "What did you say the name of the company is?"

"Prexilane."

"Sounds familiar." She drummed her fingers on the table, eyes tilted up to the ceiling. I waited. "They make an antidepressant for new mothers who have postpartum depression. Kelly was on it for a while after Colton was born, though I don't know why on earth she thought she needed it when she had me just around the corner to help. She came off it pretty quick, though—said it made her feel crazy. Anyway, they're always advertising it on TV—you'll know it when you see it." She took another sip of her coffee, momentarily lost in thought. "If this Ben fellow was involved in that, it's no wonder he could afford his own plane. He must have made a mint off it."

"Looks that way. I just wish I knew what Ally was doing with him."

She smiled at me sadly. "Don't you think they were probably involved romantically?"

I thought of his smug, polished face and winced. "I just don't know if I see her with him."

Linda raised an eyebrow. "He was good looking and he was rich. I think most girls see themselves with someone like him."

"Ally isn't most girls," I snapped. I saw the look on Linda's face and I knew I'd hurt her, but I couldn't bring myself to apologize.

"Of course she wasn't," Linda said, and I hated her for using the past tense. "Look, I've been thinking . . ." She stared down at the table as though uncertain of how to continue. She took a deep breath. "Have you thought about a memorial?" I looked at her questioningly. "For Ally," she said gently. "I think it might help you if . . ."

I felt a flutter of panic. "They haven't found her body, Linda. How can I have a funeral for her when there isn't a body?"

There was an awful look on her face, tenderness mixed with pity, and I looked away. She reached out and took my hand. "I'm not suggesting a funeral," she said. "Just something where people can come and pay their respects. There are a lot of people in this town who loved Allison, and who love you. It could be good for you. Help you get some closure."

I pictured a lid closing on a coffin. "I don't want closure," I spat. "I want to know what happened to my daughter."

I tried to pull my hand away from her but she held on tight. "I know you do," she said, "but you might never know."

I felt the familiar lump form in the back of my throat and the black chasm open up inside my chest. "Please don't say that," I whispered.

"I'm not saying it to be cruel," Linda said gently. "Trust me, if there was any way I could give you the answers you're looking for, I would. I know that there are people out there working day and night to find out what happened on that plane, but you know how these things are. There are no guarantees." She squeezed my hand. "I just want what's best for you."

"I know." Linda always wanted what was best for me and for everyone she loved. I sighed. I knew when I was beaten. "Nothing over the top," I warned. "No churches. No black. And no lilies— Ally hated lilies." I hated them, too. The church had been full of them at Charles's funeral, and the smell lingered with me for days.

"Whatever you want." She glanced at the clock and scraped back her chair. "I've got to pick up the kids. Is there anything you need from outside? I could come back after I drop them off . . . ?"

I shook my head. The computer whirred impatiently in the background. I wanted to be left so I could get on with my research.

She got up and picked her bag up off the counter. "I'll be over tomorrow. If you need anything in the meantime . . ."

I smiled up at her. "I know where to find you."

I watched her leave, and then I cleared her mug from the table and dumped it into the sink. I reached up and touched my face and realized it was wet. I'd been crying. Linda was right. No matter how much I learned about what happened, it ultimately didn't matter. A plane had crashed. Ally was dead.

Allison

I sleep underneath the Winnie-the-Pooh tree, its great big hollow staring down at me, and dream of being pinned in acres of the white pima cotton sheets that dressed our bed. I reached for him, but I got tangled up in the soft cloth, and the weight of the sheets held me down. I could sense him, though, feel the gentle dip in the mattress that would lead to where his body lay, smell the scent of him, soap mixed with the slightly sour tang of his breath. I kept fighting, arms outstretched, fingers searching, but the more I struggled, the more trapped I became, the acres of freshly laundered sheets binding me tight.

In the seconds before I open my eyes into the early pink light, I'm back in San Diego. Not the apartment I shared with Tara, with its banged-up old refrigerator covered in takeout menus and save-the-dates, and my little room at the end of the hall filled with prints I'd torn out of art books and impractical shoes and half-drunk cups of coffee (black, how my mother taught me to drink it). This was the house in Bird Rock, with its cream leather sofas and sea views from the patio out back. Ben's house. I close my eyes and see the double closet filled with expensive clothes, and the surround-sound system, and the gleaming Italian range, and the bafflingly complex espresso maker I'd never gotten the hang of.

"Coffee?" he'd say, already sliding across the vast tangle of white sheets and out of bed. I would listen to the rumble and froth and trickle of the coffee machine and he'd appear a few minutes later holding two steaming cups, and he would hand one to me with a kiss and slip back into bed and I would reach for him, pulling him on top of me while the coffee cooled on the bedside table.

In those seconds before waking I reach for him just as I had in my dream, before my eyes start open and I remember everything all over again.

I got the hang of things pretty quickly. Most nights, the bar was open to the public, and I soon learned how to charm an extra couple of bucks out of Joe from accounts who just wanted to blow off a little steam and have a pretty girl pay him a little attention. After a week, I'd made enough money to move out of my car and into a Motel 6 in Kearny Mesa.

But the real money, the girls told me, was made at private events. Once a month, a cloud of wealthy white men descended on the bar like black-tied locusts, handshakes at the ready, gold Amex cards burning a hole in their wallets. They were the great and the good of San Diego—politicians, lawyers, businessmen, real estate moguls— brought together under the guise of charity fund-raising, though I don't think any of them could have named the cause.

Dee told me to stick close to her on my first event night. "We'll work a table together," she said as she carefully applied liquid eyeliner before the start of the shift. She caught my eye in the mirror and winked. "They won't know what hit them." Our uniforms were swapped for cocktail dresses, and our job was to sit at the tables looking pretty and keep the champagne flowing and the guests happy. How you provided that happiness, we were told, was open to interpretation.

The guests arrived at eight p.m. sharp. The men varied in age from their early thirties to their late seventies, but each one of them shone with the polish of money. Dee and I were assigned to a VIP table of six at the front of the room. I was placed between a silver-haired banking executive and a paunch-bellied VP of an aerospace company. I smiled as I poured champagne into their outstretched glasses and then poured myself a half glass. We were expected to drink at these things, but it didn't pay to get messy.

It started almost immediately. The banking executive took my hand in his while the aerospace VP's hand crept up my bare thigh. I glanced across the table to see a man old enough to be Dee's grandfather openly staring down her dress. The aerospace VP's hand reached the hem of my dress. The banking executive asked me to fetch another bottle of champagne, and I felt his hand graze my ass when I stood up. Panic began to well up inside me and I signaled for Dee to follow me to the bar.

"What the fuck is going on here?" I hissed as I handed her a fresh bottle of champagne from the fridge.

She took one look at my face and pulled me into the stockroom. I watched as she tapped out a line on the back of her hand. "You just need to loosen up. Here," she said, offering it to me, and I took it in one sharp inhale. She waited for the drug to hit my system. "Look, you want to make some money?" I nodded, numb. "The guys out there are harmless—they just want to have a little fun. If you play nice with them, I promise you won't be living in that Motel 6 for long."

A flush of shame crept up my neck. "How did you know?"

She shrugged. "I saw the key in your bag." She held a hand up to my face, and for a second I was reminded of the way my mom would stroke my cheek when I was sick. "We've all been there, sweetheart. You're going to be fine," she said. "Just do what I do." I nodded and followed her back to the table.

There was a crisp hundred tucked under my champagne glass, and the banking executive winked when he saw me clock it. "I hope we're going to become good friends tonight," he said, and I forced a smile and slid back into my chair.

"Sure." I reached over and knocked back the rest of my champagne before folding up the bill and tucking it into my bra. The coke was buzzing through my veins by then, and I felt invincible. "We'll be great friends."

I lay there for a few minutes, listening to the breath rasp in my chest and the chickadees singing their morning greetings to each other. *Oh yes*, I think, *that's right. I'm fucked.* I tug my arms out from underneath the blanket and stare at my fingertips (still gel manicured, they really are durable), which have turned blue and numb. Not a good sign. It's been cold overnight, colder than I was prepared for, and even now my breath is visible in foggy little puffs.

I have to move. I have to find the path today, or water. Anything, really, other than this fucking tree. I sit up too quickly and the trees around me swoon. I lie back down, gently this time, and wait for the world to stop swirling.

Breathe.

Maggie

I sifted idly through the mail stacked on the counter. Most of the envelopes were addressed to Charles. He'd been a member of countless of-the-month clubs, none of which I'd gotten around to canceling. Outdoor Monthly, Amateur Geology Society, Cairn boxes, Angler's Association, Astronomy Club: each month the boxes would arrive, and each month I'd carry them down into the basement where they'd stay until—well, I didn't know when. I couldn't imagine getting rid of them, even though I knew it was a terrible waste. Every month I thought I should really track down where these things were coming from and cancel. There were other packages, too, from far-flung collector friends who would still send him specimens they thought he'd find interesting. I didn't have the heart to tell them to stop. And so on most days I'd flick the light on in the basement, walk down the creaking steps, stick the new boxes on top of the old ones, and close the door behind me.

God, I wished he was there with me then. He would have known what to do.

There were a couple of pieces of mail for Ally, too—a clothing catalog she'd signed up for when she was a teenager and had never canceled, a solicitation from a women's refuge charity, a bank statement from her local account. We'd opened it for her when she was ten. I still remember the look on her face when we'd brought her to Saint Mary's Credit Union and handed her a hundred-dollar bill. The account was long dormant—the last time I checked there was just a couple hundred in there, ticking over and earning next to no interest. We'd talked about closing it out, but there never seemed to be enough time when she came home, and then she stopped coming.

The statements still turned up every month like clockwork, though, and I'd shove them in the desk drawer and forget about them until the next month. I set the envelope to one side. I guessed I'd finally have to do something about it.

I sat back down at the computer and stared at the blank screen, and for a second I wondered what in the hell I was doing. Ally was dead. At least that was what everyone kept telling me. What was the point of digging around the life she hadn't wanted me in? But the feeling didn't last long. It was overpowered by a voice telling me to keep fighting for Ally. She wasn't gone, not then, not for me. My fingers found the keyboard. I'd searched for Ben and Ally separately, but not together. It seemed as good a place as any. I typed in their names and hit Search. Reams of hits came up on the screen, all about the crash. The details blurred past as I scrolled down the list, until my eyes locked on a headline from the *San Diego Chronicle*. BEN GARDNER AND FIANCÉE KILLED IN PLANE CRASH.

There was a photo of them together accompanying the article, their smiling faces appearing pixel by pixel until finally, there she was, standing in a long dress made of lilac silk. I could see the hard edge of her collarbone. The thought of it made the reel start up again in my head, and I had to shut my eyes against the vision of her burned bones lying at the pit of some mountain. I opened my eyes when it finally passed. The diamond ring on her finger sparkled in the camera's flash.

They were engaged.

The piece linked to their wedding announcement, made a few months earlier.

Mr. and Mrs. David Gardner of La Jolla, San Diego, would like to announce the engagement of their son, Ben Gardner, to Allison Carpenter of Maine. The groom is a graduate of the Whitman School of Business at the University of Syracuse and is the CEO of the pharmaceuticals company Prexilane. The bride is a graduate of Boston College. The wedding is planned for September 8.

The wedding was meant to have been in just a few months, and she hadn't told me about it. She hadn't invited me. She hadn't wanted me to be there.

I looked at the picture of the two of them. Did Ally look happy? It was so hard to tell. She was smiling, all right, but there was something about her eyes that wasn't quite right. She was wearing the necklace, the gold locket Charles had given her. That gave me a little comfort. Ben looked so damn smug standing next to her. He was wearing a suit that even I could tell was a good one, and he had the look of someone who always got exactly what he wanted. I'd seen his type at Bowdoin, rich kids who thought they were doing the world a favor just by existing. I wanted to reach through the picture and throttle him.

I remembered Linda saying something about Prexilane developing some kind of wonder drug, so I googled his name again, this time with the name of the company. My eyes lit on a link to a piece in *Time* magazine. I clicked on it and leaned in to squint at the screen.

HEALTH

Mother's Little Helper?
ONE MAN'S QUEST TO END POSTPARTUM DEPRESSION
Dee Sefton, February 23, 2015

Being the mother of an infant is always steeped in challenges. The sleepless nights, the constant worries about your child's health, the struggles of breastfeeding: all of it can take its toll. But for some, bringing a new life into the world can come at a much higher cost. Recent statistics show that one out of every five women will experience postpartum depression after giving birth, with symptoms ranging from mood swings to difficulty bonding with her child. However, it's thought that only 15 percent of women suffering from the condition receive proper treatment. Ben Gardner wants to change that.

"It's a game-changer," says the CEO of pharmaceutical giant Prexilane Industries. For the past three years, his company has been spearheading research about the causes of postpartum depression—and they've hit a breakthrough. The FDA is in the final stages of approving Somnublaze, a pioneering new drug that targets postpartum depression.

"Somnublaze is the first-ever antidepressant that's been specifically developed to treat postpartum depression," Gardner says. "With it, we hope to revolutionize the lives of new mothers and the lives of their children."

If the FDA clears the drug next month, as it's expected to do, millions of American women may soon be free of the shackles of postpartum depression so they can get back to doing what they do best—caring for their babies.

That must have been the drug Linda was talking about. She was right, too. I had heard of Somnublaze—hell, everyone had. It was advertised on TV every ten minutes, some polished-looking blond woman with too-white teeth holding a baby in one hand and a briefcase in the other. "Now I can have it all!" She beamed, before the voice-over kicked in. "Why not ask your doctor if Somnublaze is right for you?" I'd seen something on the news about it having the fastest take-up of any prescription drug brought to market.

I still remembered the early days with Ally, when she'd be up three times a night and Charles and I would both get up early to go to work, both of us bleary eyed and snappy, the very bones of us aching with exhaustion. It felt like living under a heavy rain cloud, just waiting for it to pour. Even so, I don't think I would have chosen to put something like that into my system. Our generation believed in sucking it up and keeping quiet. We didn't talk about how we felt. Times had changed, though. Now everyone wanted to tell you about their diagnosis.

I looked at the photograph of him that accompanied the article, all white teeth and rolled-up shirtsleeves. I pictured him holding her hand, kissing her, bending down on one knee and offering up a diamond. The images came too easily and I had to squeeze my eyes shut against them.

No. I didn't care what kind of a saint they made him out to be. It was because of him that she had been on that plane. And that meant that I was going to do my damnedest to know every single thing about him.

Allison

My head throbs like the worst kind of hangover. I reach out for my bag, catch the zipper, and pull. There isn't any water left, but there is still a little food, and I need all the energy I can get. My fingers find a handful of nuts. I count out four and feed them into my mouth one by one. Their jagged edges catch in my throat and I fight not to gag.

Another month, another event. I was a pro by then, and Dee and I were assigned the best table in the house. A real estate mogul. A former film producer. The chairman of a major defense company. A politician vying for a Senate seat. A hedge fund manager. And the CEO of a pharmaceutical company.

I was sitting between the real estate mogul and the politician. The politician wasn't paying me much attention—he was too busy trying to butter up the chairman of the defense company—but the real estate mogul's eyes had locked on me like a laser from the moment I took my seat. It was only nine p.m. and he'd already grabbed my ass and propositioned me to spend the night on his yacht. "It's a big one, I promise," he'd said with a wink, and then he lunged at me.

I was about to fend him off with a giggle and a feint to the left when someone clamped a hand on his shoulder and pulled him back. I looked up to see the pharmaceutical CEO standing over him, mouth drawn in a tight line, fist already clenched. "Don't be an asshole." His voice was surprisingly calm. The real estate mogul stood up, knocking his champagne glass and his chair over in the process. A hush descended on the room.

"Don't fucking touch me," the mogul hissed, but I could see the fear in his eyes. The CEO was nearly half his age, and you could see the outline of muscle underneath his tailored white shirt.

Dee caught my eye and motioned for me to do something. If things escalated, the night would be ruined, and we'd walk out of there with nothing. "Boys," I said in my sweetest voice. "Please." I placed a hand on the mogul's chest and ran my fingers down the lapel of his jacket. "Why don't you sit down while I get you another glass of champagne, okay, sweetheart?" The mogul nodded petulantly and bent to right his chair.

I looked at the CEO, whose fists were still clenched. I took him by the arm and led him to the bar, where I asked the bartender for two shots of tequila. I handed one to the CEO and we downed them without a word. I sagged against the bar as the liquid burned my throat.

The CEO wiped his mouth with the back of his hand and managed a smile. "Sorry about that," he said quietly. "That guy's a prick."

I squeezed my eyes shut for a moment. The tequila had started to do its work but it wasn't enough. I wasn't yet numb. I looked up at him and shrugged. "Comes with the territory, I guess." I saw the look on his face and forced a smile. "It's not a big deal. He's harmless. He just wants to have a good time."

He shook his head. "He didn't seem harmless."

I held the smile and signaled the bartender for another round of shots. "It's fine," I said, with more conviction than I felt.

He looked around the room with open disgust. "I don't even know what I'm doing here. I thought this was supposed to be a fund-raiser, but this . . ." He shook his head. "You shouldn't have to put up with it." I felt a wince of shame. He was revolted by this place. By me. And for a second, I was, too, before it was replaced with a surge of anger.

Who was this man—with his $3,000 tuxedo and his Hollywood-perfect smile—to tell me anything? "I know you're trying to help,"

I said quietly, "but I really don't need it." I tipped back the second shot and slammed the glass onto the bar top. I glanced at my reflection in the mirrored bar and tucked an errant hair back in place. "I've got to get back to work."

He held up his hands. "Fair enough." He downed his shot and placed a twenty under the empty glass for the bartender. "I'm getting out of here anyway." He reached into his breast pocket and pulled out a business card. "If you ever need anything, call me." He pressed the card into my hand. "Take care of yourself."

I watched him leave before I read it. BEN GARDNER, CEO, PREX-ILANE INDUSTRIES. A telephone number was printed underneath. I slid the card into my bra and walked back to the table. "Where did our little friend go?" the mogul asked as I sat back down. He was smirking but his eyes still held a glimmer of fear.

"His mommy called," I said, pulling my mouth into a pout. "He can't play with us anymore."

I watched his face visibly relax. "That's too bad." He slid his hand under the table. "But I'm sure you and I can have plenty of fun just the two of us."

After a few minutes, I feel strong enough to make another attempt at getting up. I'm still dizzy, but I'm able to make it to my feet and pack up camp. Before I set out, I tear the last of the button-down shirt into thin strips. I'll mark my place this time, so I'll know if I'm doubling back on myself. The hollow of the tree yawns at me as I tie a scrap to one of its branches.

I stop and stare at it, the white fabric stark against the bark. I tear it off and rub it in the dirt before tying it back on. I can't afford for it to be noticed by anyone but me.

Maggie

I didn't sleep again. Couldn't. I just lay in bed letting the slideshow play out behind my eyes.

Terror. Pain. Blood. Fire. Bone. Ally. Only then, there was a new image: Ben Gardner smiling out at me from the photograph, all white teeth and ice-blue eyes.

I got out of bed as soon as the early-morning light started creeping through the slats in the blinds. Barney gave a plaintive meow from the end of the bed as I shifted out of the covers. It was just before six in the morning.

I went downstairs and opened the door to the backyard. I hadn't set foot outside since I'd first heard the news of the accident, and the feeling of grass between my toes gave me pause. The sky was still pink, and most of the yard was still dark, but the sun had started to break through the trees, hitting the top of the swing set.

I should have had it taken out years earlier. The slide was dotted with patches of rust, and one of the swings was missing a seat. It was a safety hazard, probably. I wouldn't trust the cat on it, never mind a kid. Charles and I had talked about getting rid of it every year, made grand plans about replacing it with a vegetable patch or a rose garden, though my heart had stopped a little when Charles suggested a beehive. Bees made me nervous. But regardless of our plans, the swing set was still standing at the end of every summer.

The truth was, neither of us could bring ourselves to throw it away. He never said as much, but I'm sure he could picture Ally swinging on that swing every time he looked out into the yard, her little pigtails flying out behind her, her cheeks red from the excitement. We never said this, either, but I think both of us imagined a little grandson or granddaughter out there someday, too—though of course we would have had to fix it up first.

I could still see her running up to me and pointing at her scraped knee after she'd gone flying one day. "How did you manage to fall off the swing?" I'd asked her as I cleaned the dirt out of the cut.

She looked down at me, eyes wide, and shrugged her small shoulders. "I wanted to see what would happen if I let go."

My bones felt heavy now, standing in my bare feet on the lawn. I couldn't bear being there one more second. I had to get away.

I showered and dressed and was on the road by nine. Owl's Creek was wide awake. The bakery on Main had a line out the door, people waiting for their morning coffee, kids clutching white paper bags filled with muffins and sandwiches for summer camp. I watched a harried mother pull her little girl down the sidewalk on one of those scooters they all had then. The girl was blond and pigtailed and her mouth was wide open in a wail, her eyes scrunched up against whatever injustice had occurred. The mother caught me looking, and I gave her a sympathetic smile. Lord knows it's not easy.

I took the lake road out of town and merged onto Route 1, thick with commuters heading to Bangor or Portland. I didn't mind. Traffic eased after Freeport and I found myself driving past familiar landmarks. The Motor Court Motel. The big red sign for C&R's trading post. The turn-off for Piper Farm. I see the signs for Brunswick Airport and know I'm almost there. I took the next exit and curled my way toward Bowdoin.

I parked on Federal Street behind Stowe Hall and made my way up to the quad. The campus was quiet in the summertime but there were still the occasional students sprawled out on the lawn with books, sleeves rolled up and legs bare, or hurrying past with a backpack on their shoulders and a frown pulling at their mouth. It was all so familiar—for twenty years I'd crossed this quad and seen kids just like those—but that day I felt like an intruder. I felt like that most of the time then. Like a stranger in my own life.

I walked past the tall arched windows of the Hawthorne-Longfellow Library and through the sliding glass door. Doug was still sitting there in his chair, same as ever. He got to his feet when he saw me.

"Maggie! What a good surprise! What are you doing here?" He flinched and I watched him remember. "I heard about Allison. Christ, I'm sorry. What a thing to happen."

"Thank you, Doug. How's Betsy? She still working?"

"She retired last year. She's driving me crazy—every day it's, 'Where have you been today? When are you coming home?' At nine o'clock in the morning, she's asking me what I want for dinner. Nine o'clock in the morning!"

"It's a big adjustment. She'll get there. What about you? It's about time you called it quits, isn't it?"

"Me? Never. The day I stop working is the day I die!" He pounded on his desk to emphasize the point.

I rolled my eyes. "I bet my hat that in a year you'll be on a round-the-world trip with Betsy, sipping mai tais on a cruise ship somewhere in the Pacific."

He shook his head. "If you think that, you're crazy. You here to see Barbara? I saw her come in a few minutes ago. You know where to find her, right?"

I promised to say goodbye on my way out and made my way into the library. The cool hush hit me immediately, along with the sickly sweet smell of carpet cleaner mixed with stale paper. The room was almost empty, just a couple of students dotted among the long wooden tables. I padded through the stacks to the reference desk at the back. There was Barbara, steel-gray hair wound into a tight bun on the top of her head, pencil stabbed through it. I raised a hand in greeting and she rushed out from behind the desk and wrapped me in a hug.

"It's good to see you," she whispered. Her voice carried and several people looked up at us from their books and narrowed their eyes. "Come on, let's go to my office."

I followed her through the staff door and through the labyrinthine corridors to the cramped office we used to share. My desk had been taken over by stacks of books and drifts of paper, as I knew it would be. She gestured toward it as we sat down. "Sorry about the mess. How are you?"

I shrugged. "As well as I can be, I suppose."

"Well, I won't waste your time with my condolences, but I hope you know you have them. Now, what can I do for you?"

"Just trying to piece together a few things, that's all. Do you think you could set me up on a computer?"

"Sure thing." She led me to a row of machines in the back. "Let me know if you need any help, even though I know you won't," she said, and then she left me to it.

I remembered what Jim had said about Allison being in some kind of trouble. Had he meant legal trouble? I clicked on the Pacer icon on the screen and typed in my login credentials, hoping they were still valid. Pacer is an electronic database of court records across the country, so if Allison had any kind of police record, it would be on there. I plugged her name into the search engine and hit Return. The computer whirred into action.

Just one entry. I double-clicked.

Agency Case 38-471
IN THE DISTRICT/SUPERIOR COURT
OF THE STATE OF CALIFORNIA
JUDICIAL DISTRICT OF PALM SPRINGS
AFFIDAVIT by Police Officer
In Support of Complaint
State of California
Plaintiff
Vs
ALLISON CARPENTER

Case number 8YU-11-39GT

I, Jerome Ramsay attest to the following and state:

On 2 August 2016 at approximately 12:55am I was dispatched to 622 N Palm Canyon Dr., Palm Springs, for report of reckless driving. MATCOM dispatch informed me that a female had called 911 to report that a woman driving a blue Mercedes S-Class was swerving between lanes. The female also reported that there was a man in the passenger seat.

I arrived at the scene at 1:03am and quickly located the vehicle, which was driving far below the legal speed limit and veering erratically across the road. I flashed my lights several times but the vehicle failed to pull over, and a short pursuit ensued until I witnessed the person in the passenger seat take the wheel and pull the car over to the side of the road. I approached the vehicle and found the operator, a woman in her late twenties, to be clearly over the legal limit for alcohol and possibly under the influence of narcotics. When I asked her for her license and registration, she produced a California state driver's license that identified her as a Ms. Allison Carpenter of 2799 Adrian Street, San Diego CA. The car was registered to the passenger, a man in his early sixties named Mr. John Dwyer, also of San Diego. He did not appear to be under the influence of drugs or alcohol.

Ms. Carpenter refused a breathalyzer test and I arrested her at the scene for suspected DUI and placed her in the back of the police vehicle. I instructed Mr. Dwyer to follow us in his car but he did not appear at the station.

Ms. Carpenter was released on bail later that morning.

Jerome Ramsay, Police Officer

Subscribed and sworn to or affirmed before me at Palm Springs, CA on 08/03/2016

I scrolled through the rest of the documents, but they'd either been sealed or blacked out. No formal charges were ever filed against Allison, and the case had been dropped.

What on earth had she been doing driving around in that condition with a man my age? I wondered. And how had she managed to get out of the charges? From the police notes, it looked like a pretty open-and-shut case.

I sat back in the chair. *My God, Ally*, I thought. *What were you thinking?*

"Excuse me."

I looked up to see a man with a shock of thick gray hair and small, round glasses looming above me. "I'm sorry to interrupt, but did you by any chance used to work here?"

"That's right." It had been four years since I worked there. I was surprised anyone remembered.

"I thought you looked familiar. I'm sorry, I can't seem to remember your name . . ."

"Maggie," I said.

"Maggie, of course." He smiled and the corners of his eyes crinkled. He looked kind. "I'm Tony. Nice to see you again."

"You too," I said, though I couldn't for the life of me remember having seen him before. Still, there had been so many people to walk through the doors of the library during my time there—there was no way of knowing all of them.

"Do you mind?" He sat down in the chair next to mine without waiting for my reply. "My knees," he said, smiling apologetically.

"They can't handle much these days. An hour or two of sitting down and they're cooked." I thought of the strange aches I woke up with, the dull pain in my hip if I sat for too long, the way the bones in my ankles clicked when I walked. He leaned forward and rested his hands on his thighs. "So, what brings you back to Bowdoin?"

I studied him. He looked like a nice enough man, but I didn't like him sitting down uninvited and asking questions about my business. It put my back up. "My computer at home is broken," I lied. "I thought I'd come here while I wait for it to be repaired." There was a pause and I realized he was waiting for me to ask him a question. "And yourself?" I asked reluctantly. "Are you a professor here, or . . . ?"

"Me? Oh, no!" He let out a laugh that was louder than strictly allowed within a library. "No, no, I'm just one of those sad old retired guys who uses his senior discount to take classes."

"That's nice." I'd seen his type enough to know that he was probably divorced or widowed. Married men his age didn't audit classes. Their wives did, to get away from them, but the married men tended to stay at home.

He shrugged. "It fills the time. Just started art history and French literature, God help me. Next semester I'm moving on to archaeology."

"Very ambitious." I turned back to the computer screen, hoping he'd take the hint.

I felt him hesitate. Out of the corner of my eye, I watched him open his mouth and waited for the next question, but instead he closed it again and pushed himself up onto his feet. "Well," he said, "I'll leave you alone. I just wanted to come by and say hello. I was always sorry I didn't introduce myself when you were here, and then one day you weren't here anymore and I kicked myself for missing my chance. But here you are."

I held up my hands. "Here I am."

He gave me a wave before wandering back to his desk. I felt a twinge of regret for giving him the brush-off. He was probably just a lonely man looking for a little conversation. Harmless. I glanced at the stack of books on his desk—Proust, Berger, Maupassant. A hell of a way to spend a summer. I should have been kinder.

I pushed the thought aside and turned back to the computer. I had work to do. I brought up the National Transportation Safety Board, typed in the details of Ally's crash, and hit Return.

NTSB Identification: CEN36FA455
14 CFR Part 91: General Aviation
Accident occurred Sunday, July 08,
2018 on Electric Peak, CO
Aircraft: MOONEY AVIATION 3

Injuries: 2 fatal

This is preliminary information, subject to change, and may contain errors. Any errors in this report will be corrected when the final report has been completed. NTSB investigators either traveled in support of this investigation or conducted a significant amount of investigative work without any travel, and used data obtained from various sources to prepare this aircraft accident report.

On July 08, 2018, about 1700 mountain time standard, a Mooney Aviation 3 airplane, N65EF, was destroyed by impact forces and post-impact fire following an apparent loss of control near Boreas Mountain, Colorado. The airplane was registered to and operated by a private individual under the provisions of the 14th code Federal Regulations Part 91 as a personal flight. The flight originated from Chicago Midway International (MDW) and is thought to have been destined for Montgomery Field Airport in San Diego, California (MYF), where the plane departed from on Friday, July 06, 2018, but no flight plan was filed. The pilot and passenger were fatally injured.

The initial impact point was located about ten feet south of the main wreckage and contained the airplane's nose landing gear. Based on the position of the airplane and the impact point, the airplane was traveling in an easterly position at the time of impact. The entire airplane was almost completely consumed by the post-impact fire that ensued, making recovery from the wreckage difficult. The pilot's remains have been recovered and his identity has been confirmed by his next of kin. The passenger's body has not yet been identified at the time of writing. The seriousness of the crash and the state of the wreckage indicate that fatality is certain and that the passenger's body was likely thrown clear of the aircraft on impact, though conditions at the site make a full investigation difficult. No anomalies could be found with respect to the engine or engine accessories; however, the extent of the fire damage precluded a complete examination and testing of components. There is some evidence that the crash site had been interfered with before investigators arrived on the scene. It is thought the interference was likely due to local wildlife.

At 1600 MDT the local weather observation for Boreas Mountain reported wind from 340 at 9 knots, 10 miles visibility, clear sky, temperature 73F, dew point 25F, and altimeter 30.21 inches of mercury. Weather is not thought to have been a factor in the crash.

An iPhone with the ForeFlight mobile application was recovered from the accident site and sent to the NTSB Recorders Laboratory for examination and download.

I sat back in my chair. So Ben's body had been found. Shannon and Jim must have known but decided not to tell me about it yet. Didn't want to get my hopes up, I guess. It was clear from the report that the investigators thought she was dead, even if they couldn't find her body. I reread it. "Thrown clear of the aircraft." "Local wildlife." I didn't want to picture either, but of course I did, one after the other. "Fatality is certain." I stared at those words until my eyes unfocused and my vision started to blur.

The necklace, though. They'd found her necklace. How could they have found her necklace but not her?

If they'd found his body, that meant his parents would know now, too. Mr. and Mrs. David Gardner. Had they spent much time with Ally? Did they know her well? I had to talk to them. I had to ask them what they knew.

I stood up too quickly, and for a second, the room swam.

"Maggie? Are you all right?" I looked up to see Tony staring at me from his desk, face full of concern. I waved him away and gathered my bags.

The green of the quad was a blur. All those kids sitting on the grass or walking in twos, heads dipped together, talking and laughing. God, they looked so young. Did all of them have lives they kept secret from their parents? Did they go home on break and sit around the dinner table and eat the food that their mothers cooked for them and laugh at their father's jokes, all the while knowing that they had secrets they would never share?

Allison

The clouds arrive thick and fast, blown in on a strong breeze that kicks up just as the sun begins to make its way home for the evening. I watch them gather above me, the gray stalking across the blue, enveloping it in its cloak and smothering the sun. The air presses down on me like a fat thumb. And then, like a sheet being ripped in two, the clouds break and the rain starts to fall.

It's slow at first, a gentle patter on the leaves, but it quickly turns to a roar. I hide beneath a canopy of trees but the water drips through, and I'm soaked to the bone in minutes.

The temperature plummets. There's nowhere for me to hide, and none of my gear is waterproof. My teeth chatter noisily in my skull, my arms pinned tightly across my chest. Fear starts to scratch. For the first few minutes of the storm, I'm frozen to the spot by shock and indecision and the weight of my now-soaked bag. I stare down at my shaking hands as though they aren't my own.

His breath was hot on my face and I had to stop myself from grimacing as he traced the outline of my mouth with his finger. "Such a pretty girl."

I leaned across the bed and took another bump. Dee had been right: It had been over quick, and I'd barely felt a thing. Like I wasn't even in my body at all.

I gathered the sheets around me and walked to the bathroom. A row of halogen bulbs framed the mirror and I squinted into the light. My pupils were wide and jet black, crowding out their rims of green. They looked strange to me, foreign and alien. Unrecognizable.

"Hurry up, baby!"

"In a sec!" I called. My voice echoed off the marble floor.

There were miniature soaps lined up on the sink, a sewing kit, a shower cap. I decided I would take all of it before I left, along with the little bottles of shampoo and conditioner and lotion and one of the thick robes that hung in the closet. I didn't need any of it, but it didn't matter. I felt it was owed to me, along with the stack of twenties I knew he'd leave on the table. I'd have to wait until he left to take them in my hands—"Don't touch the money in front of them," Dee had said, "it makes you look cheap"—and then I'd raise the bills to my face and inhale their scent of leather and metal and soap.

See? I thought as I walked back into the bedroom. *Easy money.*

Move. You have to move.

I stumble, legs heavy. I take a few steps forward, rainwater streaming down my face, plastering my filthy hair to my forehead, blurring my field of vision. The rain is torrential, hurling itself angrily to the ground like a raging toddler. I try to take a deep breath and get a lungful of water instead. Splutter and choke.

Okay. Stop. Just wait.

I throw my bag to the ground, where it lands with a wet squelch. My fingers have begun to blue again, and I tuck them tightly into my armpits to warm them. It's grown so cold so quickly, and the trees give only some shelter from the wind howling through the forest. I can feel my toes beginning to numb in my soaking sneakers, the nerve endings stinging before they go dead.

I can't stop. If I stop, I'll die. And I've come too far to die now.

I bend down and try to pick up my bag, but my shoulder screams and I let out a guttural roar as I drop it back to the ground. For a second, I'm convinced I've wrenched my arm from its socket, but after a few minutes the searing pain recedes to a dull throb. So ordinary now, this white-noise pain. So familiar.

Breathe through it. That's what my mother would say. I was always getting hurt as a child—too-long legs and too-big feet always ready to get tangled up in one another—and I was forever turning up at the back door with a scraped knee or a split lip.

Breathe through it, she'd say as she dabbed at the scrape with rubbing alcohol. *I know it hurts, Ally, but just breathe through it.*

Breathe.

The pain in my shoulder dulls enough that I can hear myself think, not that I know what to say. I'm cold. I'm wet. I'm lost in the woods. Somewhere out there, they're looking for me. They could be in these mountains right now, tracking me down like a dog. And there's nothing I can do about any of it.

I pace around my bag, hoping the movement will force the blood back into my toes, but it feels like I'm walking on a bed of needles. It's dark now, though I can't tell if that's down to the thick clouds covering the sun or the fact that it's late. Time feels like a slippery, unwieldy thing. The rain hasn't let up at all—if anything, it's getting worse. It feels like the storm is getting comfortable now, and bedding down for a long night.

There's no point in trying to push on farther.

I pull out the canvas and try to prop it up like a tent with a few loose branches as poles, but it collapses almost immediately. Anyway, it's not waterproof, at least not fully, and it's already soaked. There's no way I can build any kind of shelter for myself with it, or with anything else I have with me.

I pull my bag under the biggest tree I can find and fold myself up against its trunk, knees hugged to my chest. The rain drips through the pine needles.

I close my eyes, just for a second.

Maggie

I picked up the phone and dialed the number that Jim had given me, but no one answered. I left another message on the machine, but I didn't hold up much hope for them calling me back. It'd been two days now, and I still hadn't heard a word from Ben's parents. I knew they were grieving, but I was grieving, too. That didn't give them the right to ignore me. Not when my daughter had been engaged to their son. Not when he was responsible for her death.

The internet wasn't much help, either. I typed their names in carefully—David and Amanda Gardner; have you ever heard a more moneyed pair of names?—but nothing much came up. David was registered as on the board of a local charity, and Amanda was mentioned in a few society pieces—contributing the flower arrangements for the Audubon Society annual gala, that sort of thing—but other than that, the two of them were internet ciphers.

I typed in Ally's name again. Pages and pages of entries came up about her death. I clicked on one of them and scrolled past the crash report to her photo. It was the same one they'd used on the news: blond, thin, fancy. Nothing like my Ally. I inched my way down to the comments but quickly stopped reading them. Who were these people, these ghouls? How could they say these things about a dead woman, let alone my daughter?

Jim had mentioned when he'd called that he didn't know when I'd be getting Ally's belongings from San Diego. They'd tracked down the house she'd lived in with him—he gave me the address after I'd worked on him for a bit. I looked it up on the internet and used the street view to zoom in. I could see a hedge wall and a high gate, and then beyond it a glimpse of sandstone and glass.

My daughter had lived in that house with a man she was engaged to and whom I had never met. The shock of it still took my breath away.

I don't know why I'd been so surprised to learn they'd been living together—I knew it was normal for people their age to live together before they were married; I wasn't some kind of nun—but still, it had taken me aback. I tried to imagine her clothes hung next to his, her books propped up on a nightstand next to the bed, her shampoo lined up on the edge of the bathtub. And now it would be a long time before I could claim her things and bring them home. My blood had boiled when Jim had said that. For my own daughter's clothes, her hairbrush, her perfume—for any last scrap of her, I'd have to fight.

I thought about those first days after we brought her home from the hospital. She was a big girl when she was born—nearly nine pounds, God help me—with cheeks as round and red as crab apples. Charles and I had waited so long for her to arrive—we'd been trying for years, and were the oldest couple in the delivery ward by almost a decade—and by then we'd known it would just be her, a little family of three. We would stand by her crib and stare at her as she slept, watching her tiny chest rise and fall, both of us scared to blink or move or heaven forbid sleep in case we missed something. That lasted only a couple of weeks, of course, until sleep deprivation nearly drove us both insane. Still, I remember those days as some of the happiest of my life. After all those years of trying, the fact that she existed—that she was ours—felt like pure dumb luck.

She got colic when she was two months old and didn't seem to stop crying until she started to walk, so those golden days were short lived. But the feeling that it was just three of us in this thing together stuck around.

I'd taken to wearing Charles's ring again. It felt like a talisman, heavy and reassuring on my thumb. I slid it past the knuckle and read the inscription etched on the inside. C&M ALWAYS AND FOREVER. I sighed. Why do we kid ourselves about these things? I wondered. Nothing was built for forever. There would always be someone left behind.

The sound of Linda coming through the door made me jump. I wasn't sure how long I'd been sitting there—maybe ten minutes, maybe a couple of hours. Time had become thick and syrupy, hard to get a handle on. She walked in carrying a few letters and a shallow cardboard box. "It's addressed to Charles," she said, nodding toward the box.

"Just stick it on the counter. I'll figure out what to do with it later."

She sat down across from me at the table and nodded toward the notepad that lay open in front of me. "What's all this?"

I pulled it closer to me and stared down at my notes. "Trying to know more about what happened with Ally. Ben's parents aren't returning my calls, and I can't get through to anyone at that bar she was working at."

Linda's eyebrows shot up. "You called the bar?"

"The number was right there on the website!" I cried, suddenly defensive. I knew she would think I was going overboard.

Linda sighed. "I just don't know if this is healthy for you. Making phone calls, writing lists . . ." The corners of her eyes creased with concern. "Nothing you do is going to bring her back to you."

"They still haven't found the body," I pointed out.

She nodded. "I know," she said quietly, but I could see the pity in her eyes and I turned my face away.

"It's bullshit," I muttered under my breath. I had been planning on telling her everything I'd found out, but then I felt a flash of impatience. What was the point in telling her all that? She wouldn't understand. No one did. "I just want to know what happened with my daughter," I said. I didn't want to have to explain myself to anyone. Not then. I didn't say any of that, though, and the silence stretched between us.

"I'm sorry," she said. "I can't imagine what you're going through, and I don't want to upset you even more, it's just . . . I think it's best if you let things rest, otherwise you're going to drive yourself crazy. I only want what's best for you."

I told her I was tired and needed to lie down for a while, and she gathered up her things and headed for the door. "I'll come around tomorrow and we can talk more about plans for the memorial," she said, gathering me in for a hug.

"I won't be in tomorrow," I said. "I've got a doctor's appointment in Bangor."

"The day after, then."

I shook my head. "I've got errands to run all day. Look, why don't you just go ahead with whatever you feel is right. I'm sure you'll pull something perfect together."

For a second, she looked like she was about to ask me something, but in the end she just closed her mouth and pulled me in for another hug. "Of course. Don't you worry about a thing—just leave it with me."

I waved her off and then sat and listened for her car to turn down the street before logging back on to the computer. I clicked on an email in my inbox and hit Print.

I didn't have a doctor's appointment the next day, and I sure as hell wasn't meeting with any funeral director about Ally.

The printer spat out the e-ticket one line at a time, and when I picked it up off the tray, the ink was still damp.

Tomorrow morning, before the sun rose in the sky, I'd be on a plane bound for California.

If they wouldn't come to me, I'd go to them.

Allison

A phone is ringing. It's far away at first but now it's closer, urgent, the shrill sound clasped tightly against my ears, pressing. Insistent.

I startle awake.

Darkness. Nothing but darkness. No difference between the world and the inside of my eyelids. Black.

The wind rattles through the trees overhead. The cold is inside me now. It's both a weight pressing down and a liquid flowing through, acute and infinite.

I feel around until my fingers grasp the strap of my bag. Pull it closer. Food. There's still food. My hand dives into the bag, comes up with a Luna bar. Dumb fingers fumble at the plastic wrapping. There. It's open.

Lips crack as they part. Taste blood. Tongue a thick slab of meat filling up. Take a bite. Jaw cracks. Teeth work and work but the bar remains, solid chunks stuck to molars. Swallow. Choke.

The rain. Pat the ground until you find a fallen leaf. Raise to your lips, suck the water down. The bar loosens, slides down the throat. Another bite. Chew. Swallow. Suck. Repeat. For a second, there's calm, and then the revolt begins.

Stomach wrenches and then, bent double, eyes screwed up like pinpricks. My body is shivering badly now, shaking violently, guts twisting. I try to still myself but I can't. I'm a rag doll being shaken from within.

Get up. Get up.

Legs stumble. I can't feel my feet, or fingers, or face. I touch my hands to my ears to prove they're still there. The parts of my body feel like stars loosely gathered in the same universe, remote and disconnected. Clothes snag on branches.

But the pain—the pain is gone.

It'll be back. I can already hear it stalking me, its footsteps light across the sodden ground. I have to move before it catches me. There's time. I can still escape.

What's a pretty girl like you doing in a place like this?

This jacket is too heavy. It's holding me back. Anyway, I can't feel the cold anymore; I can't feel anything. Toss it to the ground, move on. Move. It's coming, I can hear it. The pain and the cold are coming for me, and I don't know if I can outrun them this time.

"There's nothing to you." That was what he'd said to me, the next time we met. I'd been late for work, hungover and strung out and squinting into the too-bright sun. I wasn't paying attention to where I was going and—*bam!*—I ran smack into him on the sidewalk. His coffee spilled everywhere. I was mortified, mumbling apologies and offering to pay for dry cleaning, but he just laughed. "There's nothing to you," he'd said, wiping the coffee from his cuff. "You're like a little sparrow. Here, let me help." At first, I wasn't sure if he remembered me. After all, it had been dark inside the bar, and a couple of months had gone by. But then he looked up from gathering the contents of my bag and smiled. "It's Allison, right? I'm Ben." I already knew.

He handed me my bag, and I gave him my most dazzling smile. "Can I buy you another coffee?" I asked, nodding to his empty paper cup, and he nodded and said, "Sure, but I'm buying."

Sitting across from me at the cramped table, he'd licked the foam from his top lip and asked if I was still waitressing. I thought of my dingy studio apartment, and the damp heat of a stranger's breath on my neck, and the smell of the jail cell—old sweat mixed with cheap perfume and fear. I met his eyes and waited to see judgment, but there was nothing there but polite curiosity. I realized that he didn't know the truth, and nearly wept with relief. In his eyes, I was a blank slate. I could be anyone.

In that moment, it was clear to me that it was fate. This man, with his handsome face and his kind smile and his expensive wristwatch, had tried to save me once before. This time, I was going to let myself be saved. I could already feel myself sloughing off my old life. Already, I knew I loved him.

One step. Another. I think, maybe, that I should run.

Come on, sweetheart. Don't get cute with me. We both knew what this was. Don't pretend like you're innocent.

My eyes finally adjust and within the swirl of blackness I can see darker shapes and lighter shapes and they all whizz past me as I run, legs pumping, lungs filling with the sweet, clean air, twigs snapping and leaves squelching and body darting between the thickly packed trees and under the low-slung branches. In this dark I am light light light. Have I ever been this fast before?

I can feel my father's hand in mine, tugging me along. "Faster, Allycat, faster!" We are running full throttle down the hill around the back of the house. My little legs are unsteady, barely catching me as I tear down the hill, the recklessness filling me with a sort of hysteria. Stop! I'm shouting, Stop! But I don't want to stop, not really. I want to keep almost-falling forever, the wind whipping at my face, the fizzy feeling in my stomach, like a pancake midflip, joy and terror in equal measure.

He stirs creamer into his coffee and taps the side of the mug with his spoon. A smile plays on his lips. You wouldn't want your fiancé to find out about your little brush with the law, would you?

The ground rushes toward me.

All you've got to do is help me. That's all.

Stars. I can see stars. Up there, through the trees. A whole ocean of them.

Allison. Get up, Allison. What are you doing, lying there like that?

I open my eyes and see him standing over me, eyes glowing in the darkness, two bright spots of blue in the black. He is reaching down now, hand extended, but I'm back on my feet again and I am running, stumbling, tumbling.

I didn't mean to hurt you. You know that, don't you? But in the end, you didn't give me a choice.

The cold is gone now. All I feel is a drowsy sort of warmth.

A daisy nods its lazy head at me and I snap its neck with a sharp tug.

See a daisy pick it up, all day long you'll have good luck.

No, that's not right. That's not how it goes at all.

He loves me. He loves me not. He loves me. He loves me not.

The petals won't be pinched. My fingers won't work.

How will I know if he loves me?

The trees are growing taller. Or maybe I'm shrinking, like Alice in Wonderland when she drinks from the little vial. Where is the cake that will make me grow tall?

Can you read me another story?

No, Allycat, it's time for bed.

Bed. Yes, bed. A bed of moss for a mattress. I lie down gently. The trees bend to tuck me in. *Shushhhh*, their leaves whisper. *Shushhhhh.*

There you go, Allycat. Snug as a bug in a rug.

My eyelids are heavy. I blink up at the sky. Once. Twice.

Goodnight, trees.

Goodnight, stars.

Goodnight, moon.

Dee's face rises up before me. "It's easy money. Trust me."

The nights started bleeding into each other, the days disappeared by sleep. We stashed rolls of cash everywhere—in our sock drawers and lockers and in the vents in the break room. I had never seen so much cash before.

"Just smile and be nice. That's all they want, really. A pretty girl being nice to them."

Aftershave and stale liquor. The sound of laughter burbling up inside me, forced. The rasp of stubble on skin.

"You don't have to do anything you don't want."

Do you know what a wad of bills smells like if you close your eyes?

"They'll get it one way or another. You might as well make them pay."

It smells like blood.

Ally, it's time to wake up.

My mother's hands gently shaking me.

C'mon, Ally, it's time.

My eyes start open and fear floods through me. A gap of light has opened up, and through that gap a siren is wailing. I'm in trouble. Deep trouble.

Stay awake, Ally. Just stay awake.

I try to get up but my legs don't work. It's as simple as that, really. They just don't work. My hands pad around me, searching. I hit on a rock, a sharp one, and dig my palm into it as hard as I can. The pain shocks through me, clearing my mind like a gust of wind.

Yes. That. I need to feel that.

Clumsy fingers fold themselves around the rock, and I squeeze it as tightly as I can. The sharp edge of the rock digs into my skin until finally the pain breaks through.

Up. Get up.

I haul myself onto my elbows, then my knees. There's a low-hanging branch above and I reach for it, snaking my arms around it and pulling myself up. It takes every ounce of my remaining strength but I'm on my feet, rock still clutched tightly in my hand, the pain biting at my palm.

She's standing in front of me in that blue fisherman's sweater she wears all winter, her hair scraped back from her face, her hand outstretched. I reach out and her fingers wrap around my wrist.

I'm sorry, I say, for everything.

She shakes her head.

Just keep going, Ally. Just keep going.

Maggie

I'd forgotten that the airport was in the middle of the city, right next to the beach. As we swooped in for landing and I saw the white sand stretched out beneath us, I remembered the time Charles and I had come there to visit her. Charles had gotten out of the airport, already sweating from the heat, and had taken one look at the ocean opposite and said, "Who knew that airplanes needed a sea view?" He hadn't liked San Diego—too pleasant for his tastes—but I had. The bright blue sky that never seemed bothered by a cloud, the deep blue-green of the ocean, the way that the water was lit up in Technicolor at night, each of the tall buildings refracting a different color onto its surface. It was a place that wasn't worried about looking a little over the top, and I respected that. It reminded me of Linda. I couldn't have lived there, of course, but I was happy to visit.

The sliding glass doors of the terminal opened and the dry warmth hit me as I stepped onto the pavement. Up in Maine, the summers are different, the air thick and humid, coating your skin in a sticky film, making you feel like you're being made heavier just by breathing it. In San Diego, the air seemed to gently wrap itself around you, like a caress.

I'd rented a car—a little two-door Honda—and I jingled the keys in my hand as I searched for it in the lot. The black wheeled suitcase I dragged behind me bumped against my heels as I walked. I don't know why I bothered to pack so much. I knew I wouldn't be there for long.

The car was tucked between a pair of four-by-fours at the back of the farthest row. I popped the trunk, hauled my suitcase inside, and then settled myself in the driver's seat and tried to figure out what the hell I was supposed to do next. I had a map I'd bought from the rental place even though the guy on the counter had looked at me like I was crazy—"Don't you have a phone?" he'd asked—and a scrap of paper with three addresses written on it. I studied them for a minute, marking each place on the map with a ballpoint pen, and then sparked up the engine and pulled out of the lot.

The car nearly conked out on the climb to La Jolla. The engine struggled each time I hit the gas, and I could feel the transmission hesitate before it shifted up a gear. The road had been carved straight through the rock, and on either side, houses clung to the cliffside like a collection of matchboxes, looking like a stiff breeze would be enough to blow them away.

Spindrift Drive hugged the coastline, fringed with tall green hedges grown to obscure the mansions lurking behind. I squinted at the numbers on the gated drives. A man pruning a rosebush squinted at the car as I rolled past. I guessed they didn't get too many Honda Civics up in La Jolla.

The Gardners' house was a hulking cube of glass and concrete, one of those buildings that look like they have descended from outer space rather than having been built up from the ground. I recognized it from the *New York Times* piece I'd read. According to the article, it was a "postmodern masterpiece," though I was more inclined to agree with the Gardners' neighbors about its being an eyesore. At least from what I could make out from where I stood, on the sidewalk on the wrong side of a tall wrought-iron gate. I rang the buzzer and waited. No response. I stretched up on my tiptoes and peered around the corner to the circular drive. A black Bentley was parked at the top, followed by a dark green Jaguar. Someone had to be home.

I rang again, leaning heavily on the buzzer this time. Finally, the intercom stuttered and spat. "Hello?" It was a woman's voice, heavily accented. The housekeeper, I guessed.

"I'm Maggie Carpenter," I said, trying to keep the tremble out of my voice. "Allison's mother. I'm looking for David and Amanda Gardner."

"Sorry, they're away." The intercom cut out.

I buzzed again. The voice crackled out again. "Yes?"

"Is there anyone else I could speak with? I've come a long way, and I'd like to talk to someone about my daughter."

"Sorry. I'm not allowed to let anyone onto the grounds when the Gardners are away. Sorry." The intercom cut out again, this time for good, no matter how many times I hit the buzzer.

I stood on the sidewalk for a minute, listening to the sound of the waves crashing into the rocks below and the low moan of a nearby lawn mower. A red sports car with tinted windows rolled past, too slow for it to be anything other than deliberate. I didn't believe for a minute that the Gardners weren't in that house, but it didn't matter—they weren't talking to me.

Well, if they wouldn't, maybe somebody else would. I tried the house on the left first, but no one answered the bell. I thought I saw a curtain twitch in an upstairs window, but it could just have been my eyes playing tricks on me. When I pressed the doorbell for the house on the right, I heard the patter of footsteps and a woman pulled open the door in her dressing gown. I told her my car had broken down and I needed to phone a tow truck, and she ushered me inside. It's amazing how trusting people can be when they see an old lady in distress.

I got as far as the parquet floor entryway when I admitted my car hadn't really broken down. Still, her eyes didn't show any fear, just confusion mixed with a little pity. "Are you lost?" she asked, and I shook my head and told her I was looking for the Gardners, that I was Allison's mother, that I just wanted to talk to someone about her, and did she know them, and did she know their son, and did she know my daughter? But I saw her face slam shut as soon as I mentioned their name, and soon I found myself back on the other side of the gate and her door closed tightly against the world again.

Whoever the Gardners were, and wherever they were hiding, they'd briefed the neighbors beforehand. I didn't think there was much point in knocking on any more doors—it was clear no one was going to talk.

I turned and headed back up the hill toward my car. The red sports car roared past me just as I was climbing in, leaving a wake of hot, gasoline-scented air behind it.

I drove to the Motel 6 on Pacific Highway too fast, my mind wandering back to the empty-eyed mansions up in La Jolla. I checked in and sat in my room, watching twenty-four-hour news and eating a tuna sandwich I'd picked up at a gas station on the way. The place was done out in Crayola colors—orange carpets with bright blue accents—and I had to keep closing my eyes to get a rest from it. Outside, I could hear the splashes and squeals of kids as they played in the pool.

They weren't talking about Ally anymore. Whenever they mentioned the plane crash, she was just an afterthought. Ben was the main event now. There were infographics that charted the sales of Somnublaze, interviews with his peers in the pharmaceutical industry, exterior shots of the Prexilane headquarters with solemn-faced journalists speaking in respectful tones about him. I stared at the skyscraper on the screen. I'd driven past it on my way to the hotel, just a quick glance and then it was gone. You couldn't escape him, though, or that magic pill of his. San Diego was peppered with billboards advertising it, the blond woman's smile stretched ten feet wide, holding a giggling baby with eyes as blue as the sky, and underneath, that same damn slogan. "Now I can have it all!"

I wanted to phone into one of these news programs and ask them why they weren't talking more about my daughter. She was a person in her own right, not just a passenger or a fiancée or a "glamorous companion," as some slick-haired asshole had referred to her. She was smart and kind and funny and worth ten of him. Twenty. She was the girl who'd insisted on choosing the hamster with three legs from the pet shop because she was sure no one else would love it. She was the college student who had written an op-ed for the newspaper about the lack of protection against sexual assault on campus.

She was the woman who had read to her father for hours as he lay on the sofa staring up at the ceiling, fists clenched against the pain. She was a light in this world and now she was gone, and no one seemed to give a damn except me.

I checked the time—quarter to eight. Time to take a shower and freshen up before I headed back out for the night. I was drawing the curtains closed when I noticed a man standing next to a bright red sports car in the parking lot below. I watched as he climbed into the car and peeled off into the dusk.

Allison

She led me here, my mother. She must have. I asked her for help and forgiveness and she delivered me one more time. How else can I explain how I woke up on the floor of a cabin, a fire (that I must have lit, or maybe it was her) still smoldering in the coal furnace?

I strip off my clothes and stare down at my naked body. My bad shoulder throbs and I can see that a dark bruise has appeared. My skin is red and mottled from the cold, my fingertips still blue and stinging as the blood forces itself back into them. My toes are swollen and oddly shiny, as if the skin has been polished, and the soles of my feet are puckered and tender to the touch. There's a jagged red smile on one of my palms from where the rock cut into the flesh. I'd gripped it so tightly, I'd drawn blood.

His house in Bird Rock was like something out of *Architectural Digest*. When he first told me about it, he said it was his favorite place in the world, and as soon as I stepped foot inside, it had been mine, too. I wanted to be folded into its cool white walls and fall asleep listening to the murmured hush of the rock pool.

So when, after a few weeks together, he asked me to move in with him, I said yes. I tried to put him off helping me move—I didn't have much, just a couple of bags of clothes and a few books I'd salvaged from Tara's place—but he insisted, and soon we were pulling up to the low-slung building in Logan Heights in his Tesla. I watched him take in the apartment, the cracked paint and the drunk neighbors you could hear through the walls and the smell of damp cigarettes that permeated everything.

"Let's get you out of here," he said, and slung one bag over each arm and headed out the door. We were silent on the way home, me stealing nervous glances at his profile, his jaw set tight.

When we pulled up to the house in Bird Rock, he switched off the engine and turned to me. "What were you doing, living in a place like that?"

I stared down at my lap. Shame swept through me. "What do you mean?"

I felt his eyes on my profile. "What kind of a life were you living?" I heard the accusation in his voice, sharp as a dagger.

I forced myself to look at him. He had to see my eyes if he was going to believe me. "I was waitressing," I said, as calmly as I could manage. "You know that."

He was silent, and in that moment, I was sure that he could see straight into my soul, right down to its dirty, putrid core. He knows, I thought, panic rising in my chest. He knows about all of it: the drugs, the hotel rooms, that jail cell in Palm Springs where I prayed to a god I knew wasn't listening. I could hear the rumble of a far-off engine and the hum of the cicadas and the faint snip of the gardener's shears from two houses down and the thumping roar of my own heart. I closed my eyes and waited for him to say the words. *It's over.*

I felt his warm hand cradling my chin. I opened my eyes and met his. "I hate that you had to serve drinks to those assholes, and I hate that you had to live in that shithole apartment." He shook his head. "Something could have happened to you living there."

I let myself feel a sliver of hope. He wouldn't be talking like that if he knew the truth. He wouldn't feel concern for me. He would feel disgust. I managed a shrug. "The apartment wasn't as bad as it looked."

"Brave girl," he murmured. He brushed the hair back from my neck and smiled. "I promise you'll never have to struggle like that again. Okay?"

I took in a deep, stuttering breath, like I'd been underwater for a long time. I nodded and let myself fall into him, too wrung out from adrenaline to answer. It was over. He loved me. He believed me. I really was saved.

I take a minute to look around the cabin. It's a small, squat room, low ceiling and tightly braced with neatly jointed two-by-fours. There are four windows, one for each wall, all of which have their blinds tugged down snugly. It's dark in here, but there's a candle stub sitting on top of the chest in the corner along with a pack of matches, and with shaking hands I manage to light it. The door is jammed shut but the frame is splintered, and I can see now that I must have broken it to get in. That explains the freshly blackened shoulder. How did I find the strength? I think again of my mother's strong hands. It was her somehow. I know.

There's a row of high shelves stacked with canned food—I spot a jar of pickles and my heart soars—and a jerrican of water. Inside the chest, there's a wool blanket that smells like wet dog and a few more candle ends and even a thick-bladed hunting knife, its edge blunted but useful nonetheless. There's more coal for the furnace, too.

A thought jolts through me. My bag. Shit, where is it? I cast my eyes around the place, already cursing myself for having lost it, but there it is, shoved neatly against the far wall. It's the same bewildered relief I felt on countless mornings waking up with a thudding hangover and a deep sense of unease, only to find my wallet still tucked inside my bag and my phone resting peacefully on the nightstand. Maybe hypothermia works the same as drunk logic—everything goes out the window except for an abiding sense of responsibility toward personal belongings.

I take a deep breath and exhale. Water. Canned food. A roof over my head. A stove. Crazy how so little could make me feel so rich.

I hang my damp clothes on the railing outside to dry. It's a child's drawing of a day, yellow sun high in the bright blue sky. I look back at the house. It's a funny place, no more than a wooden box on stilts. I can see now that it's a hunter's blind. I recognize it from hikes I took with my dad as a kid. No wonder it feels abandoned—hunting season doesn't start until the fall, which means the place has probably been shut up since last winter. I'll open the blinds when I get back inside, let some air in. Maybe I can stay here for a few days, heal up, get some strength back. Hopefully any trail I've left behind was washed away by the rain. Hopefully I'm safe here, at least for a little while.

I sit on the top step and tilt my chin up to the sun. I eat a few pickles, careful not to swallow them too quickly. My stomach will be the size of a pea at this point, or a pearl. My hand reaches for the necklace before I remember again that it's gone. I touch the sharp ridges of my collarbones. A month ago, I would have given anything to have collarbones like these. Now they just remind me of how fragile I am, how vulnerable.

You're nothing but a bag of bones, my mother used to say when I came home from college, even though we both knew it wasn't true. The bagels and the keg beer caught up with me after the first semester, but I didn't manage to outrun them until my senior year, when I lived in an apartment with two other women and subsisted on bags of salad leaves and Foreman-grilled chicken breasts lightly spritzed with I Can't Believe It's Not Butter. That was the first time I learned that eating could be a competition, and that eating the least could give the winner a sort of power. Of course, by February my skin was terrible and my hair was like straw. I was in a fucking terrible mood all the time, too. But the power . . . I didn't want to give up the power that came with being thin. So I joined a gym and taught myself to like kettlebells and cardioblasts in the same way I'd taught myself to like I Can't Believe It's Not Butter. (I could believe it, I really could.)

I consider my body carefully now. In the sunlight, each slender hair on my arms shines with its own specific halo. The stubble on my shins that I usually keep so carefully in check looks like the iron filings in that kid's game with the magnet and the moustache. My skin is alternately blistered, bruised, bitten, and rubbed raw, and there's a mulchy, slightly fetid smell coming off me. My stomach—the focus of so many early-morning mirror inspections—is flat to the point of concave, and my hips have slimmed to near nonexistence.

It's not just five days of eating like a squirrel and almost-dying that's done this to it. No. This body is the product of a whole lifetime of careful winnowing. I've been so good at it, I've almost disappeared.

When I get out of this, I think. Ha. Okay, if. If I get out of this, I'm going to eat the biggest fucking bagel of my entire goddamn life, and I'm going to keep eating bagels and Mars bars and eggplant parmesan and whole fucking wheels of cheese, and I will never, ever try to take up less space ever again. I will stretch these limbs of mine out wide and I will not budge, not an inch, not ever again.

Maggie

I waited for the sun to go down before I set out for the Gaslamp Quarter. I had the bar marked out on the map, but when I got there, the sign was for Ruby's, not Sapphire's. The bouncer working the door explained that they'd changed management recently. Not a very imaginative new manager, I thought. I asked if he'd known Ally but he shook his head before parting the curtains and letting me through.

The place was so dark that at first I couldn't have seen my hand if I'd held it in front of my face. There were low tables scattered around the room, and a small platformed dance floor in the back. The customers were nearly all men, and the waitresses—tall, gorgeous creatures in short skirts and impossibly high heels—were all women. I took a seat at the bar in front of the skeptical-looking bartender.

"You sure you're in the right place?" he asked, cocking an eyebrow at me. I ordered a gin and tonic and tried to stop my hands from shaking as I pulled my wallet out of my purse.

I waited until I had the drink in front of me and had placed a twenty-dollar bill on the counter to ask him.

"What's the name again?" he asked, leaning in and straining to hear above the relentless din.

"Allison," I shouted above the thumping music.

He shook his head. "Doesn't ring a bell with me, but I've only been here six months."

"Is there anyone else I could ask?" I saw him hesitate, wondering if I was going to make trouble. "Please?"

He shrugged and jerked his thumb at a redhead jabbing her

finger at a screen behind the bar. "Ask Dee," he said. "She's been here forever."

I thanked him. I sipped at my gin and tonic—watered down—and waited for the right moment to catch her. It finally arrived when she came around the bar to grab a bottle of champagne from the fridge. "Excuse me," I shouted, and she looked up, face already locked in a mask of pleasant impatience.

"Jimmy will be with you in a sec, sweetheart," she called, nodding toward the bartender.

"He told me to talk to you. He thought you could help me."

She rolled her eyes but flashed an indulgent smile and propped her elbows up on the bar. I decided I liked her. "Okay, but make it quick—I've got a customer waiting."

"I was wondering if you knew my daughter, Allison. Allison Carpenter."

Her smile faded. "Oh shit," she said, and suddenly I saw the face behind all the makeup. She looked young and scared. "You're Allison's mom?"

I nodded. "Did you know her?"

She glanced toward the door, as though she were expecting Ally to come through it. "Yeah," she said softly. "She was my friend."

The bartender appeared and tapped her on the shoulder. "Table eighteen's getting restless."

She picked up the champagne bottle and two empty glasses. "I can't talk right now," she said hurriedly. "Can you meet me after my shift?"

"What time?"

"Midnight. I'll wait for you outside."

I nodded. "I'll be here."

She was about to move away but turned back. "Be careful, it gets a little dicey around here late at night. If anyone asks you for anything, just keep walking. And tell Juan I said to look after you. He's the guy on the door."

I watched as she straightened her spine, tilted her head back, and fixed her features into a smile before sashaying toward the man waiting at table eighteen. She bent neatly at the waist when she placed the bottle on the table, and I watched his hands skim the edge of her skirt as she poured.

I looked away. There was a strange feeling about the place, an undercurrent of something stronger than the overpriced, watered-down drinks. I flagged the bartender when he passed. "How come all the customers in here are men?"

"I guess they like the atmosphere," he said with a sad smile, and I tipped the rest of my drink down my throat, climbed off the stool, and made my way out into the night.

I wandered around for the next few hours, looking into the steam-fogged windows of dim sum restaurants and Mexican cafés, past the open doors of bars where fists of noise punched out into the street. There were empty corners where the homeless had spread out sleeping bags, and people stepped over and around them like they were boulders in a current. I tried to make sense of what I'd seen back at the bar. Had Ally really been one of those miniskirted girls being pawed at by sad old men in suits?

I wished she'd come to me. If she'd needed money that badly, she could have come to me—I would have given it to her. I would have given her anything.

She must have hated me. The thought filled my head like a balloon, pressing out all other thoughts. She must have hated me to have worked in that place rather than ask me for help.

I was back outside Ruby's at quarter to midnight. I didn't go in this time—I couldn't face it. Juan smiled and asked if I was cold, offered to run inside and get me a cup of tea, bless him, even though the night was still warm. I shook my head and asked him about himself, where he'd come from, what he was doing there, but he shrugged and said that he was just passing through. It was the sort of place where you spent your time waiting for something else to come along.

Dee came out at ten past midnight. She was in baggy jeans and sneakers then, but she still had a full face of makeup. She took me by the arm and led me to a diner tucked down an alley. The lighting inside was too bright, and as we slid into one of the red leather banquettes I could see where her mascara had bled into the fine lines under her eyes. She wasn't as young as I'd thought.

"You want anything?" she asked, signaling the waitress without looking at the menu. "Coffee?"

I shook my head. "If I have coffee now, I'll never sleep. Just a glass of water for me, please."

She nodded and ordered herself a cup of coffee and a grilled cheese sandwich. "I know I shouldn't," she said, patting her flat stomach, "but I'm always starving after a shift."

We made small talk until the waitress arrived with our drinks. I watched as Dee poured a long stream of white sugar into her coffee. "I like it sweet," she said, catching my eye and winking. I smiled back. Yes, I liked her.

"So you and Ally were friends?" I prompted as I took a sip of ice water.

Dee's face lit up. "Oh God, yeah. Totally. She was like a little sister to me or something." She shook her head and her eyes clouded with sadness. "I can't believe she's gone."

I leaned across the table. "Dee, did you speak to her before she got on that plane? Did she say anything to you—anything about him, or where they were headed, or why?"

Her eyes stayed on the table. "We weren't really talking much lately."

My heart sank. "You weren't? How come?"

She shook her head again. She picked up the sugar dispenser and tipped it upside down, letting a thin stream of sugar pile up on the table and then swirling her finger through it.

"Please, Dee." She wouldn't meet my eye. "This is important. Why weren't you two talking?"

She shrugged. "He thought I wasn't good enough for her, I guess." She swept the sugar off the edge of the table and into the palm of her hand, then tipped her head back and emptied it into her mouth.

"Ben thought that?"

She nodded. A few of the sugar crystals had stuck to her lip gloss, and I had to fight the urge to reach across the table and wipe her mouth. She was thirty-five if she was a day, but she was like a little girl playing dress-up in her mom's too-big high heels.

"Did you meet him?" I pressed.

Her eyes went back down to the table. "Only once. He came to pick her up after work one night." Her face darkened. "He didn't say much. We invited him in for a drink but he wouldn't come inside. He just sat outside in his fancy sports car and waited for her." Her eyes darted to mine. "After that, she just sort of . . . disappeared. She still worked at the bar for a few weeks, but it wasn't the same. You could tell her heart wasn't in it. Then one day, she just comes in and quits. No notice or anything. Just got her stuff and walked out." She shook her head. "I had to pull doubles for two weeks to cover for her."

"That doesn't sound like her." Every teacher she'd ever had, every boss at every summer temp job she'd held down, all of them had said the same thing: Ally was reliable. You could set a clock by her. She'd never skip out like that, especially if it meant making things difficult for a friend. "Did she give a reason?"

Dee laughed, and I could see the silver of her fillings. "She didn't have to. It was obvious."

"Him?"

"He didn't want her to work. He wanted her all to himself in that house in Bird Rock." She shook her head. "It was like he cast a spell over her or something. As soon as I saw them together, I knew she was a goner."

She glanced toward the door and I felt her knee jigging under the table. She was getting antsy, and her grilled cheese remained untouched in front of her, the orange cheese leaking out of the bread and congealing on the plate. I didn't have much more time. I wanted to keep talking to her for as long as I could. "Here," I said, signaling the waitress. "Let me buy you something else. A piece of pie or something."

She shook her head. "I'm good, thanks." I watched her fingers tap nervously on the mug. "I should be going actually," she said, glancing up at the clock. "I'm meeting someone in a half hour."

"At this time of night? Isn't it a little late?" I knew I sounded like someone's nagging mother, but I couldn't help it. It's who I am, I thought. Was.

She reached across the table and squeezed my hand. "You're cute," she said. She started gathering up her bags. "You want some money for the check?"

I waved her away. I had to stop myself from giving her a wad of cash from my wallet and instructing her to get a few more hot meals into her. She had the look of someone who was permanently hungry. "If you remember anything else about Ally—anything at all—you give me a call, okay?" I wrote my number down on a slip of paper and handed it to her. She nodded and tucked it in her bra but her eyes were on the street now, and I could tell I'd lost her. As she headed out into the night, I knew I wouldn't be hearing from her again.

Allison

I polish off the last bite of pickle and head back into the cabin. It's my second day here, my second night sleeping under a roof with a fire in the furnace and a wool blanket tucked around me. The cuts covering my body are starting to scab over, and the ache in my muscles is starting to lessen. I'll have to leave soon. I can't stay in one place for too long. But right now, it's heaven.

I set to unpicking the knots in the length of cord I found inside the hope chest. My fingers are clumsy and blunt, my nails ragged. All the while, the ring on my finger winks up at me. The diamond is dulled with grime but it still manages to sparkle.

He proposed at Sunset Cliffs after a long day at the beach. We were sun kissed and sandy when he'd dropped to one knee, and when I kissed him I could taste the sea on his mouth. Everything about that moment was perfect, because it was about the two of us, no one else.

I wanted to keep it just between us for a while, like a treasure, or a secret, but he insisted on an engagement party. He said his family would be hurt if we didn't celebrate with them, and that his clients expected it. "I want to show you off to the whole world," he'd said, kissing the inside of my wrist.

He bought me a dress for the party—Prada, shell pink, silk. I was in the shower when he left for work, and when I came out, it was laid out on the bed like a new bride. It was the most beautiful thing I'd ever seen. I rushed to get ready so I could try it on, but when I finally did, the zip wouldn't close. I checked the label. It was two sizes smaller than my natural size, and a size smaller than the last dress he'd bought me, a month before. I didn't have the heart to tell him it didn't fit. I didn't want to point out that he'd gotten it wrong, not when the gesture was so sweet and the dress so perfect.

I went to the gym twice a day for two weeks. I ran and lunged and spun and squeezed and tucked and squatted, and then I sat in the sauna until I felt faint and flushed with righteousness. Every drop of sweat was a step closer to purification, to redemption. I ate steamed fish and vegetables and drank water with lemon and maple syrup and cayenne pepper. The weight dropped off until my cheekbones were two sharp razorblades slicing through the oval of my face.

Every night, Ben told me how beautiful I looked, his little sparrow, and I knew it was worth it.

I met with Amanda every afternoon to pick out table settings and linen and canapés and signature cocktails. We planned the guest list, chose the invitations. Cream is tasteful, Amanda said. White is cheap. I raised the idea of inviting Dee, but Ben stroked my hair and explained that the engagement party was more of a networking event than a social one. It wouldn't be appropriate. I'd understood. More than anything in the world, I wanted to be appropriate. He had saved me from that life, and I would do anything to fit in with the new one he'd given me.

I thought about calling my mother. Sometimes I would get as far as dialing her number, but I never pressed the Call button. She would want to know about my life, and I couldn't think how to answer her. I imagined telling her that I was engaged to a man she'd never met, one who was so rich it meant that I would never have to work again, and that I spent my days alone in a house I didn't own that someone else cleaned. And my old life . . . I was sure that she would know about it as soon as she heard my voice. She was my mother. She'd spent her life knowing things about me before I'd known them about myself. How could she not know about that? I put the phone away and pushed her out of my mind.

I took a laxative. Two. The stomach cramps would wake me in

the night and I would lie awake and picture the fat being sloughed from my bones.

I convinced myself that there was power in abstention. There was satisfaction in keeping my mouth closed and shaking my head. No, I said, over and over. No, thank you.

On the night of the party, the dress zipped up easily. When we walked into the room, everyone stopped and stared. I scanned the room for a friendly face before I remembered there wasn't any, and then I arranged my face into the smile I'd practiced in the mirror. Pretty. Demure. Saintly. Like I belonged. The women crowded around me and told me how wonderful I looked, how slim and chic. They asked how I'd done it but I just smiled and shrugged and said love, it must be love.

I start opening the blinds on the cabin's plexiglass windows. I want sunlight to flood the place. I want to nap in a patch of it like a cat. I want to luxuriate, even for a minute. I want to forget.

My foot catches on something and I tip forward. I try to stop myself from falling but it's too late, and I land hard on my knees, my bad hand scraping along the carpet, reopening the wound.

"Fuck," I mutter, and then again, with all my might, *"Fuck!"* The sound echoes off the walls of the hut. I take a deep breath, then another, and turn to see what's tripped me.

It's so small, it's a wonder I find it at all. Just a little indentation in the wood beneath the carpet, and next to it what feels like a thin raised lip. I scrape my fingers back and forth across it. Is it just a knot in the wood? No, it feels too smooth for that. I sit back and shrug the bag onto the ground. I bend down and touch the spot again. Definitely not a knot. A scrap of wood left over from when they carpeted, maybe? A stray nail? I can't move it, though. It feels like it's fixed to the floor. It feels intentional.

I scramble over to where the floor meets the wall and try to pry the edge of the carpet up with my fingers. It won't budge. I grab the knife from my bag and wedge it between the carpet and the floor, leveraging it like a crowbar. The staples pop one by one until I can finally get enough of a grip on the carpet to peel it back in a couple of firm tugs.

There, in the middle of the bare floor, is a tiny metal latch securing a hidey-hole cut into the plywood.

I open the lid. In the flickering light it's hard to see inside, but I can just make out the edge of a thin, shallow box laid into the hole in the floor. In the box, nestled in a soft scrap of cloth like a newborn baby, lies a gun.

A hunting rifle. The barrel is long and thin, the butt made from polished walnut. I pick it up carefully and hold it in my arms. It's lighter than I expect, no more than five or six pounds. I rest it on my shoulder and look through the scope, framing the window in the crosshairs. A thrill runs up my spine.

My father had owned something similar. He'd gone deer hunting a couple of times a year, though he never seemed to enjoy it—he'd always come back to the house pale and drawn afterward, handing the parceled meat from the carcass to my mother before retreating to the basement for the rest of the night. He'd even taken me and my mother along with him once, after I'd nagged him about it. I'd been too young to shoot—I was only nine, still at the age when death was both thrilling and unimaginable—but I remember the feeling of surprise when my mother lifted the gun to her shoulder and squinted through the sights.

"She's always been a better shot than me," my father said when the bullet struck the deer between the eyes. I remember the pride in his voice when he'd said it, and the regret that flashed across his face when he'd watched me stare down at the dead deer and begin to cry.

"This is my fault," he said, shaking his head. "I never should have agreed to take her."

My mother had reached out and taken his hand in hers. "It's the way of the world," she said, her voice soothing and gentle. "She has to learn."

I move quietly now, as though someone might see, and lean it against the wall. Its long leather strap pools on the floor. I pick up the box of bullets and toss them in the bag. No sense in carrying an unloaded gun, not now, not out here. I glance at the barrel of the rifle peering toward the sky and something inside me loosens.

This is a new sort of power, I think, tucking the rifle by the side of the door.

And this one, I think I like.

Maggie

I left the motel late the next morning, after I'd checked out and stashed my suitcase with reception. I was leaving that night, even though I'd only just gotten there. I'd be jet-lagged something awful, but I didn't want to be away for too long in case some kind of news came in, though I wasn't sure what. Plus, I had the memorial to attend. My heart sank at the thought.

It was another perfect day, blue skies and seventy-eight, and the sun glinted off the hoods of the cars in the lot. I remembered the red sports car from the day before, and wondered again if it had been the same one that I'd seen in La Jolla. Of course not, I told myself. To think that was to give in fully to the shadowy paranoia that had been dogging me ever since I'd gotten the news about Ally, and besides, I was in California: land of the red sports car. It was just a coincidence, nothing more.

I headed to Ben's house first. I still couldn't think of it as Ally's. I headed back up La Jolla Boulevard and took a left onto Sea Ridge Drive, and it struck me suddenly how close it was to the Gardners' house. I wondered if Ally had liked being so close to her future in-laws. I pulled up outside the house and pressed the buzzer. I didn't expect anyone to answer, but the speaker crackled almost immediately and the automatic gate groaned open.

The house was bigger than it seemed from the outside and, to my eyes, uglier. It was a low-slung bungalow made up of different-sized sandstone boxes that blinked out at you from behind enormous tinted windows. The roof was painted a dark brown and jutted aggressively into space, like someone sticking his chin out before a fight. There were a couple of palm trees sprouted from a stretch of lawn so green and manicured it looked like it had been cut from a golf course, and as I walked up the path, a network of hidden sprinklers suddenly ticked into life. I guess water bans didn't apply in Bird Rock.

A middle-aged woman was waiting for me at the door, a bottle of spray bleach dangling from one hand. She was wearing a black tunic with a name badge that read "Teresa" and a look of impatience on her face. I took a deep breath and said the line I'd practiced in the mirror that morning just in case I made it through the gates. "Hello, I'm from Sutton Realtors. The Gardners asked me to come over and appraise the property."

Teresa scowled. "They didn't tell me someone would be coming today. They usually tell me in advance."

A sweat broke out across the back of my neck. "There was a last-minute change of plans." She remained in the doorway, immovable. "Please," I said, in the most officious voice I could muster. "I'm on a very tight schedule today. You could call the Gardners and confirm but I don't think they'd be very happy about being disturbed. Do you?"

We stood at an impasse for another minute, but eventually she stepped aside and let me through. "I'm leaving in five minutes," she called as she headed off down the hallway. I heard a door slam.

The house was stunning, and not in a good way. Don't get me wrong, I could tell it was beautiful, even if it wasn't to my taste. Everything was white and pristine and expensive looking. It was a place I wouldn't trust myself to sit down in, never mind drink a glass of red wine. It's more that I felt physically stunned by it. Standing in the middle of this enormous glass box and looking at all the fancy things that Ally had been surrounded by drove home how little I'd known her. Had my daughter really been someone who would have liked all this stuff? Would she have felt comfortable sitting on the cream sofa, or padding around the plush carpet in her socked feet?

I thought about our family Christmases, the three of us sitting around the living room, drinking Baileys and making our way through a box of Russell Stover chocolates, *White Christmas* on the television. Ally would have on her old track sweatpants and the Rudolph sweater she pulled out every year, and the end of her ponytail would dangle over the arm of the couch as she dug through the chocolate box looking for one with a raspberry filling. Had she ever lain down on this sofa like that? Had she ever fallen asleep on it, mouth open slightly, soles of her feet pressed together, eyelids fluttering as she dreamed?

I couldn't picture it, not for a second, but there were a lot of things I couldn't picture her doing, and it seemed like every day I was proved wrong.

I peeked into the kitchen, where Teresa was on her hands and knees scrubbing the floor. Must be a strange job, cleaning a house that nobody lived in. From her reaction, it seemed I'd guessed right—the family was planning on selling the place. I could picture the Realtor's ad, peppered with words like "luxury" and "exclusive" and "high-end living."

The master bedroom was more of the same, with whitewashed floors and a floor-to-ceiling window that framed a view of the ocean. A king-size bed dominated the center of the room. I looked away. I didn't want to think about the bed. There was a desk tucked into the corner with a vanity mirror propped on the top. Ally's desk. But where was her jewelry? Her makeup? The girl I knew would have covered the desk with perfume and hair spray and tiny compacts of shimmering eye shadow, and tube after tube of lipstick. Charles used to complain about the number of beauty products she kept lined up on the side of the bath. Every morning, we'd hear a crash as he tried to get into the shower followed by a quiet curse. I pulled open the desk drawer: empty. The inside of it had been wiped clean.

I crossed the room to the closet and yanked it open to reveal a row of neatly pressed button-downs in whites and pinks and pale blues, and a hook garlanded with ties. I moved to the other closet. Trousers looped over hangers, suits giving off the dull gleam of expense. The shelves were stacked with polished wing tips and a single pair of battered tennis shoes, and a selection of leather belts coiled like snakes.

Not a single piece of her clothing. Not one.

I was frantic now. I moved to the bedside tables, pulled open drawers, looked under the bed. There wasn't anything of her, not a trace. Had she really lived there? Maybe I'd had it all wrong. Maybe she had another apartment, separate from him. Maybe they'd given me the wrong address. Maybe I was going crazy.

That's when I saw it, tucked into the thick pile of the carpet: a long blond hair. I plucked it out with my fingernails and held it up to the light. The very tip of it was chestnut brown. It was Ally's. It had to be.

I heard a noise behind me and turned to see Teresa standing in the doorway, arms crossed, a scowl slashed across her face. "My shift is over and they don't pay overtime. If you want to stay longer, I'll have to call Mrs. Gardner."

I climbed to my feet. Seeing her closet cleared out like that had wiped out all my pretenses. I was here as Allison's mother, and I wanted answers. "Where are her things?"

She shrugged, her face a defiant blank.

The familiar anger surged. They wanted to erase her—all of them—but I wouldn't let them. "I'm her mother. I have a right to my daughter's belongings. They belong to me now. They have no right—"

"He did everything for that girl." Her voice was quiet, almost a hiss.

My eyes snapped to hers. "What was that?"

"He gave her everything, but she didn't appreciate it. She took it all for granted." She folded her arms across her chest. Her body was thickset, her shoulders filling up much of the doorframe. I was suddenly aware that I was alone in a house with a stranger, and that no one knew I was there. Her eyes bored into mine, steady and unblinking. "Your daughter didn't deserve him."

"You're right." The blood thundered in my ears, deafening. I was scared but I wouldn't let her see it. "She deserved better."

She shook her head. Her mouth was a piece of string pulled tight. "Get out."

It was only as I was driving back downtown that it struck me: when I'd blown my cover like that, she hadn't seemed surprised in the least. It was almost like she'd known who I was the whole time.

Allison

I hear it before I see it: the low hum of an engine and the pop of tires on gravel. I glance out the window of the cabin and see the front end of an SUV nose out of the woods. The bold green letters on the side spell out UNITED STATES PARK RANGER: POLICE. I can see the outline of two men behind the windshield.

The car doors slam shut and there are heavy footsteps in the dirt. "You see anything?" A man's voice, deep and close.

My mind races. Just on the other side of this flimsy door is salvation. It's warm clothes and a comfortable bed and a hot meal. God, the food. Still-warm baguettes slicked with salted butter. Cheeseburgers, rare and juicy and draped with bacon. Chocolate layer cake with vanilla frosting and sprinkles, the kind my mother used to make for my birthday. Guacamole.

"Doesn't look like it." Another man's voice, at a slightly higher octave. Also close.

If they know you're alive, they'll find you.

I can hear them scuffling around outside, pacing the perimeter of the building. The silhouette of one of them appears in the window, momentarily blocking out the sun, and the light in the cabin dims.

I might die in these woods. I've already almost died a few times. How many more chances will I get?

Just say something. Open the door and let them see you. I need help. Say the words. Please, I need your help.

Do you know who you're dealing with?

"You seen this?" The deep-voiced man. He sounds excited.

"You think it's recent?"

"Looks too clean for it to not be."

I must have left something outside, a scrap of laundry left to dry in the sun, a sock maybe, or a pair of underwear. I feel embarrassed. Exposed. Scared.

When everything comes out in the wash. If they know what you've done, they'll kill you.

I press my back against the wall.

"Let's check inside."

My eyes dart to the door. The frame is splintered but the lock—a heavy padlock—is still swinging from its latch. Can I make it in time? I don't have a choice—I have to try. My heart thuds in my chest as I dart across the floor. Footsteps on the stairs, heavy and quick. My hand grips the lock but my fingers are shaking, fumbling. I can't get the shackle to fit into the hole. Boots scuffle on the landing. *Come on, Ally. It's now or never.* There's a click as the lock snaps together. I hear one of them push against it from the other side, the warped frame straining under the pressure. I press myself against the door and lean all my weight against it, willing it to hold. I can hear the rasp of the man's breath as he strains under the effort.

"No good," the higher-voiced man says finally, and the pressure on the door stops abruptly.

I can feel the heat of their bodies as they stand on the stairs, considering their options. I'm holding my breath, my heart high and loud in my chest. My lungs start to scream. *Leave*, I shout silently. *Leave now.*

I hear them shuffle and sigh. "Fuck it. Let's go."

One of them gives the door a final shove, and then I hear their footsteps retreating down the steps and across the gravel and the car doors slam and the engine spark up and the crunch and pop of the tires as the SUV pulls away. It's only when I can't hear the engine anymore that I let myself breathe, and by that point I'm seeing stars.

That was it. My one chance at rescue, gone.

Everyone has his price. You never know who's been paid.

But maybe, just maybe, I've saved myself again.

I was in the shower when I heard him come through the door, his keys landing with a clatter on the kitchen counter. I rinsed the conditioner out of my hair and hurried to towel myself dry. When I stepped out of the bathroom, I found him sitting on the bed cradling a glass of whisky in his hand.

"You're home early!" I said, bending down to kiss him, but I stopped short as soon as I saw his face. "What's wrong?"

He wiped a hand across his face. "Nothing," he said quietly. "Just a tough day at work, that's all." There were dark smudges under his eyes, and his skin was pale and waxy. He looked exhausted.

I sat down beside him and pulled him toward me. "Do you want to talk about it?"

He shook his head. "No."

I stroked his back as he stared into his glass, listening to the silence settling around us. I felt the first whiskers of fear. Normally he came through the door brimming with excitement. He'd sweep me into his arms and tell me about his latest triumphs at work as he opened a good bottle of red. I'd never seen him like this. Defeated.

Eventually he let out a sigh that seemed to come from some deep, forgotten part of himself and raised his eyes to mine. "Do you think I'm a good person?"

My first reaction was to laugh—it was such a ridiculous thing for him to ask—but then I saw that he was serious. "You are the best man I know," I said, taking his hands in mine. As I said the words, I realized they were true. He had rescued me, taken care of me, loved me. I owed him everything. "I can't imagine a better man. I am so lucky to have you."

The shadows parted and he smiled at me. "I'm lucky, too," he said, pulling me down on top of him. "I'm the luckiest man in the world." He pushed a few damp strands of hair from my face and pressed his forehead to mine. His eyes were almost black in the dark, and they stared into mine as if searching for something.

"What is it, baby?" I whispered. "Talk to me."

He shook his head and tugged at the cord of my bathrobe. "I

don't want to talk," he said. "I just want to be with you." His hands were warm as they slid up my body, his mouth soft as it made its way down my neck and stomach. He teased me with his tongue until I was begging for him, and when he finally pushed his way inside me, I was already coming.

Afterward, we collapsed into each other, our limbs tangled in the damp sheets, our breath heavy. I watched his chest rise and fall in the half-light and tried to silence the voice in my head that told me happiness like this could only be fleeting.

In twenty minutes I'm packed up and headed east, the cans of soup rattling in my bag, the jerrican of water sloshing by my side, the rifle slung around my neck. The familiar pain strikes up again, gaining with each step until, by the time the cabin is swallowed up by the woods, the symphony is in full flight.

Maggie

Most of the pharmaceutical companies in San Diego were up the coast in La Jolla or Del Mar, but not Prexilane. It was downtown, right on the waterfront, in a glass-and-steel skyscraper that stretched up into the clear blue sky. I parked in an Ace lot off West Ash and walked down to the pier, the air smelling like fish guts and gasoline.

I wasn't sure what my plan was. I didn't have much of one, if I was being honest. I knew he wasn't there. I didn't have an appointment to see anyone, or even a name to give a receptionist. But it felt important to try.

There was a wide concrete plaza out front edged with neat boxes of red and yellow carnations. The sun glinted off the glass of the building, and I had to shield my eyes as I approached. It was nearly lunchtime, and a few people sat on benches outside, eating their packed lunches while reading books or poking at their phones. It looked more like a scene from a movie than real life, but maybe that was just California. All this sunshine felt unnatural to me.

The receptionist watched as I approached the wide wooden desk. "Excuse me," I said, reaching up and smoothing down my hair. I put on my most trustworthy smile. "I was wondering if you could help me."

She nodded, and her eyes wandered back to the big black monitor stationed in front of her face.

I cleared my throat. "I was wondering if there was someone at Prexilane who could talk to me. My daughter, she—"

"Name?"

"Maggie," I stammered. "Margaret Carpenter."

She nodded and typed something on her keyboard. "Name here and sign," she said, tapping on a piece of paper on the desk. I printed it out in careful letters and scrawled out my signature in the box next to it. She handed me a laminated scrap of paper with a little metal clip affixed to the back. "Forty-third floor, elevator B."

I took the pass and clipped it to the edge of my blouse. It smelled faintly of the old mimeograph machine we used to use in the library years ago, before they bought the fancy Xerox. "All right," I said with a nod. "Well. Thank you." I hesitated. The marble lobby was enormous, the size of a football field. I didn't have a clue where elevator B was.

The woman must have caught the look on my face and took pity on me. "To the left," she said, nodding toward a far-off corridor. "You'll see the signs." Her eyes turned back to the monitor and her fingers flew across the keyboard.

I felt a flurry of nerves as the elevator took me up to the forty-third floor. I wasn't sure what I was doing there, or what I expected to gain. The doors opened into another lobby, this one done out in cream and brown leather. Another receptionist—blond this time, and smiling—was sitting behind a large wooden desk. She smiled at me brightly as I stepped off the elevator. "Welcome to Prexilane! Please, take a seat. Mr. Hutchinson will be out in a minute."

I stared at her quizzically. I had no clue who Mr. Hutchinson was, as I was pretty sure he wasn't expecting me. "I think there's been some kind of mix-up."

She looked up sharply. "You're not from Hyperion?" I shook my head. Behind her, through a frosted glass door that was half-open, I could see the office in a state of commotion. She followed my gaze and swiftly shut the door. "I'm sorry," she said, recovering herself. "I thought—" She shook her head apologetically. "Sorry, it's been kind of a crazy day. How can I help?"

My palms were sweating. I clasped them together and stepped forward. "I'm . . . well, my daughter, Allison, she was engaged to Ben Gardner, and . . ."

The woman's face crumpled. "I'm sorry for your loss. Allison was a sweetheart. We were all so shocked to hear about the accident."

"Thank you. I was wondering if there might be someone I could speak to, someone who might be able to tell me—" What? What was it I wanted to know? The woman watched me patiently, her eyes full of sympathy. *Come on, Maggie. Pull yourself together. Ask the damn question.* "Is there somebody I could talk to about her? Or about Ben?"

She blinked up at me. "Do you have an appointment?"

My fingers fumbled with the laminated pass. "No, like I said, I don't have an appointment, but I was hoping there might be someone . . . You see, I've come all the way from Maine, and I can't seem to get ahold of Ben's parents, and . . ."

I saw the shutters come down over her pretty green eyes. "I'm sorry," she said, shaking her head. Her blond ponytail swished neatly back and forth. "I can't help you if you don't have an appointment."

The frosted glass door opened and a clean-cut man in a dark gray suit shoved his head through. "Have they turned up yet?"

The receptionist stiffened. "Not yet," she said in a false-bright voice. I could see the tension on her face. The man cursed under his breath and slammed the door shut.

"Well, maybe that man could spare a few minutes? After all, I know his appointment isn't here yet." I ventured a conspiratorial smile but she didn't return it.

The phone on her desk rang and her gaze flicked to it impatiently. "Look, I'm really sorry about your daughter, and about you coming all this way, but there's nothing I can do."

I felt a well of desperation open inside me. "Maybe you could speak to me, since you're here? I won't take up too much of your time, but you said you knew Ally, and—"

The phone rang again, and this time her hand hovered above it. "I'm sorry, but I really have to get back to work." She gave me one last pitying glance before picking up the phone. "Good afternoon, Prexilane Industries."

I straightened up and nodded. I understood that I'd been dismissed, and I wasn't about to lose my dignity, not again, not here. I hit the call button for the elevator, and when it opened, a pair of suits pushed past me into the Prexilane reception area. Mr. Hutchinson's appointment, I guessed. At least he'd stop shouting at that poor receptionist.

I watched myself in the mirror as the elevator descended. My eyes were bloodshot and puffy, my skin waxen, and there were gaunt hollows under my cheeks. I looked like a ghost. A goddamn ghoul.

I pushed my way through the revolving door and squinted into the bright sunshine, my eyes blurred with tears. The courtyard was nearly empty now, the lunchtime crowd having slunk back to their offices for another afternoon at their desks, so I sat down on one of the benches to wait until my bearings returned. The sunshine was relentless, and the wooden slats of the bench were hot to the touch. I dug around in my purse for the bottle of water I'd tucked inside. It was lukewarm, like drinking bathwater.

All this way, and for nothing. She'd lived in this city for almost a decade but I could barely find a trace of her. It seemed like everyone who knew her had just let her slip away. They had neglected her, and now she was gone.

I could rail against all of them—Ben, Dee, the Gardners, those men in that seedy bar—but deep down I knew who was to blame. I was her mother. I was supposed to take care of her. I let her cut me out of her life without so much as a fight. I'd failed her. And I was failing her all over again.

There, under the bright glare of the California sun, I broke down and wept.

Allison

By nightfall, my steps slow to a shuffle. I can't think about how many miles I still have left to go. I can think only about the miles I've already covered, and I know that I'll get there in the end. I drop my bag where I stand, pull out the canopy cover, and tug off my sneakers. The day has done a number on them—the fabric is caked in dirt and the rubber soles are starting to pull away from the seams. Nike's finest apparently isn't up to the challenge of a week in the Rockies.

I open a can of soup with my knife—chicken noodle—and drink it straight from the tin. Unheated, the broth is gluey, oversalted, but I don't care. The noodles slip easily down my throat along with the tiny cubes of carrot. I finish the can within minutes and wash it down with a few gulps of water.

I lie back and close my eyes. What I wouldn't do right now for an ice cream sandwich, the kind with the two chocolate wafers made out of God knows what, the sort that leaves a smudge of residue on your fingertips that can be scraped off with your teeth, and a thick slab of too-sweet vanilla ice cream. Or a grilled cheese made with fluorescent-orange cheese that oozes out the edges of thickly buttered Wonder Bread. But most of all, I want a drink. A stiff one.

All the drinks in my life. All the cold beers chugged from Solo cups, tepid glasses of white wine sipped at networking events for the magazine, shots of tequila laced with wine slammed after shifts at the bar. And champagne, whole lakes of it, poured out at countless parties.

————

"Would you like a refill?" The white-shirted waitress bowed low as she refilled my glass before disappearing into the crowd. I watched her retreating back longingly. I wondered what they were saying to each other back in the kitchen. I could picture it, the stainless-steel tables lined with canapés waiting to be offered to San Diego's great and good, the waiters jostling with each other as they came through to refill trays or sneak a quick cigarette. They would be gossiping about us, whispering about who was too drunk and who was hogging the salmon tarts and which of the men were handsy. I would have given anything to be in there with them, rather than out here, trying to make small talk with the other wives and girl-friends while the men slapped backs and brokered deals.

I watched Sam lean in and whisper something in Ben's ear and saw Ben's face darken. Secrets. Always secrets. Sam's role at the company was murky—Ben called him his fixer, but he wouldn't explain what exactly Sam fixed. I'd pressed him on it once, after Sam had appeared on our doorstep at quarter to midnight and the two of them had disappeared into the study until the early hours, but when he finally climbed into bed, he just kissed the top of my head and said, "It's business, baby girl. Just business."

These events were business, too, even though they masqueraded as pleasure. Tonight was the opening of a gallery, though I hadn't seen anyone looking at the art. Before each of these events, Ben would squeeze my hand. "Knock 'em dead," he'd say, before desert-ing me to join the other men. But I never did knock 'em dead. The other women tolerated me, but I could never get past their bland politeness.

"Have you tried these miniburgers?" I looked up to find a woman frowning at me. She was holding up a tiny hamburger like it was a piece of evidence. I shook my head. "They're disgusting." She pushed it into her mouth, wincing as she chewed. "The food at these things is getting worse." She wiped her hand on her navy trousers and thrust it toward me. "I'm Liz."

"Allison."

She was older than I'd first thought. Her blue eyes creased at the corners, and her red hair was threaded with silver. She had a sweet face, I decided. The kind you could tell smiled a lot. "You're Ben's fiancée, right?"

I felt a swell of pride as she glanced at the diamond on my finger. "That's right."

She reached out and took my hand. "It's a stunner," she said admiringly as she held the ring up to the light. She winked at me. "It suits you, too."

"Thank you," I said shyly. She let go of my hand and I felt a loss. I wanted my mother in that moment, very badly.

I felt a pair of eyes on me and looked up to see Sam watching us from across the room. Our eyes met and he looked away. I'd mentioned it to Ben once, the fact that Sam was always staring at me, but he'd just laughed it off. "Can you blame him?" he'd said, pulling me in for a kiss. "You're the most beautiful woman in the room." I'd dropped it after that, but being in the same room as him still made me uneasy. I knew the difference between being admired and being watched. Sam was watching me.

I turned back to Liz and plastered a smile on my face. "How do you know Ben?"

"My husband works for him," she said, waving vaguely toward the crowd of men congregated on the other side of the room. "Like everybody else here, right?"

I laughed uncertainly. I couldn't tell from her face if she was joking. "What's your husband's name?" I asked out of politeness more than any actual hope of recognition. The truth was, I'd never been able to keep any of the names of Ben's colleagues in my head, no matter how many of these parties we attended. They all blended into one amorphous, bland-faced man in a dark suit that smelled of money. The wives weren't much different—interchangeable blondes called Cathy and Deb wearing interchangeable sheath dresses and tennis bracelets. Liz was different, though, and not just because of her shock of red hair. She looked like a real person. I hadn't seen one of those for a long time. I felt another pang of longing for my mother and tilted the champagne glass to my lips.

"His name is Paul," she said. "Paul Ricci." She was watching me closely as she said this, her face unreadable. "Have you heard of him?"

The name *did* sound familiar. I thought I'd caught it in the whisperings between Ben and Sam, but I couldn't be sure. I smiled politely. "Of course. Ben has lots of good things to say about him."

Something flickered across her face, a shadow, imperceptible. "Is that right? That's nice to hear." She leaned in conspiratorially. "How've the ice queens been?" she asked, nodding toward the cluster of wives. "Are they playing nicely?"

I hesitated. "Everyone's been very welcoming," I said, hoping I sounded more genuine than I felt.

She bent her head back and laughed. It wasn't one of the polite titters I was used to hearing at these things. It was a real laugh, from the belly up through the throat. The sound of it startled me, and I saw several of the Chanel blondes shoot her dirty looks. "You don't have to lie to me," Liz said, snaking an arm through mine. "I know they're a viper's nest. I've known most of them for the best part of a decade, and trust me, they don't mellow with age. C'mon, I know where they've stashed the macaroon tower."

Maggie

I was almost to my car when someone grabbed me by the arm and spun me around. It was a man in his midthirties, dark haired and heavyset, with a soft jaw bristled with stubble. His eyes were red-rimmed and his face had the yellowish, waxy sheen of someone who spent most of his time indoors. "You went up there." His tone was strangely flat.

I stared up at him. "Excuse me?"

"I saw you back there." He jerked his thumb toward the Prexi-lane skyscraper. "They won't let me upstairs anymore." He leaned in toward me. His breath was hot on my face, and smelled of onions. "Did they admit it?"

I felt a spark shoot through me. "Admit to what?"

"Your daughter," he whispered. "They killed her, too, didn't they?"

My whole body went cold, as if it had been plunged into ice. I reached out and grabbed his wrist. "What do you know about Allison?"

"Allison." His eyes softened. "Was that your daughter's name? That's a pretty name. My wife's name was Rebecca. Becky."

My heart sank, and I felt empty and sick. "You didn't know my daughter?"

He shook his head and covered my hand with his. His palm was slicked with sweat. "But I know what they did to her," he said quietly. "They poisoned her with those damn pills, same as they did with my wife." He was gripping my hand so tightly now I could feel the joints in my knuckles pop.

"Pills?" I remembered the police report, and the glassy look in

Dee's eyes across the table at the diner. It all made sudden, awful sense. "What kind of pills?"

"The ones they gave her after she had Lexy. They said they would help her get back to her old self, but . . ." He shook his head. "As soon as I heard you talking to the receptionist about her and asking about Prexilane, I knew you'd been through the same thing as me. I could see it in your eyes. They poisoned her just like they poisoned my Becky, didn't they?"

His face was inches from mine now, and I had to stop myself from flinching. "My daughter died in a plane crash," I said quietly. "She was engaged to the CEO of Prexilane, who died in the crash with her. That's why I was in there. I wanted to talk to someone about her." He lifted his eyes to mine and I saw the same look in his eyes that I'd seen in my own so many times in the mirror. "What is it you think happened to your wife?"

"I can't trust you." He shook his head. "You're one of them."

"I'm not," I said, reaching out and putting a hand on his arm. "I'm just trying to get to the truth, same as you. Let me help you."

He recoiled as if burned. The man turned his bloodshot, bleary eyes back toward mine and shook his head. "I don't think anyone can help me." I watched him walk away until he was out of sight, and then I climbed into the little rental car and drove back to the motel with shaking hands.

Allison

I startle awake. It's pitch black in the woods, the sliver moon blocked out by the treetops. The steady thrum of crickets fills the air, punctuated by the occasional rustle of some small, scurrying animal. I realize, dimly, that it's the middle of the night, and that I've fallen asleep without pitching camp. I can feel the cold, damp ground through my thin leggings, and my feet have gone numb in their sneakers.

I stare blinking up into the dark. Sleep, which had descended on me so quickly, has disappeared again, and I know I'll be awake now until dawn.

"Are you sure you don't mind getting up this early?" Liz leaned down to pull her laces tight.

I shook my head. "I'm a morning person," I lied. What I didn't say was that I would have met her at any time, day or night. I was just happy to be asked. Happy to have—at least I hoped, privately—a friend.

"Me too. It drives Paul crazy. He likes to sleep in on the weekend but I'm always up as soon as the sun comes up. I hate feeling like I'm missing the day, you know?"

"Totally," I said, thinking briefly of my old life, when the day wouldn't start until six o'clock in the evening and would finish as the sun was coming up. That was behind me now—all of it. Now I was someone who got up at dawn and met her friend to run on the beach.

Liz looked up and smiled and it felt, as it often did with her, like she could see straight into me. "Come on," she said, hitting the start button on her Garmin. "Let's go."

We began at a steady, slow pace, which gradually increased as we both warmed up. She was forty-seven (she'd told me that the first time we'd gone for drinks together, in a kind of conspiratorial whisper, and I'd felt flattered) but she was in good shape, and pretty soon we were up to an eight-minute mile, our light footsteps echoing off the pavement as we headed for the shore.

"So," Liz said between breaths, "how's Ben? Is he worried about the new round of trials?"

I didn't know anything about the new round of trials, or about Ben's work in general, for that matter. I'd tried asking him about it when we first got together, but he said talking about it just stressed him out—that he liked having me as an escape. Still, I didn't want Liz to think I was just some dumb airhead, so I *mmm*'d noncommittally and asked about Paul.

"He's very stressed," she said. "Not that he'd admit it. He refuses to admit when he's under any kind of pressure, but I can always tell. He fiddles with his earlobe. He doesn't even know he's doing it, but every time he's stressed he walks around pulling his left earlobe. It's the weirdest thing." She glanced over to me. "Does Ben do anything like that?"

I racked my brain for some charming, harmless behavior to offer. The truth was that the only way I could tell that Ben was upset was in bed. He was rougher with me, and wouldn't look me in the eye, though afterward he was always doubly nice, as if to make up for it. This wasn't something I wanted to tell Liz. Instead, I mumbled something about him being a restless sleeper.

"Paul does that, too," she sympathized. "It drives me crazy. He twitches right before he falls asleep, like a dog, and it always wakes me up. Every. Single. Time."

I laughed. I loved these little glimpses of their married life. They seemed so happy together, so comfortable. I tried to imagine me and Ben when we were older, gray haired and soft chinned and companionable, but I couldn't fit the picture together in my head.

We ran in silence for a few minutes, our steps falling in sync. The streets were still quiet, just the odd early office worker clutching a paper coffee cup and the occasional whir of a street sweeper. Her voice broke through the quiet. "What do you think about Sam?"

I kept my eyes on the ground. I thought about the way he looked at me, like I was a stray cat he wanted to stroke, or trap. "He's okay," I said, careful to keep my voice neutral.

"I think he's an asshole." There was an edge to her voice I hadn't heard before. The shock of her words interrupted the rhythm of my stride and I stumbled slightly.

"Why?"

I looked over at her and saw that her jaw was clenched. "Let me give you a piece of advice," she said. "Be careful around that guy. You might think he's your friend, but he's not."

"I don't think he's my friend," I said, too quickly. The truth was that I could have counted the number of words we'd exchanged on two hands. It wasn't for lack of trying—I knew how important he was to Ben, so when we'd first got together, I'd made an effort to get to know him, but every time I asked him a question, he would shut down and leave the room. That hadn't stopped him watching me, though, his dark eyes blank and unreadable.

Liz nodded. "Good," she said quietly. "Keep it that way."

Maggie

The plane touched down in Portland at quarter to ten in the morning. I'd tried to sleep on the plane—I'd even bought myself a pack of over-the-counter sleeping pills at the airport—but I stayed stubbornly awake for the whole six hours, drifting off only as we circled Logan. I was half-blind with exhaustion waiting for the connecting flight, but as soon as we boarded I was wide awake again, staring out at the gray clouds below us, waiting for us to dive back through them and down to Maine.

I drove home carefully, hands at ten and two. I didn't trust myself to take my eyes off the road, not even for a second. A film of black dots occasionally swarmed into my field of vision and my head pounded steadily. I put the radio on, turned it to a station I hated, and turned it all the way up. Even still, I could feel myself drifting. I relaxed only when I saw the exit for Owl's Creek.

My back complained as I bent down to pick up the pile of mail on the doormat. I flicked through it quickly—mainly just bills and circulars, with just a few cream-colored card envelopes mixed in. The sympathy cards were finally starting to dwindle. I fit the key in the lock and pushed open the door. "Hello?" My voice echoed through the house. I don't know who I expected to answer. I think I just wanted to hear my voice bouncing off my own four walls. I dropped my bag in the hall and headed into the kitchen.

Everything was just as I left it. The scrubbed butcher-block table, the mugs lined up on the rack, the clock ticking and the dust motes settling. The air carried that strange stale smell it always did when the house had been empty for any length of time, like it had worked to forget me as soon as I was out the door.

I took out a box of Friskies and shook it, waiting for the familiar sound of Barney running down the stairs from under the bed, but he didn't come. I shook it again, but there was just silence to answer. He must be angry with me for leaving him. He'd be under the bed, sulking.

I poured the Friskies into a bowl and set it on the ground along with a fresh bowl of water. It'd be there for him when he was ready to show his face.

I flicked on the percolator. My eyes were gritty from lack of sleep, and my bones felt an aching sort of heaviness. The milk in the fridge was on its last legs, and there wasn't much else in there except for a sad head of lettuce and the casseroles from the Owl's Creek brigade, most of which had spoiled and none of which I could face eating. I realized I'd have to run to the store the next day for more supplies.

I fixed myself a cup of coffee and sat down at the kitchen table. The trip to San Diego was already starting to take on an unreal feeling, like it was something that had happened to someone else. I sorted the mail, unfolding bills and stacking them in a neat pile, shoving the last of the sympathy cards underneath. I pulled out an envelope addressed to Ally and saw the Saint Mary's Credit Union emblem stamped on the back. I looked at it for a second and then slid a finger under the sealed flap. An official-looking letter fell out onto the table.

ST. MARY'S CREDIT UNION
42 South Street
Owl's Creek, ME 04117

Dear Allison Carpenter,

This letter is being sent to confirm that your St. Mary's Credit Union account listed above has been closed due to a negative account balance. If you wish to reopen the account, please call us at 207-555-2222 or visit your local branch to make a deposit within ten days of the date of this letter.

Thank you for banking with us and we hope you'll choose to bank with us again in the future.

All the best,
John Howes
Customer Service Relations

I cursed under my breath and pushed the letter away from me. They must have run her account down with those damn fees they'd started introducing everywhere. "Banking charges," they called them, though why they felt they could charge for something that had always been free I wasn't sure. Didn't they get enough from people by gouging them on interest rates? I felt a surge of irritation. And for Saint Mary's to be doing it . . . I expected that sort of treatment from the big banks, but this was just a local mom-and-pop credit union. I'd go down there the next day and give them a piece of my mind, I promised myself, but then the futility of it struck me. I'd have had to close the account, anyway.

Loss swept through me with its familiar dull, heavy ache, like a riptide pulling me under, leaving me slack and spent. I needed to lie down for a few minutes. I could barely keep my eyes open as I washed out the mug and stacked the rest of the mail on the desk. I left my bag in the hall and trudged up the stairs to my bedroom. The room had the same strange smell of abandonment that the kitchen had—like I'd been gone a month rather than a couple of days.

I'd clean the place in the morning, I thought as I threw myself down onto the bed. I climbed under the comforter and waited for Barney to come out from under the bed and curl up next to me for a nap as he always did, but he didn't stir.

I propped myself up onto my elbows and peered under the bed. Nothing but dust balls and an old pair of slippers.

Barney was a creature of habit, and if he wasn't downstairs in the kitchen with me, he was under the bed. I thought of his untouched bowl of food downstairs, and the fact that he hadn't come to greet me at the door. The first cold fingertips of worry touched me, and I heaved myself out of bed. I wouldn't be able to sleep until I found him.

Ally's room was the last place I checked. The door was shut tight as it always was, and I hovered on the threshold. I hadn't been in there since just after Charles died, when I had tucked some of the things she'd left behind into her closet and out of sight. I pushed open the door and took a step in. The room was just the same as it had been the day she went to college and left behind all the accumulated detritus of eighteen years of growing up. There was her bed, with its checked comforter, and her walls tacked up with art prints and pages from magazines, and her box of cheap jewelry, and her desk, with its stack of thumbed paperbacks and its ceramic mug full of colored pens. There was the collage she'd made of her and her friends from high school at proms and pep rallies and soccer games and sleepovers. It was all exactly as I remembered, except for one thing: the smell. Sort of sickly sweet. I glanced around the room looking for the source—maybe a bottle of her old perfume had tipped over—but I couldn't find anything obvious. It all looked just the same as it always did.

I got down on my hands and knees and peered beneath the ruffled bed skirt. There, behind a box of Ally's old sweaters, was Barney. "What are you doing under there?" I asked. I stroked his fur. His body was cool and still.

I got down on my stomach and reached underneath the bed with both hands. He didn't stir when I pulled him out, or when I laid him on the comforter, or when I pressed my cheek against the soft fur on his belly. His eyes were open but the spark in them was gone, and they looked like two dull black beads pressed into his skull.

He must have been dead at least a day. Maybe more.

I don't know how long I sat on the floor cradling his head in my hands. I didn't cry, I remember that. I'd loved him, but I didn't have any tears left. Poor Barney. He'd been a good cat and deserved better. He shouldn't have had to die all alone in this big house.

He was nearly seventeen. He'd died of old age, I was sure. What I was less sure about was how he'd ended up in Ally's room when the door was shut tight.

I didn't tell anyone, but I started locking the doors after that.

The hut fell into shadow. The two men looked up and saw him standing in the doorway, his body blocking out the sun. He could smell the fear on them before he set foot inside.

—This your place?

—None of your business.

—I'm going to ask you one more time.

They stared at the Man. He noticed that the little one's hands had started to shake.

—Yeah, it's ours.

They were lying, but he didn't care. That wasn't his business.

—You seen anyone around here? A woman?

The little one smiled, showing a row of rotting, yellowed teeth. The Man looked away. He hated the sight of poor hygiene.

—Sure we did. Bunch of supermodels were here. You just missed them.

The big one was quiet. He had a tin of beans in one hand and a fork in the other, and up until then he'd kept his eyes on his dinner. Now he glared at the little one.

—Shut your mouth, Bill.

The Man took a step toward them and saw the little one flinch. All mouth, he thought.

—Listen to your friend, Bill. Now, have either of you seen a woman around here?

The big one stuck his fork into the beans, put the tin down on the ground, and stood up. The Man took another step forward.

—Sit back down.

The big one raised his hands.

—I don't want no trouble.

—Then sit back down.

The big one picked up the can of beans and sat down.

—Somebody was in here. Not sure if it was a man or a woman, but they took some stuff.

The Man's eyes didn't waver.

—What kind of stuff?

—Canned goods. Little hunting knife. Nothing big.

The little one shifted in his chair and made a noise. A kind of laugh-grunt. The Man turned his gaze on him.

—You got something you want to say?

—Son of a bitch stole my rifle.

The big one ran a hand across his face.

—Bill.

The Man looked back at the big one.

—Now, why wouldn't you want to tell me about the rifle?

The big one shrugged, but the Man could see that he was sweating.

—Don't see why it's any of your business. Wasn't your rifle.

The Man took another step forward and leaned down so he was eye level with the big one. He was close enough to smell the baked beans on his breath along with something yeasty and sour.

—It's not your place to tell me what is and isn't my business.

Silence. The big one closed his eyes.

—There were a few hairs on the floor. Long ones. I saw them when we were clearing up the mess.

—What color?

—Yellow.

—You mean blond?

The little one let out a peal of nervous laughter, and the Man clenched his fist.

—Sure. Blond.

—Anything else?

The two of them shook their heads. The Man pictured, briefly, reaching out and knocking their two skulls together. Bone against bone.

—Don't think so.

The Man straightened up. The big one sagged with relief.

—If you think of anything else, give me a call.

He held out a card with a number printed on it in thick black type.

The little one took it. He read it and frowned.

—There's no name here. What are we supposed to call you?

The Man reached out and gripped the little one by the neck. Just one squeeze, he thought. One squeeze and it would be over. But then he'd have to take care of the big one, and then he'd have a mess to clean up. The boss said no mess. He let go. The little one rubbed at his throat.

—Nothing. You're not supposed to call me anything.

He turned and walked out and the sunlight filled the space, dazzling the two he left behind.

Allison

I tug off my sneakers and place my toes tentatively into the lake. It's cold but it feels good.

I peel off my clothes and toss them on the bank. The breeze rustles the hairs on the back of my neck, my thighs, my calves. It feels strange to be naked out in the open, and I cover my breasts, suddenly shy.

I wade through a patch of tall reeds, feeling them tickle as I pass, and then with one deep breath, I dive in.

The cold knocks the wind out of me. I surface spluttering, my breath coming in ragged gasps before my body numbs itself to the temperature. I dip my head under and try to run my hands through my hair but my fingers catch in the snarls. Still, it feels good to be in the water, and I tilt my head back and let myself go under again.

The cups rattled gently in their saucers as the maid placed them on the table. "Sugar?" Amanda asked, already heaping a teaspoon into the cup and stirring it with a small silver spoon.

"Yes, thank you." I took a sip and suppressed a wince. The coffee was weak and achingly sweet, nothing like how I would normally take it. I remembered the coffee maker in my mother's kitchen, the way she would spoon heaping tablespoons of coffee grounds into the filter, the steady drip of the machine, the smell of dark roast filling the air. I took another sip and placed the cup down on the saucer. The taste was something I'd get used to, just like I had the rest of it.

"How are the wedding plans?" she asked, and then reached out and picked up a leather-bound diary without waiting for an answer. "I've spoken to the people at Torrey Pines," she said, flicking through the pages. "They can do the seventeenth, so I told them to hold it for us." She flashed us a bright smile. "Of course, it's your choice. I don't want to step on any toes."

A little fissure of panic ran through me. We hadn't discussed venues yet. We hadn't discussed anything, really, other than the occasional fantasy about running away to some tropical island and eloping. Now I realized how ridiculous that had been. Of course this was going to be Amanda's wedding. I couldn't believe I'd ever thought otherwise.

"I'm sure it'll be perfect, Mom." Ben caught my eye and winked, and I felt myself relax. The wedding didn't matter. Let her plan the whole thing, I didn't care. I had him.

David walked in, the newspaper tucked under his arm, and sat down at the table. "Sorry I'm late." He took a sip from the cup Amanda handed to him and frowned. "Why the hell can't anyone make a decent cup of coffee in this house?"

"We were just discussing plans for the wedding," Amanda said. "We've decided on Torrey Pines."

"Wonderful," he said distractedly. "Ben, could I have a word with you?"

Amanda and I watched the two men leave the room and smiled at each other politely. "Have you thought about your dress? I know this fantastic woman in Sabre Springs who designs the most incredible bespoke gowns . . ."

I could hear the rumble of their voices in the room next door. Amanda kept talking. She had the names of the best florist, the best caterer, the best wedding planner. I nodded along without really listening. The voices in the next room were louder now, the cadence more halted. They were arguing. I strained to catch the words but they were lost between the vaulted ceilings and thick walls of the house. I agreed to rack of lamb for the main course, and that figs wrapped in prosciutto would make an elegant hors d'oeuvre. There was the thud of someone's fist coming down on a table and we both jumped.

The door opened and Ben walked in and sat down. His father wasn't with him. There were faint beads of sweat around his hairline, and I saw a muscle in his jaw twitch. "So," he said, plastering a smile onto his face, "have you two planned the entire wedding since I've been gone?"

"Almost!" Amanda trilled. "Allison is going to be the most beautiful bride, isn't she?"

Ben reached out and took my hand. "Absolutely." His palm was clammy as he squeezed my hand a little too hard. "She'll be a vision."

In the car ride home, I tried to ask him what he'd talked about with his father, but he brushed it off. "Nothing," he said, reaching over and running a thumb across my cheek. "Just family stuff." But I saw the muscle in his jaw twitch again.

The sores that cover my body sting. I scrub at the dirt encrusted on my shoulders, my shins, between my toes. I rub with the heel of my palm, scrape with what is left of my fingernails, but the dirt still won't budge. I need soap, or a hot shower, or both. Eventually I give up. I slip back underwater, open my eyes, and see only a murky green, the sun a faint white glow above.

I think of all the hours I spent making myself pretty. The mani-pedis and cuts and blowdries and laser hair removals and rejuvenating facials. The foils and the steams and the juice cleanses. I wanted to be coveted and admired and adored, like a pampered little cat, or a shiny trinket in a shopwindow. I wanted everyone to look at me, and for the most part, everyone did. Sometimes too much.

And now here I am, stripped down, filthy, covered in bites and scratches and wounds. Unrecognizable. I think of myself sloughing off another layer of skin, revealing the tender flesh underneath. I'll be brand new after this. I'll be someone else completely.

I stare up at the sky and watch the clouds float past above. The world is almost big enough to make me forget what led me to this place, the moment that shattered my perfect glass-encased world and sent me spiraling into the splinters.

Almost, but not quite.

Maggie

There was a package waiting on the doorstep when I got back from the grocery store. It was addressed to me, and the return address was from Colorado.

I hurried into the kitchen, dumped the grocery bags on the countertop, and sliced the box open with a pair of scissors from the drawer. Inside was a padded envelope and a typed note addressed to me.

Dear Mrs. Carpenter,

Enclosed are the personal effects of Allison Carpenter retrieved from the site of the noncommercial plane crash that occurred on July 8, 2018. These items have been processed and cleared for release into your custody.

On behalf of the Central Regional Office of the NTSB, please accept our condolences.

Best wishes,
Bruce Logan
Case Officer
National Transportation Safety Board

I tore open the envelope and shook it. A thin gold chain snaked out and spooled onto the table.

I raised a hand to my heart and stared at it. It was a little tarnished now, sure, and the thin gold locket had been dented, but there was no mistaking it. It was the same necklace that Charles had hung around her neck a few years earlier.

I plucked it off the table and held it up to the light. I flicked open the locket, and the familiar photograph of me and Charles stared back. I flipped it over and read the inscription. *God protect him as he travels, by air or land or sea, keep him safe and guide him, wherever he may be.*

I threaded the chain around my neck and fastened the clasp.

Maybe one day I'd have to let go, but right then, I was going to keep fighting.

Allison

I should go. I've stayed here for too long now, and the light will start to fade soon. I stare out across the lake. The light catches on the surface and sparkles like fireflies.

"Excuse me? Excuse me, Miss Carpenter?" I turned to see the salon receptionist hurrying toward me, blond ponytail bouncing as she ran. "Someone dropped this off for you when you were inside." She held a small white envelope in her french-manicured hand.

My name was written across the front in neat handwriting. I ripped it open and a slip of paper slid out into my hand.

WE NEED TO TALK.

Underneath was a phone number, but no name.

I caught the receptionist by the arm. "Who gave you this?"

The receptionist looked stricken. "I jumped off the desk for two seconds to get more towels and it was there when I got back. Sorry. Is it something important?"

I forced a smile. A metallic taste formed at the back of my throat. "No, not really. Thanks, Kelly." I folded the piece of paper and slid it into the pocket of my bag before pushing my way out the door and into the bright sunshine.

I was meant to have lunch with Liz, but I tapped out an excuse on my phone and hit Send. She was a friend, but she didn't know anything about my past, and I couldn't afford to let anything slip, even to her. I was too rattled to sit down and make nice over Cobb salads and too much Chablis when my old life was knocking at the door.

I was sure it was him. I could still picture his hands with their thick fingers reaching across and grabbing the steering wheel, and the flash of blue lights in the rearview mirror. The pit of my stomach felt heavy and sour. "Just leave the talking to me." That's what he'd said when we were waiting for the officer to approach, but I could tell by his voice that he was terrified. He'd been angry afterward and told me that I owed him. He'd claimed his payback again and again, but it was never enough. He always felt entitled to more.

I wondered how he'd tracked me down. I'd made sure not to leave a forwarding address when I left Tara's, and I wasn't listed on the deed or the bills for the house in Bird Rock. Ben caught a glimpse of the missed calls on my phone one morning and asked who was calling me in the middle of the night. "Have you got something to tell me?" he'd teased. "A secret boyfriend or something?" I'd pretended it was a wrong number and blocked it the next day.

But now, it looked like he had found me, and he wanted to talk.

I pulled my sunglasses down over my eyes and set off west, toward the beach. I needed the air. I chose a table at an obscure café on the south shore and ordered an iced tea, my hands shaking as I lifted the straw to my lips. It was a beautiful day—seventy-two and sunny, just like always—and the beach was filled with tourists taking pictures of the bright blue sea. There were people like me, too, rich women idling the day away while their husbands worked in one of the high-rises that peppered the skyline.

There were old versions of me, too, if you knew what to look for: women whose jewelry was expensive but whose clothes were cheap, whose skin was a shade too pale from days spent sleeping the sunlight away, whose nails were just a little bit too long to be respectable, a little too red.

The line between the two was so thin sometimes, it hardly seemed there at all. Squint and you'd miss it. Did women from both tribes look at me and see one of their own? Or was I an outsider to both of them now?

I pulled the scrap of paper out of my bag and stared at it until the numbers swam. Someone had followed me to the salon and waited until the receptionist left to slip the note onto the desk. It was calculated, deliberate. It made the hairs on the back of my neck stand on end.

If Ben found out the truth about my old life—the whole truth, not just being a waitress at some seedy bar and living in that crappy apartment—it would be over. How could he love someone like that? I could conjure up the disgust on his face, the disappointment, the hurt. I would no longer be the woman he loved. I would be something else, something cheap and monstrous. An embarrassment.

I pushed the image out of my head. He wasn't going to find out. I'd make sure of it.

I finished my iced tea, gathered my bag, and tossed the scrap into the trash on my way out.

Whoever was looking for me could keep looking. I was on the other side now, and I wasn't going back.

Maggie

I made it to Bowdoin in record time. The campus was still in its summer slumber, and I passed only a few people on my way to the library. Doug was seated on his perch at security and sent me through with a wave and a smile.

Entering the cool hush of the library felt like walking into a sanctuary. Here was calm and quiet and order. Here were answers for me to find.

I found Barbara and asked her to set me up on the same computer. The man from the other day, Tony, came and sat down shortly after I arrived, another stack of books in front of him. He smiled and gave me a wave when he caught my eye.

I looked up the record of Ally's plane crash to see if there had been any updates. Still no body. Still no definitive cause for the crash. Of course I knew that Jim would've told me if anything had changed, but I wanted to see for myself.

Next I looked up the address of the house in Bird Rock to see if it was on the market. Sure enough, there was a listing for it on the website of a fancy-looking Realtor. "Live the high life and surround yourself in luxury in this modern and spacious bungalow. Located in the heart of Bird Rock and only seconds from Windansea Beach, this house offers high-end finishes and breathtaking sea views." The list price was north of $3 million.

I tried tracking down a few more leads but came up empty handed. After an hour of fruitless searches and dead ends, I sat back from the computer and folded my arms across my chest. I'd hit a wall.

The memory of the man in the Prexilane plaza suddenly surfaced in my mind.

I typed the word "Prexilane" into the search engine and scrolled through the results. There was a piece in Bloomberg from the week before speculating about a sale. "Acting CEO of Prexilane denies rumors of a sale to Hyperion Industries—but insiders say it's only a matter of time." Hyperion Industries—the name rang a bell. It clicked after a few seconds: the receptionist had mentioned Hyperion when I'd first turned up at the office. I smiled to myself. No wonder there'd been so much commotion when I arrived—they thought I was coming to buy the company.

The rest of the entries about Prexilane were standard business fare. I needed to get more specific.

The stricken look on the man's face as he talked about his wife's death, the anguish in his eyes . . . He'd said they'd given her the pills after she'd given birth to her daughter.

I pictured the smiling blond woman on the billboard. Somnublaze.

The first few pages were medical websites explaining Somnublaze's use for treating postpartum depression. I clicked on one at random but didn't find anything out of the ordinary—the article described the circumstances under which it would be prescribed and the side effects, which were minimal: headache, nausea—nothing more than you'd expect from taking any medication. I clicked on a *New York Times* article that described it as a wonder drug—"For many new mothers, Somnublaze is the key to feeling like themselves again." Those were the words the man had used in the plaza, who claimed they'd given his wife the drug to make her feel like herself again. Another article hailed it as one of the major developments in pharmaceuticals this decade.

The reviews, too, were glowing—hundreds of women claiming that it had saved their lives, that they had been staring down into the abyss and Somnublaze had lifted them out. "Thank God for this drug," one woman said. "I wouldn't have made it through without it."

I sat back in my chair. I'd been led on another wild-goose chase. It seemed like, whatever flaws I might suspect him of, Ben had developed a drug that helped people. Maybe the man in the plaza really had been a lunatic.

Still, I couldn't let go of the thought that I was missing something. A thought struck me: every single one of the search results I'd clicked on had been positive. I'd been using the internet long enough to know that it wasn't normal for reviews to be universally positive. People used the internet for two reasons: to find out information, and to complain. It didn't matter what about—if it existed, they'd complain about it. Hell, there were people out there who'd left bad reviews about *North by Northwest*, and I couldn't imagine anybody not liking that movie. Something didn't sit right about the fact that no one was complaining about Somnublaze. Hadn't Linda said her daughter-in-law stopped taking it because it made her feel crazy? If she'd had a negative reaction to it, there must have been others who had, too.

I went deeper into the search. The next forty pages of results were the same—more articles about Somnublaze from medical websites and news agencies, more patient reviews, all uniformly positive. The better-known sites dropped away, and smaller, more obscure sites took their place, but the tone didn't change. Somnublaze was nothing short of a miracle, and no one had a bad word to say about it.

It took me until page seventy-four to find something. It was a message board for new mothers. The thread was long defunct, but the conversation was still there. The subject line was just one word: HELP.

Posted: September 14 2016 3:49 by **Curls384**

I was diagnosed with ppd when dd was 4 weeks old. My doctor prescribed Somnublaze and I've been taking it for 6 mos now. At first it made a huge difference. I felt like myself again, and I could finally bond with dd. Lately I've been having mood swings. I'll be happy one minute and so angry the next—angrier than I've ever been. Has anyone else experienced this?

Posted: September 14 2016 10:11 by **RebeccaCC**

I've been on Somnublaze since ds2 was born 3 mos ago and it's helped so much. No mood swings. Maybe talk to your doctor? Could be a Vit D imbalance?

Posted: September 16 2016 1:32 by **Curls384**

Doctor has suggested upping my dosage from 20mg to 40. My vit levels are fine. Today I got so angry with my dd that I had to lock myself in the bathroom to calm down. I'm scaring myself. Why am I so angry??? Can anyone help? Please, I'm desperate!

Posted: September 16 2016 11:55 by **GeorgiaPeach**

Is there someone you can talk to—a family member or a friend or a therapist? Does your DH know you're feeling this way?

Posted: September 21 2016 14:33 by **GeorgiaPeach**

Did you speak to someone? Have you got help?

Posted: September 23 2016 17:04 by **GeorgiaPeach**

You're in my prayers.

Posted: November 6 2016 15:47 by **Moderator**

This thread is now closed.

The conversation ended there. My heart went out to that poor woman—she sounded genuinely scared. Maybe it didn't have anything to do with the pills. Maybe the upped dosage worked for her, and she was feeling better. I read through it again. GeorgiaPeach had been scared for her, too. The moderator's message felt too final.

It didn't prove anything, though. She was just one woman. I had no idea what her situation was, or if how she was feeling had anything to do with Somnublaze or Prexilane. It was just a single drop in an ocean of praise. Still, I wrote down the Web address. Just in case.

I checked my watch: it was nearly three thirty. I should get going before rush hour set in, I thought. I was gathering up my things when I felt a tap on my shoulder.

"Excuse me." I looked up. It was Tony. "Sorry, I don't mean to hassle you or anything, but I'm about to go out for a cup of coffee and wondered if I could persuade you to join me." He looked down at me and tilted his head to one side. "I hope you don't mind me saying, but you look like you might need it."

I bristled. I couldn't understand why he was so interested in talking to me. Something about the way he looked at me—like he could see straight through my skin—made me feel exposed and embarrassed. Did he know who I was? About Ally? Maybe he was a journalist, sniffing around for information. Or just some sick stranger looking to get close to tragedy, like the people who turned out to gawk at car wrecks. "No, thank you," I said curtly, and I turned my back and waited for him to leave.

I could feel him hovering behind me. "I'm sorry," he said softly. "I just thought you might like some company."

I listened to him shuffle away, and my heart sank. The man was just trying to be nice. It was paranoid to think it was anything more sinister than that. Hadn't I decided the last time I was up there that he was probably lonely? And then I'd been rude to him, again. I didn't want to go home yet, and a cup of coffee might be nice, especially one with someone who didn't know me, and didn't pity me. I got up and walked over to where he was sitting, a pile of books stacked on the desk in front of him. I had a quick look at the titles. He was on to the impressionists now. He looked up at me as I approached, his face like a scolded puppy. "I'll take that cup of coffee if you're still offering," I said, and his face cleared.

We went to the coffee shop in Smith Union. I sat down at one of the plastic tables while he went up to the counter and ordered, and I watched him as he stood in line. He was a good-looking man for his age, still trim and with a full head of silvery hair. He'd have been handsome when he was young. He caught my eye and smiled and I looked away, feeling like I'd been caught.

"Here you go," he said, handing me a paper cup. "They didn't have regular so I got you something called a flat white. I hope that's okay."

"I'm sure it will be," I said. "Thank you." I watched him take a sip, and as he wiped the milk from his upper lip I realized I was happy I'd accepted his invitation.

"So," he said, propping his elbows on the table, "are you going to tell me what it is you're researching? From the look on your face, I'm guessing it's some serious stuff." I didn't say anything. I wasn't ready. Tony ran a hand over the stubble on his chin and sighed. "Sorry, I'm being nosy again. My wife was always telling me that I asked too many questions."

I raised my eyebrows. "You were married?"

"Widowed. Four years now." I saw the same pain in his eyes that I saw in my own and nodded in recognition.

"Me too. Two years."

He sighed. "Well, I'd tell you it gets easier, but that would be lying."

We smiled sadly at each other. "I figured as much," I said. I took a sip from my cup. The coffee was too creamy for my taste, but it was good enough. "Can I ask what happened to . . ."

"Diane. She had a heart attack. We played golf that morning and I'd gone to take a shower. When I came out, she was lying on the couch. Already gone." His eyes filmed over and I could see he was reliving it all over again. I imagined him coming out of the bathroom and finding her slumped on the cushions, all the life suddenly sucked from her, and my heart broke for him.

"I'm sorry," I said quietly, and his eyes returned to mine. I could see an understanding there that I hadn't seen many times before. I was the first person among my friends to lose a husband. Everyone was sympathetic, of course—kinder than I could have imagined—but they hadn't really understood. No one can tell you how it feels to see the body of the person you love and know that he's not really there anymore. It's like a cheap magician's trick. Crueler than anything I could have imagined.

"What about your husband?" he asked, tearing open a packet of sugar and stirring it into his coffee.

I looked away. "Charles died of colon cancer." It was the truth, almost. The cancer had been killing him. I could still hear the steady drip of the morphine feed. "It's unlocked," the doctor had said on his last visit, nodding toward the safe where the morphine pump was stored, and then he'd said goodbye and walked out the door. He hadn't said anything else. He didn't have to.

I should have told Ally I was going to do it. I wanted to protect her, but in doing so I had robbed her of the chance to say goodbye to her father. I understood why she hated me. I still hated myself sometimes, even though Charles had asked me to do it. I knew, too, that I had acted selfishly. He loved her best—as he should, she was his daughter—but I had loved him first, and there was a part of me that had wanted to love him last. She was his daughter, but I was his wife. I had watched him turn from a kid of eighteen into a man and a husband and a father and then I watched cancer hollow him out, and I had wanted to keep the last remaining piece of him to myself. Selfishness, pure and simple. But it was love, too, even though I knew I wouldn't have been able to explain it to her.

Tony shook his head. "Nasty stuff. I'm sorry you had to go through that."

You don't know the half of it, I thought. I nodded. "I'm sorry for what you went through, too."

His mouth twisted into a smirk. "Getting old sucks, doesn't it?"

I laughed. "It certainly does. These kids don't know how lucky they are," I said, gesturing toward a table of students. "Not that I'd want to be eighteen again."

He shook his head. "God forbid." We were silent for a few minutes, just sipping our coffees and looking at the kids milling around the union, buying slices of pizza and sitting and laughing in groups of threes and fours.

I sneaked a glance at him. Yes, he would have been handsome when he was young. The lines around his eyes had settled into patterns that suggested he'd laughed a lot over the course of his life, despite the sadness he carried in his eyes. He had the face of someone who was kind. I felt something building up inside me. "My daughter was in a plane crash," I said, too loudly.

Tony looked up at me, stricken. "Jesus."

I nodded. "Everybody thinks she's dead, but they haven't found a body." Now that the words were out I felt lighter, almost giddy. Like a fire hydrant being opened up on a hot day. "I'm trying to get to the bottom of what happened, but it feels more and more like I'm just chasing my own tail. I'm trying to make sense of it, but I'm starting to think that there is no sense in these things."

He ran a hand across his face. "God, Maggie. I don't know what to say. I'm so sorry for your loss."

I shook my head. I don't know why I thought he'd understand, but I was frustrated now that he hadn't. "That's just it—I can't bring myself to believe I've lost her. We weren't in touch over the past couple of years, and I keep learning all these things about what her life was like, and it's like hearing about a stranger. I have to know, though. Even though I know I should just let it rest, I can't. I have to know everything I can. I'm looking things up now that don't have anything to do with Ally, just in case they lead me to her somehow. Does that make sense?" I allowed my eyes to meet his. "What am I saying? I know it doesn't." I felt a flush of embarrassment. What was I doing, telling a stranger things like this?

His eyes were so gentle then, so kind. He nodded. "Of course it does."

I looked away. "Well, you're the only one who thinks so. Everyone else thinks I'm crazy." I stared down at the top of the Formica table. "It's her memorial tomorrow. My friend organized the whole thing, thinks it will give me closure." I let out a short laugh. "Somehow I don't think that'll happen."

He shook his head and smiled. "I remember when Diane died, and my buddies came around with six-packs and we all ended up just getting drunk in silence. No one said a damn word all night, until finally Bobby Maguire started talking about the Dodgers and everyone sort of relaxed. What else was there to say? No one has answers for these things. No one can understand how you're feeling. That's the thing about it—even when you're surrounded by people, you're still completely alone. You've got to deal with it whatever way you can." He ran a hand across his stubble again and sighed. "Sorry, I'm probably not being much use here."

I felt suddenly shy, like he'd seen me without my clothes on. I folded my arms across my chest. "It is what it is." I glanced at the clock mounted on the wall. Almost four. I reached out and drained the last of my coffee. "Well, I'd better get going."

He checked his watch and grimaced. "Me too. I've got to get back to the books. I've got to write a paper on *Swann's Way* by Friday." He leaned across the table conspiratorially. "You got any idea what he was talking about?"

I shook my head. "I tried to read it once but I didn't get on with it. Too flowery for me."

"Good. That makes two of us."

We threw out our paper cups and walked out of the building together. The heat had gone out of the day and the sky was a whitish gray and overcast. It would rain later.

Tony shoved his hands into his pockets. "Thanks for keeping me company."

"My pleasure. Thanks for the coffee."

"Anytime."

We stood there for a minute, both of us unsure how to leave. "Well, goodbye," I said finally, thrusting my hand toward him. We shook hands awkwardly, and I felt myself blush. *Stop it*, I scolded myself. *You're acting like a fool.* I could tell by his face that he felt silly, too, which made me feel both better and worse.

"You take care of yourself, Maggie," he said, pushing his hands back down into his pockets. "I hope I'll see you again soon."

Allison

I scrounge through my bag. There isn't much left from the cabin—a single can of soup and a handful of crackers. Hunger gnaws. I stab open the tin with the dulled point of my knife and drink. I catch the inside of my lip on the jagged metal edge, and the taste of blood mixes with the taste of alphabet soup. My favorite when I was a kid.

"Allison!"

The way the man called out my name made my stomach clench. When I had passed him farther up the block I saw him staring at me, but I didn't think twice about it. Men stared at me all the time. Part of being a woman meant being common property as soon as you set foot outside. You got used to it early, learned to set your face a certain way, to avoid eye contact, to keep walking. But then he called out my name.

He was behind me on the sidewalk. I could hear his footsteps gathering pace and I picked up my own. My fist tightened around the strap of my purse and I started to formulate a plan. There was a shop a few doors down—I'd duck inside and ask for help.

A hand grabbed my elbow. "Allison, please. I just want to talk to you." I jerked my arm away and spun around, ready to fight. It was broad daylight. Someone would see us before things got too bad. Someone would intervene.

The man standing in front of me had the sort of hangdog face that suggests a life of continuous disappointment. His eyes were widely set and slightly rheumy, like he was in the grip of a fever, and there was a shock of unruly gray hair on top of his head. I'd never seen him before in my life. He didn't look like someone who was a threat, but then again, I was old enough to know that people were capable of anything. "Don't touch me," I said, in my iciest voice.

"I'm sorry." He shuffled back a few paces and held up his hands. "I didn't mean to scare you."

"You didn't scare me." Rule number one: never show fear. "How do you know my name?"

The edges of his mouth curled into a tentative smile. "I've been trying to get in touch with you."

My eyes narrowed. "You're the person who sent the notes." After the first came another, and another. The people who'd given them to me couldn't say who they were from—it was like they had just materialized out of thin air. But now here he was, standing right in front of me. Flesh and bone. "What do you want?"

He held up his hands, as if to show he was unarmed. "Like I said, I just want to talk."

I folded my arms across my chest. "What if I don't want to talk?"

He took an uncertain step toward me. "I didn't want to do this," he whispered.

I took a step back. "Do what?"

He fiddled nervously with the hem of his shirt. "I know about your little car ride in Palm Springs."

A bolt of fear ran through me, icy sharp. "I don't know what you're talking about." The slick black spool of highway. Flashing blue lights in the rearview mirror. I felt a wave of nausea come over me.

The man was studying my face. "Your fiancé doesn't know about it, does he?"

I was silent.

"There are a lot of things he doesn't know about you." It was a threat, but he said it almost kindly, and his eyes were filled with something close to pity.

We went to a coffee shop down the street. It was midday, and the place was crammed full of office lunchtimers looking for their caffeine fix and freelance types tapping away on their laptops. I avoided their eyes as I walked to the counter and placed my order. It felt like the whole room was watching. *They know about me*, I thought. *Everyone knows.*

We settled into a table tucked in a back corner and fell into silence until the waitress brought our order. The man tore open three packets of sugar and emptied them into his coffee. "Sweet tooth," he said with an apologetic grin, and I had to hide my hands under the table to stop from slapping him.

I watched as he slowly stirred his coffee, took a sip, poured in a splash of milk, sipped again. All the while, the feathered wings of panic gathered themselves and started pushing up into my throat. This man—this stupid, useless old man—was going to take everything away from me, and all he cared about was getting his coffee right. I hated him. Finally, I couldn't take it anymore. "Who are you?"

He tapped his spoon on the side of his mug and set it down in the saucer. "It's not important."

So that was the deal: he knew me, but I couldn't know him. Even though he knew things about me that could take the man I loved away from me, things that could destroy the life I'd created for myself. "Look," I blurted out. I felt too hot, tearful. "I don't know what you know about me, but—"

He held up a hand to stop me. "Relax. I'm not interested in what you got up to at that bar, or the kind of company you used to keep."

I stared at him dumbly. "You're not?"

He shook his head.

"Then why did you—"

He tilted his head to one side and smiled. "I needed a way to make you talk to me. To listen."

I sat back in my chair. "So you're not going to tell Ben about my past?"

He shook his head. "As much as I'd love to hurt the guy, I don't want to hurt him in that way. No, I'm not going to tell him. Your secret is safe with me."

I should have felt relieved, but the sourness in the pit of my stomach remained. This man wanted something from me. Something I knew, instinctively, that I wouldn't want to give. I wanted to push back from the table and run away as fast as I could. But I knew I couldn't do that. He'd already proved that he had ways of finding me, and he might not be so nice about my past the next time. "What do you want?" I asked quietly.

He took a sip of his coffee and stared at me above the rim. "How much do you know about your fiancé's company?"

I let out a laugh, startling us both. "Prexilane?" I shook my head. "I don't have anything to do with it."

He nodded patiently. "I know you don't. That wasn't my question. My question was, how much do you know about it?"

I thought about the nights Ben came home late from work, exhausted but exhilarated because of a breakthrough they'd made in the lab. The way he talked about his desire to help people, to heal them. "I know that he makes drugs that save people's lives."

He gave me a sad little smile. "Is that right." He took another sip of his coffee. "Have you ever heard the phrase 'manipulation of equilibrium samples'?" I shook my head. "How about 'selection bias'?"

I felt a fizz of anger. "What does this have to do with anything?" The itch to run out of the café returned.

"What if I told you that Prexilane has been manipulating their own drug trials, and that people have gotten hurt as a result? Some have even died."

I flinched. "Ben would never do something like that. He cares about people. He wants to help them."

Now it was his turn to laugh. "The only thing he cares about is money. Just like the rest of them."

"No." The anger in my voice startled us both. "You're wrong."

I was prepared for this man to drag me through the mud—I deserved it—but I wouldn't let him talk about Ben like that. He was a good man.

He sighed. "Drug companies have been doing it for years. Think of the opioids screwing over middle America—you think they got to market based on sound research?" He shook his head. "They're all at it. You have no idea the kind of side effects some of these drugs can have on innocent people."

"All drugs have side effects," I pointed out. "Haven't you ever seen a drug commercial? Half of it is taken up with listing side effects." My voice was shaking and I had to work to control it.

He gave me a pitying look, like I was some stupid, silly girl who didn't know anything about the world. "Those are just the side effects they want you to know about."

I rolled my eyes. "Drug companies are regulated by the FDA. They have to be tested, go through research . . ." I trailed off. I was out of my depth now, just repeating phrases I'd heard. "There's a process," I said, more confidently than I felt.

He smirked. "Oh, sure, there's a process all right. The process of being bought and sold to the highest bidder. You think the FDA is above a little bribery?"

I hated him. He was just like every other patronizing man I'd ever met in my life, and there'd been so many—hundreds of them—all eager to pat me on the head and tell me not to worry my pretty little head. But this was worse. He was trying to tell me I didn't know the man I loved. I wouldn't let him. "You don't know what you're talking about. You're crazy," I hissed.

He slapped the table, hard. The room fell silent. A baby started to cry. "Don't call me crazy." His eyes were bright now, as if gripped by fever. "I am *not* crazy."

I shoved back in my chair and got to my feet. He was scaring me now, but I didn't want to let him see that he'd rattled me. I didn't want to give him the satisfaction. "I'm leaving," I said, hoisting my bag over my shoulder. "Don't contact me again."

He peered up at me, his eyes boring into mine. "Your fiancé is killing people," he said in a low voice. "He and his people have destroyed lives to cover it up. Don't you care about that?"

"You're a liar," I spat. But he had opened up a little fissure of doubt inside me. I thought of the whispers Ben shared with Sam, the way he would startle awake at night, the sheets drenched in sweat, the dark moods that sometimes followed him home from work and trailed after him for hours. My heart thumped in my chest, and my head swam. I needed to get out of there. I needed air.

I pushed my way out into the brilliant sunshine and took off in a run. The man in the café was sick, deranged, a fantasist. I never wanted to see him again.

The Man sniffed the early-morning air, and the coal-fire scent of cold filled his lungs. He took out his phone and dialed.

—It's me.

—Not yet, but I'm close.

He lit a cigarette with red-raw fingers and took a drag. The smoke when he exhaled was mingled with condensation, and he watched as the fog drifted down the mountain in tumbling whorls.

—Don't worry, she won't.

He took another drag, scuffed his heel at the blackened circle of scorched earth. He glanced down at the patch of matted grass and frozen mud and smiled. She was getting sloppy. Tired. It wouldn't be long now before she made a mistake.

—Yes, sir. I'll make sure of it.

He hung up the phone, slid it back in his pocket. He took one last drag and curled the smoke out the side of his mouth. He ground out the cigarette, picked up the butt, placed it in his pocket next to the phone.

His boots were still damp, the tips of the laces were frosted with ice, and he stomped his feet hard to get the feeling back into them. He was sick and tired of being out there. He was ready for this to be finished.

He gazed out east. The land stretched before him, patient.

She was out there somewhere, waiting for him.

He would find her, and it would be soon.

Maggie

Today is the day of my daughter's memorial.

The words appeared before I'd even opened my eyes, and they cycled through my head as I got out of bed and pulled Charles's old terry cloth robe around me.

I felt weighed down with dread. All those people, all those eyes on me. I wasn't sure I could stand it. I forced myself to think of it as an opportunity. This wasn't me giving up on Ally. It was a chance to talk to people who knew her, who may have spoken to her over the past two years. Maybe I'd learn something new that would help.

I could hear Linda's voice downstairs, arguing with someone over a tent. She'd been there since seven, taking care of all the last-minute details. She was still angry with me for having gone off to San Diego without telling her, though she wouldn't admit it. I could tell, though, and I felt guilty as hell about it. She was trying her best to help me and I was being ungrateful in everything I did.

I forced myself into the shower and then into a dress—yellow with a pretty floral pattern that Ally had helped me choose years ago. No black today. It was snug on me the last time I'd worn it, but now it zipped up without any trouble. I glanced at myself in the mirror and put a hand to my face. I looked thin, my cheeks hollowed out, my mouth pinched. The dress hung off me like a sack. How had I lost so much weight in so little time? I rubbed a little blush into my cheeks and flicked on some mascara. It was the best I could do.

I stopped outside Ally's room on my way downstairs. I hadn't been in it since the day I found Barney dead, and I hesitated when

I placed my hand on the handle. It was cold to the touch. I turned it and pushed the door open.

I sat down on the edge of the bed, the frame creaking beneath my weight, and looked around the room. I spotted it before I realized I was even looking for it—the old shoebox filled with pictures that she kept on top of the wardrobe. I pulled it down and took off the lid. It was stacked to the brim.

A photograph of Ally and Charles was resting on top, her smiling in her high school cap and gown, him gazing at her with such a look of pride and love and awe. I remembered taking it. It had been boiling that day and the backs of my legs had stuck to the metal folding chair. Ally had made a speech about old friends and new beginnings—the usual sort of graduation speech, but beautiful nonetheless—and I'd sat there sweating gently into my sundress and wondering how on earth I'd given birth to this beautiful, confident girl. Charles had held my hand through the ceremony, and by the end of it both our palms were slicked with sweat, but we didn't care. Oh, we were happy.

I remembered his funeral. Me sitting in the long black car that smelled of pine air freshener and ammonia and stale cigarette smoke from the driver's coat. The crinkle of the paper mats under my sensible black heels. The feel of Linda's hand in mine, powdery cool. The sight of the coffin in the hearse ahead as we drove through town. I stared out the window and watched the ghosts of us drift past. Me and Charles when we were first married, giddy and young in our ridiculous bell-bottoms, on our way to the movies. Me and Charles pushing Ally in her stroller, people on the street stopping us to fuss and coo over the little dark-haired bundle tucked in a blanket. Me and Charles just before he got sick, when we thought he just had a persistent stomach bug. We'd gone out to dinner but had to leave halfway through because he was in so much discomfort. We went to the doctor the next day.

That's the thing about living in the same place your whole life.

You can see shadows of your former lives on every corner. You can't escape them.

I can't remember the funeral service. I know it happened, because I have the program tucked between the pages of the ancient family Bible downstairs, but I can't remember a single thing about it. The mind is funny that way. It protects you from the things you shouldn't know and shouldn't remember.

I wondered if I'd remember this day.

I put my hand to my face and my palm came away wet. I'd been crying. The realization made it worse, and soon my chest was heaving and my throat ached and I wondered if I'd ever be able to stop.

There was a knock on the door. Linda poked her head around the frame. "You okay in here?" She took one look at me and her face crumpled. "Oh, honey."

"Barney died." I didn't know I was going to say it until it was out of my mouth, and we both knew it wasn't the reason I was crying, but it didn't matter. I knew I didn't have to explain myself to her.

"I'm sorry," she said, and her voice was full of pain and sympathy. I knew she wasn't talking about Barney, either, though we'd both loved that old cat. She sat down next to me on the bed and put her arm around me, and I let myself sink into her for a minute, breathing in the familiar smell of fabric softener, perfume, and lemon-scented Pledge. "I'm getting your blouse all wet," I said, but I felt her shake her head and pull me closer. We stayed like that for a long time. Finally I took a deep breath, one of those shuddering ones that come after a long cry, and pulled away. "Is it time to go?"

She checked her watch. "Almost. You want something to eat before we go? There'll be food there but I wasn't sure if you'd want something beforehand, maybe settle your stomach?"

"No, thank you." The thought of eating anything made my stomach turn.

She reached out and touched the locket resting at the base of my throat. "Pretty."

I nodded.

"I'm glad it made it back to you."

Linda drove us there in her pink Cadillac. It was a beautiful day, and the air smelled of freshly cut grass and lilac. From the passenger seat, I squinted into the sun and tried not to think about where we were headed. "You stay as long as you want," Linda said, reaching over and squeezing my hand. "As soon as you're ready to go, I'll take you home."

I nodded. All I could think about was who would be there, and what I would say to them, and how they'd look at me. I was shaking by the time we pulled into the parking lot of the high school. It was already half full and teeming with people. A few of them stopped and looked as I got out of the car, nodding their heads before carrying on into the park. I reached into my bag until my fingers wrapped around the little orange pill bottle I'd tossed in before we left the house.

"Come on," Linda said, taking my elbow. "Let's go."

"Just a second," I said. "I think I forgot something in the car." I opened the car door and ducked down to where she couldn't see me. The pill caught in my throat before it went down.

I didn't want to remember this day after all.

We walked past the high school—a flat brick sixties relic I went to long before Ally did—and over to the fields out back. They were used for sports during the school year, their surfaces marked out in white chalk and scuffed by cleats, but now, in mid-July, it was just one long expanse of patchy, sun-bleached grass. A group of teenagers—the high school drama club, I found out later—were standing in the middle of it singing a Beatles song a cappella.

"They're her favorite," I said quietly.

Linda slipped her hand in mine. "I know."

There was a long folding table that had been pulled out from the cafeteria on which people were placing cakes and bowls of potato chips and big casserole dishes of macaroni and cheese. A couple of men were manning a barbecue—an industrial-size one; God knows where Linda got it from—and the smell of burgers and hot dogs filled the air. The grass was dotted with people, some I recognized, some I didn't, clutching paper plates and talking in groups of twos and threes. Little kids swung from their parents' arms, faces smeared with ketchup and chocolate ice cream.

Linda looked at me closely. "Is it all right? It's not too much, is it? Just tell me if it is and we can go."

I shook my head. "It's perfect." I could feel the pill starting to work, rubbing out the sharp edges. "Thank you."

"You're welcome. Now, do you want something to eat? I can get you a seat somewhere so you can just sit and watch and not be bothered by anybody?"

"I'm fine," I said. "You've done enough. I think I'll just wander around."

I watched Linda bustle off to check on the buffet table and took a minute to survey the crowd. There were old teachers and soccer coaches of Ally's, people I'd grown up with, faces I recognized from the bank and the grocery store and the post office. It seemed like half the town was there, and the sight of it filled me with a kind of warmth. Even if this town was haunted by ghosts, it was also full of people who cared about each other.

I was staring off into the crowd when I felt a tap on the shoulder. "Maggie?" I turned to find Tony holding a clutch of white carnations dotted with baby's breath. "I wasn't sure what the etiquette was, so . . ." He held them out to me but I was too dazed to take them. I hadn't told him about the memorial. Had I? I couldn't think clearly enough to remember. "I saw it in the paper," he said, sensing my hesitation. "I thought I'd come down and pay my respects." He looked down at the flowers and shook his head. "I'm sorry, it was a stupid idea. I shouldn't have intruded." He looked so helpless then, like a scolded child.

I reached out and took the bouquet from him. "They're beautiful," I said. "Thank you. It was sweet of you to come."

Silence expanded between us like a balloon. It felt like a dream. I was here. I was at my daughter's memorial. He looked around and surveyed the field. "It's a great turnout. Your daughter was obviously loved by a lot of people." I followed his gaze. All these people, there for Ally. All these people, convinced that she was dead. The grief hit me again like a wave and I felt myself sway. Tony reached out and placed a hand on my elbow to steady me. "Do you want to sit down?"

I shook my head. "I'm fine. The sun must be getting to me."

He nodded. "It's hot out today. Can I get you some water?"

"Honestly, I'm fine. Let's find a little shade."

We walked together across the field. It was flooded with people now, and the air was filled with the sounds of people chatting and laughing and enjoying themselves. Ally would have gotten such a kick out of seeing it. There was a little part of me that believed I'd tell her about it one day, and I clung to that.

"Is that her?"

My heart lurched. I followed Tony's gaze to the photograph of Allison in the light blue dress resting on an easel. Linda must have had it blown up for the memorial. I nodded.

"She's beautiful."

"Thank you." The other photographs of her, the ones in which she was blond and too thin, nudged into my head, and I pushed them away. No. This was how I wanted to think of her that day, in her light blue dress with her face tilted toward the sun.

Tony scuffed a shoe on the grass. "I hope you don't take this the wrong way, but . . ." He hesitated. "After our conversation the other day, I was thinking that you might need someone to talk to, and I'd like to be that person. I think maybe I can help, or at least listen. I don't want to put any pressure on you or anything, but I was wondering if maybe you'd like to go out for coffee sometime. I know I'll probably see you at the library again, but frankly I don't want to wait until then if I can help it." He ran a hand through his hair. I could see that he was nervous. "I'm impatient, too," he said with a smile. "Add that to the list of things my wife—" He swallowed the rest of his words and shot me an uncertain look.

The pill silenced any suspicion I might have felt. He was just a nice, lonely man who wanted some company and was trying to help. There wasn't anything sinister behind it. I nodded. "How's Wednesday for you?"

His face broke into a smile, and even the sadness in his eyes seemed to recede a little. "Wednesday's great. Is there somewhere in particular you want to go?"

"There's a place a few towns over in Felton called Sunnyside Café—sweet little place. I'd rather not meet in Owl's Creek if that's all right with you. You know how small towns are."

He nodded. "Sure. How's three o'clock for you?"

"Perfect." I realized I was already looking forward to it.

I blinked and found Shannon standing in front of me in her uniform. She smiled at me shyly and I resisted the urge to gather her up in my arms. She looked so young. "I don't mean to bother you but there's a couple over there," she said, nodding toward a well-dressed older man and a brittle, nervous-looking blond woman. "They want to meet you."

I stared at them. There was something familiar about them, especially the man, though I couldn't quite put my finger on it. "Did they say what they wanted?"

She shrugged. "Just that they wanted to meet you."

It didn't matter if I couldn't place them, I guessed. They'd come to Ally's memorial and if they wanted to talk to me, they could. "Tell them to come over," I said. I turned to Tony to apologize but he was gone, and I saw his back striding through the crowd toward the parking lot. I realized I was still holding the flowers in my arms and put them down on the table beside me.

I watched the man come toward me, the blond woman by his side. He was tall and broad shouldered, his dark hair still thick and streaked with silver, and his eyes a dark blue. Maybe he was someone I worked with at the university, I thought. Though I wasn't sure why he'd feel the need to go through Shannon to be introduced if that were the case. His wife, or whoever she was to him, was like a perfect little doll, all slender limbs and cherry-red mouth and honey-colored hair. She reminded me of the photograph of Ally, the one of her in the fancy dress.

The realization finally broke through the syrup as he stepped toward me and extended his hand. It was David Gardner. And the beautiful woman on his arm, the one who reminded me so much of Ally, was Amanda. After all this time, I was finally meeting them. I blinked a few times and willed my mind to clear.

"Mrs. Carpenter, I'm so glad we're finally meeting," he said smoothly, placing a firm hand in mine and leaning in to kiss my cheek. "I'm Ben's father, David." There was a smell coming off him, something musky and citrusy and no doubt expensive. It instantly gave me a headache.

"I know who you are," I said, taking a step back and stumbling slightly on the uneven grass. They were the people who hadn't bothered to return my phone calls. They'd brought into this world the man who'd taken my daughter away from me. I took a deep breath and steadied myself. "Please," I said, "call me Maggie."

"Maggie, allow me to introduce my wife, Amanda. Ben's mother."

Before the words were out of his mouth, she had launched herself at me, her thin arms wrapping around me tight. "I'm so sorry," she whispered into my ear. My face was buried in her hair and I could smell hair spray mixed with perfume. Shalimar.

I extricated myself from her grip. "Thank you," I said quietly. "I'm sorry for your loss, too." My tongue felt thick in my mouth. I looked into the woman's eyes and saw heartbreak there, and for a second I felt sorry for her. I shook my head. *Pull yourself together, Maggie. Remember who they are.* "Did you get any of the messages I left for you?"

Amanda blinked quickly, like a cat who'd been sprayed in the face with a water bottle. "No," she said, the corners of her mouth turning down. "We didn't, did we, David?" David shook his head. "We've been away . . ."

"What about your housekeeper? Did she mention that I stopped by the house?"

Amanda's blue eyes widened. "You were in San Diego?"

I watched her face, but it didn't register anything beyond bland surprise. "I spoke to her," I said. "And your neighbor, too. You didn't hear?"

She frowned. "Like I said, we've been away. Still, Pilar should have mentioned this . . ." She placed a hand on my forearm and her eyes clouded with concern. "I'm so sorry you went all the way there for nothing."

I thought of the empty closet in the house in San Diego, the bare vanity table, Ally's presence eradicated except for a single hair. The anger cut through the haze. "It wasn't for nothing." My voice was terse and I saw the shock register on her face, a single ripple and then the smooth surface reappeared.

Amanda squeezed my arm. "Well, I'm just glad we're here now. We don't want to impose—we know that this is your day—but when we heard about it, we felt like we had to come over here and pay our respects in person."

Surprise registered through the fog. "How did you hear about it?"

"Oh, there was something in the paper about it. Someone sent us a link and we bought our plane tickets the next day." I didn't see how news of an event in Owl's Creek could have made it all the way across the country, but then I remembered that Ally was public property. I hadn't watched the news in days: I didn't know what they were reporting. "Your daughter was very special to us," Amanda continued. "She was a wonderful young woman. We have such wonderful memories of her, don't we, David? She made Ben so happy. They were like two little peas in a pod." The image of Ally swaddled in her baby blanket swam in and out of my head, fast as a minnow.

David nodded distractedly, his eyes assessing the crowd. "She was a great girl. If you'll excuse me . . ." Amanda and I watched him stride across the field toward the buffet table. David pulled a bottle of beer from one of the garbage cans full of ice, unscrewed the top, and took a long pull.

"You'll have to excuse my husband," Amanda said with a brittle laugh. "He hasn't been himself since Ben's death. It's hit him very hard."

I saw the dark circles under her eyes that no amount of makeup could disguise, and the worried set of her mouth. I couldn't deny it: this woman was suffering, and in spite of myself, I felt a swell of pity. "It's been hard on all of us," I said quietly.

She looked at me gratefully. "It's a beautiful memorial," she said, gesturing around at the field. "I wanted to do something similar for Ben—something informal, you know, and welcoming—but David insisted on a private service."

"You've had the funeral?" The news knocked the wind out of me. They had their son's body. They'd had the chance to say goodbye to him one last time. I might never get that same chance. My fingers trailed to the necklace around my neck. I had so little of her. They had so much.

Amanda nodded. "Yes, on Friday. It was held in the church where Ben was baptized. Where he and Allison were meant to be—" The words caught in her throat and I could see she was struggling not to cry. "I don't want to make a scene. I promised myself I wouldn't do this, it's just . . . seeing all of these people here for Allison, and meeting you, well—" She started crying in earnest now, tears streaming down her cheeks, and I found myself putting an arm around her and pulling her toward me. "It's just all so awful," she sobbed.

I watched David walk toward us from over the top of her bent head. "We should go," he said to Amanda. He didn't seem to notice that his wife was crying her eyes out, or that I was comforting her.

I looked up at him, dazed. "You've only just got here."

Amanda pulled away from me and wiped at the streaked mascara under her eyes. "David has some family business in Portland in the morning, so we're going tonight."

His face remained blank and impassive. "Well," I said, "it was very nice of you to come all this way. I'm sorry we didn't get the chance to talk more."

Amanda gave me a small, shy smile. "Maybe we could have dinner tomorrow, if you're free? We don't fly back to California until Thursday, and David's business will be finished by lunchtime tomorrow. Isn't that right, David?" He grunted. "We could come back up here for dinner before we leave. It looks like such a charming town. I'd love to see more of it."

It was all happening too quickly. I couldn't process it all, couldn't think. I willed my mind to clear. "There's a place on Main Street called Chloe's that's nice. I don't know if you like French food . . ."

"It sounds perfect. Eight o'clock?" She pressed herself against me in a hug. I could smell the faint traces of her perfume, bergamot and vanilla.

I watched them drift across the field into the parking lot, Amanda leaning heavily on David. She stumbled once and he reached out with a steadying arm and pulled her into him. She looked like a little china doll compared with him.

"How are you holding up?" Linda was standing next to me, face clouded with worry. "Shannon told me who they are. I thought about coming over, making sure you were all right, but I didn't want to interrupt."

"I'm fine." My head felt cottony and light. "They're coming back here tomorrow. We're going out to supper together."

She watched me closely. She always could read me like a book. "Come on," she said, putting an arm around me. "Let's get you home."

Allison

The housekeeper came most afternoons, which meant I had to get out of the house. I didn't like the way she told me to lift my feet when she was vacuuming, or tutted when she found strands of my hair in the drain. I didn't like the way she looked at me, like I was a visitor who had long outstayed my welcome.

So on days when she came, I made myself scarce. I went to the beach sometimes, but mainly I just drove around. Sometimes I made it as far as Carlsbad, where I'd park and watch the skateboarders clatter around the wide dome of the park, or I'd bring my sneakers and run around Lake Calavera. Once I went all the way to Los Angeles. I got close enough to see the smog lifting off the city but I turned around at the first snarl of traffic. Ben didn't like it if I wasn't home when he got back from work—he said he wanted to see my face as soon as he could, to wipe away the day—and I didn't want to be late.

The truth was, it didn't matter where I went. All of it was so much killing time. I had to keep busy, or else my mind would start to take me back to places I wanted to forget.

I drove south to Pacific Gateway Park and watched the gulls wheel in lazy circles across the sky. I tried to read the book I'd brought with me, but it couldn't hold my attention. My mind kept pulling me back to the coffee shop, and the man's red-rimmed eyes staring at me as he spewed lies across the table. He was crazy, I told myself. A lunatic. But every time I shoved his voice out of my head, it would come creeping back in. Relentless. Eventually I packed up and headed back, driving slowly to make sure the cleaner would be gone.

The door wasn't locked when I got home. I pushed it open and called out to Teresa, expecting her to appear around a corner holding a dust rag and a disapproving look, but instead I heard a man's voice coming from the back of the house. My heart caught in my throat. It wasn't Ben.

"Hello?" Silence. I dropped my bag in the hall and headed into the kitchen. I slid a knife out of the butcher's block with a shaking hand and held my cell phone in the other, finger hovering above the emergency button. I heard a muffled thump in the other room. "Who's there?"

"Allison? Is that you?" Sam appeared in the doorway of Ben's study clutching a sheaf of papers, his broad shoulders filling up the frame. He didn't look surprised to see me. Definitely not as surprised as I was to see him. He gestured toward the knife I still held in my hand. "You planning on putting that down?"

I dropped the knife on the counter. I felt like a fool. "I— I just wasn't expecting anyone to be here. Is everything okay?"

He waved the papers in the air before dropping them into his briefcase. "Ben asked me to swing by and pick up a couple of things. Work stuff." He moved too easily for such a big man, like a dancer, or a cat. It made me uneasy.

I told myself to stop being ridiculous. Sam was Ben's closest friend, his second in command. I'd known that he had a key to the house. It was totally normal for him to be there. "Did you want a drink or something?" I asked. Good. Act normal.

"Sure." He settled himself on the couch, his arms looped over the back.

I hadn't expected him to say yes. "White wine okay?"

He shook his head. "Just water for me."

I poured two glasses of water from the Brita before changing my mind and pouring myself a glass of the good Chablis we kept in the fridge. I took a few big gulps before heading back to the living room, and by the time I sat down opposite him its warmth was already snaking its way into my bloodstream. He was wearing too much cologne, and the air was thick with orange and bergamot, like he was marking territory with his scent.

"So." I cast around for something to say. "Everything good with you?"

"Fine, thanks. You?" He took a sip of water and placed his glass down gently on a coaster on the coffee table. He was not a man who left marks.

"Good! Great!" My voice was high and too bright. I took a swallow of wine and forced myself to smile. *There's no reason to be nervous*, I reminded myself. *Sam is just being friendly.*

I heard Liz's voice in my head telling me to be careful around Sam. "You might think he's your friend," she'd said, "but he's not."

"Good to hear. What were you up to this afternoon? Anything nice?"

"Not particularly. I went to the park today and read my book. I'm not that into it, though. The book, I mean." I was gabbling. "I might stop and read something else. How about you? Are you a big reader?"

"No." I waited for him to say more, but the silence stretched. He studied his carefully manicured fingernails. "Allison, have you been contacted by anyone recently?"

I felt the shock register on my face and took another sip of wine to hide it. "What do you mean?"

He looked at me evenly. "Has anyone been in touch with you recently—a stranger, maybe, or someone from your past?"

My head spun. Maybe he wasn't talking about the man in the coffee shop. Maybe he was talking about someone from my old life, one of the men who'd left messages on my phone late at night. The fist in my stomach tightened. "Not that I can think of," I managed, shaking my head.

He picked up the glass again, and I noticed the whiteness of his knuckles. "Are you sure about that?" I could feel him studying me. *You don't know what he knows*, I told myself, *so act like there's nothing to know.*

"I think so." I couldn't bring myself to meet his eyes.

"You think or you know?"

I was silent. I could hear my heart thudding in my chest, and I was convinced he could, too.

There was a smile fixed on his mouth, but his eyes were hard, unreadable. "A pretty girl like you, I'm sure you get approached all the time, but I want you to think about this carefully."

Acid built at the back of my throat and I forced myself to swallow it down. I thought back to the man in the coffee shop—was it possible that someone had seen us talking? Had there been anyone in there who looked familiar? My mind raced. All I could remember was a bunch of young mothers killing time with their babies and a few freelancers typing away on Macs. No one I knew. If I'd seen anyone, I would have turned around and left.

Sam leaned forward and rested his elbows on his knees. *His beautiful suit*, I thought. *It'll crease.* "You're not in any trouble, Allison. I'm trying to look out for you here. If anyone's bothering you, I want to know about it."

I hesitated. The man in the coffee shop wanted to hurt Ben. He was unhinged, deranged—who knew what he was capable of? Maybe telling Sam about him was the right thing. Maybe he could protect Ben. But if Sam confronted him, he might tell Sam about my past, and Sam would tell Ben, and it would be over, all of it, and I'd be left with nothing.

I couldn't risk it. I had to pretend I was ignorant. It was the only path to take. "No," I said finally. "I haven't spoken to anyone."

He let out a sigh and got to his feet. "If you change your mind, you know where to find me." He picked up his water glass and brought it into the kitchen. "I'll see myself out."

I waited until I heard the door click shut behind him, and then I swallowed down the rest of the wine in my glass and poured myself another. I checked the clock. Ten to six. Ben would be home by seven at the latest. We were supposed to go out to dinner with one of the investors and his wife. Ben had chosen the outfit he wanted me to wear before he'd gone to work that morning, a black dress with a high slit. "I want you to knock them dead tonight," he'd said when he pulled it out of the closet. "It's important."

I tipped the full glass to my mouth and finished it in a few quick swallows. The alcohol worked its magic, and already the shock had started to numb.

Sam had come there specifically to ask about the man in the coffee shop—there was no doubt in my mind. Which led to the question: If he was so concerned with what the man in the coffee shop said to me, did that mean that the man might have been telling the truth about Prexilane?

I thought back to the trial my father volunteered for after he'd gotten his diagnosis. The doctor told him this drug had proved successful in the first round, with tumors shrinking by as much as 80 percent. Now they wanted to try it on a larger sample size. He signed up on the spot. His diagnosis was terminal, with no more than a year to live. He had nothing to lose—at least that's what he thought.

The weight started dropping off him almost immediately. Within a few weeks, he was half the size he had been, just a ravaged husk of the man he'd been. We begged the doctor to withdraw him from the trial, but he refused. "Once you're signed up, there's no going back." So we watched as his life expectancy dropped to six months, and then three. We watched him disappear in front of our eyes, and there was nothing we could do about it.

"That's the risk you have to take," Dad said as he lay on the sofa, eyes wide and haunted in his thin face. "If you don't gamble on science, you don't win."

He had such faith in the system, and I'd followed him down the same path. Yes, the drugs don't always work, but their intention is always to heal. It's never to hurt.

But maybe he'd been naive. Maybe we both had.

I felt lost. A wave of homesickness washed over me so strongly that I braced myself on the counter to stop my knees from buckling.

Mom. The word pushed up my throat and pressed against my lips. I wanted to hear her clear, calm voice tell me that it was going to be okay, and to feel her fingertips scratch the place between my shoulder blades like she did when I was a kid and couldn't sleep.

I picked up my phone and tapped in the number I knew by heart. My finger was hovering above the Call button when I heard the sound of a key in a lock and the front door opening. "Hello?" Ben's voice called out from the hallway. "Sweetheart, are you here?"

I dropped the phone on the counter and shoved the half-empty bottle of white back into the fridge. "I'm in the kitchen!" My heart pounded in my rib cage. I looked at my hands gripping the countertop, nails perfectly manicured, diamond sparkling on my finger. I'd been a fool to think I could call her out of the blue after all this time. She wouldn't recognize me anymore. I barely recognized myself.

Ben came through the door, his tie loosened, his blue eyes sparkling. He wrapped his arms around me and lifted me off the ground. "I missed you," he whispered into my hair, and I tilted my chin up to accept his kiss. This was the only home I had now. There was no going back.

Later, before we went to dinner, I was sick in the toilet, the white wine coming back up as greenish-yellow bile. I made sure he didn't hear.

Maggie

I sat in the car outside Chloe's for a quarter of an hour, watching the time tick by on the dashboard clock as I went from on time to late, then later still. Chloe's was glass-fronted and candlelit, and I could see Amanda's and David's dim shapes in the window, heads bent together in conversation. Of course they would have seated them at the front. Chloe's was the type of place you went for special occasions—anniversaries and birthdays and graduations. It was the sort of place where I'd tell Charles to put on a tie before we got in the car, or at least a shirt with buttons down the front, but they still wouldn't be used to people like Amanda and David—people whose wealth shone out of every pore, and who didn't have regular clothes and good clothes, just clothes.

I didn't want to go in. I knew I had to, for Ally's sake, and probably for my own, but I didn't want to. I found myself dwelling on things after the memorial, doubting Amanda's sincerity when her eyes filled with tears, thinking David was more rude than stand-offish. I thought about the unanswered phone calls, and the big house up in La Jolla with its shuttered windows like dolls' eyes, and the house in Bird Rock stripped of all traces of my daughter. No, I didn't want to spend time with these people, but like so many things in life, I didn't seem to have a choice.

Amanda was on her feet as soon as I walked through the door. She was wearing a billowing white dress, all elegant folds and drapes, and I felt oafish in my sensible slacks and floral-sprigged blouse. When she hugged me, I could feel the tiny bones in her back through the fabric of her dress and had to stop myself from shivering. She tittered and fussed around me as I settled down at the table, and she sat down only when I had a napkin tucked onto my lap and a glass of water at my elbow.

David offered a polite handshake and then turned his eyes back to the wine list. He didn't get up.

I realized I was nervous. Now that I was there, what was I supposed to say? I could feel a flush coming on, the sweat pooling in the small of my back and dampening the armpits of my blouse. I took a sip of water and forced myself to calm down. "How was Portland?" I asked finally. I hoped they didn't notice my hand shaking when I put the glass back down on the table.

"Just precious," Amanda said, beaming. She tucked a honey-colored lock of hair behind her ear. "All of those little shops along the harbor are adorable!"

I nodded in agreement. "It's a cute little city. They've got some nice restaurants down there, too. James Beard winners and everything." Not that I'd been to any of them, but I'd read about them in the paper.

She gestured around the room and smiled. "Well, I'm sure here will be wonderful, too. The menu certainly looks exciting! There's so much to choose from . . ." She picked up the laminated bit of paper and studied it with a furrowed brow.

I didn't need to look at it myself. It was the same as it had been for the past fifteen years—duck confit and cassoulet and escargot for the adventurous. I hadn't thought I was hungry, but now that I was sitting there surrounded by the smell of garlic sautéed in butter, I realized I was starving.

The waiter arrived and we ordered. Steak for David, beef bour-guignonne for me, and a frisée salad for Amanda. "Aren't you going to be hungry?" I asked, even though I suspected it was rude to mention it. They probably had a whole ream of etiquette rules they followed, and I was sure I was breaking most of them. I wondered briefly if Ally had known them.

She let out a tinkling laugh and continued to shred the bread roll she'd been working on for five minutes but had failed to take a bite of. "It'll be plenty for me," she demurred.

David ordered a bottle of wine—red, expensive—without asking what either of us would like and then settled into his seat and pulled out his phone. "Just need to check a few things at the office," he said, frowning into the dim screen light.

He was a handsome man, David. There was no denying that. Amanda was pretty, of course, but David had the bones, even if there was a little extra meat on them now. I could see Ben in him clearly, at least from the pictures I'd seen. Same eyes. Same jaw.

Amanda grasped my hand in hers and smiled at me. "I'm so glad we're doing this," she cooed. "Your daughter was very special to me, and losing her and Ben . . ." Her eyes dampened, and she dabbed at them with her napkin. "It felt like losing two children at once."

I fought to keep my face neutral. Ally had been my daughter, not hers. I swallowed my anger with a mouthful of wine. "You two were close, then?"

Her face took on a dreamy look. "We spent every Thursday afternoon together wedding planning. Oh"—her hand grasped mine again, and I fought not to pull it away—"you should have seen the things we had planned. She was planning on having a dress made for her, though there was a gorgeous Vera Wang she had her eye on, and we'd reserved Torrey Pines for the reception. White roses, candlelight . . ." She sighed. "It was going to be a beautiful wedding."

"Sounds very nice," I said. I tried to picture Ally in a fancy white dress, gliding down a candlelit aisle. She and I had never talked about weddings much—she hadn't been one of those little girls who dreamed of a big white wedding. I'd always had the impression she didn't care much about marriage, period. But then again, things change. "I didn't know anything about it."

She gasped and raised her hand to her mouth, which had shaped itself into a perfect pink 0. "Maggie, I'm so sorry. I didn't even stop to think about—"

"It's fine," I cut her off quietly.

She placed her hand over mine. "Allison told me that the two of you weren't on the best of terms." I could see that she was choosing her words carefully, and shame swept over me. She knew that I'd failed as a mother. "I was hoping that things might clear up before the wedding. I'm sure she would have wanted you to be there . . ." The words hung above the table. She didn't believe what she was saying, and neither did I. We both knew my daughter hadn't wanted anything to do with me.

I placed my napkin on my plate and pushed out from the table. The hot flush had returned, and I could feel the sweat gathering in my hairline. I needed to get away. "If you'll excuse me, I'm going to run to the bathroom." Amanda watched me, stricken. David's eyes barely flickered from his screen.

The ladies' room was painted a garish pink, with a tufted stool tucked in one corner. I turned on the taps and ran cold water across my wrists. In the mirror, my face looked mottled and too shiny, like I'd just run for a bus. The mascara under one of my eyes had smudged, and my hair had escaped its clip, strands of it standing on end around my head like a halo. I looked like a crazy person.

I couldn't get rid of the image of Amanda and Ally cozied up together on a sofa, their heads dipped low over wedding magazines, their blond hair mingling. Had Ally gone dress shopping with her? Had Amanda sat in one of those plush reception rooms and waited for her to emerge in some frothy white creation? "Your daughter was very special to me." Had Ally thought of Amanda as a mother? Had she so expunged me from her life that she'd sought out a replacement?

I thought of Amanda's pretty, sweet face, and her tinkling laugh, and the warmth of her hand on mine. If Ally had, I couldn't blame her. I hadn't deserved Ally, not after what I'd done. I felt a sob threatening to build in my chest and blinked away the first tears.

I placed my forehead on the cool mirror. "Pull yourself together," I whispered to my reflection.

I saw that the entrées had arrived when I got back to the table.

David and Amanda had left theirs untouched, and my napkin had been neatly folded into a fan and placed on my chair. David poured a second glass of wine for himself and filled our glasses another few inches. I took a sip and felt my cheeks flush an even deeper red. I'd never been much of a wine drinker, and it was making me feel hazy and slow witted.

Amanda's eyes were on me, watchful. "I'm so sorry if I upset you," she whispered, bending her head toward mine. Her fork was poised above her plate of frizzy lettuce, frozen.

I tucked the napkin around my lap and waved her away. "You didn't," I said. I attempted a bright smile. "It's fine."

I felt her eyes still on me as I cut into the meat. "I know," she said, shaking her head sympathetically, "I know. It just comes over you sometimes, doesn't it? There are mornings when I wake up and for a split second, I forget what's happened. And then I blink and it all comes rushing back."

I raised my eyes to hers. I expected there to be something in them, some glint of calculation, but they were clear and blue and searching. "It's like living it all over again," I said finally. It felt good to admit it, and good, too, to see the understanding in her eyes.

"Yes," she whispered. "Yes, it's exactly like that."

David's phone started ringing, making all three of us jump. He snatched it off the table and hurried out the door without a word to us. Amanda gave me an apologetic smile. "You'll have to excuse him," she said. "He's under a lot of pressure at work."

I shook my head. "You don't have to explain."

"Ben's death hit him very hard," she whispered. "It's been such a . . . difficult time." I glanced over at her. Her fork was still balanced on the edge of the plate, her salad untouched. She looked like a lost little girl, waiting for her mother to pick her up and take her home.

"I'm sorry," I said, and I meant it. "What sort of business is David in?"

"Oh, something to do with finance," she said, brushing the word away as if it were a bad smell. "I don't really understand it."

I nodded. "And you? Do you work?"

She let out a little tinkling laugh. "No, not for years. I'm on the board of the San Diego Museum of Art, and I have a few pet charities. Enough to keep me busy."

"I understand Ally wasn't working when she was with Ben," I said carefully. "Do you know why?"

Amanda looked at me indulgently, as though I was a small child who needed her hand held crossing the street. "She didn't need to," she said. "Ben had more than enough to make her very comfortable."

I pushed a mushroom around my plate with my fork. Could it really have been that simple? Ally hadn't had to work, so she hadn't worked. It was so alien to the way we had raised her, so at odds with the young woman I'd known. I wondered if she'd at least kept her own money. I'd always told her how important it was for a woman to be independent. *Even if your relationship is solid as a rock*, I'd said, *it's always good to put a little something aside for yourself, just in case.* I thought about the empty wardrobe. Had she kept anything for herself in the end? Or had she really been left with as little as it seemed? I put my fork down and sighed. It was now or never.

"Do you know what happened to Ally's things?"

Amanda pushed a lock of hair off her forehead with a manicured hand. "What do you mean?" There was the flicker of something behind her pale eyes and I knew then that she was playing dumb.

"I went to the house in San Diego." My heart was pounding in my chest and I wondered if she could hear the nerves in my voice. I felt like a kid confessing to the teacher about cheating on a test. "I was curious," I explained. "I wanted to see where she lived, maybe take her things back with me."

"You should have called," she said coolly. I could see from the way she held her jaw that she was angry, and I felt my own anger surge once again. The warmth that had built up between us evaporated instantly.

"I think you know I tried, but you didn't seem to want to answer the phone," I said pointedly. "Anyway, I went to the house and none of her things were there."

She shrugged. "Maybe she didn't keep much there."

"I don't think you're understanding me," I said, though I was damn sure she did. "Her clothes, her jewelry, her books—all of it was gone. There wasn't a trace of her in that place."

Amanda smiled tightly. "I'm not sure what you want me to say."

"I'm asking you to tell me what's happened to my daughter's belongings." I was speaking deliberately slowly, but still my voice was shaking. "She was my daughter, which means her things belong to me now. I want to know where they are."

She shook her head. "It's not that simple, I'm afraid. Allison merged her life with my son's life and—not to put too fine a point on it—she was completely dependent on him." She spoke like she was explaining the idea of bedtime to a truculent child. "She was living in a house that was owned by Ben, and everything that belonged to Ben—including the contents of that house—are now tied up in probate until the will has been settled. So," she said, spreading out her hands, "my hands are tied."

I stared down at my plate as the humiliation swept through me. I'd let myself be taken in by her, and for what? What was I doing there, sitting across from this woman, asking her about Ally like a dog hunting for scraps, when she clearly wasn't going to give me a damn thing? I'd had too much wine, and my head had already begun to throb. I wanted, very badly, to go home.

"I'm sorry," I heard Amanda say, and then her fingers were on my wrist. The hard edge had dropped away from her voice again, back to its pillowed softness. "I've upset you again."

I kept my eyes on my dinner. I didn't want her to see that they were filled with tears. I could bear a lot of things in this world, but I couldn't bear letting her see me cry. It was what she wanted, I could feel it in the way she was studying me, like I was a lock she was determined to pick. "I'm not feeling very well," I managed to say, and then I scraped my chair back from the table and got steadily to my feet.

There was a burst of warm air. David walked through the door and settled himself back at the table. "I'm sorry about that," he said, fixing his napkin back in his lap and picking up his fork. "It was the office."

We both watched wordlessly as he started working away at his steak.

"Maggie isn't feeling well, sweetheart," Amanda said, putting a light hand on his wrist. "She's going to go home." He glanced up at me and frowned.

"I'm sorry to hear that. Would you like me to get you a cab?"

I shook my head. "I'm okay to drive myself home."

He nodded and I felt myself being dismissed. "Well," he said, turning back to his steak, "goodnight."

Amanda jumped up and followed me out to my car. "I'm so sorry that the evening hasn't ended well," she cooed. "I hope you know I would never want to upset you in any way."

"I'm fine," I said, waving her away. "It's just a headache. Thank you for a very nice evening." I attempted a smile but it came out more like a grimace. She reached out and pulled me into her and I allowed myself to be embraced. The heady smell of her perfume filled my head and it started pounding in earnest. I disentangled myself from her arms and climbed into the car. She was still waving as I pulled out onto the road, her face livid red in the reflection of my taillights.

Allison

By the time I'm a hundred yards away, I can see that it isn't so much a cabin as a large building pretending to be a cabin, complete with fake-log cladding and a pitched roof. There's a stretch of manicured grass out front, and a tall wooden fence ringed a clearing out back. A small blue sign hangs from a hinge and swings lightly in the breeze. The letters, painted in red, spell out "Chuck's Trailstop."

My stomach gurgles excitedly. Who knows what delights line Chuck's shelves? Boxes of Wheat Thins and Cheez-Its. Bags of Wise potato chips in exotic flavors. Ice-cold cans of Diet Coke and Arizona iced tea and cellophane-wrapped snack cakes and oh my God, what if they have those little tubs of cheese dip?

I eye up the store from my perch. It's a risk, of course. Maybe one I shouldn't take. I still have a few crackers left over from the hunter's blind, and I could try to hunt something with the rifle, though that seems unlikely, seeing as I don't know how to shoot. I also know that I'm borderline starving and I'm not sure how much longer I can keep going on so little fuel. The jerrican of water is almost empty and I have no way of knowing when I'll find water again.

So I don't have a choice, really.

I have to go in.

But if I'm going to go in, I have to make sure that I call as little attention to myself as possible.

I put a hand to the ungodly rat's nest that used to be my hair. My leggings are stained and ripped, my arms covered in scrapes and bites, and my sneakers—well, they're barely shoes at this point, more like pieces of rubber loosely strapped to my feet. I can't even begin to imagine what I smell like. I'm carrying a leather overnight bag instead of a backpack, I'm wearing inappropriate clothing that's torn and filthy, and I have a stolen rifle swinging around my neck.

There's work to be done.

I dust myself off as best I can and wipe my face on the back of my sleeve. I dig out the sweatshirt—still relatively clean, miraculously—and pull it over my head. The sun is baking down and I immediately start to sweat. I rake my fingers through my hair, snagging on thickly coiled snarls. Christ, I wish I could cut it all off. I tie it back with a length of string and hide it under the hood. I dig into the pocket of my bag and pull out a few soggy bills. Nine dollars, to be exact. All the cash I have to my name. I tuck it into my bra.

I need to go in there looking like your average day hiker, not some nutcase survivalist, meaning I can't take the gun or my bag inside. There's a thick bank of shrubs near the path, so I chuck the bag and the rifle behind it, arrange the branches to make sure everything's fully hidden, and head for the shop.

A bell chimes my arrival.

The first thing that hits me is the air conditioning pumping through the vents. My arms prickle with goose bumps and I'm suddenly grateful for the baggy sweatshirt. The second is the smell. I sniff the air, trying to place it. It reminds me of something. Parking lots in summertime. Backyard barbecues. My mouth starts to water.

There they are, glistening as they slowly rotate in the glass case perched on top of the counter. Hot dogs. My stomach gives a plaintive growl.

"Can I help you?"

I turn to find a man in his early thirties in a Cubs baseball cap towering over me. I can't bring myself to feel fear. All I care about right now is my hunger. I smile and avoid his eyes. "Can I have a hot dog, please?"

I feel him take in my dirty clothes and tattered shoes in a single glance. "Sure thing." He walks over to the case and opens it. The smell hits me afresh, salty and fatty and rich. He tongs a hot dog into a bun and hands it to me. "That'll be two dollars. Ketchup and mustard are on the side," he said, nodding toward the service station.

"Thanks." I pull the bills out of my bra and hand them over the counter.

He pinches the bills between two fingers and slides them into the cash register, his eyes flickering across my face.

I can't wait any longer. I take a bite. The tensile skin gives way beneath my teeth and the salty flesh fills my mouth. The bread wads itself between my teeth as I chew. I swallow and take another bite, then another. The man watches with detached interest.

"You want another?" he asks as I polish off the last bite.

I nod as my tongue works a bit of gristle from a molar.

He picks up the tongs. "You're not exactly dressed for the trail," he says, nodding at my sneakers. "You been out long?"

I shrug and try to look casual. "Just a day trip."

He points to a reddish-brown stain on my leggings. "Looks like blood. You hurt?"

I shake my head. "Just mud. I slipped."

He looks for a minute as though he's going to say something else, but instead he gets another hot dog out of the case and hands it to me. I set to work and finish it in a few swift bites. "You're pretty hungry for a day tripper," he says, taking two more wilted dollar bills I scrounge out of my bra. "Where'd you start from?"

I wipe my mouth with the back of my hand and stall for time. "Just over the ridge," I say finally. "I can't remember the name of it."

He's watching me more carefully now. "You out here on your own?"

My antennae go up. I'm filthy and smelly and battered and bruised but I'm still a woman on my own and I know that there's still no end of terrible things that could happen to me because of it. I shake my head. "My friends are down by the river."

He goes to the window. "I can't see them."

I feel a prickle of fear at the base of my spine. "They're probably just around the corner. I should go find them." *Get out get out get out.* "I'm just going to grab a couple things," I say, retreating into the aisles. "I'll just be a sec."

He gives me a funny little smile. "Take your time."

I try to quell the rising panic and force myself to concentrate on the task at hand. I want to run but I need the supplies too badly. A jar of peanut butter—$1.99. Sold. A pack of survival biscuits. $2.50. I hate myself for eating that second hot dog. I can already feel the fat from it sliding through my intestines. I'll pay for it later.

I make my way back up to the counter and place the items on the counter. I palm a Snickers from the shelf below and place it on the counter, too. "Have you got someplace I can fill up my water bottle?"

He jerks his head toward the window. "There's a pump round back. Help yourself."

"Great." My eyes meet his for the first time and I realize they're a soft, warm brown. They remind me of my father's eyes, and I see the same familiar kindness in them. I let myself relax just a little. "Just out of curiosity, how far is it to the nearest town?" Wherever it is, I wouldn't be able stay there, but maybe I could sneak a night in a motel while I got some money together, take a shower, eat a hot meal.

"Just over the mountain," he says, nodding east. "About twenty miles. That'll be $4.99."

I shake my head when he tries to give me my change. "Just put it in there," I say, gesturing toward the Take-a-Penny dish. I can't imagine a scenario in which a single penny will do me any good. "What's the best way to get there? The quickest route, I mean."

He raises an eyebrow. "On foot?"

"Yeah."

He shakes his head. "It's too far to get to on a day trip."

"It's not for today," I say, too fast. "It's just if we come back again. My friends and I."

He hands me the plastic bag. "There's a trail that takes you up the mountain. It's not too steep, but you'll want proper hiking boots for it, not just sneakers. You just follow that until you get to the other side and then you'll want to hook a left when you come to the pond. The main road is down the bank and it'll take you straight into town."

"Great," I say. "Thanks. I'll remember that for next time."

"Remember to bring the right clothes next time, too, and some more food. You could get in trouble coming out here unprepared."

"Thanks for the tip," I say, backing toward the door. "I'll be like a Girl Scout next time, I swear." I pull open the door and am about to leave when it catches my eye. There, stacked in a neat pile in a wire stand, is the *Denver Post*. A leader tucked at the bottom of the front page snags my vision. TOWN MOURNS PLANE CRASH VICTIM—PAGE 3. I pick up a copy and pull it open.

I recognize the photograph they've run of me from one of the countless charity galas we attended. I stare at the woman, blond and polished as a new penny in a black sheath dress, and feel no connection. This woman isn't real. She was something decorative designed to hang nicely off an arm. More important, according to the thick black type below, she's dead.

Allison Carpenter, 31, fiancée of Prexilane CEO Ben Gardner, was killed when her plane went down in the Colorado Rocky Mountains. Gardner was also killed in the crash.

A bubble rises inside me and bursts. They've got it all wrong but it doesn't matter, because it means I'm free.

I glance farther down the page and see another photograph, this one smaller. My heart catches in my throat as my mother stares back at me.

"You all right?" the man calls from the counter.

"Fine!" My voice is strangled and too loud. I hold the paper closer to my face. There she is. I can see her clearly now, standing in a field wearing that yellow dress we bought together years ago, shading her eyes from the sun. She's aged. The skin has loosened on her neck and jowls, and bags darkly under her eyes. She's too thin. She looks tired. Guilt wrenches at my gut. I did this to her.

I read the caption underneath.

Owl's Creek, ME: Maggie Carpenter, mother of Allison Carpenter, at the town's memorial for her daughter.

That's when I notice it. The necklace around her neck winks at me, familiar as my own hands. In the background, shadowed and blurred but undeniable, I see his face. My blood turns to ice.

I wheel around. "Do you have a car?"

"Excuse me?"

"Do you have a car?" I don't have a choice. I have to trust him.

The man frowns. "Sure, but I—"

"I need to get to the nearest town as soon as possible."

He raises an eyebrow. "I thought you had a car close by."

"It'll take too long," I explain impatiently. "I need to go now. It's an emergency."

"What's happened?" Concern washes over his face and I realize I was right to trust him.

I shake my head. "I can't say."

He hesitates. "I've got a shop to run. I can't just drop everything just because you tell me you need to get somewhere in a hurry."

"I promise, I wouldn't ask if it wasn't important." He looks at me and I can see he's wavering. "Please."

He nods, just once. "Give me ten minutes to close up shop."

"Thank you. I can't tell you how much this means."

"Don't worry about it," he grunts. And then, "Do you want to tell your friends you're going?"

I look at him evenly. "We both know I don't have any friends out there."

He smiles. "I'll meet you out back."

I run to get the gun.

Maggie

I saw him before he saw me. Five minutes late, hair still wet from the shower, and with a harried expression I hadn't seen on him before. He spotted me and waved before making his way up to the counter. He mimed a drinking action at me—*Do you want one?*—and I pointed at my still-full coffee and shook my head. I watched him chat to the waitress and laugh when he struggled to find his wallet in his own back pocket. When he'd finished ordering, he took a seat across from me at the table and smiled.

"Sorry I'm late," he said, running a hand through his hair. "I'm all over the place this morning."

"You're fine," I said, waving away his apology. "I'm always early for everything. Drives people crazy."

"Nothing wrong with being early."

I laughed. "There is when you're clogging up their waiting room."

The waitress came around and set a cup on the table in front of him. Hot chocolate with whipped cream, from the look of it. He must have noticed my eyebrows being raised because he shrugged and looked sheepish. "Don't tell the doctor," he said, dipping a spoon into the whipped cream and sticking it in his mouth. "I've got a bad sweet tooth."

I nodded. "Salt's my thing." Charles used to tease me about it. He called me the potato chip queen of Owl's Creek. "Not that I'm allowed much of it anymore," I added ruefully.

He smiled sympathetically. "Cholesterol?"

"Blood pressure." The doctor had tried to put me on medication, but it made me light headed, so I'd stopped it and changed my diet instead. I still missed potato chips.

He took a sip of his hot chocolate and wiped the cream from his mouth with the back of his hand. "How was the rest of the memorial?"

I thought of David and Amanda turning up out of the blue, and our stilted dinner the night before. I didn't want to get into that, not then, so I shrugged and said, "Oh, you know, fine. Good to see so many people."

He nodded encouragingly. "Seemed like a nice turnout. A lot of people loved your daughter, that's for sure." He lifted the mug to his mouth and hesitated. "Sorry I had to run off like that."

I glanced at him across the table. I'd been wanting to ask him, but I was afraid it would sound rude, or worse, but now he'd opened the door himself. "Where did you go?" I asked, keeping my voice light.

He shifted in his seat. "I felt like maybe I was imposing a little. Showing up like that . . ." He looked uncomfortable admitting it, and I felt myself soften. "I thought maybe you'd think I was weird or something."

I felt a wince of regret. He'd turned up trying to do something nice, and I'd made him feel he was in the wrong. I straightened my shoulders and looked him in the eye. "No. I was glad you came."

"Good." He fumbled with his spoon and started tapping it on the side of his saucer. *Clink clink clink.* A dark shadow had spread across his face.

"Tony, is there something on your mind?"

He looked up, surprised. "Me? No. Why do you ask?" He followed my gaze to the spoon in his hand and put it down gently on the saucer. He smiled sheepishly. "I'm sorry. Nervous habit. I don't know what's got into me today. Tell me," he said, reaching across the table to take my hand. "How are you holding up?"

I tried not to think about the warmth of his fingers on mine. "Oh, you know. Getting by."

"Maggie," he said softly. "You can be honest with me." There was that look in his eye again, like he could see straight through to the heart of me. I felt my defenses slip away.

I sighed. "Everyone seems to think that I'm not dealing with my grief properly, that I'm being irrational by not accepting what happened to Ally." I raised my eyes to his. He was watching me steadily, waiting. "Do you think I'm being irrational?"

He shook his head. "It doesn't matter what I think. What do you think?"

"I don't know," I said. "I know I should be trying to get on with my life, but it all feels like a smoke-and-mirrors game. Just when I think I'm getting somewhere, starting to understand what happened with Ally, starting to accept it—poof!—it disappears right in front of me." I sighed. "I feel like I'm losing my mind."

He squeezed my hand. "You're not losing your mind."

We were silent for a minute, the swish and whir of the coffee machine rumbling in the background. My fingers reached for the necklace. I held the cool gold disk for a moment before letting it go.

"Pretty," he said finally. "The necklace, I mean. Is it new?"

"No," I said quietly. "It was Ally's. They found it at the crash site."

He nodded. "Must be nice to have it." He reached out as if to touch it and stopped himself, but I could still feel the ghost of his fingers on my skin, and an electric current seemed to run through me. I pulled away and he smiled apologetically. "Didn't mean to make you jump."

I shook my head. "I'm just a little jittery, that's all." I wondered if my cheeks were burning as red as they felt. I scolded myself for being so ridiculous. "The parents of the pilot came," I said abruptly. "They were the people who came up to me right after you and I were talking. I don't know if you saw them—fancy-looking couple?"

He shook his head.

"Well, they were there. We had dinner last night, too."

He looked at me sharply. "You had *dinner* with them?"

I shrugged, suddenly defensive. "They came all the way from California. I didn't feel like I had much of a choice."

I waited for him to tell me I'd been a fool, but he just nodded. "Well, I guess that makes sense. What did they say?"

I thought about David's staring at his phone and Amanda's brittle laugh. "Nothing." It was half-true: they hadn't said anything useful. Still, the evening gnawed at me. Amanda's charm had turned cold as soon as I pushed her for something she didn't want to give, and David had been so distant, so remote . . .

I looked at Tony sitting across from me, his paunch hidden behind his rumpled T-shirt, his big hand with its gnawed cuticles resting on mine. Surely I could trust this man. Or at least I wanted to, badly. "I went to her house in San Diego," I said finally. "The one she shared with that man." I told him about the housekeeper giving me the cold shoulder, and the place being stripped of anything of Ally's.

The color drained from his face as I talked and I saw his hands gripping the edge of the table. "Did you tell his parents about this?"

I remembered the carefully controlled anger in Amanda's voice when I'd asked her, the floral smell of her perfume, the fuggy, underwater feeling of too much wine, and felt a flush of renewed humiliation. "Amanda told me they were tied up in probate." Now that I'd brought it up, I didn't want to talk about it. I picked up the mug to take a sip and then remembered it was cold.

He shook his head. "It's bullshit." I looked up at him sharply, startled by the anger in his voice. "You're her mother. You're her next of kin. Her things should go straight to you. I thought . . ."

He trailed off and I waited for him to continue. "You thought what?" I prompted, but he just shook his head and scowled. It felt like he'd retreated to some remote part of himself, one that I didn't have access to. "Well," I said eventually, "I'm not sure what to do. I suppose I could get a lawyer involved, but it seems crazy to chase after something I'm not even sure exists anymore." I put my hands up. "Who knows, maybe they've already chucked everything out."

He sat back in his chair and rubbed his face with his hand. "Those bastards," he muttered. His eyes met mine and I was surprised to see they had filled with tears. "People like that think they can get away with anything."

I stared at him. "What do you mean, people like that? You don't know them." I felt suddenly off balance, like a trapdoor had opened up under my feet.

"Of course I don't," he said sharply. "It's just that . . ." I watched him cast around for his next words. He was being careful, too. "They're rich, right?" I nodded. "Well, that's what I meant. Rich people think they can get away with anything. They treat people like us—normal, hardworking people—they treat us like dirt." His face was red, his eyes shining. People in the café were starting to look over at our table. "They ruin people's lives and then they laugh about it, because they don't care about anyone but themselves and their precious pile of money. Someone should stop them. You know that? Someone should make them stop. They shouldn't be allowed to get away with it."

He wasn't there anymore, I could see that. It scared me a little. I placed my hand gently on his. "Tony," I said quietly. "Tony?"

He seemed startled to see me. The anger receded from his eyes, replaced by a horrified sort of contrition. "I'm sorry. My wife always told me I was too hotheaded. I didn't upset you, did I?"

"You scared me a little," I admitted. "I mean, I appreciate you getting angry on my behalf, but—"

"I know, I know, I got carried away. Shit." He looked embarrassed, like a dog caught chewing up a newspaper. "I guess it's the old sixties socialist in me," he said. "Always rooting for the underdog."

I gave him a smile and felt the balance between us return. "And I'm the underdog?"

He returned the smile, though his held a sadness in it. "Afraid so," he said. He leaned across the table and plucked the locket off my chest. I could feel the warmth of his fingers on my skin through my thin cotton shirt, and the electric current charged through me again. "My wife had one of these, too," he said, weighing it in his hand. "But hers was silver. She kept a lock of hair hidden behind the photograph—her mother's." He kept hold of the locket in his palm and raised his eyes to mine. "It's good that you have it now. Make sure you keep it close to your heart." The insistence of his gaze unbalanced me, and I was sure now that I was blushing. I pulled away and the locket slipped from his hand and fell back against my chest.

There was a tension between us now, though I couldn't tell where it was coming from. I could feel him willing me toward something, like he was his own center of gravity and I was being pulled into it. I put a hand to my forehead. I felt suddenly, deeply tired.

Tony placed his palms on the table and leaned toward me. "Maggie, you think she's still alive, don't you?"

"A part of me does," I said, and as the words came out of my mouth I realized they were true. "They never found her body, and the necklace . . ." I shook my head. "Even if she is gone, I need to understand her, and him, and everything that went with it. Does that make sense?"

"It does." He reached over and patted the top of my hand. "Keep going, Maggie. Keep digging. You'll get to the truth, I know it." His fingers slid underneath my palm. "But make sure you're careful. These people . . ." He shook his head. "Just be careful, that's all. I wouldn't want anything to happen to you."

Allison

The smell of me has filled the cab of the truck—the tang of dried sweat coupled with something rotten—and I roll the window down to let the air in. After I've walked for so long, traveling at this speed feels treacherous, and my eyes hurt from trying to single out the trees as they whiz past.

I think about the blurred face in the photograph. If he's there, it means they won't be far behind. I should have been more careful. I should have known they wouldn't let it rest. I should have known they'd come after her, too.

"So, what's this big emergency?" The man's voice cuts through the silence and I jump. I forgot that someone was in the truck with me, even though he is driving.

"A family thing." I keep my eyes on the passing trees.

"You read about a family emergency in the newspaper?" I can hear the incredulity in his voice. Fair enough. I barely believed it myself, and it was my life.

Still, I'm not looking for conversation. My head's too full of my own shouting voice to concentrate. "Look," I say, "I appreciate the ride, but I'm not really up for talking."

"Fair enough."

I steal a glance at his profile. He has a nose like a hawk and a strong, square jaw, like something that should be carved into Mount Rushmore. One hand rests on the top of the steering wheel, the other on the stick shift. It's like being driven by GI Joe.

I turn my face back to the window. I can see the mountain crowning in the distance, its snow-capped peak looming over the landscape. It's hard to believe I was on that mountain just a couple of days before, clinging to the side and praying for mercy.

The driver clears his throat. "You're that girl, aren't you?"

I look at him. His eyes are fixed on the road. "What girl?" I keep my voice neutral, uninterested, but panic swells inside my rib cage.

His eyes dart toward me. "The one from the plane. I recognized you from the news."

I shake my head. "I don't know what you're talking about." *Play dumb*, I remind myself. *Don't give him anything.*

He smiles, and my throat tightens. "I wasn't sure at first. You look a little different from your photograph, though I suppose that's to be expected under the circumstances. But then I saw the look on your face when you were eating that hot dog. People only get that look when they're desperate from hunger, and you don't get desperate from hunger on a day trip."

"It was a long day." I've misread him—he isn't one of the good ones. Maybe he's one of theirs, sent here to find me. Maybe he's just your standard psychopath who wants to chop me into pieces. Or maybe he's just an average Joe sensing a paycheck and a moment of fame for being the man who brings a damsel in distress back to civilization. It doesn't matter: all paths lead to trouble.

He sighs impatiently. "There's no use in trying to say otherwise. I know you're the same girl who was on that plane."

My hand grips the door handle and I give it a tentative tug. It's locked. I'm trapped. All I can do is try to bargain with him. "What do you want for keeping quiet?"

He looks at me now, a quick glance, but enough for me to catch the surprise on his face. "What do I want?"

I nod. "What do you want?"

A short laugh. His eyes go back to the road. "I don't want anything."

I don't like the fact he's playing coy. It most likely means someone's already promised him something. I try again. "I'll have money soon. Once we get into town. I could give you some."

"I told you, I don't want anything." We lapse into silence. My animal brain is screaming now. Maybe I can grab the wheel and force him to the side of the road. But then what? I'm in the middle of nowhere, weak and exhausted, and he's twice my size. He'd overpower me in a second. I study the window. Could I reach around and open the door from the outside? How fast are we going—fifty? Sixty? Will I survive the fall, or die on the asphalt? His voice cuts in suddenly, interrupting my thoughts. "Look," he says quietly, "I don't know what happened on that plane or how you managed to survive or where you're going to next. It's not any of my business. But I see a young woman such as yourself on her own like this and possibly in trouble, and I have to ask if there's anything I can do to help. So. Is there anything I can do to help?"

My fists tighten. *Don't believe him. You can't trust him.* "You're already helping me by driving me into town," I say, fighting to keep my voice light.

He grunts. "Anything else?"

"You're doing plenty," I say. *I don't want your help. Your help is a trick.* Then, as a gamble, "Just don't tell anyone you saw me."

He nods, his eyes locked on the road. "You've got my word." Silence settles between us again. My heartbeat begins to slow. A squirrel darts out from the brush and stops dead still in the middle of the road. The truck swerves to avoid it but the squirrel takes off in the wrong direction and slips under the wheel. We feel the slightest of bumps as we roll over it. The crunch of its tiny bones is drowned out by the hum of the engine. The man curses under his breath and I see the regret flash across his face. I glance in the rearview mirror. It's just a smear of blood and fur on the pavement now, and before long it's out of sight.

The man clears his throat. "I couldn't help but notice that you have a hunting rifle."

The fear grips me again. Is this how he does it? With my own gun? "That's right."

Another darting glance. "You know how to use it?"

"Sure," I say, as confidently as I can muster.

"You sure about that?"

I falter. I watched my parents, but that doesn't mean I know. Watching and knowing are two different things. But if I admit that, will he use it against me?

He senses my hesitance. "Why don't I teach you how to use it properly?" he offers, eyes fixed on the road. "Just in case you need it."

He's offering me a choice. I can accept his help, which may or may not be genuine, or I can reject it. I realize, with a resigned sort of horror, it doesn't matter: if he's going to kill me, he will. There's nothing I can do about it. I stare out the windshield. I guess I should choose the option that might end with me knowing how to shoot a gun. "That would be good," I say finally.

We pull onto the shoulder and hike a few hundred yards into the woods. My heart is pounding now, the adrenaline coursing through me. I keep the rifle close to my side.

We walk until we reach a clearing. I fight the urge to run. *Don't let him see your fear*, I remind myself. *Fear is a trigger.*

"Okay," he says, gesturing toward the gun. "Give her here."

I pause for a minute. My fingers are clutching the barrel of the rifle so tightly, they've turned white.

He notices and smiles. "I'm not going to hurt you, I promise. I'm just going to show you how to load it." He holds out his hand.

I regard his outstretched hand warily. "Can't you show me while I hold it?"

He smiles and shakes his head. "You don't have a very trusting nature, you know that?"

I hug the rifle to my chest. "Learned from experience."

He watches me for a minute. "Okay, you hold her, I'll load. First, you want to make sure the muzzle is pointed away from you—and me, for that matter." He gently moves the muzzle so it faces a line of trees in the distance. "Next, you want to pull back the bolt. Now look in the chamber."

I peer inside.

"You see anything in there?"

I shake my head.

"Good. That means it's clear." He picks up a few bullets from the box by his feet. "You want to load in a few rounds. This gun'll hold three shots at a time." The bullets click into place. "Okay, now that she's loaded, you want to push the bolt back into place. This moves the shots into the chamber. Got it?"

I nod.

"Great. That's the safety. If it's up, it means if you pull the trigger, nothing will happen. If you flip it down, you're ready to fire. Now go ahead and flip it down."

I flip it down.

"You want to brace the butt of the gun on your shoulder joint—like this." He lifts the gun and gently rests the butt against my shoulder. "Good. Now, with this arm, you want to steady the muzzle, and then you place your other hand on the trigger. Got it?"

I nod.

"Now take a couple of big breaths to steady yourself. Look through the crosshairs and find your target. Got one?"

I focus on a knot in the trunk of a pine tree about ten yards away.

"Got it? Good. You're ready to shoot. You always want to fire on an exhale, so take a deep breath, let it out, and pull the trigger."

The recoil knocks me back and he catches me just before I fall. The crack of the rifle has left my ears ringing and the reverberation echoing through the woods. I rub at the sore spot on my shoulder from where the rifle kicked back, and feel yet another bruise start to bloom.

He smiles at me. "You okay?"

I nod. My mouth has gone dry. I don't feel okay, not at all.

"Try again," he says encouragingly, "and this time, try to hit the target."

I focus my eye on the crosshairs. I brace the gun against my shoulder, lock my arm, and take a few deep breaths, the smell of gunpowder filling my lungs. I think of my mother, the light way she held the rifle, how her body stilled before she took the shot. *Calm*, I think. *Steady*. I breathe out and pull the trigger.

I stagger back a step but manage to keep on my feet this time.

"Not bad," he says, nodding approvingly. "You almost got it. You want another try?" I shake my head, and he laughs. "Fair enough. You might turn out to be a decent shot one day. C'mon, let's head back to the truck."

I realize, with a sense of flooding relief that makes my knees buckle, that I'm safe. He's not going to hurt me after all. He really did just want to help. My stomach wrenches violently and I hold up a hand. "One second," I say, before stumbling into a thatch of tall grass. The contents of my stomach empty noisily on the ground.

"You okay there?" he calls.

I rasp out a couple of breaths standing hunched over the remnants of the two hot dogs. "Fine," I croak. I wipe my mouth with the back of my hand and head back toward him. "Sorry you had to hear that."

He shakes his head. "I've heard worse. I'm Luke, by the way." He offers me a hand and I take it.

"Allison," I say. "But I guess you knew that already."

We climb back into the truck and Luke swings us back onto the road. He goes back to staring out the windshield and I go back to staring out the window. My stomach is still sour and the taste of bile won't leave the back of my throat. The adrenaline has deserted me now, and I feel exhausted. The trees blur into a wall of green.

We pull into the town around six o'clock. It announces itself with one of those old-timey wooden signs—WELCOME TO BUCKSHOT CANYON! POPULATION 2,960—and quickly reveals itself to be one long street filled with half-shuttered shops and the occasional neon-lit bar.

"Think there's a motel around the corner," Luke says, and sure enough, we find ourselves parked outside a white stucco building with a vacancy sign posted out front. There's a yellowish light coming from one of the windows on the ground floor, and I spot a woman sitting behind a desk, staring into space, her mouth chewing mechanically. "I can't vouch for the rooms," he says, "but I'm guessing they'll be better than where you've been staying." Luke opens the door of the cab and hops out. "You coming?"

I linger. "How much do you think it is for the night?"

He glances back at the motel. The small parking lot is deserted except for a rusted-out Honda, and the railing on the second floor looks like it's been kicked loose. "If it's any more than thirty bucks, you're getting ripped off."

"Okay." I still don't move.

He leans back into the cab. "Don't worry, I can cover you, if that's what you're worried about."

I shake my head. I've already accepted too much from him. I can't accept any more. "I don't want you to do that."

He grins. "Well, I don't think you've got much of a choice."

He's right, I don't. Not unless I want to try skipping out tomorrow morning, but that's risky. It could draw attention. I could get caught. Finally, I nod gratefully. "I'll pay you back. I'll have money first thing in the morning. I'll send it to you, just give me your address."

He folds his arms across his chest. "The shop doesn't pay much but it pays enough for me to let a girl have a room with a hot shower."

"I'll pay you back," I say again, insistent. I can't bring myself to rely on a man's credit, not anymore. Not ever again.

He walks around the side of the truck and opens my door. "We'll see about that. Now let's get you into a room."

He swings my bag over his shoulder and strides toward reception. The heels of his boots click on the pavement.

I swing open the door to find him already peeling off two twenties and handing them to the clerk. There's a television mounted above the door and her eyes never leave it, even as she counts out six singles in change. I glance up to see what she's watching. Judge

Judy is seated on her perch like a crow, yelling at someone for not keeping her receipts. The receptionist hands the key over to Luke, who hands it to me along with the six dollars. "In case you get hungry for something other than peanut butter," he says with a shrug.

I walk him back to his truck and watch as he climbs in. "You going to be okay?" he asks, the roof light like the moon's glow above him.

"I'll be fine," I say, not believing it but not disbelieving it now, either. I've learned enough to know not to question these things. "Thank you. I can't tell you how much——"

"Don't mention it." He sticks an arm out the open window and places a hand on my shoulder. "I don't know what happened to you out there, and I don't know where you're going or what sort of mess you might find yourself in, but you strike me as the surviving type, so I'm not going to worry about you."

There's a charge from his fingertips as they touch my skin, and I imagine inviting him upstairs to my room. It would be so easy to let it happen. The heat of another person. The taste of his mouth on mine. The feeling of safety, however fleeting or imagined. Instead, I smile and tap the hood of his truck. I can't let him get dragged under with me. I have to see this through on my own.

He starts up the engine. "Well, goodbye, Allison. It's been a pleasure." He tips an imaginary hat and throws the truck into reverse. The wheels kick up a cloud of dust and I watch until his taillights disappear.

Maggie

I tossed my keys onto the counter and heaved myself into a chair. I was jittery from the extra caffeine and my nerves were frayed. I replayed the conversation with Tony in my head: the look on his face when he told me to be careful, and the way his mouth tightened into a thin line when I asked what he'd meant by it. He just shook his head and repeated his cautions, and then a few minutes later he made his excuses and left. I didn't know what to make of it, or of him, and our meeting had left me with a strange taste in my mouth.

I looked around the kitchen. The countertops were grimed with coffee stains and toast crumbs, the tile floor was scuffed and dull, and the mail was stacked in a precarious pile on the desk. The whole place looked like it was behind a filmy pane of glass. I'd always prided myself on keeping a clean home, but looking around I could see that I'd let the place go. I was embarrassed to be living like this. Embarrassed that I'd let people into my home in this state.

I pulled myself to my feet and rummaged around in the cabinet under the sink for cleaning products. Windex in hand, I set to work cleaning off the stove top and wiping down the windowpanes. Balled-up, grease-smudged paper towels collected in my wake, and slowly but surely the kitchen started to look like itself again. The caffeine hummed through my veins as I tackled the desk with a bottle of Pledge. A layer of dust came up with the first swipe, and I scolded myself again for letting things get so bad.

I straightened up the pile of mail and moved to shove it into the cabinet above the desk, promising myself I'd look through it next. A letter slipped out from the bottom of the stack and fluttered to the floor. I picked it up, my back groaning in complaint. It was the letter from the bank saying it was closing down Ally's account.

I read it over and felt myself getting angry all over again about the bank running down her account like that. I knew I should just let it go, be glad that a piece of paperwork had taken care of itself, but the injustice of it still rankled. I finally decided to go down there myself and give them a piece of my mind.

I shoved the cleaning products back under the sink, pulled on a fresh T-shirt, and headed out into the muggy late-afternoon air.

The bank was getting ready to close by the time I got there, with just one window still open, the rest of them shuttered. Wendy waved to me from the window and came out to give me a hug.

"I'm sorry I couldn't make it to the memorial," she said, pushing her glasses up on the bridge of her nose. She nodded toward the closed door of an office in the back. "Peter wouldn't give me the time off, the jackass." This was said in a theatrical kind of stage whisper, though her voice still echoed through the place. "Linda was in here earlier and said it was a beautiful day."

"It was." Wendy had gone to high school with us, and the six of us—me and Charles, Linda and Jim, Wendy and her husband, Mike—used to get together to play cards or go out to supper together. That changed when Charles died—Linda and Wendy encouraged me to still join their card nights, but it wasn't much fun being the fifth wheel, so I stopped coming and eventually they stopped asking. Still, I had a fondness for Wendy. Everything about her was just a little bit bigger than you expected—her voice, her laugh, her jewelry. She was oversize in nearly every way.

"Now," she said, smiling her too-big smile, "what can I do for you today?"

I pulled the letter out of my bag and handed it to her. I watched as she scanned it, her smile turning to a frown. "I'm sorry," she said, handing it back to me. "Somebody should have given you a call rather than sending a letter like that." She shook her head. "It's these damn computers—everything's automated these days."

"It's not the letter," I said, brushing away her apology. "That account's been dormant for years, which means the only way it would have gone to zero is if the bank was charging for use of the account." I felt myself getting hot and flushed as I spoke, the old anger coming so quickly to the surface. "What I want to know is why a bank like Saint Mary's—a local bank that my family has been using for God knows how long—is charging their customers like they're some big corporation. It's not right, Wendy."

She shook her head sympathetically, and when I'd finished she led me over to one of the too-firm armchairs that lined the side of the office. "I'm sorry you've gone through all this," she said as she handed me a paper cup of water. "I think there has to have been some kind of mistake. The thing is, we don't charge our customers banking fees."

I lifted my eyes to hers. "You don't?"

She shook her head. "The board suggested it a couple of years ago, but Peter wouldn't stand for it. He thinks it'll be bad for business, and for once he's right." She looked at the letter again. "Do you mind if I have a quick look into this?"

She scurried back behind the teller window and I heard her clacking loudly at a keyboard followed by a series of sighs and tsks and gasps. Finally, she emerged with a sheaf of printouts in hand.

"I'm not technically supposed to show you these as you're not the account holder, but given the situation . . ." She handed them to me and busied herself with straightening out a stack of leaflets while I scanned them. They were Ally's bank statements from the past year. The account, unlike what I'd assumed, was far from dormant. In fact, over the past few months, she'd been making steady deposits—each a few hundred dollars—followed by one withdrawal that wiped out the whole balance. Every last penny.

I squinted at the date listed next to the withdrawal: it had been made just a week before the plane had gone down.

Allison

I look at my key. Room 113. I swing the bag over my shoulder, tuck the rifle under my arm, and trudge up the steps to the first-floor mezzanine. Mine is the last one on the row.

I turn the key in the lock and push open the door. The smell of cigarette smoke and mildew and stale sweat hits me before I set foot inside. I flick a switch and a fluorescent light flickers uncertainly overhead. The carpet is red-and-blue plaid and worn bare in places, a queen-size bed marooned in its center, a pair of flat pillows lying limp on the floral-sprigged comforter. A cheap pine wardrobe squats in the corner next to an unplugged minifridge, and a fan spins lazily overhead.

I drop my bag and the rifle and kick the door shut. Already my own stink has begun to overpower the other stinks in the room, and I wonder if I can find the energy to take a shower. Instead, I drink gulps of bathroom tap water from a cloudy toothbrush glass and try not to look at my reflection in the mirror. I'm not ready to see myself, not yet. I peel off my clothes and leave them in a pile on the bathroom floor before turning out the light and climbing into bed.

It's still early, only just twilight, and I can hear the hum of cars as they drive past and the occasional blast of a stereo. I get up and check the lock on the door and slide the chain through the bolt, then press my ear to the door. I listen for the muted sound of the television in reception but can't catch it.

I stare at the phone cradled on the bedside table. Cream-colored, plastic, with a note taped to the base warning that long-distance calls will be charged. My fingers itch to pick it up and dial her number, but I can't risk it. They might have bugged her phone, and no one can know that I'm coming until I get to my mother's door. Not even her.

The mattress creaks beneath my weight and a spring digs into my shoulder blade. The heat has gone out of the day and I can feel the air moving beneath the fan's blades through the thin sheets. It's strange, being in a bed. My back has grown used to the hard ground, and the yield of the mattress feels like I'm lying on top of an enormous marshmallow. The silence is strange, too. No crickets chirping, no mournful hoot of an owl. Just the occasional murmur of a passing car and the steady, low whir of the fan.

I reach for the remote on the bedside table and press the red power button. The TV sputters to life. There's no cable and the reception is hazy and everyone's face is a strange, lurid orange, but the noise that fills the room is instantly soothing. I flick through the channels. An old episode of *Friends*. *Dr. Phil*. *Entertainment Tonight*. All this has been here while I've been out there. Same as always.

I land on a twenty-four-hour news channel. A blond woman in a bright red dress tells me that the stock market has fallen six points today and that there are worrying signs for the economy ahead. A gray-haired man in a gray suit shakes his head grimly at her before turning toward the camera. "Tonight, police are investigating a woman accused of placing her partner in critical condition following what some are calling a violent rampage. Witnesses describe seeing Melanie Traynor screaming and holding a knife while her young children looked on—"

I click off the TV. I've seen enough.

It took three days after Sam came to the house for me to dig the scrap of paper out of the ski boot in the back of my closet and dial the number. He hadn't sounded surprised to hear from me. "You ready to hear what I have to say?" That was it. No questions about why I had changed my mind. It was like he'd known I would

243

change it all along and wasn't interested in hearing the details. We arranged to meet the next day.

He barely glanced up when I met him at the bench in Murray Ridge, just lowered his newspaper an inch and nodded for me to sit down. It was a Monday afternoon, and the park was deserted except for a pair of young mothers pushing pigtailed toddlers on the playground swings and a college kid in a pair of cargo shorts walking a pack of unruly dogs. In the distance, a lawn mower hummed. When the breeze shifted, I could smell the lemon-crisp scent of freshly cut grass.

I sat down. "Ben's business partner, Sam—he came over to the house and was asking questions about you." The man lowered his paper. I saw the shock register on his face, along with something else. Fear.

He cursed under his breath. "What did he say?"

"He didn't say your name or anything"—not that I knew it, I realized—"but he asked if I'd been approached by anyone about Ben's business."

"What did you say?" His eyes bored into mine.

"I told him I didn't know what he was talking about."

"Do you think he believed you?"

I thought about Sam's inscrutable face as he questioned me, the anger in his voice when he realized I wasn't going to tell him what he wanted to hear. I shook my head. "I don't know."

He stood up abruptly, sending the newspaper that had been tucked neatly beside him flying. "Forget it."

"What do you mean?"

"It's too risky. Just forget the whole thing. Pretend you never met me. That guy . . ." He ran a hand across his mouth. "You don't know what he's capable of." His face drained of color, and he suddenly looked ten years older, and scared shitless.

Sam's hands suddenly loomed into my vision, with their neatly manicured fingernails and flat, meaty palms. He held them close to his body, fists tensed, like a boxer waiting for the chance to throw a clean punch. Fear rushed up my throat, bitter and acidic.

Sam was Ben's best friend. His second in command.

And now I knew for sure that he was dangerous.

I close my eyes and will myself to sleep, but I can't stop seeing the photograph from the paper. She looked so tired, like a woman who'd been beaten up by life. I didn't think I'd ever seen her like that. Growing up, she'd been the strong, sure hands that would lift me off the swing set, the arms that had held me when I cried. My father had been filled with magic, his eye always lighting on something new, his desire to know the world addictive and intoxicating, but my mother had been the earth.

And then she took him from me.

I can still feel the nub of the carpet under my bare feet, and the smell of sickness in the air—antiseptic mixed with sour breath and bedsheets that turned fetid, no matter how often they were changed. I'm standing in the doorway. My father is lying on the sofa, his eyes lightly closed, his face drawn and jaundiced. At first, I think she's holding his hand, but then I see that she has one hand on the morphine pump and the other on his chest and that her face is wet with tears and then her eyes meet mine and I know, I know that he is dead.

It wasn't that she had done it. I knew, deep down, that it was what he wanted, and that he would have asked her to do it. It was that she had done it without me. And, worse, that he had, too. He had taken himself away from me, and in that moment I had hated them both for their selfishness, for thinking that I was too weak to face it, for cutting me out. That's how I felt: as though I'd been surgically extracted from them, like a vestigial organ that had proved itself useless. Of course, now I can see that I was the selfish one. What my mother did was an act of love, pure and simple, and I rewarded her by taking my love away.

I push away the shame. No. I've punished myself enough for one lifetime. I think of the photograph in the newspaper, the locket around her neck, the face looming at the edge of the frame. I have to go back, even if I'm terrified. Even if I know I probably won't make it out. Even if she's found out everything I did, and hates me for it, just like I hated her. None of it matters now. I have to save her.

I get up and pad across the room to my bag. I unzip it and plunge my hand in, feeling around the lining for the heavy edge of card. I nudge it toward the slit in the lining and pull it out.

I flick the passport open and look at the photograph. I stare back at myself, blond and tanned. I'm smiling at the camera but my eyes look frightened. The name underneath is not my own. It's the name I chose to fit the person I was going to become, exotic and mysterious, a mermaid washed ashore. It was going to get me to Thailand. At least that's what the guy I paid in cash had promised.

I pull out the ticket that's tucked between its pages. One way to Phuket. I try to imagine the sun on my skin, the white sand spread out in front of me, the scent of coconut milk and jasmine in the air. The turquoise of the ocean. I look at the ticket again. The flight is meant to leave from LAX in a week. I thought it would be over by then. I thought I'd be free and clear.

I slip the ticket back into the passport and slide it back into the lining of my bag. Maybe it's not too late, but first, there's work to be done.

The Man was waiting for him outside the shop. His boots were covered in dust from the trail and he was smoking the end of his last cigarette.

—Can I help you?

—A pack of Marlboro Reds.

—Give me a second to open up.

Luke unlocked the door and flicked the light switch. It was early but the sun was already hot. He'd have to stock the fridges with water.

He walked behind the counter and picked a pack of Marlboros off the shelf.

—You need matches?

—I'm good.

—That'll be $5.65.

The Man handed him a ten.

—Cigarettes are cheap out here.

—I guess that depends on where you're coming from.

—Not from here.

—Yeah, I figured.

Luke handed the Man his change and waited for him to leave. Something about the Man unsettled him. He looked too comfortable in himself. Like his bones were too loose in his skin.

The Man slid the cigarettes from their cellophane and tapped the pack in his palm.

—Where did you take her?

—Where did I take who?

—You know who.

They stared at each other across the counter. Luke felt a trickle of sweat slide down his spine.

—I don't know what you're talking about.

The Man placed his hands on the counter and leaned forward. Luke could see the black curve of his eyelashes now, the stubble marking his upper lip, the dip of his cleft chin.

—You're going to tell me where you brought that girl one way or the other. I recommend you choose the easy way. The Man smiled.

Luke could smell the tobacco on his breath.

—Though I do admit I enjoy the hard way, if that's the way things go. Luke felt his knees buckle.

Maggie

I sat with the bank statements spread out in front of me on the table. I felt a strange kind of comfort in knowing that she'd kept something back for herself, some shred of independence, though it was mixed with a sense of unease. Why had she decided to use this account after so many years? Was it because she was trying to hide something, or protect herself from something—or someone? Nearly two thousand dollars withdrawn in a single day, all in cash. What had she needed it for?

I remembered what Amanda had said about Ally not working. "Ben had more than enough to make her very comfortable." Like she was a child, or an invalid. But if it was true—if she really hadn't felt the need to work because he provided for her—why would she have felt the need to secretly squirrel away money in an old account? And it *had* been a secret. I was sure of it.

I thought about what Tony had said about David and Amanda, how wealth made people like them think they could get away with anything. It seemed to remove them from the dirty business of how the money was made, too. Amanda didn't seem to have much of a clue about what David did, though I couldn't tell how genuine she was in her ignorance. Amanda was a woman who wanted you to think she was just a pretty face, but underneath, she was sharp as a tack.

I googled "David Gardner businessman," "David Gardner finance," and "David Gardner San Diego," but nothing much came up—mainly just brief mentions of him and Amanda in relation to Ben. Amanda had said he'd been doing some business in Portland, so I tried that, too, but came up blank.

I sat back and stretched my arms over my head. I'd slept badly the night before, and my back was stiff and complaining. I stared at the blinking cursor on my screen and considered my next move. It was hard to avoid having an internet footprint, especially if you had money, but it looked like David had managed it. But I knew that avoiding the public was one thing. Avoiding the government was another.

I logged onto the Securities and Exchange Commission's database and typed in David's name. Reams of impenetrable entries popped up. I made slow work of scrawling through them, and can't pretend I understood much of the language—all "quarterly reports" and "statement of acquisition"—but one phrase appeared over and over: "Hyperion Industries." My pulse started racing. That was the company that the receptionist had mentioned when I'd gone to the Prexilane offices, the one I'd later read had been looking to buy out the company.

I typed it into the database and up popped an entry for a company registered in San Diego, California. David Gardner was listed as the sole director. David had been trying to buy his son's company.

The arthritis in my hands was acting up again thanks to all the time I'd spent at the keyboard, but it receded to background noise as my fingers flew across the keys. I typed "Hyperion Industries" into Google and came back with page after page of articles detailing Hyperion's ruthless reputation as a corporate raider, buying up ailing companies, stripping them of their assets, and selling the bones for a profit. The words "hostile takeover" came up again and again. "Hyperion Industries is the pirate of the financial world," said one piece in *Forbes*, "and unwilling shareholders are made to walk the plank."

It kept going. An airline in the 1980s, a chain of grocery stores in the 1990s, a steel manufacturer in the early 2000s: all of them had been stripped and sold by Hyperion.

And now David wanted to do the same to Prexilane.

Outside, I heard the rain start up again, and I got up to close the windows. My eyes felt grainy from staring at the screen for too long and my shoulders ached, but adrenaline pumped through my veins. I was still staring into the woods, but one by one the trees were taking shape.

Allison

It's the sun that wakes me, streaming through the slats of the blinds and creeping around the edges of the door. I open my eyes and stretch, every muscle straining. I can't remember falling asleep— just the hours spent watching the ceiling as my mind raced—but in the end I slept deeply and blankly and the edges of it still blur the perimeters in my head. It takes me a minute to remember where I am, and why, but then the pieces slowly come together and I close my eyes against it.

Sam watched me even more after that day at the house. I could feel his eyes on me whenever we were in the same room, tracking me like I was his prey. At parties, I'd look up and see him staring at me, face inscrutable, fists clenched tightly by his sides.

What he didn't know was that I was watching him now, too.

I asked Ben casual questions about him: How long had he known Sam? Where had he grown up? How did he spend his free time? Ben fielded the questions bemusedly. "Why?" he'd said when I asked if Sam had a girlfriend. "Are you interested?"

I'd let out a peal of laughter that jolted us both. "No!" I said. "He just seems lonely, that's all."

Ben had smirked at this. "Don't worry about Sam. He is not exactly sitting at home waiting for the phone to ring."

When Sam came to the house, I would linger by the closed door of Ben's study, straining to hear their conversation. Most of it was indecipherable—talk of deliveries and actuals and forecasts and net growth. But one night, I heard them arguing. Fear prickled at the base of my spine. I thought of Sam's broad shoulders, his large hands, his cold, calculating eyes. He was capable of violence, I was sure of it. Ben's body had the lean, ropy muscle of a long-distance runner. He was fit, but he wouldn't stand a chance against someone like Sam. He'd be snapped like a twig.

I pressed my ear against the door and held my breath.

"I thought you took care of it." This was Ben, his voice low and steady, but I could hear the anger coiled inside it. I'd never heard him sound like that before.

"I did." Sam's voice was softer, almost pleading. "They want more money. They say—"

"I don't care what they say. Just make it go away. Remember, you're in this just as deep. If I go down, you're coming with me."

I heard footsteps approaching and pressed myself against the wall just before Sam burst through the door and rushed down the hallway. Ben emerged a few minutes later, relaxed and smiling. I had moved to the sofa and was pretending to read a book.

"Hey, baby," he said, leaning down and kissing the top of my head. "Let's go out for supper tonight. Sushi, maybe?"

I smiled up at him. "Sounds great."

I watched him lope down the hallway and thought of the clenched look on Sam's face as he came out of the study, and the way his voice had wavered during the argument.

I realized then that it wasn't that Ben was scared of Sam. It was the other way around.

I swing my legs off the edge of the bed and pull myself onto my feet. The blood drains too quickly and I stumble drunkenly into the bathroom, bracing myself on the edge of the sink. I lift my eyes to the mirror and watch the shock register on my own face. I don't recognize the person staring back.

The skin on my nose is flaked and peeling, and my lips are cracked and bloodied at the edges. There are hollows below my cheekbones now, my skin tanned a deep nut brown and peppered with a constellation of freckles. My eyes are still the same washed-out green, but the skin around them has gained faint, spidery lines. There's something else that's different: a hardness that seems to come from the back of my skull. I wonder if other people can see it in me, too.

I raise my hands and untie my hair. The honeyed blond tones poor Kai had gone to such lengths to perfect are now a brassy yellowish white, bleached and dried out from the sun. Thick coils of it spring from my head like Medusa's snakes, and now my fingers can't make their way through more than an inch without snagging. I finger the scab covering a wound on the back of my skull. The blood is matted into the hair around it, crusted and stiff. Jesus, I think. What a mess.

I'd spent years growing it out, carefully shampooing its lengths and massaging conditioner into the ends. I'd wanted hair that would stream seductively down my back or tickle a man's bare chest as I leaned over him in bed. I'd wanted hair that I could use as a tool or a weapon.

He'd loved my hair. He'd come up behind me sometimes and take a lock of it in his hand, as if he were weighing its worth.

I can't wait for it to be gone.

I fetch the nail scissors from my bag. It's slow work, methodical, gathering thin bunches between thumb and forefinger and snipping close to the roots, but eventually I'm left with a head of messily cropped dark hair. There's a pile of tangled blond straw in the sink, and I scoop it up and shove it into the trash. It looks faintly absurd peering over the lip of the can, like one of those long-haired little dogs that girls in San Diego carry in their Louis Vuitton totes. I resist the urge to reach down and pet it. Instead, I run a hand across my new spiky tufts and admire my reflection. My cheekbones are like razors, my eyes two shining stones. Now I look how I feel: streamlined and bullet smooth.

I turn on the shower and climb in. I turn the dial all the way into the red, and steam quickly fills the air. I position my whole body underneath the showerhead and let the water pour over me, blistering and painful. I unwrap the complimentary disk of soap and lather it between my hands. The water in the tub turns gray as the accumulated grime slowly sloughs off me. I slide my hands over my legs, my shoulders, my stomach. Each part of me is different than it was: slimmer and sinewed and dotted with patches of thick, calloused skin.

I take a deep breath, pour shampoo into my cupped hand, and wash my newly sheared head. It feels like washing a kiwi fruit. I rinse off and step out onto the bath mat. There are still half-moons of dirt packed under my nails and I pick them clean before drying off. I examine the wound on my thigh, now a jagged red-black seam running up my leg, its teeth smiling at me. It should have had stitches. I smile back before padding naked into the bedroom and gathering my clothes.

I pull on the dirt-encrusted leggings and one of the sweat-stained T-shirts and force my feet back into the sneakers I swore I'd never put on again. The movement reignites the smell trapped inside the fibers, and the stench hits the back of my throat. God, how was poor Luke able to stand being in the truck with me for that long? Once I get my new clothes, I'll have to burn the old ones, though who knows what kind of ghouls will be released in the flames.

The pawnshop is shut when I get there, so I spend four of my six remaining bucks on a cup of coffee and a blueberry muffin and sit on the stoop waiting for it to open. The caffeine pulses through me and the muffin is almost unbearably sweet, the sugar coating my already-furred teeth. I remind myself to pick up a toothbrush after this, and some toothpaste, as well as new clothes and shoes.

A burly looking man with a longish white beard turns up at ten to nine and pulls up the metal shutter with a screech. I stand up and brush myself down. I'm nervous, I realize, and eager to impress.

"Can't come in here with that," he says, nodding toward my coffee. I dash across the street and chuck the paper cup into a garbage can. When I get back, the door is open and the lights are on and the man is already squatting on a stool behind the counter, a newspaper spread out in front of him. I wonder briefly if I'm in it.

"What've you got?" He doesn't bother to look up.

I slide the ring off my finger and place it on the counter. He keeps his head bent low as he picks it up but I can see his eyebrows raise. He pulls a loupe out of one of the desk drawers and peers at the diamond through the lens.

"This yours?" His voice is neutral, but I can feel the doubt in it already.

"Yes." My voice sounds false and too bright. *Relax*, I chide myself. *You're not doing anything wrong. It's your property, and you have every right to sell it.*

He raises his eyes to mine and I see him take in my cropped hair and dirty clothes. "You sure about that?"

I nod, a little too eagerly. "It was my engagement ring." He grunts, and I can tell from the look on his face that he can't imagine any right-minded man proposing to me, never mind one brandishing a three-carat flawless solitaire. It's fair enough—if I were him, I'd think I was lying, too. If I close my eyes, I can still picture Ben down on one knee in front of me, holding out the little black velvet box like it was the key to the world. "It's mine," I say again, but I choke on the word. I stare down at the ring sitting in a stranger's meaty palm and feel the acid pain of my old life being burned away. I swallow it down.

He shakes his head, and for a minute, my heart sinks. And then I see him look at the diamond again, and I realize he doesn't care if I'm lying. A diamond that size has that effect on people. "I don't have the cash to cover this," he says, blowing out his cheeks. "Even if I did, there's not a lot of call for $30,000 engagement rings around these parts."

My heart flutters in my chest. I need this money, badly. *Keep calm*, I tell myself. *Hold your nerve.* "What can you give me? I'm open to offers." I hope I sound casual, but I know I sound desperate by the smirk that flickers at the edge of his mouth. He knows he's got me.

"Seven thousand."

"Fifteen." It's not even close to what I'd hoped to get for it, but I guess plans have changed. Fifteen thousand would give me enough money to get myself to Maine and make a start on a new life once all this is finished. If I live to see it finished.

He stares at the ring. I can see the wheels turning in his head. He knows he won't see something like it in a place like this again, but it's a lot of money for him up front—maybe too much. Finally, he lets out a long sigh. "I'll give you ten and that's my final offer. You'll have to give me until tomorrow to get it to you."

I shake my head. "It needs to be today."

His eyebrows raise and I realize he wasn't expecting me to accept the offer. I should have pushed back one more time, asked for $12,500. It doesn't matter—it's too late now. He knows he has me over a barrel. "Well, sweetheart," he says, his smirk fully intact now, "I guess you're out of luck."

I nod. I know enough to know when I'm beaten. "Fine. No later than ten a.m., though. And I'll need that seven you mentioned up front."

He studies me for a long minute, and then heaves himself off his stool. "Give me a minute." He walks into the back room and I hear a series of beeps. A code being punched into a safe. He returns with a stack of hundreds held together by a rubber band. "I'll give you five," he says with a smirk, "because I'm a nice guy." I reach out to take the bills and he holds them just beyond my reach. "The ring stays with me," he says.

I feel a flurry of panic. "Shouldn't we sign an IOU or something?"

"You gonna give me your name?" I don't say anything and he laughs. "I didn't think so. Look, I'll give you my word, all right? I ain't in the business of screwing people over, and I don't intend to do it to you."

"What do you call ten thousand dollars for a thirty-thousand-dollar ring?"

"Business."

I drop the ring into his palm and he hands me the stack of bills. I tuck them into my sports bra, where they bulge conspicuously. "Ten a.m.," I say.

He grins. "I'll be here with bells on."

I walk out of the shop and stand on the sidewalk for a minute. The bills feel heavy against my chest and I can feel the skin underneath turning clammy. I look down the street, scanning the storefronts for something useful, though I know that's unlikely. Towns like this stopped having useful stores on their main streets years ago, hollowed out by strip malls on the outskirts of town. Just like Owl's Creek. Which means I need to get to a strip mall on the outskirts of town, which means the first order of business is to get myself a car.

I duck my head back in the shop. The man looks like he's been expecting me.

"Where's the nearest car dealership?" I ask.

"Blowing through it already, huh? 'Bout two miles from here. Take a left at the end of Main and follow Route 32. It'll be on your right after about a mile and a quarter. Chet's, it's called, and that's his name, too. Can't miss it, or him."

Chet's is right where he said it would be. A row of multicolored flags tacked up on the low-slung cement building wave a half-hearted greeting, and there's a row of dusty cars lined up in front. Chet must have seen me walking up the road because he's standing outside waiting for me in a pair of grease-stained overalls, an expectant smile stretched across his face.

"I hear you're in the market for a new car," he calls out before I've even set foot in the parking lot.

My footsteps crunch on the gravel, and my lungs fill with the smell of motor oil. "News travels fast around here."

Chet's a few inches shorter than me, with a round face and pink cheeks, and the bottoms of his overalls pool over his thick-soled boots. He shrugs affably and wipes his hands with a rag. "Bill called from the shop to give me a heads-up. Told me I had a pretty young lady coming to see me and I'd better be presentable. So, what sort of thing are you looking for?"

"Cheap," I say, thinking of the wad of cash stuffed in my bra. I need to hold on to as much of it as I can. "But something that won't break down on a long drive."

"How long?"

"The East Coast," I say vaguely.

He lets out a low whistle. "How cheap?"

I think for a minute. "You have anything for a grand?" I know I'm lowballing him, but the higher I start the higher he'll go, and I can't afford to be ripped off the way I was at the pawnshop. I need every penny of that money, especially if the guy doesn't cough up the second half tomorrow.

He laughs. "I do, but I wouldn't count on it getting you to the East Coast. The best I've got for you is this old gal," he says, slapping the roof of a Subaru station wagon. "She don't look like much but she's dependable. She'll get you where you need to go, no problem."

A high-stakes cross-country journey in a Subaru: just like I'd always imagined. "How much?"

"Thirty-five hundred." He shoots me a sideways glance and I can tell he's sizing me up for a reaction.

I shake my head. "I'll give you two."

He sighs and runs a hand across his face. His fingers still carry traces of grease, and they leave black marks down either side of his mouth. He offers up an apologetic smile. "You know I'd love to help a pretty little lady like yourself, but I've got a business to run here."

I fold my arms across my chest. Chet's poker face isn't as good as the guy at the pawnshop's, and I can tell that he's itching to make a sale. There can't be much business out here in the middle of no-where, judging by the layer of dust on the car hoods. "Two and a half in cash and throw in a dealer's plate."

He pulls a face. "What do you want a dealer's plate for?"

"It doesn't matter." I don't want him to ask questions. I just want him to sell me the car so I can get out of here.

He passes a hand across his face again, and this time a deep smudge appears on the tip of his nose. "Three and you got yourself a deal."

I fudge the paperwork, signing Amanda's name in place of my own. The idea of her being the proud owner of a used Subaru is enough to tip me into hysteria, and I peel out of the lot gulping down laughter and struggling to see the road.

I asked Chet to point me toward the nearest Walmart—I knew there'd be one, there always is—and he'd told me it was a couple of towns over, in Ponderosa. I drive carefully, taking it slow and waving cars past when they stack up behind me. I know that driving this way is probably more conspicuous than speeding, which is what everyone else seems to do on these long, wide, near-empty roads, but I'm too nervous to go above fifty. My head feels clouded, like it's stuffed full of that pink insulation foam they used in houses during the eighties, and I'm worried I'll lose con-centration and crash.

I walk through the swooshing sliding doors and feel the blast of air conditioning hit my scalp. I'm suddenly self-conscious, aware of my short hair and dirty clothes that still carry the smell of dried sweat. The irony of being the worst-dressed person in Walmart isn't lost on me, and I allow myself a little smile as I grab a cart and head quickly toward the beauty section.

I spent hours haunting the aisles of drugstores in San Diego, swiping nubs of eyeliner on the inside of my wrist and smudging them to see how they'd blend. I could afford to go to the fancier places, of course, where black-smocked women flocked around me, cooing over my complexion and pressing free samples into my hands, but I liked going to Rite Aid and CVS better, the brightly lit rows of cosmetics holding the familiar promise of a new self, or at least a concealment of the old.

Now I roll past the eye shadow trios and candy-colored nail polishes and blunt plugs of lipstick without a second look. I feel a faint thrill at my lack of interest, like a teenager changing the dial when her former heartthrob comes on the radio. I realize, with a shock, that I'm not interested in being pretty. What can a new lipstick offer me now?

I toss a toothbrush and toothpaste into the cart, along with a stick of deodorant and a pack of bandages. My toes have started bleeding again; I can feel the slippery squelch of blood in my sneakers. I head for the clothes department and throw in a three-pack of white T-shirts and a pair of jeans. A new bra, a pair of underwear. A six-pack of athletic socks. I find a pair of plain white sneakers in the shoe department and toss them into the cart, too. I want to dress anonymously, invisibly. I want to be anyone.

I take a detour to the hunting aisle. I figure they'll take one look at me and turn me away, taking me for a lunatic or a vagrant, but instead the guy at the counter hands me the box of ammo without batting an eye. I hurry to the checkout counter before he has time to change his mind.

I bundle the bags into the trunk of the Subaru and drive back to the motel. The cleaner is changing the bed and gives me a look of open disgust when I walk in. I see the sheets piled up in her cart, the white cotton smeared with dirt and sweat. I smile apologetically and wait outside on the walkway. There's a red plastic chair next to my door and I sit down heavily and rest the bags at my feet. I stare out across the parking lot. Mine is the only car in the lot apart from the receptionist's Honda.

I feel the box of bullets against my foot and wonder just what I plan on doing when I get to my mother's house. Every option I come up with is histrionic and absurd, like something out of one of those telenovelas the maid used to watch while she cleaned the house. Then again, my life has been histrionic and absurd for a while now. I should be used to it.

———————

Ever since overhearing the argument between him and Sam, I found myself studying Ben's every move, looking for some kind of clue. I started noticing how often he went into his study when he took a call, the way he locked his laptop in a drawer at night, the fact that he always changed the subject when I asked about work, demurring that he was too tired to discuss it, or that I'd find it boring.

I was getting nowhere. I called the man from the coffee shop again and begged him to meet with me. He knew something about what Ben and Sam were into, and I needed to know what it was.

He took a little convincing. "I told you," he said, "it's too dangerous. If they even begin to suspect that we're talking . . ."

"They won't," I said. "I'll be careful." There was silence on the end of the line. "You're the one who approached me in the first place. You can't just trigger a bomb at the center of my life and then walk away when it starts to smoke. You owe it to me to tell me what the hell is going on."

We met at the park. He reached into his briefcase and pulled out a sheaf of photographs. "Here."

I flicked through the photos. They were mostly of women, though there were a few photographs of babies, too, gazing up at the camera with huge clear eyes. "Who are they?"

"They're people who've died because of Somnublaze," he said quietly.

I looked at him. "But—why would a child be on an antidepressant?" I held up a photograph of a little boy no more than a year old. "Why would a doctor prescribe something like that to him?"

He smiled sadly. "He didn't take the drug. His mother did."

I shook my head. I didn't understand.

"Somnublaze was specifically marketed to women with postpartum depression," he explained. I stared at him blankly. "One of the side effects is temporary psychosis."

It took a moment for it to sink in, and when it finally did, I went cold. "You mean these kids were killed by their own mothers?"

He nodded once, and turned to gaze out across the park. It was a beautiful day, the clear air carrying a tinge of sea salt, the sky a bright cobalt blue. It felt wrong to be talking about such dark things.

I remembered a story one of the customers at the bar told me, about how he'd been alone in his house late one night and had seen a stranger staring up at him from the street below. When he caught the stranger's eye, the man charged his front door, headbutting it over and over until the frame splintered. The customer locked himself in his bedroom, pushed a desk against the door, and called the police. By the time they got there, the stranger had forced his way into the house, only to drop dead on the stairs. He'd staved in his skull breaking down the door. There was blood everywhere, the customer told me, eyes wide. It turned out that the stranger was a happily married man with two kids he adored and a good job. He'd just snapped—that's what the police told my customer. Like he was a piece of peanut brittle.

People just snap. But to kill your own child . . . "What makes you think it was Prexilane that made them do it?"

"I saw an early study," he said. "It ran for a year. At the end of it, a half dozen of the participants had experienced some kind of psychotic breakdown. One of them went mute for a week. One of them washed her hands until the skin cracked and bled. One of them had a psychotic break and banged her head against the bathroom wall until she knocked herself unconscious. Her husband found her on the floor, covered in her own blood." He shook his head. "It was horrible. Just horrible."

"I don't understand," I said again, but the truth was, I was beginning to. Like it or not, I was starting to understand. I felt the wooden slats of the bench digging into my back and pressed myself against them. I wanted to feel the pain. I wanted to remind myself that this was real.

He shifted his weight toward me. "They shortened the trial lengths. They knew that the side effects would only kick in after prolonged exposure to the drug—three months at least—so they shortened their clinicals to eight weeks."

"If this is true, how did it make it past the FDA? Surely there are safety nets in place to prevent this kind of thing?"

He laughed bitterly. "There are people everywhere who are happy to look away for the right price. Even there." I saw his fists tighten. "And those who aren't willing to play ball—" He shrugged. "Well, they have ways of dealing with them, too."

I stared at him. His face was lined, his eyes pouched and heavy. He looked like a man who'd gone one too many rounds with life, and had lost. "How do you know all this?" I asked.

A pause. "I used to work for them."

"For the FDA?"

He nodded.

"What happened?"

He kept his gaze down on the grass. "Let's just say we didn't end on the best terms."

When he lifted his eyes to mine, I was surprised to find they were filled with tears. "You were the guy who wouldn't play ball?"

He looked away. "They tried to pay me off at first, and when I wouldn't leave it alone, they spread lies about me. They didn't just take my job away." He shook his head bitterly. "They took everything from me, and they didn't give a shit. Just like they don't give a shit about these people they're poisoning."

I glanced back at the photograph of the little boy. His eyes were a chocolate brown, with irises so big they almost edged out the whites entirely. "You're saying that the people at Prexilane know about this? That Ben knows?" Even saying his name felt like a betrayal.

He nodded and passed a hand across his face. "I'm sorry."

"But—why would they do it? If they knew the side effects, why would they still put the drug out on the market?" There was one last shred of hope inside me, and it was hanging by a thread.

He sighed. He looked exhausted, like he hadn't slept in weeks, maybe months. "Why does anyone do anything? Postpartum diagnoses have skyrocketed in the past decade. There's more awareness than ever, and with that awareness comes the search for a magic pill to stop it, and with that magic pill comes—"

The last thread inside me snapped. Ben loved me, but he loved something else more. I knew this because I loved it, too, and I had done things for its sake I couldn't bring myself to name. I had seen glimpses of the same compulsion living inside him, driving him on. "Money," I said quietly.

He smiled sadly. "It makes the world go round."

I thought of the house in Bird Rock, our bed with its vast expanse of white cotton sheets, the closet filled with beautiful dresses, his voice when he called out my name. I closed my eyes and watched it all disappear. I took a deep breath. "Tell me what to do."

Maggie

I sat back in my chair and let out a sigh. For all intents and purposes, Prexilane was a success. So why would it be entertaining an offer from a slash-and-burn operation like Hyperion?

I thought of the commotion I'd overheard at the Prexilane offices, the way the receptionist's eyes had become guarded as soon as I started asking questions, the look on the suited man's flushed face when he'd asked if Hyperion had arrived. I couldn't say I knew much about corporate business, but I knew panic when I saw it. What I couldn't figure out was what was causing it.

I flicked back through my notes, hoping to find something that might help point me in the right direction. In the section of notes about the trip to San Diego—Christ, I thought, that already seemed like a lifetime ago, though it had only been a week—I spotted a website address scrawled in the upper left-hand corner. The address of the postpartum forum where those women had been discussing Somnublaze.

I typed the address into the search bar and hit Return.

Not Found

The requested URL/fgererg was not found on this server.

Additionally, a 404 Not Found error was encountered while trying to use an ErrorDocument to handle the request.

I felt like I'd had the wind knocked out of me. How could I have been so sloppy? I should have gotten in touch with one of the women, asked her about her experience, seen if it had something to do with the pills she was taking. I allowed myself to get distracted and I lost a piece of the puzzle. I'd let Ally down.

I got to my feet and poured the dregs of my cold coffee down the sink. I was anxious, restless. Ants under the skin—that's what Charles used to call it. I couldn't sit at that table for a second longer. I needed to do something with myself—anything that would distract me from that blank computer screen and that stupid blinking cursor.

I trucked down to the basement, balancing an overflowing laundry basket on my hip. The air held the familiar tang of must and damp. I pushed the laundry into the machine and poured in a capful of Tide and set it away. The forum thread nagged at me. Why had it been deleted? Was it a technical glitch, or had someone intentionally taken it down? And was it just a coincidence that it had disappeared right at the moment that Prexilane was about to be sold off? The more I found out, the less I seemed to understand—it was like trying to sift sand with a fishing net. But one thing stuck: Ally believed in what was right, and I was sure now—to my core— that Ben had been mixed up in something bad.

When I got back upstairs, a little winded from the climb, I did what I'd always known I was going to do and picked up the phone and dialed Tony's number. He was the only person I wanted to talk to about all this. I wasn't sure why, but I was sure that he was the only one who would understand.

He picked up on the first ring. Just the sound of his voice down the line calmed me. "Tony, it's Maggie. Sorry for calling like this, but I need to talk to someone."

"I'm happy to talk to you anytime. What's going on?"

"It's probably nothing . . ." I hesitated. Now that I had him on the phone, I wasn't sure where to start. The bank account, Hyperion, the deleted website . . . all of it swarmed through my head.

"Whatever it is, you can tell me," he prompted gently. It wasn't the first time I felt like he could read my mind, but it still took me by surprise, and I found myself wondering what kind of luck had brought him into my life just at the moment I needed him. It felt like the first piece of luck I'd had in a long time.

"I found something out about David Gardner's company today." I explained my recent discoveries in one long breathless sentence, Tony making encouraging noises down the line to show he was listening but otherwise keeping quiet.

"And you're sure they were talking about Hyperion when you were at the Prexilane office?" he asked when I'd finished.

"Sure as death and taxes."

"And the forum thread disappeared between then and now?" His voice sounded tight.

"That's right. But I can't be sure it's not just a coincidence," I added hurriedly. I didn't want him to think I was some kind of conspiracy theorist. Everyone else around me seemed to think I'd lost my mind—I didn't want him thinking that, too.

I didn't have to worry, though. He let out a low whistle. "Sons of bitches," he muttered under his breath before catching himself and apologizing. "I don't mean to curse. What else did you find?"

I took a breath. "Ally was hiding money. She was making regular deposits into a local account up here, and she took all of it out the week before the crash. Two thousand dollars, cash. What would she need that amount of money for?"

"To get away." He said it so quietly I almost didn't catch it.

"What did you say?" There was a muffled, strangled noise, and I swear I heard him start to sob. "What did you say?" I said again, and my own voice sounded hollow in my ears. I gripped the phone so hard I was surprised the plastic didn't snap. "Tony, do you know something you're not telling me?"

There was a pause, and I heard him heave out a long, shuddering sigh down the line. "I never should have got her mixed up in this." Ally. He was talking about Ally.

"Tony, please," I begged. I was shaking so hard that my teeth were chattering in my skull. "If you know something about her, you have to tell me."

Finally, he cleared his throat. "You're right," he said softly. "It's time you knew the truth."

Allison

I spent last night in the hotel room, flicking aimlessly through the channels and thinking about what was coming. The only time I left the motel was to run across the street to the gas station to buy a couple of grayish hot dogs, a pack of Ho Hos, and a fifth of whisky. I left most of the Ho Hos but drained the whisky, eventually passing out to the sound of Ina Garten making a soufflé.

I check the clock—the pawnshop will be open in half an hour. Time to go. I shower, shave my legs, brush my teeth, comb my hair. It feels important to be clean. I dress in the new underwear and white T-shirt and stiff blue jeans before packing my things and throwing my bag into the back seat of the Subaru. It's still early but the day's heat has already settled around the town like a thick blanket. The door of the car is hot to the touch. I tuck the rifle and the box of bullets under the passenger seat.

I walk across the parking lot to the motel office and pull open the door. The same receptionist is still staring up at the television screen, though now she's watching a property show.

"Are you ready to see your new kitchen?" the host trills, and I find my gaze drifting up toward the screen, eager for the big reveal.

The receptionist snaps her gum. "You checking out?"

My eyes flicker to hers and then back up to the television, where a woman is crying over an oven. "Yeah. Should just be for one night. I paid up front for the first."

She smirks. "I thought it was your friend who paid."

I shrug. I can tell she's trying to get a rise out of me, but I don't have time to get into a thing with this woman. "Same difference. It's thirty-four, right?"

"Thirty-eight. We had to charge you extra because the sheets were so dirty. The maid said she had to bleach them twice." She snaps her gum again to punctuate the point and I will myself not to blush. I don't care what she thinks about me, I remind myself. I don't care what anyone thinks.

"Here's forty," I say, peeling off the bills and handing them to her. "Keep the change."

She counts out the bills and shoves them into the register. "You cut your hair?"

My hand reaches up to my sheared head. I'm still not used to the feel of it underneath my fingers. "Yeah. Time for a change."

She nods approvingly. "It looks cute."

"Really?" My eyes prick with tears and I'm instantly mortified. Am I really that pathetic? Like a dog who's been kicked again and again and then rolls over when someone offers him a bone? I wipe my eyes roughly and manage a smile. "Thanks. Well, see you."

"See you." Her eyes have already trailed back up to the screen, where a young couple are now crying over a dining set.

I drive the Subaru the block and a half to Main Street, past the empty storefronts and the bars with dark frosted windows and the lone diner with its faded sign advertising two-for-one breakfasts on Mondays. I park in front of the pawnshop. The owner is standing out front waiting for me, the shutter already half open.

"Right on time," he says as I hop out of the station wagon. "See you got yourself a new set of wheels. Chet look after you all right?"

I remember the look on his face when he handed me the keys, like a little kid who'd just sneaked a cookie without getting caught, and smile. "Yep."

He looks around the front of the car. "You still got the dealer's plate on it."

I nod. "He's letting me use it until I can pick up my plates from the DMV."

He raises an eyebrow but doesn't comment. "Come on then," he says, nodding toward the shop.

We both duck under the shutter and into the shop. Inside, it's dark and cool. He disappears into the back and reappears with a stack of bills. "It's in twenties," he says with a shrug. "All I could get."

"That's fine." The wad of bills is too thick to fit in my pocket so I end up cradling it awkwardly in my hands. "Well, I should get going. Thanks for your help."

"You're the one I should be thanking," he says. He looks at me for a minute, the silence settling between us. "I hope you won't mind me asking, but what's a girl like you need with all this cash?"

I shrug but don't say anything. I don't have time to answer questions, and the less he knows, the safer I'll be. Him, too, probably. "I should get going," I say, glancing pointedly at the Subaru outside.

"Sure," he says. "I hear you've got a long ride ahead of you." He and Chet must have talked after I left the dealership. I wonder what else they had to say about me. I notice that he's stalling and realize he has something to say—something he doesn't want to. He reaches up and scratches the back of his neck. "Somebody was looking for you."

"Oh yeah?" I try to sound casual but I can hear the slight quiver in my voice. "Who?"

He shakes his head. "Wouldn't say. Tall fellow. Dark hair. Didn't look like he was from around here."

I don't know anyone who matches that description, but I know immediately who it is. "What did he want?" I don't need to ask—I know that, too. He wants me.

"Wouldn't say that, either. Just described what you looked like and asked if I'd seen you." He pauses and nods at my head. "Except he said you were blond."

My eyes search his face. "What did you tell him?"

"Told him I hadn't seen a pretty blond stranger round here in nearly twenty years."

The breath whistles out of my lungs. He's bought me some time. I don't know how much, but it's something at least. "Thank you."

"No need to thank me. Whatever business you've got, it's your own." He looks at me steadily. "Still, I think it's best you're on your way now. No telling who else he'll be asking, and some people around here've got big mouths."

I nod. "I'm leaving town now."

"Well. Good luck." He picks up the newspaper, flicks the pages out, and smooths them down on the counter. "You take care of yourself."

I walk out into the blinding sunlight and straight into the car. I slip the money out of my jeans and shove it under the front seat. It'll have to do for now.

I'm sparking up the ignition when I see him. He's leaning against a lamppost and even though I can't see his eyes behind his sunglasses I feel them on me and know he's been watching me. Waiting. He reaches into his pocket and steps off the curb.

I punch the gas and drive.

He showed me how to download the spyware onto my phone. "You see?" he said, tapping at the screen. "It's easy." I nodded, though I felt sick with fear. He saw this and smiled at me reassuringly. "You'll do fine." He dropped a chip into my palm and wrapped my fingers around it. "Download everything," he'd said, pointing to my closed fist. "Keep it hidden. Somewhere he would never think to look." He nodded toward my necklace. "Do you always wear that?" I looked down at the Saint Christopher's locket my father had given me and nodded. "Then that might be a good place to hide it."

I hesitated. "Why aren't you doing this yourself? Why did you come to me?"

He smiled a sad sort of smile and shook his head. "No one would believe me," he said quietly. "They've made sure of that." He leaned forward and took my hands in his, and I noticed again the dark circles under his eyes. He looked like a man who hadn't slept in weeks, months, maybe years, and I wondered what exactly he'd gone through to get to this point. "Anyway," he said quietly, "you can get close to him in ways I never could. He trusts you." He reached over and took my hand. His eyes burned into mine. "Before you do this, I want to be sure that you know what you're getting into. If they suspect you, even for a second——"

I shook my head. "They won't. I'll be smart about it. Even if Sam doesn't trust me, I know Ben does. He would never think I'd do anything to hurt him." As soon as I said it, I knew it was true, and the thought of betraying him was a hot knife running through me. Still, I had to know the truth. I couldn't live my life without knowing who I was getting into bed with every night.

He must have seen that on my face—desperation mixed with determination—because he sat back down heavily on the bench and took my hand in his again. We sat there in silence for a minute, both of us thinking our separate thoughts and feeling our separate fears. Eventually he looked up at me and nodded, just once. "We can't meet again. If they see the two of us together, it'll be game over."

The thought left me feeling stranded and at sea, but I knew he was right. He'd led me to the path, but I had to go down it on my own.

"You have to protect yourself. He'll be watching you, Allison. If you think, even for a second, that they're on to you, you have to disappear. Do you understand?" I nodded weakly. My mouth was dry and my tongue pressed itself against the roof of my mouth and stuck there. "You'll need money. Do you have any?" I shook my head, humiliated by the admission, but he didn't flinch. "Put aside a little every week, in amounts he won't notice. Keep it somewhere safe. You'll need the cash for a passport and a plane ticket if you need to disappear."

"I don't think it will come to that," I said, managing a smile. It was all so absurd.

He stared at me for a long moment, and I struggled to hold his gaze. "Please. I need to be sure you know what you're signing up for."

I realized he was serious. "Fine. I'll do what you want."

"Good." He kept his eyes on mine. "Are you sure you want to do this?"

I thought about what I was agreeing to. I would be betraying the man I loved, the man who had rescued me from a spiral of self-destruction and made me into someone brand new. I would be risking my future. If what he was saying was true, I might even be risking my life. But I knew that if I didn't do it, I would never be able to find my way back to myself again. I would be lost forever.

"I'm sure," I said, as confidently as I could muster.

"Good." He stood up and gathered the scattered pages of his paper off the bench. "Someone will be in touch about the passport." He held out a hand and I took it. "It was a pleasure meeting you, Allison. You look after yourself."

"You, too—" I faltered. I realized I didn't know his name.

"Anthony," he said. "But my friends call me Tony." He turned and walked away across the freshly mowed grass, the paper tucked neatly in the crook of his arm.

It was the last time I saw him.

Maggie

The world, in that moment, seemed to slow almost to a stop. I could hear the blood rushing through my veins, and the sound of the ticking clock in the kitchen, and the rustle of the leaves in the trees outside. A swirl of dust motes sparkled in the air. The colors seemed brighter, too, like the Technicolor they used in the old movies Charles and I used to watch on Sunday afternoons. The deep red of the tiled kitchen floor. The acid green of the apple sitting on the countertop, waiting to be sliced. The bright gold of the sunlight as it streamed through the window. It had stopped raining, I realized, and the sun had come out.

"Maggie? Are you there?"

I blinked, slowly. Yes, I was still there. "What is it? What do you know about Ally?" My voice didn't sound like mine. It was strangled and too high, like my throat had been stripped by something caustic.

"I can't tell you over the phone." He sounded panicked. "I'm coming over."

I looked frantically around the kitchen, with its worn Shaker cabinets and chipped worktops and its empty, barren fridge. Suddenly the idea of him—this stranger, this man—in my house felt all wrong. "I don't think that's a good idea."

"You're right. They might have bugged your place. We shouldn't even be talking over the phone. Meet me at the coffee shop in twenty minutes."

The world seemed to tilt and I had to brace myself on the counter before my knees gave way. "Tony, you're not talking any sense. You sound crazy."

"I'm not crazy!" His voice was angry, manic.

I felt a fissure of fear jolt through me. I didn't want this man in my house. "I'm not saying you're crazy." I was using my most soothing voice, the one I'd used for students who used to come to me at my desk at Bowdoin, ashen faced, and announce that they'd deleted their term paper. "Just tell me what's going on and we'll figure it out."

"But if I tell you . . ." There was a muffled sound down the line and I realized he was fighting back tears. "I'm so sorry, Maggie. I'm so sorry. I've been wanting to tell you for so long, but I didn't know how. I got her mixed up in all this. It's my fault she's dead."

My heart was pounding in my chest, and my stomach was filled with cold, heavy dread. "Please, just tell me what you know."

He was silent for so long I thought he'd hung up, but then his voice came through the phone, quiet and reed thin. "She was investigating Prexilane. I told her what they were up to and she was gathering evidence on them, recording phone calls . . ."

"What do you mean, she was investigating them?"

"They killed her because she was trying to expose them. Your daughter was very brave. A hero. That's what I wanted to tell you. That's why I came all this way . . . I never thought you'd get mixed up in it, too."

"Please, I don't understand—"

He took a deep breath. "The necklace, Maggie. It's all in the necklace."

The line went dead.

"Tony? Are you there?"

But there was no one there. Just the dial tone ringing in my ear, and when I tried to call him back, the phone just rang and rang.

2,105 Miles to Go

Allison

I've been on the road for a couple of hours, the hum of the engine lulling me, the snippets of talk radio filling the car and then dropping away under a haze of static. It's late afternoon, and the fingers of terror have slowly loosened as the road spools out in front of me, but the image of the man in the sunglasses is still imprinted on my mind.

I'm sure of two things: I've never seen him before in my life, and he's been sent to kill me.

How long, I wonder, has he been following me? Was he up there in the mountains? Was he looking in on me as I slept in the cabin? Did he see me get into Luke's truck back at the trail shop, or in the motel, as the TV flickered across the darkened walls?

Deep in my bones, I know the answer. Deep in my bones, I've known he's been with me the whole time, just one step behind, the scent of me always in his lungs. The thing is, spying is easy. I know that from experience.

A part of me still didn't believe what I'd been told in the park that day. Part of me agreed to install the spyware on Ben's phone and listen in to his conversations in order to exonerate him. *He's innocent*, I thought, as I waited for him to fall asleep. *This is all just a misunderstanding, and once it's cleared up, I can keep living this life.* The belief stayed with me as I sent the spyware to his phone by text, typed in the password I'd memorized, and—with one tap of a finger—watched it download. My own phone flashed up with a notification. *"619-555-3364 is now active."* *He's innocent*, I thought as I'd crawled

279

into bed beside him and pulled his warm back toward my chest. *Now I can prove it.*

I was on the treadmill in the gym below our building when the first call came through. There was the tinny sound of Beyoncé coming through my headphones, and the steady thud of my footsteps, and the heave of my breath, the thrum of my heartbeat, and then there was a clicking sound and voices in my ear.

"I just heard back from the lawyer." It was a male voice, deeper than Ben's, but familiar. "It looks like they're going to push ahead with the class action." Sam.

"Shit." Ben's voice sounded strange, strangled. "How bad is it?"

"Bad. The shareholders are already losing their shit. We need to bury this, fast."

My stride faltered and I had to grab the handrails to stop myself from falling. I hit the emergency stop button and the conveyor belt lurched to a halt. The woman running next to me glanced over at me and smirked.

"If we settle, the FDA will look to pull the product. We can still fix this." Ben's voice shook a little, and I felt a twinge of pity. "We've got R&D working around the clock. It's only—what?—three percent who are affected?"

"Eight."

A sharp intake of breath. At least Ben still had the capacity to be shocked. At least there was that. "It's a good product, Sam. It's helping a lot of people."

Sam cleared his throat. "Look, I don't like this either, but we don't have a choice. If this goes to court, we're fucked. I saw the briefing."

Ben cursed under his breath. "Anything we could point to? Drug use, family history of mental illness?" My stomach lurched. I had let this man put his hands on me, his mouth, his tongue. I had let him come inside me.

"They're clean as a whistle. The lawyers have sewn it up tight this time. She was a schoolteacher, for Chrissakes. Her husband's a social worker. No history of depression before she had the baby." There was a long pause. My vision swam and I realized I'd been holding my breath since the conversation began. "We don't have a choice, Ben. They've got a gun to our heads."

Ben let out a long breath. "How much?"

I would soon learn that that was always the question: How much will it cost? How much for their silence? How much to make this go away?

Sam cleared his throat. "Three million. Three and a half."

"Pay him four and get him to sign an NDA so tight you could bounce quarters off it. I want him to understand that if he ever breathes a word of it, we will bury him."

"Got it."

The line clicked off and Beyoncé filled my head again. I jumped off the treadmill and sprinted to the locker room, pushing past women in various states of undress and making it to the toilet a fraction of a second too late. I was sick on the floor of the cubicle, the smooth jazz playing from the locker room speakers muffling the sound of my retches.

Maggie

Everything about the place was the same as it had been when I'd come there with him. There was the same whir and clank as they frothed the milk, the same bitter smell of roasted coffee beans mixed with the synthetic florals of an air freshener, the same guitar music playing in the background. The same waitress brought me coffee along with an oversize chocolate chip cookie on a plate. "They're getting thrown out at the end of the day," she'd said with a shrug when I asked her about it, so I smiled and thanked her even though the thought of the butter and sugar coating my mouth was enough to turn my stomach.

Everything was exactly the same, but the place felt completely alien to me. The whole world felt unfamiliar and frightening, like shining a flashlight under a refrigerator and seeing the filth that had collected.

I forced myself to sit there and sip my latte and nibble at the free cookie so as not to be rude and watch the long arm of the clock swoop around in its slow circle.

He didn't show up. I knew he wouldn't, but I had to sit there anyway, just in case.

I was wearing the necklace, and kept touching it to make sure it was still there. After the waitress had cleared the table, shooting me a sympathetic glance and asking if I'd like another cookie, which I declined, I took it off and spooled it in my palm. The cup of the locket was dented and there were spots where the cheap gold had rubbed off, exposing the nickel underneath, but otherwise it looked exactly the same as it had when Charles had given it to her all those years ago.

I clicked open the locket with shaking fingers and stared at the photograph nestled inside. I could still remember when it had been taken. It was on a family vacation to Ogunquit, and Charles had been angry with me for getting us lost, and I'd been angry with him for getting angry at me when it was his own damn fault that he didn't want to bring a map, and all three of us had been hot and tired and sunburned and covered in sand. I think the photo had been Ally's way of making peace among us. "Smile!" she'd said, or more like demanded, and she'd lifted the old Canon we'd given her and snapped the picture before we had a chance to argue. Charles's smile looks genuine—he could never stop himself from smiling at his little girl, no matter how irritated with his wife he might be— but mine was tight and forced. I was probably already worrying about where we'd get groceries for the cabin, or whether I'd taken enough cash out for dinner, or if I'd remembered to lock the back door.

I shook my head. If I had it all to do again, I wouldn't have wasted so much time worrying. I would have smiled big for the camera and held Charles's hand, and when it was finished, I would have run over to Ally and gathered her to me and pressed her sandy cheek to mine. No one tells you how good you have it at the time. No one warns you about how you'll feel when it's taken away.

"The necklace." That had been the last thing he'd said to me. "The necklace."

I took a deep breath, lifted the edge of the photograph, and pried it out of the frame. There, resting in the locket's cup, was a small rectangle of white plastic the size of my thumbnail.

A computer chip.

Allison

It happens so fast. One minute, I'm alone on the road, the only speck on the long ribbon of asphalt. The next minute, there's an eighteen-wheeler hugging my right bumper and a sports car bearing down on me from behind.

It should be a simple maneuver: just merge into the middle lane to let the sports car pass. I flick on the turn signal and glance over my shoulder to check that I'm clear to move, but instead of easing back to let me in, the eighteen-wheeler speeds up. I'm blocked in.

The panic comes on quickly. It's him, it must be him.

I hit the gas. The Subaru groans and lurches forward. I watch the arm on the speedometer start to climb. Seventy. Seventy-five. Eighty. I look to my right and see the eighteen-wheeler keeping pace. I try to peer up into the cab, maybe catch the driver's eye, but the truck is too tall and his face is in shadow and all I can see is the bill of his baseball cap. My eyes dart to the rearview mirror. The sports car is just a single car length away now, close enough for me to see the Mercedes badge on the hood. If I tap the brakes, he'll slam into me, sending me sailing off the shoulder or under the eighteen-wheeler. He's flashing his headlights, warning me to get out of the way. I'm going eighty-five now but the truck is still there, boxing me in. I feel the car being pulled toward the truck's wind-suck and tighten my grip on the wheel.

I lean on the horn and strain my neck up toward the driver of the truck. *Look at me*, I will him. *Look!* All I can see is the set of his jaw and the peak of his cap. He keeps his eyes fixed on the road.

One hundred. The body of the car begins to shake. I squint into the rearview mirror. The front end of the sports car fills the entire frame now, blocking out the sun and the sky and the road behind it. The driver is alone in the car, gloved hands gripping the wheel at ten and two, eyes shaded by mirrored sunglasses, mouth pulled in a tight line. He flashes his lights again and makes a gesture with his hand.

One hundred and ten. A sign warns of a curve in the road up ahead. I'm only barely keeping the car in my lane going straight— I'll never make the turn. I can see the long black stream of the asphalt start to bend, and as I tilt the wheel into it I can feel the car grind against it. I can see the bottom of the truck's cab door painted blue with a faint metallic sheen. The Subaru drifts farther into its gravitational pull as the curve deepens. It's a matter of inches now.

They had to scrape him off the pavement. That's what Uncle Jim used to say after a bad accident. *Nothing left of the poor bastard.*

A sign blinks up ahead. MERGE RIGHT IN 200 FEET. Orange chevrons light the way. MEN AT WORK another sign screams, but there are no men in sight, just a neat line of concrete barriers directly in my path.

A cold sweat blooms at the back of my neck. I brace myself for the screech of metal on metal, the shattering of glass, the weightless, slipping journey through space. The scrape of flesh across the rough sandpaper of concrete. The crack and snap of bone. Blood spreading across the asphalt, thick and too red, its metallic smell mixing with the smell of gasoline and burning.

I'm going to die. I feel strangely calm, as though everything I've ever done has been steadily heading for this particular moment, as though I was meant, from birth, to leave this world in flight.

And then, just like that, it's over. The truck drops away suddenly and the sports car nips in front of it and speeds past, horn blaring. I ease my foot off the accelerator and guide the Subaru into the right lane, missing the merge sign by only a few feet. Eighty-five. Eighty. Seventy-five. Seventy. I steer through the hard turn and emerge on a straight stretch of deserted road. I check the rearview mirror and see the truck turn off at the exit. In front of me, the road is empty. The other car is nowhere to be seen.

There's a metallic taste in my mouth and I realize I've bitten the inside of my cheek until I've drawn blood. I try not to notice how badly my hands are shaking as they grip the wheel.

I'm beginning to think I won't make it home.

No.

I have to make it home.

Maggie

It wasn't even front-page news in the *Owl's Creek Examiner*. That honor went to the first day of football practice for the local high school team and a piece on the plans to freshen up Main Street. Instead it was buried on page 5, just a few column inches and a thumbnail image. The picture was grainy but I knew it was him. Tony.

GUEST FOUND DEAD

The body of a hotel guest was discovered in the early hours of yesterday morning. Anthony Tracanelli, 66, was found dead by a hotel maid who entered the room despite having received strict instructions not to disturb him. The maid explained that she became suspicious after overhearing an altercation in the room, though Tracanelli was alone when his body was recovered. The cause of death is still unknown but police are investigating.

I hadn't known his last name. I had never even thought to ask.

I could still hear the panic in his voice on the phone, and then the line had cut out, and now he was dead.

I had to tell someone. I had to say these things aloud, otherwise they wouldn't be real. If they were real.

I called Jim. He picked up on the first ring.

"What do you know about Anthony Tracanelli?" I didn't bother to say hello, just launched straight into it. I was too worked up for pleasantries.

"The fella who turned up in the hotel room? Not much. It's under Branville's jurisdiction, so we don't have much to do with it."

"Can you find out?"

"Why do you want to know?"

I sighed. "I know him."

"You know him? How?"

I scraped a long-set stain on the kitchen table with a fingernail and stalled for time. "I met him at Bowdoin. He told me he was retired, that he was taking classes to fill the time. We got talking, and . . ." I dug my nail deep into the grain of the wood. "We became close, I guess." I felt awful saying it, like a fool and the worst kind of traitor. Jim had loved Charles like a brother, and even though nothing had happened between me and Tony, I felt like he could still sense something over the phone.

"Right."

He was waiting for me to go on, but I was silent. I looked over at the computer chip sitting on the worktop next to the stove. This was the moment I had to tell him everything. There was no other way. "There was a computer chip in Ally's necklace," I blurted out. "It was hidden inside it. Tony told me about it. I don't know how he knew, but he did, and then the phone cut off, and now he's dead." The words were pouring out of me now, like a faucet on full blast. "He's dead, Jim, and it's because of me. I don't know what in the hell is going on here but I know it's not good, I know it's something bad and I can't make any sense of it anymore. I feel—" I hesitated, pulling the breath deep into my lungs and pushing it out again "I feel like I'm going crazy."

Jim was quiet. I could hear the gears whirring in his head, weighing what I'd said before making a judgment. He was like that: calm in a crisis. Assessing before acting. I was terrified he was going to dismiss me as being crazy. Finally, I heard him clear his throat. "Are you at home right now?"

"Of course I am."

"Stay right where you are. I'm coming over."

I set about making a pot of coffee while I waited for him. I looked down at the photograph in the paper spread out on the countertop. It was in black and white and the image was slightly blurry, but it was him. Same silver hair, same sad eyes, same warm smile. The sight of it stretched and pulled at my insides, like one of those taffy machines they have at York Beach. Anger mixed with sadness mixed with the stomach-sick of humiliation.

He had kept things from me . . . Wait. No. He had *lied* to me. He pretended he knew nothing about my daughter when all the time, he knew more than me. He harbored secrets about her, and now that he was gone, he would never reveal them to me. That's what stung the most—not the lies, but the truth he had taken with him to his grave.

I put my head in my hands. I could still feel the shock of his fingers on my skin as he reached for the necklace. I should have gone with my instincts and kept my guard up. God, I had been such a fool.

I heard Jim's cruiser coast into the drive and wiped my face with the flat of my hand. I had to pull it together. I needed him to believe me. I couldn't leave any room for doubt.

He was in the house as quick as a shot. I handed him a cup of coffee and sat him down at the kitchen table. "I spoke to the fellas up at Branville on the way over," he said, taking a sip. "They're still working out what happened."

I folded my arms across my chest. "That's what I'm trying to tell you. I know what happened. Somebody killed him."

Jim ran a hand across his mouth. He looked tired and older than his years. "Maggie, I'm going to need you to tell me everything you know."

So I told him everything. The way Tony had approached me in the library. The memorial. The meeting over coffee. His hint about the necklace, and then the chip itself, which I presented to him nestled in my palm like a pearl. At the end of it, he shook his head. "You should have come to me sooner, Maggie. You should have told me what you were up to."

I shook my head. "You wouldn't have believed me."

He pulled his head back into his neck as if I'd slapped him. "Now, that's not fair—"

"I wouldn't have blamed you," I said, holding up my hands. "I know it sounds crazy." I stared at him across the table. "I just wanted to get to the bottom of what happened to her. That's all."

He sighed. "I know, but Maggie, we've been over this. Ally's death was an accident."

"That's not what I think. That's not what Tony thought, either." The chair scraped against the floor as I pushed back from the table. A restless energy burned through me as I paced the room. "The more I find out about what she was doing in San Diego, and the kind of man Ben was . . ." I wheeled on him. "You saw the photographs. You saw how different she looked. Did you know that Ally had stopped working, stopped talking to her friends? She was cut off from everything in the world, all because of that man. Does that sound like the girl you knew?"

Jim sighed. It was the longest, saddest sigh I could imagine. "I haven't known her since she was a kid," he said softly. "And I'm sorry to have to say this, believe me I am, but I don't think you knew her, either. Hell, I barely know my own sons and I see them most weeks. It's the way of the world, Maggie. Our children grow up and become strangers to us." He reached out and took my hand in his. "Allison's gone. I wish that I could tell you something different, but I've seen the photos from the crash site and . . . there's just no way she could have survived something like that."

I thrust the plastic chip toward him, my fingers shaking as I held it up to him. "Why would she be hiding this in her necklace? It must mean something, Jim. It has to."

I could see him wavering. "Do you know what it is?"

I shook my head. "I don't know exactly, but if Ally went to the trouble of hiding it in her locket, it's got to be important."

Jim's eyes went from mine to the chip in my hand and back again. He rubbed a meaty hand across his mouth and sighed. "Give it to me," he said finally, holding out his hand. "I'll ask the guys to take a look." I opened my mouth to thank him but he stopped me. "I'm only doing this if you promise me that when we figure out what this is and it's proved to be nothing, you'll drop this once and for all." I nodded mutely, even though my thoughts were treacherous. "Good," he said, getting to his feet. He closed his fist around the chip and slid it into the breast pocket of his shirt. "I'll let you know as soon as we get the results."

I walked him to the door. "Will you let me know when they find out about what happened to him? To Tony?"

Jim nodded. A little coffee had dribbled onto the front of his shirt, and I thought about Linda trying to wash out the stain. I'd have to tell her to use vinegar. "Just don't forget our promise. You've got to leave it alone after this."

"I won't," I said, as he walked down the path toward the cruiser parked in the driveway. "I'll try."

We both knew it was a lie.

1,141 Miles to Go

Allison

I'm somewhere in Indiana, I think, unless I missed the sign welcoming me to Ohio. It doesn't matter: out here, on the flat stretch of highway, there's nothing but endless patchwork fields and the occasional box elder or red maple, their leaves glowing gold in my headlights.

There are no other cars on the road, either, just me and the endless stretch of highway, the cat's eyes winking in the pavement reflecting the stars scattered above.

I've been driving for nearly seventeen hours. All the adrenaline has been leached out of me, and I feel emptied and hollow. My eyelids are heavy. They keep pulling down over my tired eyes, and I have to force them open again, like a pair of faulty blinds.

But there's no time to sleep. No time to stop. They're out there somewhere, waiting for me. Waiting, too—maybe, God no, but maybe—for my mother. Maybe they've already gotten to her. No. I rub my fist into my eyes and press down on the accelerator. I can't think like that. I have to believe there's still time for me to get to her.

I jolt awake. The whole car is vibrating, and a deafening buzz fills the air.

I've drifted across the lanes and onto the rumble strip. I only have a split second to correct the wheel before the car grinds against the barrier wall.

My heart pounds in my throat. How long was I asleep? A second? A minute? I blink at the clock. Two forty-three. I'm wide awake now but I know it's too dangerous to keep driving. There's no way I'll make it through to the morning. I have to stop for a few hours, get some sleep. There's a sign for a trucker's weigh-in station in a half mile, and when it comes into view, I can see a couple of eighteen-wheelers slumbering underneath the flashing neon lights. I sail past. It's too risky, too exposed. I need a room with a door that I can lock behind me.

I drive for another half-dozen miles, one hand on the wheel, the other pinching the flesh on my inner thigh to stay awake. Finally, it comes into view. The sign for the motel is enormous, two stories tall at least, and the light from it casts a glow that's twenty feet around. I pull off the highway and wind my way through the sleeping streets into the half-full parking lot. I cut the engine. All the windows in the motel are dark except for one on the ground floor. I haul my bag out of the back, tuck the rifle inside, and walk up to the front door. I expect it to be locked, but it whirs open automatically and I find myself standing in a cramped lobby smelling of Pine-Sol and stale breakfast foods. There's a little bell on the desk and I ring it.

A door to the side of the desk opens and a woman emerges, blond and neat in a starched blue button-down and pressed navy trousers. She's pretty and fresh faced and looks startlingly perky for the hour, and the overall effect of seeing her is unnerving. "Good evening," she says brightly, her face splitting into a wide smile. "How can I help you?"

"I— I need a room," I stutter. "Just for the night. The rest of the night, I mean."

I half expect her to throw me out, but she just nods and turns to fetch a key from the board behind her. "Room thirty-one," she says. "Could I take a credit card?"

I shake my head. "I could pay in cash up front?"

"That would be fine. I'll also need a $100 deposit, in case of damages."

I scramble through the pockets of my bag and hand her a wad of bills, too much I'm sure. She counts them out serenely on the desk and hands back the extra. "Will you be eating breakfast with us tomorrow?"

"No," I say quickly, and then realize I won't have eaten a meal in nearly twenty-four hours by then. "I mean, yes. If that's okay."

"Of course. Our complimentary breakfast begins at seven a.m. and ends at nine a.m. Would you like a wake-up call?"

The absurdity of the situation is beginning to get to me, and I find myself swallowing back laughter. "No, thank you."

"Room thirty-one is on the third floor. The elevator is to your left. Would you like help with your luggage?" She nods at the filthy bag resting by my feet, and this time I do laugh.

"No, you're fine," I say, lugging the bag onto my shoulder. "Thanks very much."

The room is small but clean. The walls are papered in gray-and-white stripes, and there's an innocuous watercolor of a seaside town above the queen-size bed. I wash my face and watch myself in the mirror while I brush my teeth, still surprised by the sharp angles of my face and my close-cut head of hair. I draw the blinds and the heavy curtains and settle into bed. The air conditioner moans quietly, but otherwise it's completely silent. I reach into my bag and slide the rifle under the bed.

I think of my mother lying in her bed halfway across the country. I haven't been in that room for two years but I can still picture it clearly in my mind. The big oak bed bought from Jordan Marsh, the blue quilt with white flowers, the thick curtains pulled back to let in the morning light. Barney would be lying by her feet, curled in on himself and twitching in his sleep. I keep this image of her in my head as I let the exhaustion finally take me. Peaceful. Safe.

Waiting for me.

Maggie

There was only one Anthony Tracanelli who fit Tony's description, but he wasn't a mature student at Bowdoin. He didn't live in Maine, either—at least not permanently. Most of the search listings that came up had him as a resident of California. San Diego, to be exact.

I'd tried to brace myself for him not being who he said he was, but it was still a shock to see it in black and white. I took a deep breath and started scrolling through the search results. And there were a lot of results.

Most people his age didn't have much of an online footprint. Maybe a Facebook page our kids had set up for us, or a profile page on a company website if we were a big shot, but for the most part the internet is populated by the young. Unless, of course, someone has a reason to write about you. Unless you had somehow become newsworthy.

There was plenty to pick from when it came to Tony. The *New York Times*, the *Washington Post*, the *Boston Globe*—all of them had published articles that mentioned his name. I clicked on the first one that came up.

WASHINGTON TRIBUNE
FORMER FDA EMPLOYEE ARRESTED

SAN DIEGO, CA—A former Federal Drug Administration whistle-blower has been arrested. Anthony Tracanelli, 60, was placed under police custody following a raid on his home in Clairemont in the early hours of yesterday morning. Police say that they recovered indecent material from a laptop in his home following an anonymous tip. He was later released on bail.

Tracanelli worked for the FDA in research and development until May of last year, when he launched a campaign to expose what he claimed were harmful practices at the FDA. According to internal documents leaked to the press, Tracanelli accused his supervisors of what he described as "blatant delinquency in their duty of care to the American people," and went on to allege that senior regulatory officials had accepted bribes from pharmaceutical companies in order to speed up the approvals process—and in some cases, turned a blind eye to "harmful and at times fatal side effects" of drugs being brought to market.

When still in his role at the agency, Tracanelli raised eyebrows among his colleagues by demanding that pharmaceutical manufacturers provide more clinical data about the safety of their products, including longer clinical trials and double-blind data analysis. FDA managers deemed Tracanelli's requests excessive, and they were quashed. He was dismissed from his post shortly thereafter, but Tracanelli continued to pursue the matter, posting what he alleged was evidence that the FDA colluded with the drug manufacturer Prexilane on the website Whistleblowers.org. Prexilane sued the website for defamation and the post was subsequently removed.

An internal investigation was conducted following Tracanelli's departure and showed no wrongdoing on the part of the agency. While Tracanelli's allegations were deemed groundless, insiders say that a cloud remains over the agency.

Reached for comment at his home, Tracanelli denied harboring indecent material and claimed that he was the subject of a witch hunt. "This is nothing less than a setup," Tracanelli said of the charges against him. "I'm confident the truth will win out in the end."

I had to read it twice, just to make sure my eyes weren't playing a trick on me. But no, there it was on the screen, clear as the nose on my face. Tony had been investigating Prexilane. He had known Ally. He had known about the chip she was carrying around her neck. He had known about all of it.

What had he said about her again? That she was a hero. My heart swelled through the grief. She had been trying to uncover an injustice. For the first time in a long time, I felt like I could reach out and touch her. This was the Ally I knew. This was my daughter, and I was so damn proud of her.

Allison

I don't hear a thing, not even the rasping sound of his breath as he hovers above me. It's only when his hands close around my throat that I wake up.

It's pitch black in the room and my eyes open to blackness. His weight is on top of me, pushing me down into the springs of the mattress, and I hear them groan from the strain. I can feel his hot breath on my cheek and the pressure of his fingers tightening around my windpipe. White dots appear in my field of vision.

He's here. He's found me.

I scrabble to free my arms from the tangle of sheets. Every muscle in my body is tense as I claw up and out, swiping at the air, grasping at the hands that are fixed around my throat. I feel his skin tear under my fingernails but his grip doesn't let up and the white dots are expanding, multiplying. I can feel myself going under. There are stars now stretched out across the ceiling and I am falling falling falling back and up toward them, into them, weightless.

I hear a strangled wail, a cat whose tail has been trapped in the door, and realize it's coming from me. The adrenaline surges through me and my hands claw at his fingers and my legs kick out against his weight and then, with the last bit of strength I can summon before the whiteness takes me, I open my mouth wide and strain upward, searching, and when I find a piece of his flesh—I can't be sure what part—with my mouth I bite down, as hard as I can. I feel flesh tear beneath my teeth and I hear him grunt and for a second, his grip loosens. I suck in air and then I scream.

The noise startles both of us, and I feel his body tense and shift. I scramble out and away and then I'm on the floor, the carpet rough under my knees. I feel the wind on my ankles as he swipes for them and I turn and kick up at him. My foot hits something, hard, and I hear a snap and feel a sizzle of pain run down my big toe. Another grunt, angrier this time, and then he's down on the ground with me and his hands are grasping at my waist and my hips and my thighs and my hands are reaching searching scrambling under the bed and then my fingers nudge the cold edge of the barrel and I grasp it with one hand and then two but his arms are around me now and he is lifting me up so I turn and twist and swing the butt of the gun down. There's a crack and a shudder as the reverberation ricochets through my arms and then he lets go and we both land with a thud on the ground and he's lying there now and he's not moving but I don't stop. I can't. I swing and I swing and I swing and cracks turn thicker, duller, mulchier, and then I realize that my hands and arms and face are wet and when I nudge my tongue out of my mouth I can taste blood and tears and something else, something thick and dark and of this world and not.

I sit on the edge of the bed in the blackness for I don't know how long. A minute. An hour. When the lilac light of dawn edges around the curtains, I pad into the bathroom and turn on the shower and clean myself off. I don't switch the lights on to dress.

I can see the outline of the body on the floor. I approach it tentatively, careful to avoid the puddle of black around the head. I feel around in his trouser pockets until I find it. I hit a button on the phone and it lights up in my hand, casting a yellowish halo around the room.

I can see his face now. What's left of it. It's the man I saw back in Colorado, the one who was leaning on the lamppost. I knew it would be him but something inside me is still disappointed. It means the game isn't finished. He's still out there. Waiting.

The phone is just a cheap thing, an old Nokia. A burner phone, I'd guess. There's only one number in his contacts. I bring up a fresh message field and type, "It's done." I hit Send and listen to the whoosh of the envelope as it flies off into the ether.

It should buy me some time. I don't know how much, but hopefully enough.

I slide the phone into my pocket and shove the rifle into the bag along with the towel I used to clean it. I wash my hands one last time in the sink, and then I edge open the door, slip through, and close it behind me. I don't look back.

The brittle hollow of my throat aches as I hurry down the stairs and out the back door. I can still feel his hands pressing the breath out of me. I circle back to the parking lot, careful to duck under the windows, but I don't need to worry—the motel is still asleep. I toss my bag into the back seat and spark up the engine and I'm miles down the highway by the time the sun crawls all the way up the horizon.

It's only then that I let myself cry, and even then it's only for a few seconds. I can't afford to waste any more time on it, and besides, crying hurts too much.

It's happening. It's really happening. He's come for me. And if he's come for me, he'll be coming for her, too.

I punch the gas and drive.

Maggie

Sifting through Anthony Tracanelli's life was like finding different fragments of the same broken vase. It had shattered the minute he blew the whistle at the FDA.

Of course, I couldn't find anything more about what he'd discovered about Prexilane. All those records had been either sealed or destroyed, presumably thanks to the same army of lawyers who'd helped to erase the forum thread about the possible side effects of Somnublaze. They were whitewashing the internet, bleaching it of anything that could make Prexilane look bad.

I couldn't sit still. It had been a while since Jim had left—surely there was news now. I dialed his number at the police station. "Any news on the chip?" I asked, before he'd had the chance to say hello.

"Not yet. Shannon's taking a look at it."

"Shannon?" I couldn't hide my surprise. "I didn't know she knew anything about computers."

He laughed. "I know what you're thinking, but she was an expert down in Florida, apparently. Worked in a department called Digital Forensics. Bright future ahead of her down there, too. None of us could figure out why she ended up here."

"The weather," I said, recalling the look of wonder on her face when she'd talked about snow. "She didn't like the heat down there. Said she wanted a real winter."

"Well, she'll get plenty of that. Anyway, she said it shouldn't take her more than a day or so to know what's on that chip, so we'll have answers for you soon."

My heart sank. "A day? Isn't there any way to move it along a little faster?"

Jim sighed, and I could hear the impatience in his voice. "We're going as fast as we can, Maggie. You just have to be a little more patient. There is some news about your friend, though. Tony."

My stomach still lurched at the sound of his name. "Do they know what happened to him?"

"Still inconclusive, though the guy down at Branville told me they're leaning toward suicide."

I went cold. I remembered the fear in his voice on the phone. "He didn't kill himself," I hissed.

"Look, I'm just telling you what I've been told."

"Jim—"

He cut me off. "He was a criminal, Maggie." I was silent. "He was some kind of pervert—did you know that?"

He must have found out about the indecent-material charges they mentioned in the newspaper. "Yes." And then, hurriedly, "No. I mean, he didn't tell me, I just read about it online. But, look, it's not important—"

"Not important?" His disbelief was like a brick wall between us. "I looked up his case file. Do you know the kind of stuff they found on this guy's computer? It makes me sick thinking he was anywhere near you."

Images crowded into my head, things I never wanted to imagine. I pushed them out. It wasn't him, I reminded myself. He'd said himself in that article that he'd been set up. I owed it to him to believe him. Ally must have trusted him. That meant I should, too. "It's not what you think," I said quietly.

"I've seen the photographs." Jim's voice was shaking with anger. "The man was sick." He took a breath. "He didn't touch you, did he? He didn't—"

The question hung between us like a bad smell. I thought of him reaching out toward me, the electric current when his fingers brushed my neck. "No," I said finally. "He never laid a finger on me."

He let out a deep breath down the line. "Thank God."

"Jim."

"It's my fault—I should have been paying closer attention to you."

"Jim."

"You were vulnerable, and this creep took advantage—"

"Jim!" I was sick to death of people acting like I was a child. Tony had been wrong to lie to me, but in some twisted way I knew he was trying to protect me, too. He wasn't a bad man. He didn't do those things they said about him in the papers, I was sure of it. They were behind it—all of it. I just had to figure out how. "I need you to listen to me. Tony didn't take advantage of me and he didn't commit suicide. He was killed, and it's all because of Ben Gardner."

Jim sighed down the line. I could picture him sitting in his office, his shiny black shoes propped up on the edge of his desk, one hand tucked behind his head, a mug of coffee cooling next to the phone. "We talked about all this."

"No, we haven't, because you refuse to listen to me. Tony was working for the FDA. He was investigating Prexilane—that's Ben's company, Jim. He'd lodged a complaint against them and he was fired from his job and then that—that stuff turned up on his computer."

"Filth. It was filth."

"Whatever it was, it doesn't matter. What matters is what he knew about Prexilane."

"What exactly was it you think he found out?"

I looked up at the framed photo of Ally above the mantel. Her smile beamed out at me, her dark hair tucked behind one ear, her eyes shining. She looked so young. Still just a little girl. "I don't know," I said finally. "But I think Ally knew, too, and I think that's why they both ended up dead."

Allison

I stop the car on a bridge about fifty miles from the motel. I roll down the window, check that there aren't any oncoming cars, and throw the burner phone as far as I can. I hear a quiet splash as it hits the water below, and then I roll up the window, turn on the radio, and peel back onto the road.

There was a pharmaceuticals conference in Chicago, and I'd convinced Ben to take me along. He had balked at the idea at first—he didn't like mixing business with pleasure, he said, and he was worried I'd be bored—but I convinced him in the end, and we'd flown there in his Mooney, the country spread out below us like a patchwork quilt.

It was Saturday afternoon. I was in our suite at the Peninsula, towel drying my hair and admiring the hand-painted wallpaper, when the phone clicked on.

"Ricci's vulnerable." It was Sam speaking. I knew his voice by heart then, heard its low, gravelly tone in my sleep.

"What do you mean?" This was Ben. He was meant to be presenting a seminar on DNA-targeted cancer treatments in the Gleacher Center, but I could hear the thrum and rumble of street noise in the background. "He's our best researcher."

It hit me like a thunderbolt. They were talking about Paul, Liz's husband. The woman who'd taken me under her wing at that party another lifetime ago. The only person out of all of them who'd shown me any kindness.

"It doesn't matter how good a researcher he is if he's going to go to the Feds."

I held my breath, my heart thudding in my chest. Ben swore down the line. "I don't believe this. We wouldn't be in this fucking mess if he was better at his job. He's been telling me that he's close to a fix." He sounded frantic.

"It's under control. Zeman's ready to step up."

There was a long, tense pause, and it was only when Ben exhaled that I realized he'd been holding his breath, and I'd been holding mine. "Fine. Get rid of Ricci, and tell Zeman he's been promoted, effective immediately."

The call cut out. I sat on the edge of the bed, holding the phone with shaking hands. I thought of the photo Liz had showed me of their kids, three curly-haired teenagers with identical dimples. What had Ben meant when he said "get rid of Ricci"? I thought back to the fear on Anthony's face when I mentioned Sam's name. *You don't know what he's capable of.* I did now, or at least I was starting to suspect it. I couldn't stand by and do nothing. I had to warn her.

I found her number on my phone and hit Dial. *Come on*, I chanted as the phone rang. *Pick up pick up pick up.*

"Hey, Allison!" Liz's warm voice came flooding from the phone, and I felt a rush of relief. I wasn't too late. "We're not having lunch today, are we? I had it down in the calendar for next week but God knows I can't seem to remember anything these days."

"No, it's not that," I said hurriedly. "I— I think Paul might be in trouble."

"Has something happened at work? It's not his heart, is it?" I heard the panic in her voice and felt a twinge of pity.

"No, it's . . ." I trailed off. I was gripping the phone tight against my face, and my cheek was already clammy with sweat. Now that I had her on the phone, I wasn't sure what to say. How could I warn her without telling her things that could put her in more danger? "Look, I can't explain. All I can say is that you and Paul should get out of town."

"I don't understand . . ."

I could hear a muffled rattling at the front door of the suite and then the neat snick of the lock. Someone was there. I ran to the bathroom and pulled the door shut behind me. She was the only friend I had left. I had to try to save her. "Listen to me," I whispered, "he's in danger. You are, too." My voice echoed off the tiled walls. "You have to leave. Please. Just pack a bag and go. It doesn't matter where." I willed her to believe me.

"Allison, please! You're not making any sense!" Liz's voice was panicked now, and I could tell that I was scaring her.

Ben's footsteps were hushed on the plush carpet. "Baby? Are you here?"

"I have to go," I whispered. My heart thudded in my chest. "Please, just do what I said."

"But—"

I ended the call and shoved my phone into the pocket of my robe. "I'll be out in a minute!" I called. I gripped the sides of the sink with both hands and stared at my reflection in the mirror. My cheeks were flushed, eyes glassy, and I could see my pulse pecking at the base of my neck. My voice screamed inside my skull. *You stupid, silly bitch. What were you thinking, calling her like that? How do you know they still won't get to her? How do you know they won't get to you first?*

No. I shut my eyes against myself and took a breath. *You had to warn her. You did what you had to do. Now get your shit together.*

Ben smiled when I opened the bathroom door. "C'mere," he said, opening his arms, and I walked into them, numb. "Your hair's still wet," he murmured, nuzzling his face in my neck. "Did you only just get out of the shower? Lazy girl."

I forced myself not to pull away. "I wasn't expecting you home so soon," I said. "I thought you were supposed to be at that seminar."

He shrugged. "I blew it off." He leaned over and kissed me on the lips. "Come on, get ready and we'll go get a drink."

I dressed carefully, choosing the little white dress I knew he liked. I slipped into the bathroom and rubbed lotion into my bare legs and put on my makeup and blow-dried my hair, all the time thinking about Liz and fighting off swells of panic. I wondered if she was on the phone to Paul right now, relaying what I'd said. I wondered if they would believe me. *Please, let them believe me.*

I stepped into my shoes and walked back into the bedroom. Ben was sitting on the edge of the bed, my phone cradled in his hands. My stomach lurched again. "Liz called," he said, tossing the phone toward me.

"Oh." My stomach bucked. I stared at the screen. No missed calls. Bile rose in my throat. "Did you answer it?"

"I saw her name come up so I said hi." He looked at me steadily. "That okay?"

"Of course!" I picked my engagement ring up off the vanity and slid it onto my finger. The diamond sparkled in the low light. "What did you guys talk about?" I worked to keep my voice even but it sounded strangled to my ears.

"Nothing interesting." I glanced over at him, and for a split second, I was sure I saw a flash of anger cross his face, but when I looked again his features were carefully arranged in a smile. "Come here," he said, his hands trailing up the skirt of my dress.

"You'll smudge my lipstick," I said, but I let myself be pulled down onto the bed. He flipped me onto my back and pinned my arms above my head. I stared up at him. I knew every inch of his face, but in that moment, he was a stranger to me.

"Fuck your lipstick," he murmured, and then his mouth was on mine and his hands were sliding across my body, pressing, kneading, searching, before he pushed himself inside me. I wasn't ready for him, and the pain of it made me gasp, but he didn't seem to notice. I squeezed my eyes shut against it. I thought of the passport in my bag, and the plane ticket tucked inside. *It will be over soon*, I promised myself, *and I'll be far, far away.*

He came quickly and rolled off, breathless. I watched as he pulled on his trousers and straightened his cuffs and ran his fingers through his hair. "Hurry up," he said, tossing a glance my way. "We'll be late."

I made my way unsteadily to the bathroom, where I fixed my hair and reapplied my lipstick. I was used to him being rough sometimes, had even asked for it on occasion, but this had been something else. Something pointed and cruel and designed to hurt.

I pried open the back of my cell phone with shaking hands, dislodged the chip, and slid it into the locket of my necklace.

I stared at my reflection in the mirror. Somewhere in my eyes, behind the blond hair and the mask of makeup, I saw a flash of something familiar. *She's still inside me somewhere, the woman I used to know, and I'm going to save her.*

And I swear to God I will make him pay.

Maggie

I stayed at the kitchen table for hours, searching for more information on Tony. He'd been married, that much had been true, and his wife had died of a heart attack the year before he was fired from the FDA. He'd worked there for almost twenty years, without so much as a single complaint until the whistle-blowing. His coworkers all said he'd never been a troublemaker. "A spotless record," as one of the articles described it.

I felt a tug in my stomach and realized I hadn't eaten anything. I opened a cabinet door, pulled out a jar of peanut butter, and dug around the cutlery drawer for a spoon. My fingers curled around the Mickey Mouse teaspoon we'd brought home from Disney World nearly twenty-five years earlier. Ally had refused to eat with anything else for a year. Charles and I had once watched her try to eat a pork chop with that spoon and our eyes had met across the dinner table. "Should have sprung for the knife and fork," he'd said, and Ally had scowled at her plate.

I spooned peanut butter into my mouth and stared out at the backyard. In the moonlight, I could see the begonias I'd planted in June drooping heavily in their borders.

I rubbed my eyes and looked up at the clock. It was past three already. My back ached from the hours spent sitting at the table staring at a screen. I poured a glass of water from the tap, gulping it down in a few greedy swallows, and headed into the darkened living room.

I fell heavily into Charles's chair and stared blankly into space. The sounds of the summer night were coming in through the screened windows, and the room was full of the muted sounds of crickets chirping and owls hooting and chipmunks and raccoons scurrying. There was a smell, too, of humid air and damp mulch and lingering heat.

I was living in a world full of shadows.

I felt a lump form in the hollow of my throat and waited for the tears to come. What was the use in trying to hold them back now? There was no one I was trying to be strong for. No reason for me to keep it together. Ally was still gone, and with Tony dead . . . I didn't know how much more fight I had left in me. I felt old and tired and spent.

I wished Charles were there. God, how I missed that man. His calm, sure voice, the glint in his eye when he was about to tell a joke, his cool palm resting on my hip as we slept. The smell of him in the morning. The rasp of his stubble against my cheek. The way we would look at each other when Ally was in the room, a mix of pride and awe.

He would have known what to do. He would have taken my hand and squeezed it and told me not to worry, that we'd get to the bottom of all this, that it would be all right. He'd have been lying when he said it, but I'd have allowed myself to believe him, even if only for a minute. And that belief would have been a kind of grace.

Maybe I should leave this place, I thought. Cut my losses and start fresh. Sell up, move to Florida, buy a little house or a condo near the ocean. Spend my days sitting in the sunshine with the other ghosts, waiting for our chance to be reunited with all the parts of ourselves we'd lost.

I leaned back in the chair, closed my eyes, and listened to the crickets' chorus in the grass until sleep pulled me down into its depths.

172 Miles to Go

Allison

The radio stations keep switching in and out, country turning to rock turning back to country. It's giving me a headache, so I snap the dial and roll down the window, letting the highway breeze cut through the stuffiness of the car. It's a scorcher of a day, nearing ninety already, and I keep one eye on the temperature gauge. It holds steady, though, and I say a silent thanks to Chet for selling the car to me. I'm starting to think it'll get me home after all.

The car drove us through the city's Sunday-deserted streets and deposited us at Midway airport in the early afternoon. Ben held my hand the entire ride, occasionally glancing over to give me a wink. He knew I was a nervous flier, especially in the Mooney. It wasn't that he was a bad pilot—the opposite, in fact—but it was rather the size of the tiny plane compared with the vast expanse of sky, like a toy suspended by some invisible child's hand.

We walked straight through the terminal and out onto the tarmac: security measures don't apply to the rich. The plane was waiting for us, its propeller glinting in the unrelenting sun. The heat seemed to come from every direction, the air thick with fumes. Ben took my bag from me and swung it into the luggage compartment.

"Come here," he said, pulling me into him and kissing me hard. "I'm going to miss you, pretty girl."

I looked at him blankly. "What do you mean?"

"Sam's going to take you back to San Diego," he said. "I've got a couple of things to take care of here." I followed his eyes and watched as Sam strode across the tarmac to meet us, a leather bag slung across his shoulder. He raised a hand in greeting.

My mind felt sluggish, like it was working at half speed. I tried to read his eyes but they were hidden behind dark sunglasses, and all I could see was my own stunned reflection staring back. "But— it's your plane. You're the pilot."

"Sam got his license at the same time as me. Did I never tell you that? He's a real ace, this guy. Aren't you, buddy?" Ben reached out and clapped him on the back. "You'll be in safe hands with him." The two men exchanged a look, and I saw the corners of Sam's mouth twitch. The terror pierced through, like so much ice water running through my core.

"Please, baby," I pleaded, grabbing for his hand. "I miss you so much when you're away, you know that. The house is so quiet without you. I want— I just— Please—" Fear was making me incoherent. I took a breath. "I could stay with you, keep you company . . ."

He shook his head. "I'll just be working the whole time—it'll be boring for you. Better to get you back to San Diego. Liz told me you were having lunch next week—you wouldn't want to miss it." Ben read the confusion on my face. "I talked to her last night— remember? When you were in the shower?" I nodded, uncertain. His face twisted into a rigid smile. "She told me something else, too—the craziest story about you warning her that Paul was in some kind of trouble." My vision swam. He reached up and cradled my chin in his tented fingers. "I thought you loved me," he said gently, shaking his head in disbelief.

I opened my mouth but no words came. The shock of it split me in two, and I felt for a second like my head had been removed from my body in one clean strike. Liz had betrayed me. I had betrayed Ben. I was totally and utterly alone, and now I was going to die.

He took off his sunglasses and his eyes bored into mine. There was nothing in them that I recognized now, no warmth, no love.

They were the cold, dead eyes of a killer. "Ben . . ." I whispered, but my throat swallowed the rest. There were no words for us now.

He squeezed my chin, too hard, and kissed me on the cheek. "You guys had better get going if you want to keep your slot."

The blood pounded in my ears as my eyes darted around the airfield. Was there someone I could shout to for help? No. *Run. I have to run.* The airport was a few hundred yards away—could I make it? I looked at the two of them standing there in front of me, Ben's long, lean frame and Sam's barrel-chested power. I'd never make it. Even if I did, what would I say when I got there? Liz was proof that I couldn't trust anyone. Anthony had been right: when the time came, no one would be able to help me. I was on my own.

Be ready, he'd said, but in the end I hadn't been, and now I was trapped like an animal on its way to the slaughter.

Sam took me roughly by the elbow and steered me toward the cabin door. "Wait!" I cried, wrenching myself away. I was tearful now, desperate. If I couldn't run, I would beg. "Ben, please. This is all a misunderstanding."

He reached up and brushed a lock of hair from my face. "I understand perfectly," he said, and then he reached down and kissed me hard on the mouth before pushing me toward Sam. The two of them had blocked me in. I had no choice but to board the plane. I made my way unsteadily up the stairs to the cabin, the metal frame swaying beneath my weight. I could feel Sam's weight on the stairs, and the heat of his body as he climbed behind me.

The door of the cabin clanged shut and the engine began to roar. I watched Ben stride away across the tarmac. That's when I realized that there would be no last-minute rescue. I was not in a fairy tale. There would be no prince at the end of my story.

I was on my own.

Maggie

The doorbell rang, startling me awake. It was morning—I'd fallen asleep in the living room. I pulled myself out of the armchair and walked stiffly to the front door. I tried to see who it was through the little window but all I could see was a man's broad back and a head of dark hair. A salesman, probably.

I opened the door. "Can I help you?"

The man turned around and smiled. "Mrs. Carpenter," he said, laying a hand across his chest. "It's so nice to finally meet you."

Allison

At first we were silent as the plane climbed into the sky. My insides had turned to liquid, hot and slick. Sam stared straight ahead, eyes fixed on the vast expanse of blue, hands tightly clutching the controls.

As long as he was flying the plane, he couldn't do anything. But as soon as we landed, I'd be dead.

How much did they know? My fingers fumbled at the neck of my dress until I found the locket. Did they know what was inside it?

I peered down at the mountain range stretched out below us like a crumpled sheet of paper. I thought of that invisible child's hand, bobbing us up and down through the blue sky, and then of the long, weightless drop into nothing.

A plan emerged from the terror-fog. I had watched Ben fly this plane dozens of times. If I could incapacitate Sam, I could try to land the plane myself and make a run for it. It probably wouldn't work, but I had to risk it. And if I was going to die, I would at least take him with me.

I could picture the self-defense instructor from college. "Eyes nose throat stomach groin feet," she would chant, over and over. She would make us repeat the words, too, and I chanted them then in my head.

Nose. He was a big man but he was slow. When I swung my elbow I felt the crunch of bone before he could raise his hands to stop me. "What the fuck?" he shouted, his words thick, his eyes stunned as they streamed. He held his hands to his face as blood poured out from between his fingers.

Eyes. I shoved one of my fingers deep into a socket. He made a noise that didn't sound human to my ears, a strangled sort of scream. He held one of his bloodied hands up to his blinded eye, cupping it like a wounded bird. Tears and snot were mixing with the blood now, and the effluvia ran down his forearms and onto his pristine white collared shirt.

Fight. I seized the moment and grabbed hold of the abandoned controls. The plane was losing altitude. I pictured Ben's hands on the controls. What would they do to correct this?

Think. I reduced the throttle and pulled back on the column, and the plane groaned and shuddered as it climbed. Sam recovered and grabbed me by the throat. My hands slipped off the controls. His bloodied fingers clawed at me. His face was mottled, his nose already swollen, his bad eye streaming whitish pink. The engine stuttered and the power failed. I elbowed him away and tried to steady the column. An alarm began emitting a low wail.

"What have you done?" I heard the panic in his voice, and then he was shaking me, hard, my head thudding against the dashboard. "What the fuck have you done?"

Fight.

And then the plane began to fall.

He pulled me up and away by my arms and threw me against the side of the cabin. The alarms continued to blare. "Fuck!" He was panicked now, pressing buttons, pushing the throttle down, wrenching the rudder out from underneath his leg and trying to steer it straight, his one good eye skittering across the flashing control panel. But it was too late. "You stupid bitch! What the fuck did you do? What did you do?" We were falling, falling. We were weightless.

This was it. I was going to die.

No.

I'd read a story once in the newspaper about a girl surviving a plane crash. She was in a prop plane with her boyfriend and two friends. The plane lost altitude and crashed into the side of a mountain. The other three died on impact, but the girl emerged practically unscathed. She hiked down the mountain, flagged down a park ranger, and was taken to safety. When she was interviewed about her miraculous survival, she told the journalist that she'd lived because she'd stayed calm. She hadn't succumbed to panic like the others.

My mother's voice in my head. *Don't panic, Ally. Breathe.*

I took a breath, filling my lungs with as much air as they could gather, and then exhaled. Sam was in his own world now, one of pain and terror and rage. He didn't notice as I climbed back into my seat, clicked my seat belt into place, and folded myself into the brace position. His hands were pounding on the dashboard now as the alarm continued its mournful wail. *Go limp*, I told myself. *Just go limp.*

As the mountain came nearer and the carpet of green pixilated into individual trees that waved in the breeze and heralded our arrival, I reached toward him. He was screaming now, a raw animal sound, his hands clawing at the windshield. He didn't notice me unclasping his seat belt.

Head down. Brace. Breathe.

I clutched suddenly at my necklace, fingers fumbling with the clasp. I had to see their faces one last time. I clicked open the locket and gazed down at the photograph, my parents in miniature, pressed flat inside the gold disk. "I'm sorry," I said, eyes blurring with tears. "I'm so, so sorry." I clutched the locket in my fist and mouthed the words inscribed on the back: *God protect him as he travels, by air or land or sea, keep him safe and guide him, wherever he may be.*

I closed my eyes and let the earth come to me.

Survive.

Maggie

He was better looking in the photographs. In real life, there was something too angular about the set of his jaw. Still, his eyes were a deep, sapphire blue, and the smile he was currently directing toward me was wide and displayed a perfect set of white, even teeth. I could see the appeal.

"You're dead," I said, blinking dumbly.

"I know this must be a shock," he said, pushing past me into the house. I watched him take in the room in a single glance: the floral wallpaper in the hallway, the threadbare rugs, Charles's armchair with the outline of my body still imprinted on its cushion. I fought the urge to apologize for the mess.

I trailed after him as he headed toward the kitchen. "They found your body. Your parents told me there'd been a funeral."

"There was a service, yes. Very nice, too, I hear." He picked up a sheaf of papers from the table, flicked through them, set them down again. "Mrs. Carpenter—may I call you Maggie? You have a lovely home." He paced around the kitchen, fingers trailing across the countertop. "It's very . . . cozy."

"What are you doing here?"

He didn't answer. He picked up a dishcloth, refolded it, and hung it over the oven handle.

I followed him into the living room, where he took up a place by the mantel. He picked up one of Charles's little tin cars and cradled it in his palm. The photograph of Ally looked down at us. He followed my eyes and smiled. "Beautiful, isn't she?"

"What are you doing here?" I said again. Shock was flooding through me in waves.

He placed the car back on the mantel and turned to face me. "I thought it was time I met the mother of my fiancée."

I took a step toward him. "Where is she? Is she still alive? What have you done with her?"

He pulled out a chair and offered it to me, concern washing over his face. "You look pale," he said. "Please, sit down. I know this must be a shock. Please, sit down."

"I'm fine standing." I didn't want him to see how badly I was shaking.

He smiled. "At least let me get you a glass of water." He walked back into the kitchen and I heard the rattle of glass and the tap thundering into the sink. I stared around the room, dazed. Was this really happening? I asked myself. Or had I finally lost my mind?

When he came back into the room, the full terror of it all sank in. I had no idea who this man was, or what he was capable of. I had to keep myself under control. He handed me the glass and I sipped from it dutifully.

"Can I get you anything else?" He stood over me, handsome and solicitous in his rolled-up shirtsleeves. "I saw the coffee maker—I could make you a cup?"

The bile in my stomach rose and fizzed unpleasantly at the back of my throat. I shook my head. "Please," I said weakly. "I have a right to know what's going on."

"Please, let's sit."

I nodded and fell back onto the sofa, too numb or weak to keep standing anyway.

"It seems there have been a . . . series of misunderstandings," he said carefully, lowering himself into Charles's armchair. The leather creaked beneath his weight.

"I saw the reports," I stuttered. "They matched the dental records—"

He frowned. "These things are never infallible. Records get lost, or misplaced."

"So you weren't on that plane?" I thought of all the hours of research I'd done. The bright glare of San Diego, the musty hush of the Bowdoin library, the groan and whir of the old computer still sitting in my kitchen, waiting. Of all the things I'd suspected, I'd never once questioned that he was dead.

He shook his head. "A last-minute change of plans. Unavoidable."

"But— You were the pilot," I stuttered. "If you weren't on the plane, who was flying it?"

He swatted the question away like a fly. "It doesn't matter."

"I don't understand." A feverish hope suddenly gripped me. If he was alive—if he hadn't died in that plane crash—hadn't even been on that plane . . . "Does that mean Allison wasn't on that plane, either? Is she alive, too?"

He looked at me sadly and the corners of his mouth tugged down into a frown. "Allison was on the plane. I'm sorry."

I fell heavily back to earth. "But she— But you— I don't—" I stammered. I felt stupid, like the answer must be obvious to everyone but me, but I just couldn't see it.

"I'm sorry," he said again, quietly. "I loved her very much. I would have given her anything she wanted." He reached out and took my hand in his. "You see, I'm a good man, Maggie. That's something your daughter didn't always appreciate." His voice was calm and even, his blue eyes shining and unreadable. He reached toward my neck. His fingers were cool and powder dry on my skin. I flinched. He lifted the necklace from inside my blouse and studied it. "I never understood why she wore this thing," he said, weighing it in his palm. I could feel his breath on my collarbone. "I always thought it looked a little . . . cheap."

My voice came out as a whisper. "Her father gave it to her. They were very close."

He nodded toward the locket. "Do you mind." It wasn't a question. He flicked it open and gazed at the photograph inside. "You two look very happy. We were happy, too." He lifted the photograph out of the locket with his fingernail. I watched a muscle in his jaw twitch. Terror was coursing through me now, ice water in my veins.

"Where is it?" His voice was barely audible.

"I don't know what you're talking about." I was shaking violently now, like one of those paint cans in a mixer, and I hated myself for it but I couldn't stop.

"Oh no. I won't fall for that again." He smiled at me then, that broad, blinding smile. That's when I knew he was crazy. "Your daughter played me for a fool. Do you understand what it feels like be betrayed by the woman you wanted to marry?"

I shook my head. The air was suddenly thick with the threat of violence.

"Dying," he said quietly. "It feels like dying."

15 Miles to Go

Allison

I pull off at the exit and head for the crossroads. The McDonald's is still there. So is the discount mattress store. The Starbucks is new.

Granville is just south of Owl's Creek. As a teenager, I'd come here every weekend to wander the sprawling corridors of the Granville Mall. I never bought much—a pair of earrings from Claire's Accessories, a T-shirt from the sales rack in Gap, a couple of CDs from HMV. It wasn't the buying that drew us there, whole packs of us roaming the stores in our low-rise jeans and our too-loud voices. It was the feeling of having something to do, however frivolous. Owl's Creek felt like our parents' town, one that had closed in on itself a long time earlier. My father would tell me about the drive-in they used to go to, and the dances they would have in the town hall, and it all seemed so alien to this boarded-up place we haunted, with its dusty library and its Salvation Army and its diner serving eggs all day. Granville was a glimpse of the wider world, albeit a world that smelled like Abercrombie cologne and deep-fried cheese. It held potential.

And now, here I am, almost back where I started. I'd flown too close to the sun and I was plummeting back to earth at speed, my wings long gone, my hair streaming out behind me in the wind.

I take a right at the Marshalls and a left at the gas station. I don't look at the signs. I don't need to. These roads are all wired deep into my brain. I don't have to think where I'm going. I just go. Down the long road to Owl's Creek, the one with the bend I used to take too quickly, gripping the wheel with both hands and laughing as the tires screeched. Straight past the elementary school where I won third place in the science fair. A left by the playground where I had my first kiss with a boy called Andy. A right onto the street where I rode my bike during the summer. The barbershop where I had my first haircut. The old warehouse, windows still blown out. The diner, still needing a lick of paint. It's all here, just like I never left it.

I pull over in the parking lot behind the liquor store and get out of the car. My legs are so stiff that I stumble for the first few steps. It's hot, the kind of hot that makes the pavement sing. The sky is the brightest blue and I can hear the faint tinkle of an ice cream truck in the distance and remember, suddenly, that it's summer. People are on their way to barbecues, and lying on lounge chairs inhaling the smell of chlorine and sunscreen, and eating Popsicles that dribble down their knuckles before they have the chance to catch the drips with their tongues.

I pop the trunk and take out the rifle. It feels heavy in my hands and the metal is hot to the touch. I check the chamber and slide in another bullet. Three shots. That's all I'll have.

I place the rifle on the floor of the passenger seat and climb back into the driver's seat. I take a deep breath. The air carries the scent of geraniums and Joe-Pye weed mixed with a hundred freshly mowed lawns and the acrid tang of melting asphalt. All the smells of a Maine summer.

I'm close now. I'm almost home.

Maggie

A mechanical chime rang through the house. We both froze. I could see the outline of a slim figure through the frosted glass. The doorbell rang again and a voice called out to me. "Mrs. Carpenter? Are you there?" My heart dropped as soon as I recognized her voice.

Ben swiveled toward me. "Who is that?" he hissed.

"Shannon," I said quickly. "She's a friend of mine." I wondered if I should mention she was a police officer, see if I could scare him a little, but I didn't want to risk it. This was a man who had faked his own death. I didn't want Shannon getting mixed up in this mess.

A palm pressed itself against the glass. "I saw your car in the driveway," Shannon called. "Jim sent me over. I've got the results of the chip!"

I heard the breath catch in his throat. "Let her in," he said hoarsely, and he placed a hand on my shoulder and shoved me toward the door.

My feet felt like lead. I wanted to shout a warning to her, to swing open the door and tell her to run, but instead I watched myself turn the doorknob with a shaking hand and pull open the door.

Shannon smiled at me from the doorstep. "I knew you were home!" she scolded, stepping into the hallway. "What took you so long?"

"I—" I glanced behind me. The living room was empty. I looked back at her. She was in uniform, her gun holstered snuggly against her hip. I knew it was her job to protect people, but her face was so young and open, and she was so tiny, like a little bird . . . it made me want to protect her. "I was in the bathroom," I said hurriedly. "Look, it's not a great time. I'm not feeling so hot, and I was just about to lie down . . ."

"You do look kind of pale." She placed a hand on my forehead and frowned. "You don't feel like you have a fever, though. Can I get you something? A cup of tea maybe? Some Advil?"

I shook my head. "You're sweet, but I'm fine, honestly. It's probably better if you go, though. I don't want you to catch whatever I've got."

"I have an immune system like a horse," she declared, waving me away. "Besides, I think you're going to want to hear what I have to tell you. That thing you found inside Allison's locket was a micro-SD card. It's basically a memory storage device, and you can use it to record conversations, which is what she was doing. There are hours of audio recordings on that card—maybe hundreds. I haven't had the chance to go through everything, but Jim filled me in on what you'd told him and you were right—she was definitely digging for dirt on that company."

"Please, Shannon," I said, pushing her toward the door. I was shaking now, my palms clammy, dread a cold stone in my stomach. "We can talk about all of this later. I'd really rather be alone right now."

Shannon ignored me. "She knew Anthony Tracanelli, too," she continued. "There are documents from him on the chip. How did you say you knew him again?"

I fought the urge to physically shove her out the door. I needed her out of the house, right then, before she said another word. "Shannon, please—"

A muffled thud came from the kitchen, and both of us froze.

She studied me carefully, as if seeing me for the first time. I tried to keep my gaze steady, but I knew she could see the fear in my eyes. "Is someone else here?"

"No," I said, too quickly. She tried to move past me but I blocked her way. Out of the corner of my eye, I saw Ben's shadow pass across the floor. "Please," I begged. "I'm asking you to go."

"I've just made a pot of coffee."

Shannon and I turned and watched Ben pad lightly into the

hallway. His face was a mask of polite calm. "Why don't you invite your friend in for a cup?"

I waited for a flicker of recognition to register in Shannon's eyes, but none came. She shot me a suspicious glance. "I thought you said no one was here?"

I opened my mouth to speak, but nothing came out. I felt trapped in my body, like I was hovering above it, powerless. Paralyzed.

She was already pushing past me into the kitchen. Ben smiled as she passed and motioned for me to follow. It felt like the bones in my legs had dissolved.

The kitchen smelled of freshly brewed coffee mixed with that aftershave of his, a spicy musk undercut with the sharpness of citrus. Shannon was already sitting at the table, watching closely as Ben poured coffee into three mugs.

He noticed me lingering in the doorway. "Please," he said, "sit down." His voice was light but I could hear the hard edge scraping against it. I sat down at the table and tried not to meet Shannon's searching eyes. If she thought everything was fine, maybe she'd leave. Maybe there was still time. I noticed her fingers hovering lightly on the edge of her holster. She didn't think everything was fine.

"I don't think we've been introduced," Ben said as he set a steaming mug in front of her. "I'm Ben Gardner."

I watched the shock flicker across her face for a split second, but she recovered lightning quick. She nodded, just once, and said in a steady, official-sounding voice, "Maybe you'd like to explain what you're doing here."

He shook his head and smiled. "I don't think I would, actually." He picked up the sugar bowl and held it out to her. "Sugar?"

She shook her head. "No, thank you. Just milk."

He tipped a spoonful of sugar into his mug and stirred it carefully before placing the wet spoon back in the sugar bowl. I watched the sugar around it darken and fuse. "So," he continued, pausing to take a sip, "what were you saying to Maggie about a memory card?"

Shannon barely even blinked. "I'm guessing that's why you're here." She might have looked like a sweet kid, but she was cool as a cucumber now. She kept her gaze trained on Ben. "I would have thought somebody like you would have been more discreet about using the telephone."

"What do we have in this world if not our trust in people?" He scraped his chair forward. "That said, I'd love to hear what you think you have on me. I'm sure it's all just a misunderstanding."

Shannon ignored him. "A man died recently. A former FDA employee called Anthony Tracanelli." She knew that Tony had worked at the FDA, too. I wondered what else she'd found out. "Do you know him?"

Ben shrugged, but I saw the muscles in his jaw tighten. "I meet a lot of people."

"He was investigating your company. He'd been compiling evidence to prove that Prexilane misled the public about the side effects of one of its medications. Somnublaze. He was killed in his hotel room not far from here." Her eyes flickered briefly to mine, as if to temper the shock rattling through me. So it was murder, not suicide, after all, and Ben had been behind it. I felt a movement under the table. I glanced down and saw that she'd unclipped her holster now and her hand was resting on the handle of her gun. "But I guess you don't know anything about that, either."

Ben reached across the table and handed her a small jug of milk and a teaspoon. "You haven't had the milk yet. Here, help yourself."

Shannon used her free hand—her left—to lift the jug. Her hand shook slightly as she poured and the milk splashed onto the surface of the table—the only sign of fear she'd given away. Ben watched carefully as she placed the jug onto the table and picked up the spoon with the same hand.

What happened next was so quick I could barely piece it together in my mind. One second Shannon was stirring her coffee with her teaspoon, the metal chinking against ceramic, and the next she was on the floor, blood spreading out of a hole in her chest and onto the tile floor.

I was on my hands and knees, cradling her head in my arms as her wide, panicked eyes stared up at the ceiling.

The blood kept coming, so red it was almost black. I pressed my hands against it, hoping to stem the tide. I'd never seen so much blood in my life. It spread out from underneath us like a carpet, and it soaked through my jeans to the skin. Shannon's blood. How was this moment real? How could this possibly be happening? I looked up to see Ben holding a gun in one shaking hand and wiping the spilled milk off the table with a dishcloth with the other. He looked numb.

"You shot her," I said dumbly. Shannon's pale face stared up at us from the floor. I could hear the breath rattling through her chest, ragged and faint. The blood kept coming. "We have to call an ambulance," I said. "We have to do something."

He shook his head. He looked like a scared, sad little kid. "You know we can't do that." That's the moment I knew he was going to kill me. I felt tired then. So tired.

"What really happened with Ally?" I asked.

He held out a hand to help me up off the floor but I refused it. "I'm sorry," he said gently. "I never meant for any of this to happen."

And then he raised his arm above me and the world went black.

Zero Miles to Go

Allison

I pull the car to the curb a block away from the house. Outside, a little boy wobbles up the street on his bicycle, training wheels holding him steady. His mother is close behind, sipping iced coffee out of a straw, baby strapped to her chest. I wait until they pass, and then I get out of the car and sling the rifle around my neck.

I'm calm as I hop the first fence. This used to be the Walters' house—I had a crush on Billy Walters when I was thirteen and used to gaze over the fence in the hope of catching glimpses of him—but now the mailbox out front is unmarked, and the blue wooden cladding has been painted a deep green. There's a pool in the backyard now, too, and I skirt around a cluster of pool toys: diving rings, a half-inflated raft, a nest of Styrofoam noodles. I glance in the windows as I go past. It's dark inside, the kitchen empty and still, but a pair of golden eyes peer back. A large orange cat is sitting on the windowsill, eyeing me suspiciously.

I keep low and press myself against the perimeter of the fence. It's bordered by thick shrubs, and the small green leaves catch on my clothes. My jeans are sticking to my thighs, and I can feel the sweat dribbling down the back of them and pooling in the shallows of my knees.

I climb the next fence, into the Mancuzos' yard. Mr. Mancuzo was always proud of his roses, and they're as beautiful as ever, huge pink blooms yawning up at the sky. Laundry waves gently on the line: a couple of undershirts, a bedsheet, a single pillowcase. Mrs. Mancuzo died a few years before my dad. Cancer, too. From somewhere deep inside the house, I hear the forced-chipper voices of a daytime talk show. I press my back against the wall and hurry on.

Next, the McCormicks', and then the Stones', and then the Woodburys', who've left the lawn mower out in the yard to rust.

And then, finally, our house.

I peer over the fence. The first thing I see is the swing set. It's a little rustier than before, but still standing. I remember my father pushing me on that swing, higher and higher until, for the briefest moment, the chain went slack and I would feel the stomach-flip of weightlessness. I remember my mother cautioning him to take it easy—*She'll fall off!* she'd yell—but he wouldn't listen. Higher and higher and higher until I could lean back and see only the sky above my shoes.

Now, setting eyes on it for the first time in over two years, I'm struck by how familiar it all is. The grass is a little overgrown, and the usually neat rows of begonias are looking a little worse for wear, but still—nothing's really changed. Everywhere I look, I can see shadow versions of myself, and memories intersecting and overlapping until they dissolve in a sort of enveloping haze.

I take a deep breath. There is still one person alive in this world who matters to me, and she is just beyond those glass doors.

I've got to find her.

Maggie

I'm lying on the couch, but I can't be sure how I got there. Time comes in stuttered bursts. My vision blurs. I reach up and touch my forehead. My fingers come away wet, my own blood mixed with Shannon's.

Shannon. Oh, God.

My eyes focus for a second and I see Ben sitting in a chair opposite, watching. "Don't try to move," he says quietly. "It will hurt too much." His voice is almost kind.

I rest my head back on the arm of the sofa and stare up at the patterned whorls on the ceiling. Charles plastered it himself when we first moved in. I close my eyes and let the weight press down on me. I am so tired now, down to my very bones. Everything in this world is lost to me now. All I want to do is sleep.

"How did you know?" My voice sounds strange to my ears, like it's coming from far away. "About the locket, I mean. How did you find out?"

"Your phone," he says quietly, and I curse myself for not being more careful. Ben's voice breaks through the silence. "I've liked listening to you." My eyes flicker open. He's looking at me with something that's almost like affection. "You remind me of her." I close my eyes against him. I hear him get to his feet. "Who else knows what's on the microSD card?"

I can't bring myself to answer. The effort of opening my mouth is too much. He repeats the question. I hear him moving toward me. He places a hand on my forehead. It reminds me of when I was a child and my mother would lay a cold compress across my eyes when I had a fever. "Please." His voice is gentle. Soothing. I feel myself lulled by it. "I don't want to make this any worse than it has to be. Just tell me everything you know, and this will all be over." He's pleading now, desperate. I open my eyes just enough to see his silhouette, backlit by the afternoon sun streaming in through the window.

I shake my head, just a little. Ally died trying to uncover his secrets. I'm not about to let her down. Not now. Not again.

I feel a shadow fall over me and I know he's above me now. It's only a matter of time before he pulls the trigger and ends this.

I'm ready.

Allison

The house is silent as I approach it, unwilling to give up its secrets. I try the back door. Locked. I lift the potted plant to the left of the door and pick up the small bronze key tucked underneath. Some things never change. I fit the key in the lock and turn it, wincing at the sound, and slowly slide open the door.

I step inside.

The kitchen is dark except for a shaft of light coming through the window. I inhale. It smells like bleach and coffee and olive-and-thyme Yankee Candle just like always, but there is something else there now. Something feculent and metallic. That's when I see it. Her. The body sprawled on the floor, the face peaceful except for the dot of blood at the corner of her mouth and the hole in her chest. The floor is spread sticky with black blood. The smell of it overpowers me, its sickly sweetness filling my nostrils, seeping into my lungs, my skin. Bile catches in the back of my throat and I have to force myself not to retch.

I'm too late.

Wait.

I crouch down next to the body. I don't recognize her face, but I can tell that she's young. She's wearing a police uniform. I sag with relief. It's not her. There's still a chance.

There's a noise coming from the living room. A faint scraping sound. I freeze. The sound of the blood pounding in my ears drowns out everything else, and I have to force myself to quiet my thundering heart. I listen again. There's nothing now, just the steady ticking of the clock, but it feels as though the walls are throbbing. Someone is in there.

I raise the rifle to my shoulder and take a step forward. I'm at the edge of the doorway, the late-afternoon light throwing shadows into the hall. I edge my way around the frame, breath caught tight in my throat. Dad's old armchair comes into view, and the fireplace with its mantel lined with knickknacks, and the threadbare rug, and the photograph of me. It was taken when I was a senior in high school, at a professional studio off Route 32. The photographer was an old hippie, complete with worry beads and a long graying pony-tail, and he'd encouraged me to unbutton a few more buttons on my blouse and hike up my skirt a little. "Such a gorgeous girl," he'd said, almost to himself, as the camera clicked away. I'd just smiled and smiled. No one had called me pretty much yet in my life, other than my parents, and hearing the words had held a sort of power over me. When I got the negatives, I felt a little sick. There I was, pouting for some old man, my shoulder cocked toward the camera, hand balanced on thrust hip. I ended up tossing half of them in the garbage before I showed my parents. Dad had picked out the one that was now framed on the wall. It was a close-up of my face, and I was smiling with all my teeth, like the kid I'd really been.

I lean forward and crane my neck around the corner. I can see her now, lying back on the sofa, her eyes closed. My mother. It's such a normal sight, my mother asleep on the couch, hands tucked into her armpits like always, knees bent, feet tucked together. But something isn't right. Her skin is yellowish and waxy, and her eyes seem to have sunk into the bruised skin of the sockets. The breath catches in my throat. There's a mark on her forehead, deep. There's blood.

I'm too late. I've lost her. He has taken everything from me now, every single scrap of self that I'd managed to build and rebuild and scrape together and hide away. All of it is gone. I am no longer loved by anyone in this world. I have nothing left to lose.

Rage surges through me like an electric current.

He did this.

As soon as I find him, I am going to fucking kill him.

Maggie

There's a voice. It's small and faint and faraway, but it's there. I can hear it. I reach for it like a plant reaches for the sun, up up up up up into the light.

Allison

I've lost it now, all pretense of stealth. A noise swells up in my rib cage, somewhere between a scream and a howl. I charge into the living room, gun fixed to my shoulder, finger pressed tightly against the trigger. My eyes search the room for signs of movement, but there's no one else here, only my mother lying on the sofa, just like my father lay on that same sofa two years ago. I push the thought out of my skull. "Where are you?" I scream, the rifle rattling against my collarbone. "I want to fucking see your face, you fucking coward!"

There's a noise, a low, brittle rasp, and I freeze. It sounds like a bird beating its wings against the walls of its cage. It's coming from my mother.

I drop to my knees in front of her, and the rifle drops with me. "Mom?" Her eyelids flutter. "Mom, can you hear me? It's Ally. I'm here, Mom. I'm home."

Her lips part but no words emerge, just a moan from somewhere deep inside her. Relief surges through me, followed by an almost-animal urge to protect her. She's still here with me. I won't lose her now.

"Don't worry. Just relax. I'm going to get help." I touch the wound on her forehead. The blood around it has started to coagulate, and a dark bruise has begun to form. Nasty, I think, but not fatal. Relief flows through me again, warm as bathwater. "It's going to be okay," I whisper.

"You made it." I spin around to see Ben emerge from the corner, a gun pointed at my head. "I knew you would." I glance down at the rifle lying at my feet. He kicks it away and the rifle skitters under the sofa. My mother moans softly. He's looming over us both. There's blood spattered on the starched white collar of his shirt.

"Leave her alone," I say, climbing unsteadily to my feet. He keeps the gun trained on me and I hold up my hands. "I don't care if you kill me, but promise me you'll leave her alone. This is between you and me."

He shakes his head sadly. "She knows too much now." He takes a step forward. "This is all your fault, you know. It didn't have to be this way. We were happy together, weren't we?"

His eyes are plaintive. I feel a dull pain in my breastbone, like an old bruise being prodded. "Yes," I said softly. "We were happy." The ghost of a smile appears on his lips, and he reaches out and touches a finger to my cheek. A chill runs through me. "But it was a lie," I say, taking a step back. "You aren't the man I thought you were. You're a monster."

His head snaps back as if he's been struck. "And what about you? Are you the person you told me you were?" He lets out a mean laugh. "You were just some coked-up whore when I met you."

My eyes dart to my mother lying on the sofa. "That's not true."

He laughs again and takes a step closer. "What's wrong? Are you afraid your mother will find out what you were really up to at that bar and won't love you anymore?" He reads the shock on my face and smiles. "I knew all along. Do you really think I'd propose to a woman without running a background check on her?" He shakes his head. "That's what hurt the most, you know. I pulled you out of the gutter. I lied to my family about you, pretended that you were this sweet, naive little girl from Maine, brought you into my world, and gave you everything you wanted—everything." His eyes are wild now. "I gave you everything," he whispers, "and you betrayed me. So now, I'm going to take everything away from you."

My knees start to give way and I have to steady myself on the back of my dad's armchair. "You won't get away with it. They'll find out what you've done, that you're still alive. You'll go to jail."

He shakes his head. "You ended up doing me a favor. When I

341

first heard about the crash, I was angry. Sam was like a brother to me. But when the first reports came out listing me as the pilot, I realized that it might be better to stay dead. Easier for everyone." There's a weight in his voice, and for a minute I can see him again, the man I fell in love with, the one who talked about saving the world, who wanted more than anything to make people happy. With a blink, he's gone. "Once this is all taken care of, I'm going to disappear."

I shake my head. "I don't understand. If you're going to disappear anyway, what does it matter if Prexilane is exposed?"

He smiles a little half smile. "My parents are the only two people who knew I wasn't on that plane. My father agreed to keep up the pretense as long as I bought him enough time to get the equity out of the company before shit hit the fan."

The pieces fall into place, one by one. "Your parents know you're alive?" I think of the grief in my mother's eyes in the photograph from the memorial, and the pain she must have suffered thinking I had been killed in some horrific twisting wreck of metal and blood. His parents had been spared that pain. They had been spared everything.

"My father has been behind the scenes for a while now, ever since the shareholders got wind of the settlements." He looks in that moment like he must have looked as a child, small and vulnerable and desperate for approval. "I told him that I would fix it. I told all of them I would fix it, but they didn't believe me, and then you took away my chance. I was going to make things right, Allison. I didn't mean to hurt anyone. I would have made things right." He cups my chin in the palm of his hand and I feel his fingers trembling against my skin. "Why didn't you let me make things right? I loved you."

I twist my head away from his grasp. "You never loved me. You just wanted to dress me up like a doll and fuck me."

He shakes his head and smiles. "You're right. I should have just paid for it like everybody else." He lifts the gun and I watch him unlatch the safety. My vision tunnels. In a second, the bullet will be released from its chamber and it will tear through my skull and kill me. And once he's killed me, he'll kill my mother, too. I can't let that happen. I have to stop him.

My entire body tenses, my muscles like coiled spring. The blood thunders. *This is it. This is my chance.* I close my eyes and launch my body forward into space.

My forehead connects with the bridge of his nose with a crack. Shock makes him drop the gun but soon he's down on the ground, one hand searching desperately for the gun while the other holds his shattered nose. Blood pours onto the wood floor. I'm dazed, too, my head throbbing from the impact, stars spinning behind my eyes, but I can still see enough to stamp on his fingers as they wrap themselves around the butt of the gun. He lets out a howl and then swipes out at me desperately, his fist connecting with the edge of my kneecap and sending me crashing to the floor beside him. We're grappling now, arms and legs wrapped together, breath heavy, mouths searching for flesh to bite. The floor is slick with his blood and our sweat. It is all so familiar, so close to the way we used to fuck, violence almost indistinguishable from a certain type of love. He sinks his teeth into my shoulder and I scream.

He's standing on top of me now, with the butt of the gun tight in his fist, and he swings it down onto the side of my skull and the pain is shocking, literally shocking, a sort of hot white heat that sears through me. I open my eyes long enough to see him lift the gun and point the barrel and the tendons in his hand tighten as his fingers squeeze the trigger and there is the crack of a gunshot and he is falling on top of me and his weight is enough to snuff out my remaining breath.

Maggie

I'll never stop hearing the sound the gun made when it hit her, nor the sight of her falling to the ground. Lifeless.

He was standing over her, his back turned toward me. He'd forgotten I was there, I could tell, but I knew he'd remember soon enough. I had to act fast. I pulled myself up and felt around under the sofa until I found it. The rifle.

When I hefted it to my shoulder it felt just like cradling a baby. Natural. As if I'd been doing it all my life.

The safety was already off and my finger found the trigger just as he raised the gun again and pointed it at Ally. I saw her eyes open, I saw the terror in them as she stared down the barrel of that gun, and I squeezed the trigger.

A rifle like that isn't meant to be used in the home. It's meant for long-range kills. The recoil threw me back against the sofa and the smell of sulfur filled my nostrils. I looked again and saw him standing there, swaying. There was a hole in the center of his back already blackening with blood.

He fell forward onto Ally and I heard the breath whistle out of her lungs.

I tried to pull him off her but I couldn't. He was too heavy, or I was too weak. Time passed. I don't know how much. Maybe a few minutes. Maybe an hour. And then a door opened and a strong pair of hands were on my shoulders pulling me away and the only sound I could hear were the ragged sobs that I realized, after a while, were coming from me.

Allison

A weight is lifted off me.

Breathe.

"Don't move her too much," I hear a voice say. "Careful with her neck."

I open my eyes and look up at a familiar face peering down at me. "Don't worry," Jim says, "just try to stay still. The ambulance is on its way. You're going to be all right, though. You've got a nasty bump on your head, but you'll be just fine."

"Mom." I don't recognize my own voice.

"Ally," my mother says, "I'm right here, honey." I feel her hands on my face, cool and dry. Her fingers find the scar that laces around my skull. "Oh, Ally," she whispers, "what happened to you?"

"It's okay, Mom," I murmur. The pain is a mist and I have to fight my way through it to her. "It's okay. I'm home."

She leans down and kisses my forehead. "I know you are," she says. "I know."

After

Allison

"I don't think Sox fans can take much more bad news, Chuck.

"In business news, the pharmaceutical company Prexilane has seen its share value plummet since the Federal Drug Administration announced it was opening an investigation into the safety of its top-selling antidepressant, Somnublaze. Evidence has recently come to light that top executives issued bribes to FDA officials and falsified trial data in order to cover up side effects of the drug, which are reported to include temporary psychosis.

"Prexilane's former chief executive, Ben Gardner, was declared dead following a plane crash in the Colorado mountains, but it's been revealed that he faked his own death in order to extricate himself from the scandal. He was later killed in an altercation between himself and his former fiancée, Maine native Allison Carpenter, also falsely presumed dead in the crash.

"His father, David Gardner, is currently awaiting trial. We'll have more as this story unfolds."

The newscaster shakes his expertly coiffed head. "Sounds like we'll be hearing plenty more about this one, Susan."

I flick the television off with the remote. I don't want to hear any more about Ben. I'll be hearing his name enough when the Prexilane case goes to trial.

It's been two weeks since the incident, as I'm calling it now, even though it was more like the giant clusterfuck. I spent the first week in the hospital with my head wrapped in bandages, feeling like my brain had been stuffed full of cotton. Ben fractured my cheekbone when he hit me, and there's a nasty scrape on the top of my skull from where the bullet grazed it. He missed by a few millimeters, the doctor told me, shaking his head in disbelief. "You're a lucky woman," he said, and I nodded in agreement. Yes. I was lucky.

Memories come back to me in hazy flashes. The twisted metal of the wreckage. Sam's skull stripped of flesh. The mountains looming over me. The endless sky. The sour breath of the man in the hotel room as his fingers closed around my throat. The crunch of bone against the butt of the rifle. Ben's cold, flat eyes as he raised the gun at me. The sour rasp of gunpowder in my lungs. The tacky pull of blood on my fingers. The terror. The terror. The terror. And then I'll feel a cool hand on my forehead and look up to see my mother's face above me, her eyes clouded with worry. She hasn't left my side.

There's still an angry scar on the back of my skull from when I fell out there in the woods, like a row of bloodied teeth sewn into the skin, and there's a strip of skin across the top of my thigh that's shiny and puckered where the gash has healed badly. I like to run my fingers across them both and feel their hard, jagged ridges. Proof.

The officer he shot—Shannon, I later learned—survived. The doctors said it was a miracle—someone who'd lost that much blood should have been a goner. My mom wasn't surprised, though. "She's a fighter," she said. "Like you."

I'm in Owl's Creek now, back in my old bedroom. Everything feels smaller somehow, like living in a dollhouse, but I'm happy here, at least for now. There's a peace that comes from padding down the stairs every morning to the sound of the radio and the smell of freshly brewed coffee, and my mother's voice as she sings to herself.

It feels like home. That's the thing, I guess. No matter how far you go, it's always there, etched deep in your bones. Home.

Maggie

I can hear her stirring upstairs, padding across the hall on her way to the bathroom. I stop and listen, straining to hear her footsteps. It's been so long since there have been the sounds of other people in this house, I didn't think I'd ever hear them again.

I still have nightmares, and some nights the familiar loop of film starts up behind my eyes. Terror. Pain. Blood. Fire. Bone. Ally. I can still see her lying there in front of me, her cheek swollen and bruised, the top of her head bleeding. Her face so different from the one I'd known.

She *is* different now. She's not the girl she was when she was growing up here, the one who would come running down the stairs to tell Charles and me about the book she just read, or the latest cause she decided to devote herself to. She's not the young woman we went to visit in San Diego, the one in the light blue dress who lived in that messy apartment, or the pale-faced, hollow-eyed daughter who watched her father be eaten alive by cancer. I didn't know the glossy blond woman in the photographs, but I know she's not her anymore, either.

She's someone else now. A woman with a quiet strength that sometimes takes my breath away. She's the woman who saved my life, and whose life I saved in return. She's the sum of all the people she was before, forged in the fire and turned to iron.

To me, though, she's the same as she always was and ever will be. She's the baby that Charles and I brought home from the hospital. She's our daughter, and she holds inside her all the love the two of us had to give.

Acknowledgments

This book is the product of a lot of people's hard work, but of three people in particular: my husband, Simon Robertson; my best friend, Katie Cunningham; and my friend and agent, Felicity Blunt. Simon for encouraging me to stick to my guns, Katie for reminding me to keep digging, and Felicity for reading countless drafts and pushing me on. Thank you, guys. I owe you all a lot of drinks. I've been very lucky to have two brilliant editors by my side, Sara Nelson at HarperCollins and Jade Chandler at Harvill Secker, along with their incredible teams, including Mary Gaule, Heather Drucker, and SallyAnne McCartin at HarperCollins and Sophie Painter and Anna Redman at Harvill Secker. Thank you to the inimitable Alexandra Machinist at ICM who, along with Felicity, kept me sane and steered me right, and to Lucy Morris, Claire Nozieres, Enrichetta Frezzato, Callum Mollison, and Sophia Macaskill at Curtis Brown. I strong-armed several people into reading early drafts of the book: Chad Pimentel, Alice Dill, and Alice Lutyens, thank you for your gentle and helpful notes, and for not telling me that the book sucked. Finally, thank you to my family—both the Pimentels and the Robertsons—for being so generally wonderful.

JESSICA BARRY is a pseudonym for an American author who has lived and worked in London for the past fifteen years. *Freefall*, her debut thriller, has sold in more than seventeen territories around the world and has also secured a major Hollywood film deal.